THE UNLIKEABLE DEMON HUNTER: CRAVE

DEBORAH WILDE

te da media
vancouver

Publisher's Note: This is a work of fiction. Names, characters, places, and incidents are a product of the author's imagination. Locales and public names are sometimes used for atmospheric purposes. Any resemblance to actual people, living or dead, or to businesses, companies, events, institutions, or locales is completely coincidental.

Book Layout ©2015 BookDesignTemplates.com

Cover design by Damonza

Issued in print and electronic formats.
ISBN 978-1-988681-10-8 (paperback)
ISBN 978-1-988681-11-5 (EPUB)
ISBN 978-1-988681-12-2 (Kindle)

Praise for the Nava Katz series:

The Unlikeable Demon Hunter

"She's like Buffy from the wrong side of the tracks. And that's okay with me." - Heroes and Heartbreakers

"...a fun, funny, and unapologetically raunchy new urban fantasy series... a clever guilty pleasure at its best." - Fine Print

"The action sequences are terrific and the humour will have you smiling. Nava is the underdog you will cheer on..." - Uncaged Book Reviews

"The story is emotional, action packed, and fast-paced... It's an intoxicating and invigorating read." - Angel's Guilty Pleasures

"Nava's like the fun-loving, dirty-talking, drink-tossing best friend you'd want to take to the bar. But you'd also want her around, because, you know, demons." – Lady Smut

"...an original entry into the genre..." - BrizzleLass Books

The Unlikeable Demon Hunter: Sting

"I didn't think Deborah Wilde could repeat the success of book 1 in this series but somehow she did. Fantastic plot, characters, snarky dialogue and all. I'm actually giving 5 stars out two books in a row for a series and I don't remember ever doing that. Go figure. Better yet, go get these books." – The Mysterious Amazon Customer

"Chock full of complicated and total visual butt-kicking, sensual push and pull swoons, crass clever and crude hilarity ... STING -- book two in the Nava Katz series -- was a definite win for me and a solid follow up to book one. No middle book syndrome here, folks!" – HJ, Reviewer, Amazon

"My favorite urban fantasy series so far this year." – Uncaged Book Reviews

"Nava Katz is the funniest, bad-a$$, hot mess of a demon hunter you could ever want to meet." - Sunnyles, Reviewer, Amazon

1

Kissing Rohan Mitra, my delectable boyfriend of seventeen days, fourteen hours, and some miscellaneous minutes that I was above counting, was my new favorite addiction. Didn't matter if it was a soft brush of lips, a quick, almost absent-minded peck to the corner of his mouth, a hot fevered embrace, or long, slow, drugged kisses like now, in a shadowy corner of Neon Paradise, our high bar chairs pushed close enough together for our knees to touch and one of Ro's hands on the small of my back, pulling me toward him.

We'd mastered the art form under a variety of conditions: stolen in the hallway of the chapter house, between the order and pick-up windows of a Starbucks drive-thru, hell, even high off a demon kill. Those were especially delicious.

And sure, I'd been skeptical. Not being emotionally up for kissing anyone for over a year could do that to a girl. But Rohan Mitra was worth every second of waiting and more. I never wanted to break this kiss.

Oxygen, that demanding element, had other ideas. I pulled back and draped my arms around his neck, ruffling his locks that fell like dark silk through my fingers. Planning on a quick lungful before going in for more.

Then the darling boy spoke. "I didn't think you'd be any good at kissing."

I slapped the tall, lacquered table. "Boom. Officially hitting pause."

Rohan raised an eyebrow. "On what?"

"Your boyfriend status. What could possibly have led you to believe something so deluded?"

He rubbed his nose against mine. "I figured the reason you were so dead-set against it was because of some deep-seated kissing insecurities. I was prepared to have to educate you on the subject. At length."

I clicked my tongue, though hours of kiss education with Rohan honestly didn't sound so bad. "My mouth is a marvel, Snowflake. It would behoove you to remember that."

He leaned his elbows back over the top of his chair, pulling the fabric of his short-sleeved linen shirt tight around his biceps. "Behoove?"

"Yes. Not only am I astoundingly kick-ass, I am also highly erudite." I'd gotten this Word of the Day app that I was putting to good use, unlike the running app the Brotherhood made me download for training purposes. A little intellectual self-improvement never hurt. Besides, Rohan's last girlfriend was a hair away from getting her Ph.D in physics and I didn't want to lower the bar too much. "Reiterating the marvel part now since that's what you should be focusing on."

His gold eyes crinkled in either confusion or amusement. "I see."

"You doubt me?"

He rubbed his head. "One of those PDs we took out earlier really clocked me. My short term memory is spotty."

"Apparently, since you've forgotten that we're now calling them half-demons, not Practice Demons, out of respect for Leo. Also, shame on you. Blaming those poor spawn for your own shortcomings." Tsking him, I slipped my fingers into his belt loops and tugged him close.

Five minutes later, I pulled away from his mouth with a nip. "Are my stellar abilities coming back to you yet?"

Wearing a slightly glazed look, his chest rising and falling rapidly, Rohan nodded like he'd forgotten how to form words.

I patted his cheek. "Good man." I grabbed my emerald satin clutch off the table where it had fallen between his half-finished G&T and my glass of water and slowly edged myself out. Time for another circuit of the dance floor. "Be right back." I pushed my water glass at him. "Drink this so you're not all headachy tomorrow."

"Hey, wait." Rohan caught my wrist, eyes hot and insistent. "Restart the clock, Sparky."

I smiled, then mimed smacking it again. He raised the glass in cheers. What a guy.

Leaving the boy to regroup, I skirted the packed dance area. The floor pulsed from the baseline of Jamiroquai's "Canned Heat" cranked to eleven, with everyone pulling out their best *Napoleon Dynamite* moves. Glittery disco starbursts illuminated arms thrown up in abandon, the dancers having a blast with the "hits from the 90s to today" that were on tap tonight.

Along the far edge of the floor, pleated curtains framed by multicolored spotlights illuminated cozy booths. Suppressing a smile at the dismayed groan that went up from the dude-bro group over by the pool tables, I curved around the sleek bar, restroom bound.

I charged into the middle stall, locked the door, and sank down in sweet relief. This rare night out was so precious that I'd stayed totally sober to remember every moment of it. But all the dancing I'd done had required copious amounts of hydration and I'd drunk an ocean of water tonight. I peed for so long I must have been pissing out stored reserves.

On the plus side, I was so well-hydrated that my skin glowed like I'd been airbrushed.

The marathon urination gave me a chance to catch up on the scrawled graffiti. In neat red ballpoint above the toilet paper holder, someone had written: *You're a solid 8.* Underneath that in pink glitter pen it read: *Fuck that. I'm a 12½.* A sentiment I applauded. Red pen then chimed back in with: *Your ego certainly is.* To which glitter had replied: *All women are a 12½ out of 10. At least.*

Black sharpie rounded out the exchange with: **fist pump* Sisterhood.*

If I was going to be stuck in a cubicle peeing like a crazy person, it was nice to be in one with a compatible philosophic leaning and not "all girls be bitches."

Someone else had drawn a wishing well in the center of the stall door. Responses alternated between lewd comments carved into the wood, initials drawn inside hearts, and requests of cash, designer clothes, and Hamilton tickets. It was all very silly, which was why I almost didn't add the tiny snowflake to the bottom of the list.

I flushed the toilet and exited, bladder de-stressed. Though I had to wave my wrist in front of the tap's motion sensor about seventeen times before I activated it. Damn things never worked properly for me, and I kept feeling like I was a dead person or a ghost. Two women entered as I was lathering up and

I peered at their reflection in the gold gilt-framed mirror. "Christina?" I squealed.

"Nava! Where've you been, girlfriend? Campus is so boring without you. I have no one to ditch class with on mental health days." Chinese-Canadian in her mid-twenties, Christina rocked a purple pixie haircut, a sequined one-piece romper, and an astounding example of cat eye eyeliner. When I attempted that look, I always came off as an Amy Winehouse drag queen who'd been crying while singing "Love is a Losing Game."

"Oh, you know. Life." I rinsed off my hands, tearing off some dead tree from the dispenser. "It's so good to see you."

"Nava." The woman next to Christina, her blonde hair scraped into a straight ponytail worn low on her head, gave me a brusque wave. I doubted there was a sports bra under that swank suit jacket, and her pencil skirt failed to resemble the nylon workout pants I was used to seeing her in. She'd changed, but her presence was still a giant ugh.

I fumbled the toss of my paper towels, barely making the garbage can. "Naomi. You look–"

"Like she has a stick jammed up her white ass," Christina said.

"Different."

"I'm articling now." Naomi brushed some imaginary lint off her navy lapel. "That's a position in a law firm."

She knew damn well that my dad, Dov, was a law professor at the University of British Columbia, since she'd had him for half a dozen classes. Clearly not much had changed besides the clothes. I jammed my hands into the pockets of my loose black trousers before either of them could see the spark of electric magic that jumped out of my fingertips. "You're doing bitch work for the actual lawyers. Mazel tov. What are you two up to tonight?"

Christina held up a vial filled with tiny pink crystals that glinted in the light. "Sweet Tooth. Perfectly designed to give you the all-night euphoria of every lush depravity you can think of. Want in?"

"No, thanks." There was only one thing I craved these days and it wasn't some new drug. I rummaged in my small backpack purse for my hair clip to twist my sweaty locks into a loose chignon (and give Ro better access to kiss his way down my neck) when I noticed Naomi staring. "Yes?"

"Nothing." She turned away, reapplying her sheer lip gloss. "You said we were going for a drink. One drink."

"I lied," Christina said. "You wouldn't have left work otherwise." She uncorked the vial releasing a burst of cotton candy scent. "One night to cut loose. 'Life at Full Tilt,' remember?"

Ten bucks said Christina was fighting a losing battle. Naomi was buttoned up so tight, cracking Level Fun required a set of lock picks, a tire iron, and some WD40. I patted my hairdo, waiting for their debate to end so I could get Christina's new phone number. Reconnect now that my life was a bit more stable, which funnily, even with the demon hunting addition, was true.

"I've got to finish up some research for a court appearance." Smug tone, nose in the air, Naomi hadn't lost her infuriating knack of making everything she did sound sooo verrah verrah important.

"Minor court appearance," I muttered. She was articling, not trying grand jury cases.

Christina tapped her finger against the vial a couple of times to dislodge powder from the sides. "Shut it, or I'll key both your cars."

I mustered a smile. "All dropped." Christina had always been good at follow-through. "Hey Chris, I don't have your current—"

"The lawyers are fast-tracking me to making associate. There's every expectation of me making partner in record time." Naomi ducked her head, her voice dripping with false modesty. "I don't want to mess any of that up. I can't. This is too important to me. Sorry, Chris." The longing glance she shot at the vial was quick, but I caught it.

I dug my nails into my skin. Here, I'd do my one good deed for the night. "It's okay to relax every now and then."

"I'd imagine you'd know." Naomi turned away from her reflection to peer at me with bullshit sincerity. "Still on a break from school?"

Between the annoying men I hunted with and my mother, Naomi was amateur hour. My smile stayed in place. "I'm in the security business," I said. Savior of humanity, me.

"Like mall cop? Good for you."

Okay, so not so much savior of *all* humanity because if a curupira was trying to suck her brains out right now, I'd totally point out the best spot to dig in.

My smile widened, teeth bared.

Christina muscled in between the two of us, smacking my hip in warning. "You can finish all your lawyer work tomorrow." She dumped half the crystals into her hand. "This shit is like the best fuck and best chocolate all at once."

"Careful Nava doesn't steal it." Naomi popped the cap back on her gloss.

"Jesus, Naomi, get over it. I didn't steal Sean. You weren't dating him or even sleeping with him."

"I spent every weekend with him and I liked him."

"You spent every weekend with *all* of your weekend warrior group. Besides, it's not like his flirting was subtle. If you'd had a problem with us leaving together that night, you could have used your words."

"As if you'd have listened."

"Enough." Christina held a hand up. "Naomi is an uptight bitch and Nava is a party whore. Have I settled it?"

"Like Nava limits the whoring to one area, but sure." Naomi wiped a trace of gloss off the corner of her lip.

My magic slid through my veins, whispering sweet nothings like *eviscerate her.* "You don't know anything about me, Naomi, so shove your little digs up your ass."

"I know what I see." She sniffed primly. "At least I have goals."

"Big deal. You exchanged flinging yourself off cliffs for flinging yourself into work. Real growth. Christina, gimme your new number."

She held up a finger and waggled the vial at Naomi. "It's not addictive and there's no hangover. I've done it a couple of times already so yes, I do know firsthand. It's also way less dangerous than the shit you used to pull and you won't have weird bruises to explain to your uptight firm. Merely a fun night that leaves you revitalized and ready to scale those lawyerly mountains. There, I've destroyed your objections, counselor." She licked the drug off her palm. "Plus, it tastes like cotton candy."

Her PSA over, she reeled off her phone number.

The second I had it, I dropped my phone in my clutch and snapped the clasp shut. "Excellent. I'll call you. As for you, Naomi, I'm going back to my boyfriend and forget you exist."

Naomi actually snorted. "Who'd you steal this one from?"

I gave her an icy smile. "Keep running on that hamster wheel. Maybe if you go fast enough and achieve enough, no one will realize you have absolutely no personality. Just an addict, held together by insecurity and rage, desperate for a rush to make you feel alive."

Christina gasped.

Aw, shit. My eyes darted away from both their faces, my fingers fiddling with the diamante clasp. This was what happened when I let things fester. Spewage and emotional carnage.

"Fuck you. You have no idea how hard I work." Naomi's voice trembled.

Calvin Harris' "This Is What You Came For" came on and I flinched at the memory that came with it. Christina, myself, and a few others had gone back to the apartment she shared with Naomi near campus to chill. That song had pulsed on low through the speakers and the air was fogged with the sweet smell of pot.

It was the time of night when people got cozy and shared past experiences. I'd been telling them about my Lincoln Center debut back in high school. The whole room had been silent except for me and that song, and yeah, the shine of admiration in their eyes had eased the constant sting of hurt a bit. Tap had been such a sad topic for me during that period, and it had been nice that night to remember the highs and not just the lows.

Naomi had burst in, eyes bright, loudly retelling some craaaazy adventure she'd just had. *Like, the last one had been insane, but this one?* She'd nudged me to the side so she could sit next to Christina, except there wasn't enough room on the couch so she ended up half-squashing me instead. She'd sucked all the air out of the room, totally disrupting our mellow vibe and killing my tale. I'd never understood why everyone not only indulged her spotlight-hogging, but was so charmed by it.

Keeping my mouth shut since speaking out against her was pointless, I'd reached for the joint in the ashtray and lit it.

Naomi had waited for me to inhale. "Geez, Little Miss Gimme. Never enough with you." This from the woman who had literally just interrupted herself mid-story about BASE jumping. Flinging herself off buildings, slacklining it across canyons, yes, it was cool, but she was such a hypocrite accusing *me* of being extreme.

Her crew called themselves the Full Tilt Gang for fuck's sake. Half the stunts they pulled were done illegally, so her moral high ground was built on quicksand.

Christina had shot me a sympathetic smile but the others had snickered unkindly. Not ten minutes ago they'd thought I was the coolest person alive, and here Naomi had totally turned them against me. Naomi had smirked, taking her friend's arm and monopolizing her in conversation, my existence forgotten.

The same way she now clutched Christina's arm, not so much possessively as in defeat.

My gut twisted. I'd fired off a lot of smart remarks in the past, but my comment to Naomi now had been a bitch too far. I didn't want to deliberately hurt others anymore. I was doing good in the world.

I wanted to *be* good in the world.

"Naomi, I'm sorry. I shouldn't be bringing up the past. But you do deserve a night off," I said. "The earth will continue to spin. The lawyers work you to the bone and in return you get no interesting tasks, no praise, and no life. Besides, you're ridiculously smart. I'm sure you can knock out the items on your minion list in record time. Do this stuff, don't do it, but enjoy yourself tonight. Normal is important."

Naomi snatched the vial away from Christina, rolling her eyes. "I don't need you to tell me how to have fun. I trademarked that shit."

So much for my genuine, heartfelt attempt at being friendly, Bellatrix.

Christina squealed and clapped her hands while Naomi licked up the crystals. In her excitement, she failed to notice that when Naomi tossed the vial out, there was still some left at the bottom.

A cautious good time on the menu, then. Whatever worked for her. As for me, I waved bye to Christina, catching the door and shouldering past a group of chattering women spilling in.

Rohan waited for me at the end of the short hallway leading to the restrooms. His lopsided grin soothed my fraying edges.

"Hel-lo," Christina said, having followed me. "I could ride that boy into next week."

"Words spoken by many a woman with working eyeballs," I said. "Yup, he's all the catnip. But he's also more than just a hot body."

Christina gave me a searching glance. "You know this how?"

"That's my boyfriend."

Naomi's mouth fell open as she stared at Rohan. "No way. He's dating you?"

To be fair, his moss green shirt emphasized his broad shoulders and leanly muscled, V-bod. It was like his East Indian/Jewish genes had convened a summit at his conception to negotiate for maximum incredible. He was magnificent, but for me? His humor at 2AM blending me smoothies that he named after our demon kills–the Tezcatlipoca Mocha Blast was my fave–the effort he'd made getting to know Ari and Leo, and the steadfast belief in his convictions even as he helped me dig deeper into the

Brotherhood, were even more attractive. I respected the hell out of him.

"Way, baby." I said. "We don't match, but we go."

Rohan crooked a finger at me and all three of us sighed.

"I underestimated you," Naomi said.

"Yeah," I replied. "In more ways than one." I hugged Christina goodbye with mutual promises to see each other soon and headed for my guy.

Rohan slung an arm around me, glanced back at the women, then kissed the side of my head. "You okay?"

I leaned into his steady comfort. "Perfect."

The opening notes of George Michael's "Freedom" kicked in and he tugged me onto the dance floor, squirming past the other dancers into the center. He caught me around the waist, singing into my ear about roads to Heaven and Hell as we grooved to the music, all rolling hips and sinuous arms.

I was lightness and air, anchored to this mortal plane by the rasp in Rohan's voice and the gentle bite of his fingers through the thin fabric of my tank top. I caressed his cheek and he nuzzled into my hand. "Did you get yourself happy, Snowflake?" I asked, referring to the lyrics.

"I did. I am." Still, when he sang along about freedom, the insistence in his voice was more than emotive karaoke.

"Is that what it felt like to leave the band? Like you got your freedom?"

He pulled me to him, making me ride his hard thigh in the dirtiest of dancing. Cuntessa de Spluge was in Heaven. "I thought all heavy conversations were banned tonight," he said.

"Yes. Heavy conversations pertaining to current Brotherhood-witch shit are banned during date night," I confirmed, my hips in a slow, syncopated slide with his.

"But prying into my past?"

"A total go." My breath quickened, a spark low in my gut bursting into flame.

"Nice try. Pool?" he asked as the song ended, taking away my happy motion ride.

"You callous bastard."

He leaned in, his lips brushing my ears. "I want you desperate for me."

"Your arrogance isn't doing it for me."

"Yeah, it is." He waggled his eyebrows at me in exaggerated fashion.

I shot him the finger and sashayed off the dance floor.

We passed Naomi, currently the filling in a boy sandwich. She'd shed her jacket, leaving her in a lacy camisole. Good time evidently unlocked. Christina smiled at her from outside the plastered-together bodies, but her expression was a bit strained. I didn't blame her. Naomi had gone from "no" to "wheeee!" in record time and she'd been known to ditch Christina when there were more interesting–or dangerous–things around to play with.

I raced off ahead to snag a pool table, practically flinging myself bodily over it until Rohan caught up. I handed him a pool cue. "Answer my prying now. Was it a relief ditching Fugue State Five? You ever wish you had that back or some new version of it?"

Were you going to run away soon?

His expression turned distant. "Sometimes... It felt like I was living with a noose around my neck. Writing music, even performing again, it wouldn't be like that. I wouldn't be like that."

"What changed?"

He pulled some balls out of the corner pocket, rolling them over the green felt for me to rack up. "Time. Heals all wounds, right?"

Rohan had always had a dark side, which had gotten worse with the twin fallouts of fame and the demon murder of his cousin Asha. His personal demons had been front and center pretty recently on our mission in Prague and only intensified on his gig in Pakistan, so I doubted he was suddenly a paragon of mental wellbeing, but I nodded.

He bopped the tip of my nose. "Don't worry, Sparky. I'm not going back down any dark roads."

I wasn't convinced of that either. Not given the single-minded focus Rohan had shown in unraveling the mystery of what certain Brotherhood members were up to these past few weeks. But that was part of tonight's ban on serious Rasha topics, so I pushed those thoughts away.

Maybe I was overthinking things. Besides, I needed my full concentration to kick his ass. Rohan was exceedingly competitive.

The hour grew later, the music faster, the crowd drunker. Despite being jostled yet again by a stray elbow, I sank three balls in rapid succession. I chalked my pool cue, eyeing the eight-ball. "Need a safe word, baby? Because when I sink this and obliterate you for a second game, it might be more pain than you can handle."

Rohan slid his palm in a teasing glide along my belly. "Try me."

"My favorite dare." I positioned my stick slightly off-center, and with a satisfying crack, sank the eight-ball. I handed Rohan my pool cue. "Does it chafe? Be honest."

He snapped both our sticks back into the mounted wall rack. "It's a little raw, not gonna lie."

"Good. I want you to feel it in the morning. Remember who owns you." I smacked his ass, laughing at the mock-scandalized expression on Rohan's face.

He caught my wrist, tugging me up against him and nipping my earlobe. "Isn't this where you're supposed to minister to me and take away the sting like a good girlfriend?" His voice ran over me like rivulets of honey.

I mentally stomped on the memory of his ex, Lily, adjusting his scarf and quietly caring for him in a dozen small ways when we'd all been in Prague. Without having to be asked.

In the *Grease* lens on the world, which was really the only useful metric, Lily was Sandy and I was Rizzo. Rohan claimed to want Rizzo, so he should have known that the idea of me on some Sandy scale of good was laughable. I gazed up at him through half-lidded eyes. "Got something in mind, O wounded man child?"

"Since you asked." He motioned for me to fan him.

"Yeah, right."

"So hot," he whined, taking my hands and moving them ineffectually up and down. It was so humid in the club, my skin was sticky where he held my wrist. "I know these are the wilds of Canada, but don't you people know about A/C?"

Laughing, I blew air on him. "Poor pampered L.A. baby."

Motioning for him to follow, I unclasped the chain blocking access to a small stairway and led him up. At the top was a small balcony overlooking the back half of the dance floor and one of the bars. The door behind it had been jacked open to the summer night. A siren cut through the alley below, its flashing lights bouncing off the building walls.

"Befriending bouncers has its perks." I sat down on the bench, snickering as Rohan turned his face to the breeze wafting over us like a dog sticking its head out a window.

"Bootylicious" started up, and oh yes, I sang along. Rohan scoffed, with a "Figures you anthem'd this," but I didn't stop my beauteous phonetic rendition of the song.

That is until the chorus when Rohan spun, breaking into moves worthy of Queen B's backup dancers. Shimmying, he wriggled closer until, keeping out of touching range, he canted his hips up in a long slow roll, running his hand down along the hard planes of his stomach. His shirt rode up, exposing a stretch of brown skin I wanted to lick. Lower and lower, his hand slid dangerously along his waistline, then lower still.

I sat there, gaping.

Rohan jumped onto the bench, feet planted on either side of me. He tossed his head, flicked off each shoulder, grinning. Clutching the burnished gold railing behind me with one hand, he twerked his ass lower and lower, his falsetto singing note-perfect.

Fuck. Me. Where had he been hiding this?

Rohan ground against me once, twice, and I lunged for him, our mouths crashing together. He tasted of anise seed and gin, his mouth cool from the ice he'd been crunching all night.

I opened my eyes, seeking a deeper connection. Seeking affirmation that he was here and this was real and that the voices trumpeting disbelief that we *were* a we could go screw themselves.

A flash of something caught the light from the club area below and I stilled.

Rohan's eyes fluttered open. "Hey," he murmured.

I craned my neck, twisting around him to peer down at the bar.

The bartender wrestled a bottle away from Naomi. One of Naomi's hands was curled like a claw, and her expression was frozen in a snarl. She relaxed for a second, her shoulders slumping. The bartender eased up too, which was when she swiped the bottle and cracked him upside the head. He stumbled back against the bar, a few bottles cascading over his shoulder and shattering on the floor in bursts of light.

Pushing Ro off of me, I scrambled to my feet and shot down the stairs.

Most of the patrons were still caught up in their own dealings. They hadn't had my eagle-eyed view of the club and the press of bodies was too thick for anyone not in the immediate vicinity of the bar to have witnessed the attack. I impatiently shoved my way through the chatting, flirting masses until I broke through to the bar.

The clean-cut bartender pressed a bloody rag to one temple, his body angled as far away as possible from Naomi. Shards of glass speckled his shoulders and alcohol ran down his shirt in sticky rivers. Naomi sat on the bar top, legs crossed, swinging one slender ankle. She tipped a bottle of Bombay Sapphire back, its blue glass streaked with neon, one side smeared with the bartender's blood. After a single disturbingly long swig, she shook the final drops into her mouth with a couple of violent jerks.

Then, to my horror, she bit into the glass, licking off whatever remaining gin coated its insides, oblivious to the blood streaming out of her mouth along her psychotic smile.

I stood there frozen, heart racing. Clueless how to process this fucked-up tableau. Naomi's smirk was loaded with memories of every time she'd ever made me feel inadequate. I'd dealt with shit way worse than this, but there was such a cutting intimacy in her look, like she knew exactly who I was and that I'd never gotten over my weaknesses, that my past self had taken control of my brain. I froze up.

Somebody screamed right as the music cut out, breaking the spell and sending the dance floor into chaos. I ran for Naomi, but my friend Max, one of the bouncers here at the club, reached her first.

Naomi wore a matter-of-fact expression on her face as she calmly explained to Max, curling her bloody tongue around a razor sharp part of the bottle's neck to catch an errant drop of booze, that the bartender had tried to cut her off and that wasn't very "Full Tilt."

Max had never been anything other than an ocean of calm, even when breaking up a stabbing outside the front door. So when this 6'4" brick wall of a man drained of all color, clutching his phone so hard he cracked the screen, my blood ran cold.

But if he couldn't handle it, who could? My spine straightened. The past was just that, the past. I was Rasha and a hell of a lot stronger now on every level. I gave myself a mental shake and snapped into action. I pried the cell from Max's death-grip, and called 911. Then I tossed him the phone back with a barked, "Talk to them."

Light glinted off the jagged bottle neck as Naomi ran her thumb over it, her eyes not leaving mine, blood and gin dripping from her chin and meandering down her collarbone to stain her camisole in a gruesomely pretty bloom. "Nava, Nava, Nava. Always killing my good mood."

I couldn't use my magic. There were too many people around. I swallowed, hyping myself up to step closer. "Naomi, put the bottle down."

She wrinkled her nose at me, waving the broken glass. I stepped back out of neck slashing range. She took another sip, but finding it empty, dropped the bottle on the floor where it shattered.

Shards flew. One stung my ankle and I cursed.

Undeterred, Naomi picked up someone's abandoned pint of beer and chugged some back.

I reached out for the glass, my body turned somewhat, so she wouldn't see the new bouncer slowly approaching from her right. Max, still on the phone, kept a wary eye on us all. "Okay, fine. Then how about you share?"

Her expression hardened. "Always gotta steal something, don't you?"

Screw this. I rushed her, jumping back as she vomited blood, swayed, and went down like a sack of rocks.

The second bouncer caught her before she hit the ground, the beer mug rolling out of her hand onto the floor. "What. The. Fuck?" His pupils were dilated to the point of practically disappearing.

I was willing to bet the answer to that was "demons," because even with the fentanyl crisis ravaging my beloved Vancouver, this was too insidious to be human evil, but I needed proof.

I left Naomi in Max and this other bouncer's care and sprinted to the bathroom.

Grimacing, I plunged my hand into the mound of wet paper towels in the overflowing garbage, praying that their sogginess was water-based versus something requiring a tetanus shot. I was fumbling in there shoulder-deep before my fingers closed on the vial. I pulled it out, relieved that despite it being uncorked there was still some of the drug inside. I twisted up some dry paper towel to use as a lid and sealed the drug in.

Laying it carefully on the bathroom counter, I disinfected my arm with scalding water and a shit-ton of soap. By the time I hit the main part of the club again, the house lights were up and employees were directing confused patrons toward the front door, doing their best to keep them from rubbernecking.

Two paramedics strapped Naomi's prone form onto a gurney.

Christina stood beside them, the orange shock blanket around her shoulders sliding half-off under the force of her hysteria. Rohan had his arm around her, his head close to hers, speaking. She clutched at his shirt front.

I ran over, insides icy. Christina had taken the same drug Naomi had. The drug that had made her chew through glass and slice people. And Rohan was right next to her.

When I reached her, I felt like an idiot. Christina's eyes were hollow and wide, possessing none of the mania that Naomi's had. She was just terrified and at the touch of my hand on her shoulder, she fell into my arms, sobbing and repeating, "I'm sorry," over and over.

"I'll see if a paramedic will give her a sedative," Rohan said into my ear.

I gripped his hand. "Tell them she did Sweet Tooth. Let them know she can't have anything that conflicts with it." He nodded and I laced my fingers with his, giving him a quick squeeze. He gave me a sympathetic smile and left.

Smoothing Christina's hair, I absently registered him crossing the room to catch up with the first responders as they sped the gurney out. The gurney that had Naomi strapped to it. Naomi, who just an hour ago had been calling me mean names in the bathroom, who shouldn't be lying there like this, motionless. "It's not your fault."

It was *both* our faults. Lead twisted my gut. Bad enough that I'd encouraged Naomi to take the night off because I'd implied she had a stick up her ass, but to have mocked her for her past and driven her to do something she wasn't sure of? I'd taunted the universe and the universe had kicked my ass.

Christina turned her tear-streaked face to mine. "Why did it affect her and not me? What did I do to her?"

Fine questions I didn't have answers to. Yet. The one thing I was absolutely certain of? If this was some fucked up demon product, then I'd hunt it down and destroy the evil spawn with my bare hands. Cold comfort, but I'd take it where I could find it.

2

We didn't get home for another couple of hours, between telling a harried Max exactly what I'd seen and driving Christina to the hospital to get checked out. Oh, and scrolling through her contacts to find her brother Henry's number. Christina and I had hung out at university so I'd heard her talk about Henry, but we'd never met. I explained who I was and asked him to come to get his sister, since once the sedative she'd finally been given in the ER kicked in, my friend couldn't do much more than sluggishly wave at her phone.

Once he'd arrived, Henry assured me he'd get hold of Naomi's family and keep me posted. I hadn't been able to get any information out of the nurses about Naomi beyond "she's in surgery and being looked after."

I practically staggered out the ER doors, wrapping my arms around myself against the wind lashing at my denim jacket. The silence of deep night would have been a welcome relief except the earlier thump of the bass at the club still pounded in my temples and rang in my ears. My shoulders were wound tight; fatigue clawed at my eyes and brain, making everything gritty and dull.

I trudged across the parking lot. "I'm so tired that my feet don't want to feet."

Rohan was a champ. He got me to his precious '67 Shelby Mustang, settled me in, and cranked the heat.

"Thank you." I yawned, my head falling sideways against the window.

"For what?"

I pushed a dark brown strand of hair of out my mouth. "Sticking around."

Rohan started the ignition with a quick flick of his wrist. The motor roared to life, settling into a purr as he pulled out of the parking spot. His biceps flexed as he shifted gears. "Yeah, I was gonna go off and leave you. Dummy."

"Remember, you *are* a callous bastard." I yawned again, my mouth opening so wide that my ears popped. "Can you swing by the house?"

"It's late."

"I know."

He shrugged, and ten minutes later, drove around a quiet residential block so we could check out Dr. Gelman's sister's place. Dr. Esther Gelman was the witch that had given me the magic ceremony to get Ari inducted and her sister Rivka lived here in Vancouver.

Like every single other time that I'd come by, the place was locked up tight. No car in the car port, no change to the closed curtains. After I'd kind of broken in and damaged the place a few weeks ago, someone had set a new and powerful ward on the property. Anyone who got too close had the overwhelming urge to go elsewhere. It even affected me to some degree. I was overcome by a strong desire to go home and do my laundry. The ridiculousness of that idea generally reminded me it was magic at work and I could fight it, but damn, it was tough.

I had to find a way to contact Dr. Gelman, but could only think of the same idea that I was loath to do. It would have to wait. The Sweet Tooth situation was the more immediate concern anyway.

I rolled down the window to get some frigid air on my face and punched in the number for Brotherhood HQ in Jerusalem to let them know I had a case to investigate. The man I spoke to, older and with a French-Canadian accent, took the details about Sweet Tooth, assigned me a case number, and wished me luck.

"Huh." I looked at the phone after he'd hung up. "That was kind of anti-climatic."

Ro flicked on his turning signal. "Did you expect good fireworks or bad, phoning in your first mission?"

"Not sure. But note that *I'm* the hunter of record in charge, Snowflake." That was pretty cool.

He sighed. "Such domination issues."

My chuckle turned into a yawn, my lids fluttering shut.

I woke up to the emergency parking brake being engaged in front of Demon Club, the mansion housing the Vancouver chapter of the Brotherhood of David, that was located in the Southlands area of Vancouver's west side. Trust me, now that I was the first female member of this secret society, changing the name was on my To-Do List, though given the rest of the shit on there, like exposing duplicitous rabbis on the Executive, it kind of lacked urgency.

I stumbled up the front stairs. Heavy cloud cover obscured the few stars that could usually be seen. Without moonlight, the gardens were formless shapes. The house itself was quiet; no lamps shone out the beveled bay windows, no smoke escaped the multiple chimneys. The forest surrounding the house was still and dark.

I kicked off my chunky emerald heels in the foyer, sighing dreamily as my toes flattened out against the cool tile. Rohan tried to steer me up the curving stairs to my bedroom, but I shook his hand off. "Not yet. Get me the hawkweed and meet me in the kitchen? Please?"

My nap had only made my body realize how badly it craved sleep, and even slapping my cheeks as I shuffled down the shadowy hallway over the intricate inlaid wood floor failed to wake me up. I stepped through the arched doorway into the kitchen.

The under-the-cupboard lights were on, casting warm lemon pools over the dark granite counter. The room smelled faintly of garlic, which got my stomach rumbling, which led me to the brilliant idea of protein as a pick-me-up.

After placing my frozen meal of choice in the stainless steel microwave that matched the industrial fridge and glass-topped stove, I examined the vial with the remaining crystals. There was nothing special about the container. Made of glass, it had a label with the words "Sweet Tooth" written in script.

The microwave went "bing." I pulled my TV dinner out, puncturing the plastic wrap with a set of keys that I found on the counter.

An aggrieved sigh alerted me to Rohan's presence. "All the options open to you and you go for that." He poked at the plastic tray like he was scared the contents might bite him.

"I'll have you know this is the finest Fried Chickeny Delight available in No Name Form." I bit into a chicken leg. "Huh. You know what it doesn't taste like?" I asked, munching.

"Chicken?"

I dropped the leg back on the tray. "Good guess. It's chicken-esque."

"Technically, it's chicken-y."

"Yeah, I'm not sure if '-y' is a step up or down in the culinary world from '-esque.'" I crossed over to the fridge, pulled out the small jug of maple syrup, and doused the poultry-facsimiles like I was putting out a fire.

"Please eat real food. I honestly don't know how you're still alive."

"Preservatives, obviously. And quit being such a food snob. This is real." I tapped the jug. "One hundred percent real maple syrup, because I am Canadian and civilized."

"Half-right."

I took another bite. "Oh yeah. Way better now. Okay, gimme the spell stuff." I licked off my fingers, wiping them on a piece of paper towel. Millennials–major factor in the demise of the napkin industry. True fact.

Rohan tossed a Ziploc bag with a mixture of salts and chopped up bits of yellow Snowdonia Hawkweed onto the counter. The plant was incredibly rare, but what was scarcity when you had a boyfriend with a fat bank account from his rock star days? How fat, I had no idea. He'd assured me he didn't have billionaire status, but I suspected that multi-millionaire was still within the realm of possibility. I mean, dude had been the lead singer of Fugue State Five, international chart-topping, emo band extraordinaire. That said, multi-millionaire in Vancouver would scarcely have bought this monstrosity of a chapter house we lived in, so I clearly was not with him for his money. Real Housewives of Vancouver had never been an aspiration of mine. Besides, Ro could have been poor as dirt and he'd still be a prime catch.

I dumped the mixture in water, stirring it with the thin paintbrush that he'd thoughtfully brought. "Such a good sidekick."

"What happens when you use the 's' word?" Rohan sealed up the Ziplock.

"You tackle me."

He stuffed the baggie in his pocket. "And what happens when you admit that *I'm* Batman?"

"You tackle me."

Rohan quirked an eyebrow. "That all?"

I paused my stirring, perking up. "Ooooh, yeah." His nerdy role-playing had a deliciously filthy narrative. "'K. I pick door number two."

Rohan snickered. "Phrasing." I blushed from head to toe. "Don't feel bad, Sparky." He pushed my dinner to the far end of the island, ignoring my glare. "We're two consenting adults with perfectly natural urges."

"Yes, we are."

Rohan opened the fridge, grabbing the bread, cheddar, and butter. "Except for that thing you beg for which is totally depraved."

"Don't forget the mustard. And fuck you."

Rohan gave a smug lift of his right eyebrow, but pulled out the distinctive yellow squeeze bottle. "What? Again? Woman, you're insatiable."

"You are never getting laid again." I motioned at him to put more cheese on the grilled sandwich he was making me, and helpfully retrieved two plates from the white cabinets.

Ro rummaged around on the fridge shelf. "Is there orange juice?"

I pulled an unopened carton out of the cupboard holding the pots and pans and put it on the counter. "I hid this for you. Kane was sucking back the stuff like there was no tomorrow." I poured it into a glass over ice.

Once he'd chugged some back, I waved the vial in front of his face. "Thoughts. Go."

Rohan slid a generous pat of butter into the cast iron pan he'd heated, before reading the label. "'Sweet Tooth.' Catchy name. Branding and everything."

"It's all about discoverability."

"Did they snort this?"

"Licked it."

"The initial effects kicked in pretty quickly for licking it. Another point for a magic source." He placed the sandwiches in the pan, spatula in one hand, then pulled out my paper towel cover and, sniffing the drug, recoiled. "Gross. Cotton candy. Could be worse."

"Yeah. Could be watermelon scent."

"Exactly. Swear that's a demon invention." He sniffed again, more cautiously and gave me back the vial. "No other obvious chemical odor. I'd say test it and let's see what we've got."

I drummed the paintbrush against the counter. This was my first actual case and already I didn't know how to handle this. I bit my lip and exhaled. "I'm not sure how to do the spell."

"Because it's crystals, not something solid?"

"Yeah." The spell to test for magic signatures required the caster to paint a specific vine pattern on the object with the water/salt/hawkweed mixture. "There's only a tiny amount here. The drug dissolves if it's absorbed into the bloodstream, so if I add this liquid and the spell doesn't work, we may lose what little Sweet Tooth we have to test."

He flipped the sandwiches. "You want brown or golden brown?"

"Golden brown."

Rohan checked both sides, then plated my sandwich golden brown side up.

We tossed out a few options while eating, like either of us ingesting the stuff and then testing ourselves for a magic signature. Dismissed that one pretty damn quickly, given what had happened to Naomi.

Belly pleasantly full, I poured half of the remaining crystals into a bowl. That gave us a smaller sample size, but also gave us a second shot if need be. Dipping the paintbrush in the water mixture, I did my best to swirl the pattern onto the drug, then said "gallah" to invoke the spell.

The crystals dissolved, leaving us with nothing for the spell to work its magic on.

"Damn it." I tossed the paintbrush onto the counter with a clatter.

"Wait." Rohan picked up the brush. The finely-bristled tip cycled through a rainbow of colors before settling into a pulsing blue. It had absorbed enough of the crystals to give us a result.

"Demon magic for the win," I said.

"Too bad the spell can't tell us which demon," Rohan said.

"You need the magic equivalent of a forensic chemist," Ari said, padding into the kitchen in pajama bottoms and a faded blue T-shirt, in dire need of a shave. He rubbed a hand over his short blond hair.

"What are you doing up so early?" I glanced out the window at the basketball court and press of dense cypress, arbutus, and Douglas fir beyond. My twin may have been a morning person but light was only barely leaching back into the world.

"Up late reading while waiting for the storm to pass so we can get clearance to fly in. I'm going on assignment. With Kane."

There was a tense silence.

"Kane? With you?" Rohan repeated. "Wow, headquarters sure has our best interests at heart."

It was scathing, but fair. Our friend and fellow demon hunter Kane Hashimoto and Ari were no longer exactly on speaking terms after a disastrous kiss a few weeks back. Not like their dysfunction would stop them from having each other's backs, but the timing was awful.

"No way," I said, waving my hand. "I forbid this. Veto. No."

"Don't worry, Nee. Even if the weather was fine, I still have a few more days here for obvious reasons." He picked up an uneaten thigh. "Is that maple syrup? Awesome." Dipping the chicken into the golden pool, he devoured half the meat in one bite.

We Katz twins made it a point to be impressive.

Rohan winced like he was in genuine pain.

I hugged Ari around the waist, burrowing my head into his chest. My brother was the best. We'd had a bumpy few months what with me becoming Rasha during his induction ceremony, then our growing pains working together after I'd finally found a way to make him a hunter, but our "don't mess with us" status quo was restored.

"Quit smothering me." Ari wriggled free.

"What's happening in a couple days?" Rohan asked.

I snatched the paintbrush away from him using it to jab him in the chest. "There's a countdown widget on your phone."

Rohan's brows creased. "Are you sure?"

"And a back-up countdown widget."

Rohan shrugged. "Not ringing any bells."

"The reminder taped to your dresser?"

"Must have missed it under all the mess." As if. Snowflake was anal-retentive tidy.

I slapped my hand against the giant paper calendar pinned to the fridge with magnets reading *Yeah, bitch! Magnets!* The calendar contained a single entry. The large square for Monday June 19 was festooned with gold stars. "Nava's 21st birthday! Commence adoration!!" was written in all-caps black sharpie. In smaller penciled letters someone had added, "And Ari's."

"You do know the last person who joked about forgetting Nava's birthday was never seen again, right?" Ari dumped the detritus of the meal in the trash.

"Don't worry." I threw a pointed glance at Rohan. "I've already got the remote gravesite picked out should people fail in their duties. Back to this forensic chemist idea." I motioned at Ari. "Expound please."

Rohan, eating his sandwich, nodded in agreement.

"I've been thinking about it since I heard the gogota attacked you and your scientist witch," Ari said.

"Dr. Gelman. This isn't a case of She-Who-Shall-Not-Be-Named." She'd gone off-grid after the attacks. Rabbi Mandelbaum, head rabbi on the Brotherhood's

Executive, maintained she was dead. While I was getting increasingly worried about her failure to surface, no way did I believe him. Dr. Gelman was a badass witch, and she was probably taking her sweet time getting back in touch just to annoy me.

"Then those yaksas attacked the village in Pakistan. That makes the sites of the attacks crime scenes." Ari always talked faster when it came to chemistry stuff. Hand gestures, intense eye contact, the whole nine yards–it was actually kind of adorable. "Essentially, with both the gogota and the yaksas horn fragment, you removed material from those crime scenes to cast the spell. A forensic chemist does the same thing at a non-magical crime scene; they work to identify material found there. The spell that you and Ro cast was like basic magic chromatography. It led you to the discovery of the purple magic signature on both. The initial identification. Now you need someone who can dig deeper and isolate the specific components." He pointed at the vial. "Same with this. If a forensic chemist specializing in magic existed, that person might be able to tell you which type of demon was behind this. The specific component, so to speak."

My brother was a chemistry major. I'd bet a kidney he was dying to find a way to combine that passion with magic.

"That would be extremely cool." I finished up my sandwich, licking buttery crumbs off my fingers. "I wish I could do that."

"You have enough of a revolving list of powers," Ari said dryly. "Electricity, magnetizing shit, however you'd oscillated your power to almost kill Malik. It's weird."

"You're jealous that I keep rolling out new tricks." Rohan snorted, reaching for a napkin that he used to meticulously wipe off his hands. Fine. Maybe my magic *was* kind of weird, being variations on a theme rather than one ability gained all at once. But considering that all the other Rasha had ages to understand magic and what would happen when they came into their powers, and I was just mastering it on the go, I was acing the catch-up.

"How do we know these magic forensic chemists don't exist?" I asked.

"Oh, I just asked Rabbi Abrams."

"Ari!" I jumped off the bar stool, my heart hammering.

"Calm down, stress case, I didn't tell him. But hasn't he risked enough for us already? He deserves to know."

"Save your breath." Rohan removed the canister of ground coffee from the freezer, slamming the door. "We've had this conversation a dozen times."

"And for the dozenth and first." I stacked our dishes in the dishwasher. "I'm not saying anything until we know who's responsible for the purple magic. The man is a billion years old. I'm not potentially causing him to stroke out based on supposition."

They turned identical scowls on me. Even Kane had been nagging me to bring the head of our chapter on board. I was terrified to tell the rabbi. Partially because I didn't want to upset him, but mostly because he was the one rabbi in this entire Brotherhood that I trusted. How was I supposed to tell him the core of the cause that he'd devoted his life to was rotten? It didn't matter that I wasn't the one responsible, I knew what they did to messengers, and I wasn't ready to give up the fond smile he bestowed on me whenever he saw me.

"We don't have a forensic chemist," I said, "but we do have drugs with demon magic all over them." I sealed up the remaining crystals in the vial once more.

"What happened?" Ari asked.

Letting me relay the events of the night, Rohan filled the coffee machine with a new filter and grounds, sliding the empty glass carafe onto the base. He flipped on the power switch, the machine gurgling to life.

Ari squeezed my shoulder. "Geez. That's rough. Sorry to hear it."

I didn't even like Naomi, so why was I obsessively checking the clock on the wall to see if it was late enough in the morning to call Christina's brother

Henry for an update? I turned away from the clock with purpose. The only thing I could do to help right now was find the demons responsible.

"We're going to need a new paintbrush." Since the crystals had dissolved into the brush and saturated it with demon magic, it was now officially useless for further spell casting. Thanks to the spell, it would forever remain the color of the magic signature.

Generally, this didn't matter, like with the gogota's finger or yaksas horn, because we wanted that proof of the magic signature to remain, but sometimes it sucked. No amount of dry cleaning had changed the coat that I'd tested back to its natural pale green. I could have lived with a red coat, the color that Dr. Gelman's witch magic had turned the fabric, but it looked like a bad dye job and was now unwearable.

I was so done with my ongoing loss of clothing.

I took a few deep breaths, letting the sweet burbles of the coffeepot melt away stress and tension better than any ylang ylang shit. Meditation with hippy oils was all well and good for people with no worries more pressing than destressing from their morning commute, but for those of us with hellspawn breathing down our necks on a regular basis, mainlining caffeine was a must.

Rohan got two chunky ceramic mugs out of the cupboard and held up a third. Ari nodded at him. "Oh, hey. I got a lead from Christina while I was consoling her," Ro said. "She said she bought the Sweet Tooth from some skater kid who lives on her block. Told me where he hangs out. We'll start there."

"Leo and I have plans. As you very well know."

"Nava," he said, all blustery stern. "You're still going there?"

"Rohan," I mocked back in a deep voice. "We still need answers about the Brotherhood."

He sighed and passed me my coffee with its correct 3:2 ratio of milk to sugar and a sprinkling of cinnamon on top. "It's not that I don't believe you can pull it off."

I smiled at him. "I know."

Ari scrunched his nose. Initially he'd been hardcore Team Brotherhood, but after I told him the truth about nearly being killed by a modified demon, he'd come around to Team Nava. He still had some issues accepting that the organization he'd been a member of since birth wasn't squeaky clean, but actually fixing the problem was much more important to me than sweeping it under a rug to spare my twin's feelings.

Rohan took a sip of his disgusting black coffee. "How's Leo doing? Her midterms last week sounded rough."

I tipped my mug to my lips, watching him through lidded eyes. See? This. How many other guys would show compassion for a demi-goblin's summer semester course load? "She's good."

Ari dumped more sugar into his coffee. "Is there a Plan B for today?"

"Yeah," Rohan said. "Be careful. That's also plans C through Z."

"Sweet boy." Mug cradled in one hand, I headed out, swinging around the island for a quick pit stop. I rose onto tiptoe and kissed Rohan on the cheek. Damn. Even that gave me a short, intense rush of sunshine. "There's only one Plan B. Don't fuck up Plan A."

3

Leonie and I braved bumper-to-bumper traffic along the highway and out over the Portman Bridge, its coiled steel cables stretching like sails above the cars.

Eyes closed, she tilted her face toward the open window, her straight red hair streaming and her Sexy Ruby perfume scattering the scent of apricot and jasmine through the car.

The cool nip of the morning summer breeze had burned away by the time the car bumped over the pothole-ridden dirt parking lot for Eddy's Scrap and Salvage Yard, located out in the valley. Heat shimmered up in waves from the endless lines of cars.

Throwing the car into Park and cutting the engine, I pushed my oversized, black vintage sunglasses up my nose and winced when I touched my cheek, flushed from the sun streaming on it during the drive. Damn. I really needed to remember to sunscreen or I'd look like a Coppertone toad.

"You got it?" Leo scrambled after me, her flip flops thwacking softly.

I popped my trunk and unlocked a small iron box. A blue velvet bag was nestled inside. "Curious to see what a cursed diamond looks like?"

"Like that's a question."

I turned away so the reveal wouldn't affect me but at Leo's "Whoa!" glanced back.

The diamond was the size of a fat chestnut, uncut and flawless. I leaned in to admire it. To adore it, grateful that this puny being could bask in its splendor.

Leo smacked me across the face, snapping me out of the gem's compulsion. Good thing. I didn't have time to rip her to shreds for ownership, which had almost happened with Rohan when we'd first retrieved it.

I rubbed my cheek. "Thanks, you sadistic freak."

"Humans," my half-goblin bestie scoffed. "So weak." She put the diamond away, stuffing the velvet bag into her orange cotton sundress, and lovingly cupping her now oddly-shaped tit. "I always wanted a Cubist boob."

I snorted.

We made our way to the entrance of the salvage yard, my Sketcher high tops becoming more black-and-brown than black-and-white. I scanned for any hint of motion. The zizu demon we'd come to see would sense the diamond's presence any moment now and come for it.

"Hi." A cheerful middle-aged guy in a faded ball cap, his beer gut straining his dirty green coveralls with the word "Eddy" stitched in black across his heart, stepped out of a small trailer at the front gate. A wooden sign with "Office" painted on was nailed to the dusty aluminum siding. "Looking for car parts?" He chewed a toothpick between fleshy lips.

If Eddy was the demon, he should have been acting twitchy, trying to get to the jewel, but he looked like the last time he experienced tension was being squeezed out the birth canal.

"Transmission," I said as Leo chimed in with "Engine."

Eddy's brows creased, but he shrugged. "Well. Sounds like a car in need of some TLC." He took out his toothpick and jabbed it at the lot. "Use whatever you need. Engine hoists, wheel carts, we have it all. Let me know if you need a hand."

The hoists, strewn around the lot, resembled primary-colored metal swing sets mounted on fat tire wheels. In the center of each was a lift secured with heavy chain and huge hydraulic pulleys.

"Thanks," I said. "It's a bit of a project. Might take us a while to find what we need."

A boy and a girl, maybe five years old, both with wheat-blonde hair, barreled out of the office. The two stared at me with identical grave stares, dressed in gender-assigned T-shirts and shorts. Aw, the universal color-coding of fraternal twins.

Then the girl whipped a red foam block at her brother. Yup. That was universal, too.

Without missing a beat, he grabbed it, yelled, "Mine!" and ran.

Memories.

Setting his toothpick back into chew mode, Eddy grabbed the boy with one meaty hand, spun him around, and nudged him back toward the office. "Tony, Clea, cut it out. Both of you."

He herded them back inside and shut the door.

"Hug right wall?" I asked.

Leo nodded and we strode onto the lot. "Guess what?" she said. "I learned that pap tests can suck my dick."

"Mazel tov. My little girl is a woman." I pressed my hand to my heart. "I'm all verklempt."

She elbowed me in the gut. "Laugh now, but wait till you have to undergo the vaginal probe. You'll fry the poor doctor and end up locked in a military compound while they run tests on you as the Brotherhood quietly celebrates."

I shrugged. "A strong possibility. But maybe I'll find that doctor to marry that Mom had always hoped for. I'd make a beautiful Stockholm Syndrome bride."

We snickered, clearing the first long line of cars, some parked intact, others flattened and piled in high stacks. Sweat ran under my breasts and down my back. I lifted my arms up, flapping them to air out my pits. "It's four hundred degrees out here. Where's the stupid demon?"

We rounded the corner into the next wide row, trekking back the way we'd come.

Someone giggled behind us. I spun around with a "Boo!"

The two kids shrieked in delighted laughter.

"Are you supposed to be out here? It's kind of dangerous." I held out a hand. "Come on, we'll take you back to your dad."

The munchkins ran off. Also typical.

"It's fenced." Leo fiddled with her silver eyebrow ring. "They can't get out."

I was already dialing the office number. It went to voicemail so I left Eddy a message about his little Houdinis.

We picked up the pace. "Here, zizu, you jonsing motherfucker. Come get the pretty diamond." I glanced back in the direction the children had gone. "We need to wrap this up."

"Agreed." She pushed me forward a few steps. "Stay in front of me. I'm pulling out the big guns."

"I hope you mean the diamond and not your boobs," I said.

"You'll never know."

I slowed down, my shoulder blades prickling, dying to turn around and gaze upon the jewel.

Leo poked me in the back. "Keep moving."

"Don't drop the merchandise," I said sourly. "I don't have time to track down another flawless cursed diamond."

Rohan, Kane, Ari, and I had spent the past couple of weeks tracking the gem down using intel gleaned from David Security International, the Brotherhood's public persona. Actually retrieving it had been a bitch of a mission involving oversized crab demons and a taste of being buried alive.

I placed my hand on my head as a makeshift hat against the relentless sun.

"You should have bought me a Popsicle," Leo said.

"Hand over the ten bucks you owe me and you can pick your flavor."

"A real friend wouldn't have me pay up."

"Be sure to mention that when you find one." I wiped sweat off my brow, silently chanting *eyes front*. "Renege and I start charging interest. I'm not a good person like Rohan is."

"Yeah, yeah. You have the best boyfriend in the world."

"I do." I veered around the jagged edge of a rusted door that was sticking out of a stack of crushed minivans. "Plus, he knows I'm no dilettante."

"Okay, you need to stop with the app."

"Expanding my vocabulary is an interesting and useful endeavor."

"Nee." She spun me around, the diamond behind her back, and turned her heart-shaped face up to mine, her brown eyes suffused with pity. "This isn't your parents with Ari. It isn't even Cole. Rohan doesn't want a Lily imitation. He wants you."

Any heartfelt sentiment I was about to spew was kiboshed as an araculum, a spider demon the size of a kitten, skittered across my foot, training its creepy rows of eyes on me.

I screamed, jerking back so hard I smacked my tailbone on an engine hoist. "Fuuuck!"

Leo crouched down by the araculum.

"Don't touch it!" I yelled.

"I've touched worse."

"That's on you for hooking up with Drio." I hissed through the burn, rubbing my back.

The demon scurried off under a VW camper and I heaved a sigh of relief.

Until he returned.

With buddies.

My first thought was "The kids!" then I had no time to think because dozens of araculum poured from the cars, swarming us. I burst into a full-body electric current, doing a cartoony jig so they couldn't crawl up my legs. My normally ghost-pale skin turned blue, animated lightning bolts sliding over it as I slammed the monsters with everything I had.

Only once I'd dispatched the last of my attackers did I see Leo's blood-covered hands. She clutched an araculum and was exsanguinating the fuck out of it. The demon was literally deflating, its legs spasming, and its body shriveling in on itself. Its fur was so soaked, the demon resembled a bloody sponge. The run-off dripped over Leo's wrists, falling with quiet plops on her cute blue pedicure and running into the dirt next to the velvet bag laying at her feet.

Hot copper filled the air and my stomach heaved. Way to make me not care about the diamond.

With a soft pop, the final araculum winked out of existence, sucked dry. Leo had activated the sweet spot to kill it.

I forced myself not to step back and injected as much not-wigged-out cheer into my voice as I could. "Wow. Can you scent me when I'm on my period? Like a shark?"

Leo's eyes flashed red as she licked the blood off the inside of her wrist, dainty, like a cat. "No."

A tense silence fell over us, broken only by the crackle of Leo halfway unwrapping a power bar she'd stashed in the pocket of her sundress. Gotta love a dress with pockets. Even one with bloody fingerprints now dotting it. She crammed a piece of it into her mouth, barely chewing it before swallowing. "This is why I have to eat all the time." I looked blankly at her. "The redcap goblin thing. If I don't eat?" She ripped the rest of the bar open. "I crave blood. Probably have to rampage and pillage to satisfy it."

My eyes bounced around for a safe place to look because the savagery of her bloody hands and feet were an unnerving contrast to my adorable friend. "That would suck," I said carefully. "Hard to fit that in to your school schedule."

"And work. Rampaging doesn't give me extended medical."

"What happens if you do get all bloodlusty and don't satisfy it?" I braced myself. I wasn't going to electrocute my bestie but her eyes still had a slight red haze to them.

She swallowed the other half of the energy bar and the haze faded. "I'd feel inclined to sport a hat kept wet with blood. The hottest accessory for any fashion-conscious redcap." She twisted the torn wrapper, her bleak eyes at odds with her flippancy. "I'm scared one day I won't make the right choice."

I'd never seen Leo's goblin magic and she'd never volunteered, so I'd never pushed her on it before. Seeing my best friend vamp out didn't even phase me in the grand picture of what my life had become. What did phase me was the grand picture of what my life had become.

I should have reassured her that she'd always make the right choice, because at my continued silence Leo scooped the velvet bag off the ground and stomped off. "This is why I didn't want you to ever see it. Because you can't unsee it. Like that good-one-side dolphin we found on spring break."

I ran after her. "I shoot electricity, my twin suffocates people with shadows, and I'm dating Ginsu Man. We're all freaks, Leo. You're not a half-rotted aquatic mammal. You're my best friend and I love you." I pointed at her chin. "You got a little schmutz there."

Leo licked the blood off, her guarded eyes trained on mine.

I yawned and cocked an eyebrow.

A long, assessing look later, my bestie gave me a very shark-like grin that I swear involved too many teeth. "You scared of me?"

"Little bit. Yeah. Happy?" We ended up in the back left corner of the lot, a large unused space that had been bulldozed into uneven dirt in anticipation of more car storage.

"Yup." She stuffed the wrapper in her pocket, then glanced at her hands. "It's been way too long. I needed that fix."

"Don't make yourself sick. If you need to, suck 'em dry, baby."

"I always do," she said.

"Phrasing."

She patted my cheek, leaving a sticky, bloody smear. "Should have set up a safe word."

I spun in a circle, sunlight winking off the cars and cooking me alive. No signs of zizu demon life at all. "Now what? Either the diamond is a dud or the demon isn't–"

More giggling from the two chubby, and now grubby, kindergarteners. Sunlight caught their baby-feather hair tufting off their heads. Wait. Zizu had feathers. These kids had been following us for a reason and it wasn't because they were little dorks.

Bingo! "Leo! Show the diamond!"

She was already opening the bag.

Tony and Clea giggled and ran off. Nope. I wasn't playing hide and seek with a couple of demons.

I chased after them, clouds of dust kicking up at my feet. They zipped around the corner and I put on an extra burst of speed to catch up. Closing the distance, I flung my magic at them, scooping them up in my electric net.

"Kids!" Eddy skidded to a stop, his voice an anguished howl. He dropped his yellow tool box and sledgehammer.

"Back off, demon," I snarled at him.

"Nava!" Leo's face had drained of all color. "What have you done?"

The kids thrashed and screamed in my net.

Really terrified, really *human* screaming.

I'd just attacked human kids.

I carefully set them down on the ground with shaking hands, shutting down my magic. "I'm sorry," I babbled.

I'd been so sure.

The kids were ugly crying with snotty sobs. Eddy ran toward them but Leo reached Tony and Clea first, trying to calm them down.

I'd been so wrong.

I ran my thumbnail hard enough over my cuticles to rip them off. Blood welled up in half-moons.

Tony grabbed the diamond out of Leo's hand, right as Clea kicked her in the shins. Leo yowled and ran after the little spawn, but they remained two steps out of reach.

"You little assholes!" I blasted the kids, who'd morphed wings and were zigzag running trying to get lift-off. I whirled on Eddy, convinced I'd find papa demon, but he was still human, his expression glazed with pain.

"You don't understand," he said. "They're just children."

"They're demons." A ball of magic danced in my palm. "How about you?"

He held up his hands, cautiously stepping forward. "They're not evil. They're just scared."

Was he for real?

Leo snagged Tony by his leg, his blue outfit shredded over his bird body, and brought him crashing down. He tossed the diamond to his sister.

"Riddle me this," Leo said. "What's up with the purple magic?"

Tony snarled and called her a bunch of names that were troubling when said in a clear, high voice.

Clea clutched the diamond to her chest and flew to the top of a bright green engine hoist.

"Answer me." Leo raised her bloody hand. Still struggling, Tony turned his still-human, little boy face to hers, his eyes pooling with tears. Leo hesitated and the demon yanked free.

Eddy rushed me, knocking into me like a roaring bear. His ball cap sailed into the dirt.

"Quit it!" I twisted left, stumbling over my feet and barely avoiding frying the guy, my magic going wild to scorch the hoist Clea was on.

"Daddy!" Clea flew down to Eddy.

Winding my current around the boy demon's leg like a lasso, I swung him high into the air. Clea gasped but I only had eyes for Eddy. "Tell one of them to answer the question or they're toast."

Eddy wrapped a protective arm around Clea, sledgehammer at the ready. "I'll kill you before you hurt another feather on either of them."

I used every ounce of willpower to keep up my tough-girl bravado when with each of the little guy's cries as he dangled there, my heart broke into smaller and smaller pieces. My expression hardened. "You sure you can?"

Clea tugged on Eddy's sleeve. "Make her put Tony down."

Eddy glanced down at her, seeing the diamond for the first time. He blinked and reached for it. "Clea, give that to me."

"No, Daddy." She hugged it tightly, hopping away on needle-sharp talons.

Eddy lunged for her so I shot the ground at his feet. "You. Stay."

The kidling demons were starting to molt in distress, blond feathers drifting down to the ground.

I swallowed past the lump in my throat. The demons were the only leverage I had, so I increased the voltage pouring through Tony. Silver-blue sparks danced through the air.

He screamed.

"I'll answer!" Clea cried.

I released my magic and Tony plummeted to the ground. He hit, rolled twice, and lay still. If I could see him, he wasn't dead, but I still felt like a fucking monster.

Panting, I brushed stinging sweat from my eyes. "Purple magic."

"Witch and demon magic," Clea said a voice strung high with fear.

"Thanks. I've used crayons before. A partnership or coercion?"

"No true demon would willingly help a human," she spat at Leo.

"I'm special." Leo waved a bloody hand at Eddy, who'd been edging closer to the diamond. "You really want to listen to your kids and stay back."

He stopped, holding himself in check with visible effort.

"Less insulting my friend. More answering." I planted myself over her brother's body.

"Forced," she sneered. "Magic isn't crayons, it doesn't automatically combine. One magic must become submissive to the other for that to happen." Interesting.

"Binding demons." I checked Tony's chest. Still breathing. His eyes fluttered but stayed closed. "I want to know who, why, and how."

She inched closer to Tony. "I don't know."

I blocked her. "You're lying. You zizu are oracles. What have you seen?"

"Let me be with my brother." Clea trembled.

Grr. I was the biggest fool in the world. But I was also a twin. I stepped aside.

Clea knelt down and touched Tony, but he didn't stir. Her eyes turned milky and her head jerked back.

"Tick tock, goes the clock, blood to rule the might." She spoke in a singsong voice that caused goosebumps to break out along my skin. "Tick tock, speed the clock, the lovers reunite."

Peachy. Creepy nursery rhyme prophecies starting with a clock metaphor always boded so well for a happy ending.

"What the fuck is that supposed to mean?" I braced a hand against a school bus, heat and magic overuse making me dizzy, but she didn't answer.

Whatever. I had at least a partial answer to my questions and we were all going to walk out of here alive.

Eddy rushed Clea, swiping the diamond from her hand, and holding it aloft. His face was bathed in wonder.

Leo and I both sprinted for him, but Clea got to him first.

"Mine, Daddy!" She swiped the diamond away with one of her talons, slicing his flesh open. Blood was everywhere, on the ground, on the engine hoist, on dead husks of cars.

Eddy paled, clutching his arm, and crumpled to the ground.

Clea ducked her head. "Sorry."

Eddy started convulsing.

"Poison." Leo dropped to her knees beside Eddy, placed her hands on him, and shuddered.

"What are you doing?" I said.

"Drawing out the poison. Cool, huh?" She was sweating, a milky ooze bubbling out of his skin and over her hands.

"Die on me and you're so dead," I said.

She was coated in the toxin. Could there be residual effects for Leo? Some slow poisoning where we'd think she just had the flu and then bam! She's dead? I had to trust she knew what she was doing, but I wanted to knock her aside and hose her down, because in the scheme of Leo versus this guy, there was no comparison. If that made me selfish, so be it.

"All good," she said in a shaky voice. "You should get your cholesterol checked," she said to Eddy, scrubbing her hands with dirt to remove the toxins.

He turned his head and vomited.

I swallowed hard against the taste of metallic bile. Tony was still unconscious, his little boy features slack, and Clea, lip trembling, kept apologizing to her daddy. I couldn't leave these demons alive. Human life trumped demon and Eddy had already had one brush with death.

The more firmly I entrenched myself in this fight against evil, the more my moral compass was more of a moral tightrope.

"Is Daddy going to be okay?" Clea asked.

"Yeah."

She nodded and returned to her brother, trying to shake him awake.

Coward that I was, I waited until her face was bent down towards Tony's and I couldn't see her eyes before killing her. The fact that I dispatched of both demons with two quick strikes was little consolation.

Eddy cried brokenly, his entire body racked with sobs.

"I'm sorry." There was no forgiveness in the hate-filled glower he shot me. I picked up the discarded sledgehammer and stalked off.

Waves of anxiety rolled off Leo, running beside me to keep up, the diamond clutched in her closed fist.

I waited until Eddy could no longer see us, and then I wailed on the first intact car I found, obliterating its windshield and smashing its doors until they crumpled and broke off their frames.

I tossed the sledgehammer away with a shriek, my chest heaving.

Leo hugged me. "You had to do it. Him wanting to parent them, knowing they were demons? It wasn't normal. It couldn't work."

"What's so wrong with wanting normal? Maybe he couldn't have kids any other way? Maybe–"

"No. We can't obsess about maybe. This is the hand we're dealt. Normal isn't always in the cards and the sooner people face that fact, the better." Her voice was steel. Someday I'd ask her how hard it had been to reconcile herself to being half-demon.

"Eddy playing dad to demons may have been deluded," I said. "But wanting that connection? Not because of proximity or adrenaline rush bonding or because I'm the only female option in his Rasha life, but an unassailable certainty that Ro's mine and I'm his? I mean..." Fuck it. There was no way to recover from that Freudian slip.

Leo blinked at me. "Wow."

"I'm just saying it wasn't deluded of Eddy to try for everything he'd ever wanted." I spun around and walked out of the lot.

4

Hastings Skatepark was located at the edge of the Italian Gardens on Vancouver's east side. The whir of wheels on concrete overpowered the cascade of water trickling out of the faces carved into the ivy-wrapped stone pillars in the garden and running along tiled channels. However, nothing could drown out the screams from riders on the Hellevator or The Beast at Playland, the huge amusement park sitting smack dab between the gardens and the racetrack to the east.

Rohan greeted me at the skatepark's turnstile gate, sporting baggy cargos worn low on his hips and a T-shirt that had been washed so many times that whatever cool boarder logo had originally adorned it was now a vague suggestion of a line. His skateboard was tucked under one arm.

"Cute disguise," I said.

His eyes hit my face for a second, needle-sharp. I'd splashed a small lake's worth of cold water on my red-rimmed eyes at Leo's before driving here but I guess it hadn't been enough.

I edged past him into the brightly tagged, multi-level skate park, with its checkered concrete. "No Mercy" graffiti was sandwiched between a painted cartoon bunny and realistic-looking bulldog on the main bowl, while traffic beyond the park provided a soothing white noise.

"Hey." He tugged gently on my elbow. "What happened to Plan B?"

I stepped into his open arms, burying my head in his neck. His silky curls tickled my cheek and the scent of musk and iron enveloped me. Ro provided a safe harbor with his arms wrapped around me and my head tucked in under his chin. My breathing calmed and my tension rolled away like an outbound tide, my body resonating against his. He was my personal tuning fork, not for pitch, but alignment with the universe.

He kissed my head. "Whatever went down, let it go."

I shook it off. Not in a boppy Taylor Swift way. In a "cram that sucker into the overstuffed, creaking box of things in my psyche I couldn't deal with" way.

I leaned on the large "No Graffiti" sign bolted to the chain link fence and filled Rohan in on when and how magic combined and that I'd been right about demon coercion. "But wait, ladies and gentlemen. Order in the next fifteen minutes and we'll throw in a prophecy, absolutely free! 'Tick tock goes the clock, blood to rule the might. Tick tock speeds the clock, the lovers reunite.' Judging from the first part, I'd say a witch or group of them used blood as a binding agent."

"You got the how on the purple magic." Rohan high-fived me. "The timeline and lovers don't mean anything to me, though."

"Too bad we don't have an Acme Corp gadget to spit out the answers to all our questions."

"That'd be more Wayne Enterprises technology," he said.

"You are such a nerd."

"It's common sense. Acme is low-tech. You're talking major computing power."

"Super nerd." I poked him in the chest. "And don't bother to deny it, guy who insisted on wearing a different superhero costume every day in grade one."

Rohan knocked his hip against mine. "It was endearing."

A laugh burst out of me. "Your precious Romantics are the ones that called it 'endearing.' You do read your fan boards. I knew it!"

"Do not." Rohan dropped his board onto the concrete. "There's only one person here reading my fan boards, and it's not me, sweetheart."

"It's not me either," I backtracked. "Leo told me."

"Uh-huh." He got a pious expression. "My mom reads them and shares the good stuff."

"You lie like a rug. How's it going with the dealer?"

Rohan nodded at some skinny kid riding the lip of one of the bowls. "That's him. Elliot. I've been working on getting his source."

"He's good."

"He's okay." Rohan's critical expression matched his tone. "He's got decent tech but no gnar."

I shot him a blank look.

"No style. You wanna have both when you skate."

"Whatever, Tony Hawk. Go. I'll hang out, watch the park. See if I can spot any other deals going down."

Rohan kissed my nose. "Put on sunscreen. I put some in your purse this morning." He pushed off, his body one with the board as he carved a lazy semi-circle.

I blinked. I didn't know he could skate.

He rode up a graffiti-tagged curved ramp, hovering on his back wheels at the top for an impossibly long moment. Right when gravity had to make him its bitch and a wipe-out was imminent, Rohan popped his board up, catching it mid-air in both hands briefly before reversing directions. Riding halfway back down, he jumped his board onto the railing beside the ramp, skating down the edge with effortless grace and nailing his dismount.

The showoff then had the audacity to wink at me.

Twice in two days Rohan had pulled out a talent I'd had no idea he had.

Irritating, old-timey music on a loop grew louder as a colorful ice cream van pulled up to the curb. I jogged over, waiting patiently for the group of teens ahead of me to get their bounty, and ordered an orange Popsicle, since Leo had been a brat about me getting anything when we'd stopped at the store on our drive back to her place.

"I should get my boyfriend something." Wallet in hand, I scanned the menu board tacked up next to the order window while the bubbly blonde manning the truck flaked off her mint green nail polish.

I had no clue what Rohan liked.

He knew pretty much everything about me but the reverse wasn't true. Admittedly, our couple status was new but it wasn't like our relationship was. We'd been dancing around each other from day one. I was closer to Rohan than anyone other than Ari and Leo but how well did I really know him? How well was he letting me? We'd fought together, he had my back, but some of the basics were blank spaces. Cole and I had known everything about each other before we started dating, and Lily was well versed in Rohan 101.

I knew the stuff that mattered, didn't I? And I could make educated guesses on the rest of it. I scanned the menu for the most boring ice cream I could find. "A Revello, please." I collected my change and the purchases, heading back toward the park.

"Hey!" Rohan rode after a fleeing Elliot.

Stuffing my wallet back into my pocket, I unwrapped my orange Popsicle and took that first sugar-infused taste. Mmmm.

Elliot skated by and, without missing my next lick, I kicked him in the kneecaps. He flew off his board and crashed onto the grass, rolling twice. The board shot forward, pinged off a lamppost and rolled into the gutter. Elliot groaned, flopped out on his back.

I pinned him in place, leaning my scuffed-up sneaker on a pressure point on the side of his left calf, immobilizing him.

He choked out a pained gasp.

Rohan arrived, kicking his board up to stop. "Nice."

"Thanks."

Rohan squatted down. "Where did you get the Sweet Tooth?"

"Fuck. You."

"Listen, Elliot," Rohan said. "I'm not here to narc you out. But this shit is dangerous and I want it off the streets."

Elliot's cheek was all road-rashy from the fall. His shaggy hair hung in his eyes in sweaty clumps. He was stinky, clearly in pain, and not about to talk.

"Ro," I said softly, shaking my head. My Vulcan immobilizer trick wasn't doing it and we couldn't seriously hurt him. Even if he was sixteen and dealing drugs, I was full up on menacing the underaged.

Rohan stood up, reaching for his wallet. "We'll pay you for the info."

"I don't need cash," Elliot boasted.

"Because you're a drug dealing little shit," I said. "No surprise there. What exactly do you want?"

He eyed me speculatively. "Lemme see your tits."

I leaned harder on the pressure point.

"Fuuuuck!"

"I'd say that was her counter-offer. Is that ice cream for me?" Rohan asked.

"Oh yeah. Revello good?" I handed it over.

"If there's no Cornetto? Sure."

There. I could figure Ro out, no problem.

"Tits," Elliot ground out.

I lifted my foot off of him. "You useless cliché. No. But I will give you jerk-off material."

Elliot scrambled to his feet, smartly keeping half his attention on Ro, who munched on his Revello with the blandest of all poker faces.

I teased my lip to the tip of the Popsicle. Rohan raised his eyebrows, his gold eyes dancing, but my focus was absolute. I gave the Popsicle the best ten-second blow job in the history of mankind.

Rohan barked a laugh. "I knew Lolita was still in there."

I popped my lips off the icy sugar stick and stuck my orange tongue out at him.

"Dude," Elliot said, holding out a fist bump to Ro.

"Excuse me?" I bit into the Popsicle and Elliot flinched. "Why does he get the fist bump? He is in no way responsible."

"Her mouth is a marvel," Rohan added.

"Thanks, babe."

Rohan fist bumped the kid, winking at me. "Dealer. Name. Now."

"Candyman," Elliot said. I boffed him across the top of the head. He rubbed it. "I'm not shitting you," he said. "That's the only name I know."

"Too bad." Rohan's voice was cold.

"Bad for you." Elliot pulled a switchblade out of his pocket, flicking it open. "We're done."

Rohan laughed, but it was dark and held no hint of humor. He disarmed Elliot in a flash, dancing the blade over his knuckles while the kid was still gaping at him. "Not 'til I say so. How do we find him?"

Elliot swallowed and stepped back from Rohan. "I'm waaay too lowly to be allowed in his presence. I deal with middle management."

"Great." Rohan flipped the knife into his hand, blade casually pointed at Elliot. "Describe this middle man and where we can find him."

"That's sexist," Elliot said. "He's a she." He threw me a chin nod, like he'd just earned some level of solidarity with me.

"Hashtag feminism." Idiot.

Five minutes later, Rohan released Elliot with a promise that if he continued dealing, their next meeting wouldn't go so well.

"Do I get my blade back?" Elliot held out his hand.

Rohan smirked. "You wanna take it from me?"

Elliot fled.

Ro snapped the blade in half. "What a piece of shit. Guaranteed that kid would have stabbed himself with it."

Our middle woman, Aida, was a wreta, a demon with a crescent-shaped birthmark that was mostly likely the same wreta we'd met back when we were tracking Asmodeus. She'd been close to killing off some poor guy thanks to this highly addictive hallucinatory secretion of hers. I doubted her discharge was the basis for Sweet Tooth, but there were plenty of other crimes she could answer for.

Since this demon liked to come out at night, we had a few hours to kill.

I threaded my arm through Rohan's. "Come with me."

"Where?"

I pointed up at the roller coaster visible from the skatepark. "It's one of the few remaining wooden coasters in the world. You shouldn't miss it while you're here."

"Okay." Not exactly the "I'll be around for ages and we can ride it any time" answer I'd been hoping for.

We cut through the gardens, looping around to Playland's colorful front gates.

"Where's the diamond?" Ro asked.

"Locked up tight in the trunk." We'd give it to Rabbi Abrams to dispose of.

We agreed that we needed to learn if this witch or group of witches involved in binding demons was being coerced by the Brotherhood or acting of their own free will. Given the Rasha fingerprint on the metal spine that had been used to modify the gogotas that had attacked us in Prague, there was definitely a connection with our organization.

The line-up for the coaster was fiendishly long, and we couldn't exactly discuss demons and secret societies, which was fine by me. I continued paying up the bet I'd recently lost, and recounted more of the fanfic I'd written about Ro's band, while forced to listen to all the factual details I'd gotten incorrect. He delivered them in the driest, most professorial tone imaginable, with his editorials on the sex scenes particularly hilarious. The time flew by, and soon we were safely ensconced in the front seat of the car.

Though in Ro's opinion, "safely" may have been a bit of a stretch. He tugged on the slender metal bar across us, the only thing keeping us from cannonballing out of the coaster. "It's not even flush against us." He shot me a suspicious glare. "Is this going to be like that damned mini-train in Prague?"

I snickered. The car moved forward, clacking against the wooden rails in a familiar rhythm. Slowly, it bumped its way up the first big incline, taking us higher and higher above the park. Riders on the swings flew out as if to greet us, while The Beast ride soared and dipped by our heads.

I flung my hands in the air as the car paused on the precipice. It hurtled down the tracks and I screamed, wind streaming over me. My body half-pitched over the bar, my stomach dropped into my toes, and my ass lifted off of the seat.

"Fuuuck!" Rohan gripped the safety bar, his eyes screwed closed, but his grin wide with glee.

Over and over, we climbed and plunged, every part of me bouncing and rattling. The coaster curved sideways and I slid into Rohan, jabbing his side with my hip bone.

I didn't stop laughing until the coaster finally slowed with a jolt that snapped our heads back. I hopped out, pulling Rohan onto the platform with me. "Didja love it?"

"Not one bit," he said, hustling me back to the start of the line.

We went three more times, until our bones clanked as badly as the coaster. I cracked my neck, inhaling axle grease and hot concrete, and pointed to a nearby trailer. "Now you may buy me mini donuts."

"I'm gonna need a second job to feed you," he groused.

We stepped up to the cash. "Two bags," Ro said to the young employee. He glanced at me and added, "With extra cinnamon and sugar."

I squeezed my boyfriend's arm. "You're working out just fine."

We drove back separately that evening, Rohan beating me back to Demon Club. By the time I pulled in, he was already parked, sitting on the hood of his car, Skyping with someone.

"Your mom threw that shirt out years ago."

I pulled up short at the Indian-accented man's voice coming out of Ro's phone.

Rohan clutched his T-shirt possessively. "She can keep thinking that."

His dad laughed. "Coward. Are you coming home for the golf tournament?"

Another man, this one with a mild Irish accent chimed in. "We need you, son. Don't leave me alone with Dev."

"You can't get enough of me, Liam," his dad replied.

"You play golf?" I whispered. How many secret talents could one guy possibly have? Was this all rock stars or just Rohan being an over-achiever?

Rohan looked up from his phone. "Badly, under protest, and only for charity events."

"Who's that?" Dev said.

I pointed from myself to the house, trying to tiptoe away. Rohan grabbed my hand before I could escape, but I refused to be pulled into visual range.

"Nava," Rohan said. That was a nice neutral answer, right? Nothing to tip off who I was to these people, when I had yet to meet anyone from his family because it was waaay tooo soon.

"The girlfriend!" his dad announced in glee. There was a chorus of "oooohs" from the men.

I ducked my head to hide my hot blush. Ro had told them about me?

"You're embarrassing yourselves," Rohan said. "Please stop."

"Put her on," Dev demanded.

Rohan laughed at my impersonation of a fleeing cartoon character, legs pumping. He dropped an arm over my shoulders and pulled me in front of the screen.

I smoothed down my hair and waved at the camera. "Hi."

"You're even lovelier than your photo," Dev said.

I blinked. Ro had sent a photo? "Thank you. I see where Rohan gets his good looks." His dad, mid-fifties, was incredibly handsome with his twinkling brown eyes, nice biceps, and dark hair shot with gray at the temples.

My boy was going to age well.

Dev shook his head from side-to-side. "I'm generally considered the better looking of us."

"In your dreams, old man," Rohan said.

"I see it," I said, nudging Ro's hip with mine.

"You, I like," Dev said. "Him, not so much."

"It's a pleasure to meet you as well, Liam," I said to Ro's godfather, and the source of his middle name.

Liam pressed a hand to his heart, cramming Dev to one side of the screen, a sliver of golf course visible behind them. "Ah, sure look it, she knows who I am. Nava, I too, have a son. A wonderful Irish boy with eyes like the Emerald Isle itself. He's a doctor, working with the less fortunate." He threw me a "what do you think?" wink and a nod.

I laughed, instantly taking to this man with his crazy shock of pale blond hair and smattering of freckles.

"Faith and Begorrah, but you're slathering it on, Liam." Rohan deadpanned in an Irish accent.

I grinned at him.

Onscreen, the two men nudged each other. "I like how she looks at the lad," Liam said.

I screwed up my face, barely resisting the urge to hide behind my hair.

"Maya will be sorry she missed meeting you," Dev said.

I praised all the gods and goddesses I could think of that I hadn't gotten an impromptu first meeting with Rohan's mom. That shit was going to require epic preparation. And possibly Ativan. Maya Mitra was one of my idols. An Indian-Jewish woman who'd smashed through the music industry boys' club to become a top music producer. Whether being her only child's girlfriend was going to make her less or more enthused about me remained to be seen.

"Is my son treating you well?" Dev fixed an expectant eye on me.

Rohan tilted his head, trying not to smirk.

"He is," I said brightly. Then, for Rohan's ears only I added: "Dependent on his remembrance of certain cosmically important imminent events."

"Maybe when Rohan comes back for the tournament, you can accompany him," Dev said.

"Great idea," Rohan said as I gave my best noncommittal smile.

The other men laughed. We said our goodbyes and hung up.

I facepalmed. Then groaned and rubbed my face. "I can't believe you let me meet your dad and godfather with cinnamon sugar on my nose."

"Relax." Rohan tugged my hand away from my face. "They loved you. I know it was unexpected, but thank you for being so nice."

I brushed the remaining sugar off my nose. "I wasn't being nice. I liked them. Hanging with them is probably like watching a comedy routine."

"Too true. Thanks, anyway. It means a lot to me that you get along and you don't mind sharing me with them."

Sure, harmony between the girlfriend and the parental units was a good thing but his words fed into the low-grade ball of unease churning me up these days. Ro had whole-heartedly always embraced who he was. It was an amazing quality and a lot of why, as a rock star, he was so passionate and such a great singer-songwriter. He'd owned every inch of his identity.

Then he'd walked away cold turkey. Yes, he'd been messed up after Asha's death and he'd become Rasha, and those were both valid reasons, but it was like he'd totally shed something essential about himself for something else. He was a rock star until he wasn't. Then he was a hunter. Now he was inviting me to Los Angeles and really pleased that I got along with his family. That was super sweet, but I was terrified that with his faith in the Brotherhood crumbling, our really new relationship was his latest extreme, because damn, he was just going all in at warp speed.

I fixed my ponytail. "I'm gonna take a shower before we go demon hunting. Then I'll make us both dinner. There's still some Chickeny Delight."

"Yum."

I waited.

"I'm looking forward to it."

I waited some more.

Rohan pushed me toward the house. "Yes, I'll make us dinner."

I blew him a kiss, braced myself, and headed inside to pick up my show and tell. After today's zizu visit, Dr. Gelman didn't get to be off the radar anymore.

I wiped my palms off on my shorts and knocked on Rabbi Abram's office door on the ground floor.

"Hello?" His voice floated out from Ms. Clara's office.

I switched directions and pushed her door open. My Jewish Dumbledore was ransacking Ms. Clara's desk drawers. He wore one of his many black suits, a kippah bobby-pinned to his thinning white hair.

Ms. Clara's office was a shrine to order and symmetry, from the striking framed photos of Vancouver that were never even a millimeter crooked to her custom-made drawer organizers. "You mess up her desk, Rabbi, and she'll kill you."

Our resident administrator moonlighted as an in-demand dominatrix, though if Rabbi Abrams didn't know that about her, I wasn't going to enlighten him.

Ms. Clara was currently in Jerusalem, ostensibly at a meeting of Brotherhood admins. Wild, unfulfilled sexual tension with Tree Trunk, a.k.a. Baruch Ya'ari, weapons specialist and my adored mentor and friend who was based there at Brotherhood HQ, was a totally secondary agenda.

Rabbi Abrams stroked his longish, white beard with gnarled fingers. "Help me find my Kit Kats, Navela. A good Kosher treat."

The faint smell of butterscotch wrapped around him so he'd already dipped into the candy today. "No way. I got the run-down. Diabetes runs in your family."

"Et tu, Brute?"

I dropped my glance to my feet, ashamed.

"What's wrong?" He squinted at the hard cannonball saxophone case in my hand, containing all my evidence that I'd retrieved from upstairs. "What is that?"

I perched on the edge of the seat across the desk from him and motioned for him to sit. "I have some stuff to catch you up on."

He lowered his ancient, frail body into Ms. Clara's Aeron chair. "And you think I need to be seated?" He chuckled, his laughter dying off at my somber expression, and nodded for me to continue.

I lay the large sax case across my lap, fiddling with the clasps.

"Tell me."

So I did. It wasn't exactly Once Upon a Time, but there were plenty of monsters. It had all started when we'd been in Prague tracking Samson King to prove he was a demon and not just an A-list celebrity. Rabbi Abrams had confirmed that Ari was still an initiate but the regular Brotherhood induction ritual hadn't worked so he'd told me to contact Dr. Gelman, also visiting the city for a physics conference.

Dr. Gelman had a way to induct Ari and we'd had a couple meetings. During one of them, she'd slipped me a swirled green glass amulet, fairly unremarkable except for the etching of a hamsa on the inside.

Soon after, I'd been attacked by a gogota demon sporting the spiffy new modification of a metal spine. Kind of like stegosaurus spikes attached to its back that made it harder to hit its kill spot. The demon had been gunning for me, crying "Vashar!" which I later learned was the amulet's name. When I went to see Dr. Gelman, her hotel room was trashed and gogota slime crusted the curtains. She'd gone off-grid after that, contacting me once via letter with the instructions for the induction ritual. I'd been trying to find her ever since.

Demons weren't team players at the best of times, and they certainly weren't going to aid and abet the Brotherhood. The only way the gogota had come after me was because it was bound and forced to do someone's bidding. I'd still had to prove it though, so I'd traded a demonic dog collar for the actual gogota demon that had attacked Dr. Gelman, since I'd killed the one that had gone after me. Then I'd tracked down a spell to test for magic signatures. Magic came in three colors: red for witches, pink for Rasha, and blue for demons and this spell let the caster determine which had been used on an object.

There were no traces of magic on the metal spine, meaning the modification had been manual not magic. However, Rohan had dusted the spine for prints and come up with a partial print matching a Rasha, now deceased, called Ferdinand Alves. When we'd tested the gogota itself, however, the spell revealed purple magic.

The spell also turned a yaksas horn that had come from Rohan's Askuchar mission in Pakistan purple. That assignment had been brutal with the entire village being slaughtered and the Brotherhood ordering Ro and the other Rasha to burn the bodies and destroy the evidence. The attacks hadn't made sense; gogota were simple demons who wouldn't think big picture enough to care about an amulet that stopped Rasha induction rituals, and the yaksas' assault had been too targeted and out of their normal hunting ground to fall within a normal pattern for them. Factor in a witch binding demons, however, and you got a simple, plausible solution.

Rabbi Abrams listened without interruption to my story, his face growing whiter than his hair.

I faltered a couple of times, concerned the man was going to croak, but I continued through to the grand finale of the ticking clock prophecy. I'd opened the sax case and spread the spine, the gogota's fingertip, and the fragment of horn out on the desk. "Rohan already has the name of the Rasha whose print it was. He's investigating that angle but I need to find Dr. Gelman. I need her help to figure out who this witch is. I was hoping you'd talk to her sister and find out–"

"You think my Executive is behind this?" Rabbi Abrams touched his finger to a metal spike with a shaking hand. "That they would deliberately send demons to destroy an innocent village? Demons that need no encouragement to be bloodthirsty?"

I bit my lip. "I didn't say–"

He spun his chair around, his back to me.

I waited, hoping he just needed a moment to digest all of this, but no, I'd been dismissed. Out in the corridor, I pressed my forehead into the cool plaster, wondering if I'd just made a horrible mistake.

5

"What a dump." I rubbed gum off the bottom of my shoe, standing in the doorway to the empty back room in the run-down diner that Elliot had sworn was the only place he'd ever met up with Aida.

As we stepped into the main part of the restaurant, my stomach lurched at the smell of rancid frying oil. Two guys in blue mechanic's overalls sat in one of the booths, but the rest of the ten tables were unoccupied. Faded B-movie posters hung on beige walls in need of repainting.

The grizzled cook flipped pancakes. "Help you?"

Rohan marched up to the counter. "We're supposed to meet Aida."

"She's not here."

"When's she back?" I asked.

He shrugged, scraping some black grease off the edge of his metal spatula, and not bothering to look at me.

I rapped on the laminate counter. "I asked you a question."

It wasn't so much the tone of my voice when I spoke as the fact that he saw the crescent-shaped birthmark on my cheek that made him jump to attention. Painted-on, but he didn't know that. If wreta didn't enthrall you with their secretion, they enjoyed a good intimidation. I was counting on him having experienced the latter firsthand.

"She's not coming back. Told me last night she was wrapping things up and leaving."

"Where to?" Rohan said.

"No clue." He wiped his hands on his grimy apron.

I strode around the counter and the cook shrank back against the grill. "Got a home address for her?"

One of the men glanced our way but the customers were more interested in shoveling food into their mouths than being good Samaritans.

The cook held the spatula out against me like a shield and shook his head. "No clue. I swear."

We patrolled bustling downtown thoroughfares, sketchy alleyways reeking of urine with men and women shooting up next to dumpsters, upscale clubs with ESL students from the numerous schools in the downtown core dancing in large groups, and those bars you only went to when you were already really drunk and couldn't get in anywhere else. There was no sign of Aida.

Or any other demon.

"I refuse to believe that every demon in the city simultaneously took the night off." The scarcity of evil spawn was troubling. There hadn't even been any sign of those demons that flew at your face in a blur in the summer twilight that most people mistook for asshole wasps, who sucked seconds off your life as they zipped past. I seriously hated demons.

I plodded along like the walking dead, my head woozy and my shoulders weighted down like a lead jacket, passing two dudes in Henleys, ripped jeans, and distressed buckle boots, who'd probably spent way too many hours playing Guitar Hero. They screamed drunken obscenities at each other, their faces inches apart, spittle flying, as a group of girls in miniskirts, arms thrown around their crying, raccoon-eyed friend, weighed in on the relative asshollery of one of the men.

Watching the heartbroken girl, sobs wracking her slender frame, was physically painful. I reached for Rohan's hand.

The guy on the right stumbled back, his hands outstretched to the crying girl, his expression pleading as he told he loved her.

She dashed away her tears with short angry jabs. "You love the idea of me."

Rohan squeezed my fingers; I'd let go of him.

The couple held a look that bore no sign of recrimination from either of them, just tragic acknowledgment of an ending. My heart twisted; a black-and-white bad guy would have made this easier.

He half-raised his hand in a wave. The girl nodded, and her friends sprung into motion, ushering her away and leaving him alone in the middle of the street.

Rohan pulled me tight against him as we turned off the bright lights and noisy crush of the Granville strip. "Let's not ever be them, okay?" He blinked too slowly, bleary-eyed and unshaven. "Nava?"

I slid my arm around his waist matching my strides to his. "Of course not." I looked up at him. "Want to call it a night?"

"Yeah."

We blasted the A/C and I made Ro sing along to my dad's favorite shitty soft rock station to prove he was still awake while driving. After the third 70s power ballad about imploding love, I changed it to talk radio and feigned a deep interest in the state of toll bridges here in the Lower Mainland.

Back at the mansion, I flung my clothes off and collapsed into Rohan's bed. This was my second night of a lack of sleep and I hadn't had the energy to climb my stairs. The boyfriend had refused my reasonable request to carry me, so his bed it was.

I stared up at the ceiling, hating this entire day. "You think Rabbi Abrams still likes me?"

"Yes." Rohan turned off the lamp, moonlight streaming in through his blinds. He motioned for me to turn on to my side, then spooned me. "He won't sic the Brotherhood on you."

Ro shifted to let me stuff my feet between his legs and I twisted my hair up tight so it didn't attack him.

I pulled his arm across me. "I know none of what's happened is my fault, but it's all blowing open because of me." I sighed. "He's not answering my calls."

"Mine either. But he needed to know."

"And if he didn't, it's too late now." I rubbed my eyes, taking the edge off the curl of fatigue that clawed behind my eyeballs. Tossing and turning, I sank into a sweaty sleep.

I woke up an hour later by myself in a cold bed. The thin red file folder on Rohan's dresser with the little bit of information he'd amassed on Ferdinand Alves was gone. I threw my "Karma is like 69. You get what you give." T-shirt on over boyshorts and crept through the house towards the voices filtering out from the library.

I peered in at Kane and Rohan from the safety of the shadows by the door. Through Kane's pink mesh tank top, I glimpsed the black wings tattooed on his back, though not their flame-licked tips or the scorched feathers fallen to the base of his spine.

Rohan twisted the folder. "His print was on that damn spine. There's got to be something we can follow up. Look again."

I winced. Wrong tone, Snowflake. Ro knew better. He was a performer; he could read his audience no problem.

Kane planted his hands on his denim-clad hips. "I have looked. Date of birth and current status listed as deceased. There was a list of his missions and all the chapter houses Alves was assigned to, with Los Angeles as the one on record for the past year. Standard info. That's it."

"Impossible. I've never heard of him. It's a lie."

"Then it's a lie. Look, I'm sweaty, tired, and this pink body glitter itches. So—"

"Sure. Wash off. Sleep. Don't let some Rasha's betrayal interfere with you fucking your way through every guy in Vancouver."

The scent of salt that flooded the air was so strong that my eyes watered. Kane's skin turned iridescent purple, coated with his magic poison. "Come again?"

Rohan stepped back. He rubbed the back of his neck. "Sorry, man. I just—fuck."

I pressed against the wall, letting the shadows cover me as Rohan blew past, headed downstairs. He was bound for the Vault to blow off steam. Again.

I crawled back into bed but sleep was a long time coming.

Waking up Sunday morning was a painful experience. I stomped into the kitchen, prepared to snarl at anyone that got between me and coffee. I flung open a cupboard, grabbed a mug, and did a double take.

The paintbrush on the counter was back to its original color.

"I'm guessing you heard our little chat?" Kane braced his hands at the top of the door-frame, leaning into the kitchen. His lime green pajama bottoms slid a tantalizing smidge down his hip and his bare chest showed off his perfect six-pack and the barbell jewelry in each nipple. His spiky hair was a bed-headed snarl. "Stop objectifying me. It'll only depress you that you can't have any of my magnificence." He slapped his rock-hard abs.

I mustered up a weak smile, worried that my relationship with Kane had been damaged by Rohan being a jerk. "About last night. I'm–"

Kane plucked my empty mug out of my hands, effectively shutting me up. "Ro's his own person. Just because you're dating doesn't mean you have to apologize for him. You're not responsible for him." He poured himself coffee.

Wasn't that what happened when you were in a couple? You apologized for the other person? Or had that just been me for my ex, Cole, especially near the end? I had all of one whopping teen relationship to draw on, and given how strong a personality Ro was and where we were in our lives, it wasn't much of a guide. "I'm not sure how responsible he is for himself right now."

Kane took a stupid long time hogging the sugar. "He's hyper-sensitive about anyone failing him. Don't care. We've all got our hot buttons. He doesn't have to keep repeating the same script."

Mature me did not point out his hypocrisy as he went into week three of not speaking to my brother. Besides, antagonizing him wasn't going to get me the sugar any faster. I dumped a splash of milk in my coffee, then stood pressed up against him until he got annoyed enough to hand the green-glazed sugar jug over.

I finally got that first delicious taste of caffeine, picked up the paintbrush, and ruffled my thumb through the bristles.

"What's so fascinating, babyslay?"

"Last night this paintbrush was blue."

"Blue how?" Kane snagged a banana out of the bowl on the counter and unpeeled it.

"Signature spell."

"It should still be blue." He swallowed about half in one bite while I limited my inappropriate thoughts to a scant dozen or so.

I sipped my coffee. "You'd think."

Ari walked in, already dressed in black on black. Shocking. "Morning, Nee." His eyes flicked over Kane's chest for the barest second.

Kane didn't react. Or greet him. But his eyes lingered on my twin.

Sexual tension and simmering frustration, not a combo I ever wanted to experience again.

"Good morning, Ace." I poked Kane in the hip. He swatted my hand away.

Ari swiped my coffee away, took a sip, grimaced, and shoved it back into my hands.

I shook sloshing java off my fingers. "I was enjoying that."

"No, you weren't. You get a new paintbrush?"

"Nope. Wait here. I want to see something." Making a big show of clutching my coffee to my chest, I retrieved the last of the Sweet Tooth from my bedroom and brought it back to the kitchen.

I slapped the vial into Ari's hand. "Check it out. It's not pink anymore." No more crystals either, just a fine white powder.

"I see that." He inspected it. "Looks like corn starch."

Kane slow-clapped him.

I muscled in between them. "Quit being assholes. You guys have to keep each other alive in a couple days." I dipped the tip of my pinky into the powder and licked my finger. "Corn starch it is. Whatever magic element was combined with it to make the Sweet Tooth is gone."

Kane held the vial up to the light. "If the magic has a short shelf life, that makes this stuff more valuable. Limited supply."

"He's right. Oh, shut up," Ari said at Kane's gloat.

"Gawd," I muttered. I snagged a croissant from the bag on the counter and went in search of Rohan.

He'd set up shop in the library and dragged the whiteboard upstairs from the conference room. On it he'd scrawled a list of demons with any type of toxin or hallucinogen. His cramped writing covered the board.

Rohan was sprawled on one of the sofas grouped near the fireplace. Big chunks of the floor-to-ceiling bookcases were empty, with half-open books strewn over chairs, the long table that ran along the window, and the Persian carpet. "It's the list that won't quit," he groused.

He read my "Karma is like 69" T-shirt and laughed, resting his head back against the top of the sofa. "A joke for every occasion."

"I'm a regular walking comedienne," I said waspishly. Snarky comments were the last thing I needed from him right now.

"You are. You're always ready to laugh shit off. I need that."

Oh. He wasn't being sarcastic. I plopped down next to him, resting my head on his shoulder as I perused the database entry on his laptop. Lavellan: a poisonous water shrew.

"Fun new development." I told him about the evaporating magic. "Could that help knock some spawn off the list?"

"Not sure. I doubt anyone did tests on how long any of these poisons last."

"Because they'd rather kill the demons producing the poison than study them."

"Even so." Rohan settled a pillow behind his back. "How short is this shelf life? A day? A month?"

I pulled the laptop over. "Let's hope that Aida hasn't skipped town."

"At least we know wreta demons aren't responsible for Sweet Tooth." Wretas needed to be present for their drug to be consumed. The user generally sucked the secretion straight off the demon, though they could just fling prismatic drops at you to get you hooked if so inclined. It was possible that the demons had found a way to anchor their secretion in corn starch, but Sweet Tooth didn't behave the way the wreta's hallucinatory bliss did. Wreta secretions were powerfully addictive–Christina couldn't have done it a couple of times and walked away. She'd have been emaciated, sucked dry, seen her hair fall out, and also be most likely dead now.

My fingers flew over the keyboard. Our lunch detritus ended up shoved to one end of the library table, and I took the occasional pull of the bottle of Coke at my elbow despite it having gone flat, warm, and gross about an hour ago.

Our digging did yield a few notable facts about wretas: they tended to live in groups and if they didn't secrete on a regular basis, they stank like a noxious sewer. This resulted in them living close to waste-producing industries.

"Got something like that in Vancouver?" Rohan asked.

"We do actually. There's this slice of land down by the water on the east side. Houses both a chicken rendering plant and a waste reduction plant. When the wind blows the wrong way?" I plugged my nose. It smelled like Satan's sweaty sneakers and death. I opened Google Maps.

Rohan peered over my shoulder. "Look for places with lots of bamboo planted."

"Why?"

"They're excellent for filtering out formaldehyde, which is a byproduct the wreta produce. And they grow tall, allowing for privacy."

It was extremely slow going but we eventually narrowed down the possibilities to a handful of places. It took a bit of finagling to get the equipment we needed without Ms. Clara here to facilitate everything for us, but she worked her magic from Jerusalem.

The first address we went to had been demolished since its Google Maps images had been taken and the second was home to a sweet old Italian man who shared large juicy cherries right off his tree with us.

The third house had freshly-painted cream trim and stained-glass windows. We drove around back. The man wearing thick garden gloves to protect himself from the salt boxes he was stuffing into the trash aroused our suspicions; the crescent-shaped birthmark on his cheek confirmed them. The wreta didn't pay any attention to the white van with the pest control logo on the side that slowly cruised by.

We added gloves and face masks with respiratory filters to our yellow chemical suits, piled out of the van and entered through the back gate.

The demon was crouched chanting on the lawn next to a salt circle that ran the perimeter of the fence and continued around the side of the house. He paused at our approach. Big mistake.

"Where's Aida?" Rohan growled, stabbing the wreta's shoulder with his finger blades. The blades should have cut through the protective gloves. But that was a part of Rohan's magic: all of the knives without any of the clothing loss. Much to my dismay.

The demon froze. His body ran slick with his secretion, drops slashing everywhere. We would have been tripping balls if not for these handy dandy protective chemical suits.

When his drug failed to take us out, he burst into a flurry of fists and kicks, wrenching himself loose. I tackled the wreta, but he fought hard, demanding we let him finish the ward. It took both of us to pin him in place.

I elbowed the demon in the face. "Aida. Where is she?"

This just set him off again, thrashing and going on about the stupid ward and how it was coming.

"What's coming?" I said.

The wreta's panic escalated into full-blown hysteria. He grabbed Rohan's hand, using Ro's index finger blade to slice his own wrist open. Rohan rolled the demon sideways before any blood could hit the salt line and set the ward.

We didn't know what the ward was meant to do, and we couldn't be caught in unknown magic, but part of me was certain we'd regret our decision to leave the property exposed.

Rohan leaned his weight on the demon. "Where's Candyman?"

"Answer him." I kicked away part of the salt ward line.

The wreta stared helplessly at it, then grabbed Ro's finger and rammed it into his eyeball. His kill spot. He disappeared, dead, leaving only an oily puddle that seeped into the dirt.

Rohan punched the ground, his expression a feral snarl.

"'Choose death' isn't a popular slogan in the demon lexicon." I nervously scanned the backyard. "What the fuck is coming?"

Rohan put a finger to his lips and motioned to the back porch. We crept up the stairs and I eased open the kitchen door.

A scuffed navy backpack filled with cash sat on the kitchen counter next to a cell phone with no security code on it. Gotta love demon arrogance. There was no one listed in the contacts, and no data plan to check the browser history, but we found a text chain about some kind of drop in two days' time, along with a time and place. I tried calling that number but it was disconnected.

I tossed the phone into the backpack and tiptoed down the hallway, grateful that the shag carpet muffled the tread of our heavy work boots. I hit the living room doorway and recoiled, the reek of hot copper and rotting meat thick even through my respiratory filter.

I'd stopped so suddenly that Rohan slammed into my back and I had to grab the doorframe to stop myself from stumbling inside the room.

The floor was slick with blood. Demon viscera glistened under the LED overhead lamp.

Two wreta sat there, unmoving. Or well, one sat there, oblivious to the puddle of piss at his feet. The other one had been ripped apart like a chicken carcass and what was left of the five and a half foot demon was being funneled into a giant gaping maw.

The demon eating the wreta had an amorphous blobby body with skin like an oil spill, and a smaller egg-shaped head that brushed the nine-foot-ceiling. The head was featureless except for that mouth which took up most of the real estate, a massive pit sucking back its victim.

The hungry demon turned, revealing a single, perfectly formed right human arm and hand. Its nails were painted bright red. It popped the wreta's head in, its throat convulsing, and swallowed the head whole into its body that was expanding to accommodate the meal.

I'd always thought No Face from Spirited Away wasn't that scary a villain, but this demon was making me reconsider that stance.

Next, the demon grabbed a wreta thigh, like one would a Chickeny Delight drumstick, and feverishly crammed it into its mouth.

We should have let the wreta set the damn ward. I pulled a crackling ball of magic into my palm and Rohan pushed past me, his feet squelching on the bloody tile, but the demon was faster. Slurping down another wreta foot, the demon disappeared.

The remaining wreta slumped over as if released from a trance. He was hyperventilating, repeating the same word over and over again.

Oshk.

Since that was all we could get out of the wreta, we killed him. There were no other demons in the house.

The stench and violence of the kill was pressing in on me, an almost physical presence lingering in the room. I grabbed the backpack and shouldered out the back door. The second I was outside, I ripped off my facial gear, breathing deeply. I itched to rip off my work boots too, because they stank from the blood coating them. Grisly bits were stuck to the soles.

"We have to clean up in there," Ro said.

Damn. I'd managed to avoid clean-up duty so far and it figured it'd be a bloodbath that broke my lucky streak. I had no problem pulling my weight, so long as I didn't puke and make things worse.

He'd brought cleaning supplies along in case we'd needed to scour off any wreta secretions. We didn't want any humans who eventually came around to check out the residents' disappearance getting hurt. Unlike Sweet Tooth, the wreta's hallucinogens lasted indefinitely.

It took liberal amounts of sodium peroxide mix to remove all the bloodstains. Everything from the mops to our chemical suits would have to be burned.

"What's an oshk?" I scrubbed at a stubborn patch of something dark on the wall, unconvinced my thick rubber gloves were enough of a barrier between me and the goo. Clean up duty was exactly as awful as I'd anticipated. "That thing that ate the demons?"

Rohan placed a fresh bucket of water on the floor. "No clue. But if something that scares *demons* is in town? Something that had them all hiding last night?"

"Fuuuuuck."

"Yeah."

6

If the library had been a disaster before, it was ten times worse after our pointless search for any information on the oshk.

In theory, I was now recording all the serial numbers of the cash so Orwell, the Brotherhood intel department so nicknamed by Kane, could track its source. In practice, I was keeping a wary eye on Rohan and his string of Hindi-English cursing that had risen from a mutter to a couple of stages away from a roar.

I ruffled the bills. "Did you know that there are one hundred hundred dollar bills in each bundle?"

No response.

"I've got a cool half a mill here." I shook the backpack. "I'm thinking a quick Google search on countries with no extradition treaty, book a flight, and we're living large on a beach with umbrella drinks by happy hour tomorrow."

Holding this much cash was so surreal that it almost lost all meaning. Not gonna lie, I was tempted to rip open the bundles and roll naked on them, but considering we'd commandeered the cash from a demon home, refrained.

Rohan flung a book on the table; it bounced and crashed to the floor.

"Okay," I said, retrieving the book–and the laptop for good measure–and placing them on the far end of the table, "you're done."

Rohan turned glittering eyes on me, clearly wanting someone to fight with.

I spread my hands. "We're in a holding pattern and getting mad at your people isn't going to change that."

Expression thunderous, he left the room.

I zipped up the backpack, setting my list of serial numbers on top, and leaned back in my chair, my chest tight. Work, relationship, saving the world–for Rohan and I, it was all tangled up. We even lived at Demon Club. There was no space for us to breathe.

My ex, Cole, had recently told me that when my snapped Achilles had destroyed my tap dance dreams, he'd had no idea how to comfort me. He hadn't felt like I was in the relationship. I didn't think that about Ro, but the fear of watching someone I cared about revert into bad behaviors and shut me out was all too real these days.

If we didn't live up to Rohan's relationship expectations or I became the fallout in the implosion of his feelings around the Brotherhood, his pattern would be he'd dump me without another look back and waltz into whatever new identity he crafted for himself. There would be no fighting for us or working through things. We'd be us and then we wouldn't be anything.

I exhaled, hard. There might not be a way out of the pressure cooker we lived in, but maybe there was a way to alleviate some steam. I pulled out my phone and started researching my brilliant idea, leaning my elbows on the library table. This was supposed to be our honeymoon phase and honeymoon it we would.

"Sorry." Rohan reappeared in the doorway, sounding genuinely contrite.

"That's– juggling." I squinted at the four red balls in his hands.

"Yeah. One of our roadies got me into it as a stress relief."

"I can see how hot and cold running tour sex wouldn't have the same appeal." That earned me the ghost of a grin. "All those nights in the Vault. You've been juggling?"

"No. I've been beating the shit out of the bag." He switched up his moves, catching the balls underhand. "But I figured that if yelling wasn't going to help, then storming off wasn't either."

"Progress." I crossed the room and settled into one of the leather club chairs, my legs tucked underneath me. "You've unleashed a lot of talents on me in the past few days, Snowflake." I ticked the items off on my fingers. "Dancing, skateboarding, juggling."

"The dancing I learned to help with my stage presence, the skateboarding was from growing up in L.A., and we had a lot of downtime on tour. I'm also the undisputed champion of Crazy Eights."

"A true renaissance man. Or was that renaissance nerd?"

He threw a ball up, spinning to catch it behind his back. The tension in his body eased a fraction. "Admit it, you're impressed."

"I am." I bounced a ball of electricity in my hand, then divided them into two.

"Cute."

"You think?" The two balls became four, and I let them swivel on their own around my head while I scanned the page on my phone. This would do nicely. A couple of clicks and some expedited shipping and things were put into motion.

Ro laughed, the happiness I'd hoped for back in his eyes. "You're a total shit. What are you looking at? Why the smug grin?"

I put the phone away and powered off my magic. "My other boyfriend wants to hook-up."

"Great. I'll call mine. Girlfriend," he clarified, rolling his eyes at my crestfallen expression. "You're so predictable."

"You said it. Lots of downtime, a bus full of horny guys. Do the math."

"That's not–" His phone buzzed. Ro caught all of the balls one-handed, pulling the phone from his pocket. He scratched his jaw, reading the text, his expression cautiously optimistic. "Pretty up, Sparky. We're going out."

"Pretty is a step down for me, buddy. Wow. You really blew a compliment opportunity. Your other girlfriend can keep you."

"Don't want her," he said, grabbing me in a headlock to kiss the top of my head.

"Ack." I elbowed my way free. "What kind of pretty does the situation demand?"

"Mahmud's in town." Mahmud was the Rasha who'd recruited Rohan for the Askuchar job. Rohan quickly typed a response. "Told him to meet us at Lotus."

Last time Rohan and I had eaten at Lotus, we'd had an incredible meal and a disaster of a conversation. The knives had come out on both sides. Whatever could I look forward to this time? Mahmud was Rohan's friend, not just a fellow hunter. Had he told Mahmud he was dating me? Or had he left it out, since this was a professional meeting and not a personal one? What kind of look would even be appropriate for this dinner: badass girlfriend or hot comrade-in-arms?

Fuck appropriate. I jumped to my feet and snapped out a salute. "Prettying up, sir!"

"Hey." He swung me back toward him, his eyes serious on mine. "I'm not going to break us, okay?" He stroked his thumb over my hand, radiating sincerity and the depth of his affection for me. This mattered so much to him. *I* mattered so much to him.

Rohan was an all-or-nothing kind of guy and getting the full weight of his absolute attention and care made me feel like I could reach for the stars. I was living the cheesiest of clichés where he was the first person I wanted to see in the morning and the last person I wanted to talk to at night. Rohan wasn't my other half. I was a twin. I knew what other halves felt like.

He didn't complete me; he complemented me and that was a zillion times better.

To be ripped from that would destroy me.

I cupped his cheek. "I believe you." Well, I believed *he* believed it.

Fingers crossed that would be enough.

The outfit I chose was a curve-hugging black sheath with cap sleeves and a hemline that hit just below the knee. It looked almost demure until I turned around to reveal the plunging back, the fabric draping softly at the base of my spine. I paired it with red lips and red heels.

Rohan gave me a wolfish grin when I flounced into his room. He prodded me backward until my legs hit his mattress. "Show me how it comes off."

"None of that." My stomach fluttered; my push against his chest was more insistent. "I want you desperate for me."

He nipped my bottom lip, his hand sliding over the stretchy fabric to cup my ass, and pressed his erection against my belly. "Done. Take it off."

I allowed myself one inhale of his spicy, musky cologne with the underbite of iron that was all Ro, before sidestepping him. "Good and nope."

I picked up the bluish-gray tie, similar in color to my eyes, that he'd laid out to go with his turquoise shirt and slid it around his neck. Fussing over my man, a quiet intimacy. It was nice.

"Nava." Rohan gasped, his skin getting a tad purple and his eyes glassy.

I fumbled at the choking knot that got tighter the more I worked at it. Damn ties. My dad always made putting these on look so easy. What the hell was the stupid trick? Over, under—no. I tried again.

Rohan pushed my hands away, extended the blade on his index finger and sliced the thing off. The tie fluttered to the ground. He frowned. "I liked that tie."

I opened his closet and, pulling out an identical one, thrust it at him. "Please. You buy your ties in pairs."

He strung the tie around his neck. "Good ties are hard to…" He paused, his knot half-formed. "Did you snoop through my closet?"

I patted his cheek. "Of course I did."

He slid the tie down through the loop he'd created and pulled it tight, making the whole "over/under" thing look like anyone could learn it. Shrugging into his suit jacket, Rohan escorted me out of the room, his hand on the small of my back. "Try not to gape too much when you meet Mahmud."

"Is he horribly disfigured?"

Rohan shot me a what-is-wrong-with-you look. "No. He's your type."

"I have a type?"

He laughed.

I was determined to prove him wrong, but when we entered Lotus and Mahmud stood from his table to greet us? Yeah, I checked my chin for drool.

Tall, hot bod, suit tailored like a second skin—those were basic Rasha-issue. But his dark brown skin, intense black eyes, goatee, and black hair scraped back into a messy ponytail, all coupled with these full pink lips whose evolutionary function was to be sucked on? Let's just say that other than Malik who'd had a couple thousand years to perfect tall, dark, and sexy, Mahmud, despite only having maybe thirty years to cultivate his hotness, was the first man to make Rohan look a little plain.

"Hi. I'm Nava." I stuck my hand out for him to shake.

His grasp was firm, warm. "Mahmud." His husky voice curled inside me like syrup.

"Pleasure," I squeaked out.

Rohan snorted.

To be fair, my recovery time was pretty fast. This was work after all. Plus, the boyfriend standing right there.

Rohan pulled my chair out for me, and from Mahmud's assessing look, he got our status.

The waitress came to take our order. Slender, with dark curly hair, dressed in a crisp white shirt and black cigarette pants, her dimpled smile lit up her whole face. Given that the majority of other customers were middle-aged couples and a couple of groups of business men, serving us was hitting the jackpot. Well, serving the men.

"I'm Olivia. I'll be your server tonight."

"Hi, Olivia." Rohan turned his rock fuck grin on her. Power to the chick for staying upright.

I kicked him under the table. He covered the flinch pretty well, his knee brushing against mine, remaining there, connecting us. He trapped my hand loosely against his thigh as he told her which dishes we'd decided to share.

"So, Nava, what was your first impression of the Rasha?" Mahmud said.

I sipped my green tea. "You want the honest answer or the polite answer?"

His eyes twinkled as he leaned in. "Oh, now I definitely need the honest answer."

I entertained Mahmud with my initial meetings of Baruch, Kane, and Drio, while Olivia brought out sumptuous sushi rolls plated on daikon and fat pieces of melt-in-your-mouth sashimi.

Mahmud's single failing was that he was hopeless with chopsticks. Sushi wreckage was strewn across his plate. He licked off a couple of grains of rice that were stuck to his finger. "I'm a disaster. Apologies."

"You're fine. But you might want to hold the chopsticks down farther." I held mine up to demonstrate.

He adjusted his grip and tried again with slightly better results. "Not that I'm not always delighted to see your hairy ass, Mitra, but I get the sense you invited me for more than my good looks."

"Oh, he invited you for that too," I quipped.

Mahmud laughed and Rohan kicked me under the table.

"Askuchar," Rohan said. With that one word, all levity at our table fled. He topped up all our sake, serving himself last.

"What about it?" Mahmud's expression was bland.

I gripped my chopsticks, my eyes darting to Rohan's.

A flash of impatience darkened his face. "Don't play politics. This is you and me and no bullshit. There was no logical reason for those yaksas to have trekked from Nepal through India and into Pakistan. Why Askuchar? Conveniently isolated for burying evidence? That mission was all kinds of wrong, man, and you know it."

"Yeah." Mahmud scrubbed a hand over his face. "I keep seeing those villagers ravaged. Yaksas are bloodthirsty, but that? It was like they'd gone berserk."

Or they'd been forced to attack. I shook my head at Rohan, willing him not to voice our suspicions.

"How did you hear about the four Rasha that had originally been killed looking for the demons?" Ro asked.

"Got a call asking me to track. They were missing, not yet confirmed dead at that point." Mahmud held out his sake cup for Rohan to refill.

"Who called?" I expected him to say Rabbi Mandelbaum.

"Ferdinand Alves."

Rohan jerked the sake back so sharply that alcohol sloshed onto the white linen tablecloth. I blotted it up, grateful for something that would keep my head down and not reveal how all the color had drained from my face.

"You know him?" Mahmud asked.

"Not personally," Rohan said. "Heard he died."

"Yeah. While we were still in Pakistan. Car crash outside L.A."

"Demons?" I asked.

"Don't think so."

Rohan was staring at his plate, his tuna sashimi untouched, his brow furrowed.

"Do you know if he was in Prague in early April?" I said.

"No idea." Mahmud's gaze flickered between us. "You want to tell me what's really going on?"

"Just trying to understand how it all went balls up," Ro said.

"Okay." Mahmud warred with a piece of ebi sushi, sighing as it fell apart on his plate.

"Nava?" Rohan's voice was pitched low for only me to hear.

The more people in the Brotherhood that found out, the more likelihood there was of the wrong people finding out. Except our team was stymied. Kane had done all he can, my brother wasn't plugged in enough, and Rohan casually asking guys he trusted about Ferdinand was pointless. He'd restrained himself out of concern for me, because when shit hit the wall—and it was *when* not if—I'd be the first one the Brotherhood came after.

I'd told Rabbi Abrams and he hadn't exactly embraced my ideas. I still didn't know where I stood with him anymore or if he'd reported my suspicions to Mandelbaum. Mahmud seemed nice but he was a total unknown to me. Was the risk of confiding in him worth it? I stirred wasabi into my soya sauce, turning the liquid cloudy. "Tell him."

Rohan's hand tightened on mine under the table.

I didn't take my eyes off Mahmud's face as Rohan filled him in, searching for a single clue as to his feelings, but he gave away nothing, listening to the tale without interjection. I clenched the linen napkin, my heart stuttering to a stop when, at the end of Ro's tale, Mahmud trained a dangerous, glittering smile on me.

Was he going to blame me? I let my magic reach my eyes, knowing he'd see the lightning dancing there. "Yes?"

"We're going to bring these fuckers down. Whatever you need. However I can help. I'm yours."

"Phrasing," Rohan said, breaking the tension. "Jeez, Mahmud, don't steal all the beautiful women in the restaurant. This one's mine."

Mahmud winked at me. "I'm *all* yours," he said. He picked up some sashimi without having to stab it onto his chopstick, then blinked at it, surprised. "All right then."

Mahmud didn't have much other information to give us. He hadn't known Ferdinand, but he had known a couple of the dead Rasha and swore there was nothing suspicious about them. He promised to follow up with their families in case there was anything to learn there.

Rohan insisted on paying for the meal. We walked Mahmud outside and he signaled for a taxi.

As the cab pulled up to the curb, Mahmud turned to Rohan. "There's one person who might be able to tell you about Ferdinand. Same peer group and shit. Zahir."

Rohan gave him a searching look. "You sure?"

Mahmud shrugged. "I wouldn't name drop me, but yeah. Try him. Last I heard he was based in Paris." Mahmud opened the back door to the cab, then kissed my hand. "Delightful Nava, I look forward to our next meeting."

"You charmer." I grinned at him. "Thanks, Mahmud. Really."

He rolled his shoulders like it was nothing. "I always believed that being Rasha meant having each other's backs." Something flickered over his face and he raised his troubled eyes to Rohan's. "I just didn't expect the enemy to be so close to home."

Rohan couldn't stop stealing touches all the way home.

At a stoplight, he'd sneak his hand from the clutch to just barely on my knee. At a crosswalk, he'd ghost it up. And up, and up. As the sun set and turned the glass condo towers gold, his nimble fingers edged around the line of my underwear. When we only barely missed a very angry old lady crossing a residential street, I decided that vehicular manslaughter via horny boyfriend was not, in fact, something I needed to experience.

"Who's Zahir?" I said, smoothing my dress back to a pristine sleekness.

"Mahmud's dad. They haven't spoken in about five or six years, but he's Rasha too. In his fifties and still kicking around." Fifties was old age in our line of work. It was too depressing to contemplate.

Ro glided his hand along the base of my bare spine.

I twisted away from his touch, but the persistent boy failed to take the hint and leaned into me while still driving, so I scooted closer to him, prioritizing our collective safety. Also, I was weak and wanted those fizzy shivers as he stroked my skin. "You think he'll have any insights into Ferdinand's death?"

Rohan stopped the car at Demon Club's front iron gate, set into a stone fence, to be scanned. He leaned across the gearshift and, cradling my head between his hands, took my mouth with the force of tossing gas on a fire. I grabbed his shirt and pulled him to me, feverishly kissing him. Ro bit my bottom lip and I moaned. He grinned against my mouth. "I like how we fit together."

Dizzy, I clutched at him but only got empty air as he gunned the car up the drive.

"You were saying?" he said with a smug grin.

I was? His smugness amplified. I couldn't let that stand so I racked my brain and eventually found where I'd left off. "If Ferdinand had been killed on a mission, I wouldn't have thought twice about it. But a car crash? I don't like the timing or coincidence of it." I had personal experience with the Brotherhood masking suspicious deaths with car crashes à la Samson King in Prague.

Rohan parked, cut the engine, and turned to me, his eyes hot. "Know what else I don't like?"

I licked my lips, remembered that wasn't an answer and shook my head.

"Making me sit through dinner, watching you in that dress. Cruel."

"You've been copping feels all the way home."

"It's not enough."

I snickered, but when he slammed his precious car's door in his haste to get me inside, I may have set a new record for speed-walking in heels.

We barely made it into his bedroom before, mouth on mine, he pressed me back against the wall. His teeth dragged over my lower lip before his tongue slipped inside. He trailed his finger blades over my shoulder and bare back, just enough to leave faint marks that I'd shiver staring at in the bathroom mirror later.

Sliding my hand under his shirt, I skimmed my fingers along the ridges of his sculpted abs. He retracted his blades and I broke the kiss to draw his fingers into my mouth, my tongue swirling around each one in turn. Pinching his nipples with my other hand, I rubbed my bare thigh up his leg. His sigh rumbled over me.

A furious ache built to a throbbing pulse inside me.

Rohan sucked on my neck and I tilted my head to give him better access to the sensitive skin. He caressed my cheek with the back of his hand, pinning me with this filthy eye-fuck that made my stomach flutter. "Wrap your legs around me."

The position left Cuntessa flush against his hard cock, my dress hiked up around my waist. I thrust against him with a blissful moan, pushed my fingers into his hair, raking back his dark wavy locks, and slanted my mouth over his. His answering kiss was hot, hungry, and knifed straight into my soul.

I rocked my hips, my head thrown back against the wall.

"Slow down, sweetheart." Rohan ran his fingers idly along my spine, his touch sizzling against my bare skin. "On your knees." His voice was low and dirty.

I played with the soft dusting of hair on his chest. "You want something?"

"Yes," he growled. "You. On your knees."

"Whatever would I do there?"

Rohan's eyes were a gold haze, his "please" strained.

I ran my hand over him, feeling his cock jump. "If we ever break up, you're going to have a bitch of a time explaining to your new girlfriend that you have to come see me for blowjobs."

"Only you," he murmured.

My cold, dead heart grew two sizes larger. "You sure you deserve it?"

He gripped me by my waist. "I'm desperate for you."

This gorgeous, wonderful man, with his pants half off his hips and a piratical smile playing on his lips, was hard and wrecked. For me.

I slid off him, dropping to the ground and taking his trousers and boxers along for the ride. The planks were cool under my knees and Rohan was hot silk in my mouth. My lips buzzed with magic. I ran my tongue down his shaft, sucking his balls into my mouth, inhaling the sharp smell of his arousal.

He gave a content hum, but he didn't stop touching me: fondling my breasts, curling my locks around his fingers, running his hands over my shoulders with soft exhales and low groans.

I teased his dick between my lips, slowly taking him in, curling my tongue around the head. Grabbing him by his ass, I pulled him close, taking his cock deeper.

His hips started rocking, his fingers biting into my shoulders. His back arched off the wall. Salty precum hit my tongue.

My nipples puckered and grew achingly hard. Cuntessa was dripping wet and demanding attention. I moaned and Rohan pulled free with a soft pop. "What?" I said. "I was deep-throating like a champ."

There was enough moonlight to make out the amusement in his eyes, even through his fringe of thick dark lashes. "Not complaining, Sparky, but this party was about to be over before it started."

"Allow me to help you put on the brakes." I stood up, grasping the hem of my dress to pull it off but he stopped me, brushing my hands away.

Rohan inched the dress up me, feasting on every newly exposed inch, his gaze almost reverential. "Sometimes I can't believe we're finally here."

"Me too." It seemed too good to last, my dress bunched in Rohan's hands as he clutched my hips, my curls brushing his chest, and my head bowed close enough to his heart to hear its staccato rhythm. It was fragile and intense and perfect.

And for the moment, it was mine.

He kissed the pulse fluttering under my jaw, still working the dress off in the world's slowest striptease, until he had to release me to pull the fabric over my head. He dipped his head, assessing me through heavily fringed lashes. "On the bed."

I scrambled to do as I was told, on my back, leaning against my elbows, my legs falling open.

He stood over me, still erect. I felt the weight of his hooded gaze like it was the rough glide of his tongue along my curves. He sucked on his lush lower lip.

My heart was in my throat waiting for him to touch me.

He ran a hand up my thigh, tracing the path with his lips. Ro hadn't shaved in a few days, and his stubble chafed the tender skin on my inner thighs. He ran his tongue under my bikini underwear. So near and yet so far. I wriggled out of them, pitching them across the room into the shadows.

He flicked his tongue to my clit.

My breath caught. I curled my fingers into his locks. "More."

He did it again, a million tiny licks that set me aflame but did nothing to quench the clenching grip of desire. I canted my hips.

Pinning my knees in place, Rohan set his head between my legs.

I teased my nipples, increasing the pressure of my pinches.

"Fuck." Rohan groaned, his mouth wet and glistening. He covered my hand with his, making me knead my own sensitive flesh. I writhed on the sheets and begged for more in an unintelligible jumble of sounds. "Like that, do you?"

He slid a finger inside me and I moaned, that delicious familiar tension swelling and coursing through me. I tugged him up.

"What?" he said, lust glazing his eyes. "I was eating you out like a champ."

I laughed and couldn't help kissing him again, quick and hard. "Fuck me, Snowflake." He reached for the drawer of his nightstand but I stopped him.

"Ro. Can we…?" I licked my lips nervously. "I'm on the pill and I'm clean."

"I'm clean, too." We'd both been tested by Dr. Sousa, the Rasha-approved doctor who'd dug a bullet out of my shoulder a while ago. Ro sat back on his calves, his hands resting on my legs. "Are you sure?"

"I've never gone bare with anyone. Not even Cole." I needed him to understand everything I was trusting him with. I swallowed thickly. "I don't want anything between us."

Rohan brushed a strand of hair out of my face. "I don't either."

He pressed me into the mattress, still sitting back on his calves. I cupped the nape of his neck, drawing him down to my mouth, bracketing his face in my hands. Our tongues tangled; the tip of Rohan's cock pressed against me.

Rohan remained between my legs, not yet entering me. Our bodies molded together, hands caressing, mouths insistent. We pulled back, our gazes caught.

I caressed his cheek, his stubble tickling the pads of my fingers. "Hi, you."

Rohan gave me a wide-open smile, equal parts tenderness and soft vulnerability. "Hi, yourself." Oh lordy. Heat rolled under my skin and my heart danced a furious tarantella. "Whatcha up to, sweetheart?"

I skimmed my hands down his side and shrugged. "Hanging out." I sucked the hollow of his neck and he hissed a groan. I wrapped my legs around his waist. "You?"

"Making my girlfriend orgasm her brains out. Think it's a plan?"

I nodded. "A very sound one. So long as you enjoy yourself as well."

He rubbed his nose against mine. "Thank you. I shall."

I waved a hand. "Proceed, good man."

Rohan glided his hand up my calf. "I've never gone bare with anyone before."

My chest swelled with happiness at being his first this way and I couldn't keep the smile from my face.

Rohan brushed the sweetest kiss on my lips and plunged inside me.

I arched into his touch with a sigh, my eyes drifting to his. "I didn't know it could feel like this."

"Me neither." Ro's eyes gleamed in the darkness, a million shades of gold from the purity of flickering flame to the darker edge of the final intense burst of sunset.

A bead of sweat trickled down my chest to my stomach, his body pressing mine into the mattress. We were wrapped in the tangle of our heat, his heart racing, pulsing against my rib cage. I tightened my legs around him, wanting to keep us here forever, savoring this new experience of being so intimately joined.

"Can I move now?" he asked.

"Oh my God, yes, already." I thrust against him.

I gripped his clenched biceps as he propped himself up over me, thrusting with a slow roll of his hips. His heart tattoo on his left bicep peeked out between my splayed fingers.

Rolling us over so that I was riding him, he gripped my hips, his thrusts harder, rawer. He fumbled in the drawer by the bed for the lube. A squirt later, he slid his finger into my ass.

He rewarded my wanton moan with another finger. I'd never felt so full, so complete.

"You good?" he asked.

"Y-yeah." I raked my nails down his chest, shivering every time I bottomed out. Having him inside me like this, took our lovemaking to a whole new realm. We were physically and emotionally as intertwined as two people could be. I couldn't have handled this before now, and especially not with anyone else. But with Ro?

I clasped his face in my hands and kissed him.

"You're my supernova." Rohan curled up, dragging his lips over my belly, his scruff scratchy, and swirled his tongue into my navel.

I giggled and pushed him back, leaning over to capture his lips again, my hair drifting down along the hard planes of his abs. "What about you? You want anything else?" My voice was breathy. I was drowning in the twin tempos of his fingers and cock.

Rohan traced my swollen lips with his tongue. "Just you."

My orgasm raged through me, my back arching. A supernova swallowed me up and for a moment all I could do was let myself be consumed.

Rohan's expression was fierce. He drove into me, his entire body bucking, adding to my blissful after-shocks. With a hoarse cry, he came.

I flopped onto the mattress and he rested his head on my chest. I stroked his hair. "That was... almost too much and not nearly enough."

"I know." He pressed a gentle kiss to my hip. "I'll get a towel," he said, and slipped from the bed. The water in his bathroom ran for a moment and then Rohan cleaned us both up with a cool, damp cloth. He'd even brought a dry facecloth to cover the wet spot.

The covers rustled as he got back under, gathering me close against him. When he high-fived me with a dead-ass solemn expression, I laughed until my stomach was sore.

I fell asleep in a spill of moonlight and a warm arm around my shoulders. And despite my best efforts, the last thing flickering through my mind was Rohan's raspy voice playing over and over again:

Just you.

7

The morning light was a soft filter, my body boneless and half-dozy. Our limbs were entangled with my head on Rohan's chest and his stubble itchy against my forehead as we listened to rain pattering against the windows.

I traced lazy circles on his abs and he hummed, content, in a voice thick with sleep. I craned my neck to see the tiny strip of gold beneath his half-closed lids. "Last night was amazing."

"Yeah." Rohan tensed for the briefest second. My expression hardened. "Cool down. It's not morning after freak out. It's fine." He scratched his jaw. "I'd just better… shave."

He was staring at my chin which, come to think of it, stung. I darted out of bed to his mirror and let out a wail. "What have you done to me?" The skin along my jaw was rubbed raw, like I'd spent the night cuddled up with a sandpaper pillow.

Rohan sat up, the sheet pooling at his hips. "This is not all on me."

I touched my chafed red skin. Whimpered.

He grinned at me. "Want me to kiss it better?"

I opened his bathroom door. "No. I want you to never kiss me ag–"

The door slammed shut, Rohan bracing his hand against it. "Say you don't mean that."

"Obviously," I grumbled.

He kissed the tip of my nose. "I'll shave." He bent down to retrieve the turquoise shirt he'd worn last night, but I snatched it away from him and put it on. If our relationship had escalated to physical wounds, then I got to wear his clothing.

I inhaled, letting his scent seep into mine. The fabric was soft and contoured nicely to my body, hitting mid-thigh. "Keeping this," I said.

He gave a resigned nod and stepped past me into the bathroom. Only when I heard the shower go on, did I remember what day it was.

I pounded on the bathroom door to get my "Happy Birthday," but Rohan was singing under the spray and didn't hear me, even when I jiggled the knob two or seven times. I searched the bed, but there was no gift hidden under my pillow. Hanging off the mattress to check underneath only gave me a crick in my neck, raiding his drawers yielded nothing more interesting than the fact he folded his underwear, which was old news, and rifling through his closet was a bust unless you counted the lint-covered roll of butterscotch candy the sneak had hidden in his leather jacket. It was like expecting a trip exploring the coral reefs and instead getting the toilet he'd flushed his goldfish down when he was nine.

I still took the candy with me, unclenching my chokehold on the closet doorknob. This was the boyfriend who had taken Lily to Paris for dessert. He'd sure as shit remembered *her* birthday. Between the two apps and the back up paper reminder, he knew what today was. Was forgetting an honest mistake having just woken up, or a sign that I was once more with someone who was going to throw me under the bus emotionally and walk away?

As I gathered up last night's clothes, my phone tumbled out of my pocket onto the floor. There was a notification with my new word of the day.

Insouciance. Noun. An uncaring attitude, lack of interest.

I stuffed it into the middle of my clothing bundle. Rohan had probably gotten up early, and made me a fancy breakfast where he would gift me with the most amazing present ever, after he crawled back under the covers and pretended to wake up next to me.

Could happen.

I yanked the bedroom door open, ran down the hallway to the kitchen sniffing like a coke addict, and skidded to a stop at the sight of Drio dressed in raggedly cut-off sweats and a T-shirt, his feet bare, chugging back a glass of water at the kitchen sink. The sweat from his workout had caused his blond hair to plaster to his forehead, but it also made his olive skin glisten so it wasn't all gross. "When did you get back?"

Grimacing, he jerked a finger at my face. "What's happened to make you look like that?"

"I look fine."

Snorting his disagreement, he dumped the glass in the sink, his green gaze flicking over Rohan's shirt that I wore. "He's awake?" he asked in his sexy Italian accent, his face lighting up.

"Yeah, fanboy. He's in the shower. Hurry and you might get to soap him up."

Drio gave me the hand-to-arm Italian gesture of "fuck off."

"Happy birthday, younger and uglier twin." Ari strode into the room and jerked back at the sight of my chin. "Jesus. You're not supposed to really be uglier."

"All right, already." I hugged Ari back, even though he didn't deserve it. "Happy birthday, older and stinkier twin."

Ari held up a badly-wrapped, lumpy gift. "Took you long enough to wake up." I jumped for it but he held it out of range. "Where's mine?"

I gave another pointless swipe. "Upstairs."

"That better not be your new look for your new age," Kane said, entering. He poked my chin.

"You can all bite me." It was too much to hope that my fellow Rasha would be adult about my stubble-burn and not mention it. Ari gave me an exaggerated shudder of disgust and actually walked out.

He was so not getting his present.

Kane helped himself to coffee, scratching his bare belly. "Were you kissing a lizard?"

"If you're gonna insult me, at least caffeinate me first." I reached for his coffee but he held it out of reach.

"I only speak truth," Kane said.

"It's disgusting," Drio said.

I flicked his arm.

"What? This is a truth circle. You look like you went a round with a windigo. And lost." Drio waved a hand at me. "Fix yourself."

"It's not—he's shaving—" I threw my hands up in the air. "I don't need to explain myself to you, you big jerk."

Drio grinned at me.

"Love's not supposed to hurt, but when it does?" Ari sauntered back in and placed a tube in my hand. "Polysporin."

"Ha ha. Are we done taunting the vulnerable female now? Can we return to business as usual?"

"That is business as usual," Drio said.

"Walked into that one, babyslay."

"Go back to Rome," I said to Drio. I opened the oven. No waffles lovingly prepared by my boyfriend. I cracked my knuckles, nostrils flaring.

Ari waved my gift at me. "Upstairs. Move it."

There was a bit of a doorway tussle with free-ranging elbow jabs, but I got inside my room first and did a brief gloating wriggle dance. I grabbed his gift off the dresser and on the count of three, we switched presents.

I tore mine open. Inside was a multi-colored candy necklace, a huge pink candy diamond in a purple plastic setting, and a black sleeveless shirt covered in sparkles. Smack in the center of the shirt was a horned demon head made of silver crystals. It sat in a pink crystal circle with a slash through it. Ari had been responsible for many of my best T-shirts over the years but he'd outdone himself with this one.

I hugged my "No Demons" shirt to my chest. "You're the best."

"Not so bad yourself." Ari read the back of the jewel case for *Inside*, one of those moody puzzle videogames he liked so much.

As I adorned myself with my candy jewelry, Kane stepped in, holding a plastic bag.

"Still not a good look," he said.

"Says the man with the worst fashion sense in the history of mankind." I poked his leopard-print shirt. "What are you, a middle-aged divorceé? This, on the other hand?" I modeled my candy gems. "They're beeauutiful traditional gift items."

I bit off a red candy bead.

Ari swallowed the Coffee Crisp chocolate bar he had stuffed in his mouth. Wafer layers stacked with a coffee mousse and covered in milk chocolate, this exotic Canadian delicacy was the first of the six full-sized bars that comprised the other part of his gift. "Did you need something?" he asked Kane in a frosty tone.

Oy vey.

I muscled in between them. "You can't throw away a lifelong friendship." Yes, Ari had kissed Kane after being turned on by–and yeah, attracted to–Malik, this hot marid demon. And yes, Kane felt used and angry, and it probably wasn't the best circumstances for Ari to initiate a first kiss with the dude. But come on.

"I'm pulling birthday rank and demanding that you two work your shit out already."

"It's my birthday, too. And I'm older, so..." Ari crossed his arms.

"Your insouciance doesn't fly."

"I already got you a non-refundable gift," Kane said to me. "You can't have both."

"I don't need material goods. I want you to make up."

He pulled a slim cream envelope from the bag and held it up. The word "Miraj" was written on the outside in distinctive red script.

"You got me a gift certificate to the hammam?" This Turkish spa was deluxe. I'd heard about it from my mom but had never been able to afford it myself. I grabbed the envelope, and hugged him.

"Yeah, yeah." Kane pushed me off him.

I tried to peer inside the gift bag that Kane held. "Is that Ari's gift, perchance?"

"As if," Ari said.

Kane glowered at him, thrusting the bag stiffly out.

Ari took it like it might explode in his hands and pulled out a hardcover manga with a slick red and black design. "This is the limited edition."

"So?" Kane's chin tipped up a couple of notches higher.

"It's not even available in North America." Ari opened it like he was holding a priceless artifact. My brother had developed a love of manga around his tenth birthday–inexplicable at the time, since none of his other friends were into it–that had remained strong and ongoing. Not so inexplicable now. "There's a backlog on it everywhere."

Kane rubbed the back of his neck. "I got my cousin in Tokyo to get it. It's not a big deal."

Ari leafed through the book with an undecipherable expression.

"Ari," I hissed. "Thank him."

He and Kane stared at each other for a very long, tense, mutual idiot boy moment. "Thank you."

"You're welcome." Kane pivoted and left the room.

Ari put the book back in the shopping bag and unwrapped the second Coffee Crisp. "What did Ro get you?"

"That was pathetic. Get lost. I have to get dressed."

He paused, the chocolate bar halfway to his mouth, darting a glance after Kane. "When do you wanna leave later?"

"Five?"

He threw me a thumbs up, busy devouring bar two, and left, shutting the door behind him.

I ate three more candy beads.

The phone rang with Leo's special Flight of the Conchords ringtone. "I'm twenty-one!" I said in greeting.

Leo sang me Happy Birthday.

"Are you coming to the parents' house tonight?" I unbuttoned Rohan's shirt and tossed it on the bed.

"Of course."

"Will I be getting a present?" I rooted around in my underwear drawer for a bra.

"Perhaps."

"Did you know Drio was back?"

"He didn't go straight from the airport to Demon Club, that's for sure. That boy took everything out of me and then some."

I ate another couple of candy beads. "You greedy monkey."

"I heard zero complaints. He even gave me this gorgeous hand-printed scarf he'd bought in Rome."

He's buying her gifts? Holy shit! "Next time get cash," I said, trying to hang on to my phone as I shimmied into my bra. "Though I guess the scarf looks more impressive than a lonely five bucks."

"Ha. Ha."

"The no kiss thing wasn't a problem?" I threw on my new shirt from Ace and tugged up a pair of black booty shorts.

"Not yet. I'll break him." She snickered. "I plan to have my hands full with repeat performances from the Italian Stallion. Keep milking him dry."

I twisted my hair into a bun. "Ew. You know how easily I'm traumatized by visuals. I'm a delicate flower."

She snorted. "What did rock star get you?"

I squirmed and even though she couldn't see it my freaky friend sensed it.

"He didn't start your day with a gift?" she demanded. "And he lives?"

"His living is conditional to what happens when I next see him." I sank down on the bed. "We went bareback last night. First time. Ever."

Her shocked gasp was actually kind of gratifying. Her "you love him," not so much.

"No undying pledges involved."

"That was insensitive of me. Okay gotta run schmugs."
She hung up.

I stared suspiciously at my phone. Ten seconds later a phone rang in the hallway. I was out the door and ripping it out of Drio's hands before he'd finished his greeting of "Pronto."

"Gossip and die," I said into the phone.

"Hmph," Leo said, and hung up.

I handed Drio back his phone. "And you." I narrowed my eyes at him.

He jutted his chin out. "Che cosa?"

"Milked you dry, did she?"

He actually ducked his head, his cheeks flushing. His embarrassment was a rare and beautiful gift.

"Polysporin." I handed him the tube I'd grabbed when I'd heard his phone ring. "For when love hurts."

Cheered up immeasurably, I flew down the curved wooden staircase, the railings glowing with a high-gloss gleam and the scent of lemon polish.

Ro wasn't in his room. His bathroom was still steamy and his damp towel lay crumpled on his counter. Maybe he was lying in a coma somewhere. Or suffering from battle-induced amnesia. Neither of which excused the lack of a present since all gift provisions should have been made by now, but would temper my judgment on his lack of proper birthday greetings.

No such luck. He wasn't anywhere on the main floor and the downstairs offices were empty.

I poked my head in Rabbi Abrams' office, hoping I was still persona grata to him. He hadn't come in. No problem. I'd see him later at our birthday dinner. Hopefully.

I stomped down the stairs into the basement with its wide, well-lit corridors, and slapped my hand against the scanner to open the iron door to the Vault. The light changed from red to green and I threw the door open. It bounced off the concrete blocks that made up the walls in the basement, leaving a black mark on the white paint.

Rohan wasn't in the Vault either. I crossed the blue padded flooring and checked inside both the small iron room where we occasionally stashed demons and the weapons room. No sign of him.

I didn't hear any music coming from the small room down the corridor that I'd turned into my tap studio, but it was the last place to check before I searched the grounds. Or got a shovel to start digging his grave.

Sparks crunched between the soles of my feet and the floor as I stalked toward the room. Even if he hadn't gotten me a present, some guys just sucked at birthdays. It had no bearing on Ro's feelings towards me. This wasn't a test.

I stopped short of the doorway, anticipation prickling my chest, and stepped inside.

Empty.

I forced my slumping shoulders back, my chin up–

–And saw the shoe box with the fat yellow bow sitting on the lumpy sofa. I flung the lid off.

Ro had bought me custom-made, red leather tap shoes. There was purple leather at the toes and heels, like saddle shoes, and a red leather heart at the back of each shoe. Purple laces completed the look.

I clutched the heavy shoes to my chest and kissed the leather hearts, basking in how well Rohan knew me. He paid attention to the small stuff. I, on the other hand, wanted to have all his likes, dislikes, and idiosyncrasies downloaded into my brain already. Ro was nowhere near the open book I was, but I intended to carefully read his every page. I didn't want him to ever feel like I was taking him for granted.

"Sparky?" Booted heels neared.

I gave each heart one more kiss.

Rohan came over to me. "Finally found them?"

I shook a shoe at him. "You are playing a dangerous game, son. Gift contact didn't occur until an hour into Nava Day. One hour."

His eyes crinkled at the corners. "Is that a national or international holiday?"

I cuffed him upside the head. "It offends me that you have to ask."

"You put two countdown apps on my phone in the assumption I'd forget your birthday. That insult to my honor could not go unchallenged," he said. "Like them?"

I danced the shoes through the air. "They're only the greatest gift ever."

"They are." Fine. He'd earned that smug grin. "Do they fit?"

"Don't know yet." Sitting down, I stretched out my leg and handed him the shoes. "How did you know my size?"

Rohan sat down beside me and slid the shoe onto my left foot. "I got a pair of worn out taps that your mom said still fit and sent them to the shoemaker." He laced up the shoe. "How does it feel?"

I put on the second shoe, and stood up, testing my weight. They were heavier shoes than I'd had in a while but adjusting to the increased weight would give me sound advantages.

I kissed him with everything I had. Rohan cupped the back of my head, but I ducked his hold. "I have to test them more," I said. "For quality assurance purposes."

He sank onto the sofa, elbows braced on his knees, watching me. I'd never tire of the enrapt expression on his face while he watched me dance.

I broke the shoes in with a time step one of my instructors used to call the West Coast Bounce. Throwing on some dreamy ambient, I double timed my steps: open thirds, drawbacks, riffs, and a flurry of shuffles on my right foot.

"You look like you're making two sounds but five come out. How you move your feet that fast is beyond me."

I fought past my first impulse to joke it off. "This was basically my life for fifteen years." I nodded in satisfaction at my balance on my toe stands. "These shoes? Their weight wouldn't have worked if I was a Broadway tapper, but for rhythm tap?" I rapped a staccato percussion of heel stamps, taking in their deeper, warmer sound. "These have groove, and I'm a hoofer at heart."

An instrumental version of the jazz classic "Sunny Side of the Street" shuffled onto my iPhone next. I smoothed out my steps, my improvisation as light as a feather.

"Nava." I stopped mid-pullback at the serious tone in his voice. "I told Drio we wanted to talk to him."

As far as the wrong people knowing went, Drio was pretty damn wrong. "Did you."

I sat down on the couch, unlacing my shoe with a sharp jerk that only made a knot.

Rohan took my foot and unraveled the laces. "You greenlit Mahmud knowing, and Drio's good at getting information."

"Torture will do that. I also wouldn't put it past him to kill any Rasha he thinks are on the wrong side of this."

Like me.

"Drio's on our side. He wouldn't kill you." Rohan considered it. "Maim, maybe. Maiming, he definitely would do. But I hear having all your body parts is highly overrated."

I got my second shoe off without mishap. "It's not funny. Drio hates demons. He lives for the Brotherhood. Best friend or not, you can't predict how he'll react."

"I can. Drio lives for killing demons," Rohan said. "It's not the same thing."

"Are you going to tell me what the deal is between you two?" Rohan shook his head. "Stubborn. What if you pulled back on investigating this from the Brotherhood angle? Let me try and step things up with the witches."

"Like that's safer?" He squeezed my hands. "I'll be careful."

"Promise?"

Rohan pressed his mouth below my earlobe, his whispered "I promise," making me shiver.

I sighed. "Let's get this over with." Twenty-one had been my best birthday ever. Too bad I wouldn't live to see twenty-two.

8

Drio stood at the kitchen counter applying Crazy Glue to a machete grip as Rohan warmed up with the Sweet Tooth case. Drio was framed by the window, the trees outside bent almost double and rain lashing the glass. When he heard what had happened to Naomi, his hands tightened on the handle so hard that he cracked it again.

I slipped the box of Kosher salt out of the cupboard. If Drio was mad about the drugs, a quick ward might be in my best interests when we got to the actual topic needing to be raised, since The Flash over there was holding a literal machete.

"You think this oshk is looking for Candyman as well?" Drio said.

"Your guess is as good as mine," Rohan said. "The wreta might have known." He shrugged.

"We need to stop that shit hitting the streets. Addictions never end well." There was an uncharacteristic edge to Drio's voice.

"Never with demon drugs, but humans can beat addictions. If they get treatment in time..." I trailed off at the look of disdain Drio leveled at me.

He turned to Ro. "You want my help?"

"Nava?" Seated at the table, Rohan twisted around to look up at me.

I shifted from side-to-side.

Drio smirked. "You look uncomfortable. I can't wait to hear this."

"Tone down the delight," I said. "This is um, really, really not to be shared."

He sanded the handle. Its wicked blade glinted in the harsh kitchen light. "You know," he said, "it's unhealthy to keep things inside."

I swallowed, standing behind Ro with my hands on his shoulder for support. Drio didn't like having enemies. Between the torture, the flashstepping, and the fact he was a little murder machine capable of striking fast and dismembering painfully slow, he was a formidable ally.

But that was only if he took my side. We'd been through a lot together. We'd survived Prague and nearly hooked up, sure, but I didn't kid myself for a moment that I couldn't see the coldness creeping into Drio's eyes.

"Tough," I said, rolling the die. "Some secrets are meant to be a poison in your soul. So sit back and enjoy the rest of your truncated life. Welcome to Knowledge Club."

I kept the Kosher salt close and Ro half in front of me as a handy shield for the entire sordid tale. I may not have been convinced that I could set a ward faster than Drio could move, but Drio wouldn't hurt Ro to get to me.

Given how Drio had reacted when he'd learned the Brotherhood had its first female Rasha, I didn't think he'd be particularly fond of witches. Especially ones that were binding demons with blood magic.

Silent fury rolled off his tense frame, so I wasn't wrong. But he was as incensed about the possibility of the Brotherhood being on the wrong side of the fight as Rohan had been.

I edged that much farther behind Ro.

"You know I could kill you before you laid down a single grain of salt or hid fully behind him, yes?" he said, twisting the machete to examine the handle.

Eep. I jutted my chin up. "Good thing I decided to trust you then."

Rohan crossed his arms. "Drio, come on. Put the machete down."

"I knew something was going down in Prague. Why didn't you tell me then?" He leveled a glare at me.

"Our mission with Samson–"

"You didn't trust me."

I looked away.

"When *did* you decide to trust me?"

"Ten minutes ago," I mumbled.

A muscle twitched in his jaw. He tossed the machete onto the counter with a clatter, making Ro and me flinch, and marched off.

Rohan pinched the bridge of his nose. "That went well."

I hurried to catch up to Drio and tugged on his sleeve. "I'm sorry."

Drio's strides grew longer, forcing me to jog up the stairs behind him.

"You're honestly only mad that I didn't tell you? Why aren't you disputing my theory or blaming me or something?"

"If it comes to it, I'll assign plenty of blame." His eyes glinted. "But not to you. You don't blame someone for wanting to know the truth."

"You've come a long way from wanting me dead."

"Oh, I still want you dead, bella." He chucked me under the chin. "Just for different reasons."

"Should I consider you helping me as my birthday present?"

"No."

I clapped my hands. "Because you bought me something?"

"No." He turned his back to me and resumed climbing. "I'd have to like you to spoil you."

"Like Leo." I stuck my tongue out. "Yeah, yeah, I know all about your ways, Mr. Hand-Printed Scarf."

He stopped in the doorway of his bedroom, momentarily stunned. "What?"

I saw my chance and took it. "If exposing corruption in the Brotherhood isn't helping me, what would you call it?"

Drio's features twisted with pain for a moment and I held my breath thinking that I'd finally get some insight into what made this guy tick. He was such a mass of extremes, but he kept having my back.

I caught his hand. "I'm really truly sorry."

He stared at our connected hands like they didn't compute, then gently shook free. "Forget it."

He shut the door. One way or another, I was going to get to the bottom of the mystery that was Drio Ricci. And make it up to him for hurting his feelings, since I now resided in the bizarro-world where his feelings mattered.

"Nava?"

At the sound of Rabbi Abrams' voice, I hustled back downstairs, pathetically happy he'd called but equally worried he'd told Mandelbaum and I was now going to be forcibly rehabilitated for my own good. "Yes, Rabbi?"

"Esther wants to see you."

"You talked to her? Not the Brotherhood?"

"Navela." Even his myriad of wrinkles frowned at me. "I didn't speak to the Brotherhood about this. I wouldn't endanger you and everything you're doing to get to the bottom of this." He sounded supremely cranky.

I rolled onto the outsides of my feet, a smile breaking free. "I didn't doubt it for a second."

The hospital ward fluorescents cast a cold, grim light over the pale green walls, painted with sunflowers in some misguided attempt at "cheerful." The strained manic grins on their flower faces only achieved "constipated," pairing well with the stench of antiseptic and misery permeating the place.

A warning sign in electric yellow proclaimed that the patient inside was in isolation and listed the conditions of entry, such as no flowers or fresh fruit.

I donned the scrubs and gloves that the sign instructed me to don. The thirty-something black nurse in pink floral scrubs checked me over then pushed the door open, watching me through the window in the door. I smiled at her until she turned away and headed back to the nurse's station.

Dr. Gelman was a fragile waif in her hospital bed. Her black hair was shorter and patchier with more white streaks in it then the last time I'd seen her, while her olive leathery skin was red and angry like it was sunburned, making her look a decade older than her mid-sixties.

I dug my nails into my palms because tears were really a threat and she'd kill me. Adopting my snarkiest pose, I tsked her. "You don't call. You don't write. You neglect to give me the heads up about evil witches."

"Snippy." The oxygen mask over her mouth made her Israeli-accented voice harder to understand, though the face mask tied over my mouth muffled my words as well.

I sat down in the chair beside her bed, trying not to focus on the bank of monitors and medical equipment surrounding us. "You okay?"

"I'm still alive, so yes. Thanks so much for asking." Her sarcasm was sharp enough to sting.

"You were the one that so thoughtlessly crashed her immune system and didn't return my calls."

Her laughter died, coughs racking her body. I poured her some water from the carafe on the table by her bed, and holding the plastic cup to her lips, kept one hand on her back to prop her up. She was light as a feather. This woman who had single-handedly teleported me into weird caves below Prague just for funsies. Who had the most knowledge of magic of anyone I'd met. Who, right now, was shaking in bed, coughing violently into her hand as the nurse glared daggers at me through the door window for possibly bringing in some unknown contagion.

Was it possible for this to get more shitty?

"Damn chemo," Gelman said, another coughing spasm overtaking her.

"I can come back another time."

She shook her head, pushing the cup away. She placed her hands on her chest like she was helping her ribcage expand. "What's so urgent?" I hesitated and she snapped at me. "I'm not dead yet. Speak."

I caught her up on everything about my witch and Brotherhood suspicions in a matter-of-fact voice. Hoping if I didn't get emotional, I wouldn't raise her blood pressure too badly. "Do you believe me?"

None of the monitors blared. Go me.

The door opened and the same disapproving nurse came in, now wearing a mask and gloves. She switched out Gelman's empty IV bag for a full one. "Visiting hours are over."

"This is Nava," Gelman rasped.

"The one and only," I added.

The nurse closed the curtains around the bed, even though there were no other patients in the room. "Good job getting Esther attacked by a demon."

Gelman shot her an unimpressed look. "Play nice."

"I never meant for that to happen," I said.

"Uh-huh," the nurse said. Gelman poked her. "Fine. I'm Sienna." Another poke. "Old woman, you're annoying me." Sienna tugged her gloves off, loosening Gelman's hospital gown so she could tug the front of it down. The skin on her chest was dry and flaky.

Sienna placed one hand on Gelman's heart and the other on her back. "What do you want now, Rasha?"

"Perhaps as a witch," I said, "you could be a bit more supportive of the first female hunter? Sisterhood and all that."

Sienna threw me a mocking smile. "Aren't you a special Snowflake?"

I swallowed my snarky retort. Choked on it, but swallowed it. I needed Dr. Gelman's help and antagonizing her fellow witch wasn't the way to do it.

"A witch is binding demons," Dr. Gelman said.

Sienna whistled. "You sure?"

"We are." Gelman's tone left no room for doubt

Relief swam down to my toes. "Who has the ability to do that?" I said.

"No one now," Gelman said.

"The witches who knew how to do that are long dead. Which you'd know if you had a clue about magic," Sienna said.

"Even I only ever heard of one in my lifetime. Millicent Daniels. Died half-crazed with her obsession," Gelman said.

"Did you know her?" Sienna asked.

Dr. Gelman shook her head. "I'd only heard stories."

"Addictions never end well." I watched Sienna because she didn't seem to be doing anything except standing there touching Gelman, which was super creepy. "What are you doing? Because that was not on the sign's allowed activities."

"I'm trying to heal her."

I nodded. "A nurse, healer magic. That makes sense."

"You really know nothing."

"About witches? Call me Jon Snow," I said. Sienna frowned. "*Game of Thrones*? Seriously? How have you missed one of the hugest cultural phenomena in recent history?"

"Luck. All witches can heal."

"Infusion and elimination," Gelman said. Her eyes were closed but she breathed easier.

"Then why don't you just cure her?"

Sienna slapped her forehead. "Why didn't I think of that?"

"Our magic has grown weaker," Gelman said. "Sienna can't cure me but this helps."

"You're too stubborn to die," Sienna replied in a fond voice. "They don't even want you in isolation anymore."

"Magic," Gelman prompted.

"Witches' magic is based on the premise of infusion and elimination." Sienna removed her hands and shook them out. Gelman's skin was a bit rosier. "That's 'adding to' and 'taking away from.'"

"Thanks," I said. "I have a Word of the Day app."

"With your generation, I assume nothing. When you kill a demon, you eliminate its life force. If I pin you in place?"

I jerked against the chair hard enough to snap my head back, an invisible band pushing against my chest like a vise.

"I eliminate your ability to move." She released me, but only after much flailing of my hands and an order from Dr. Gelman.

I rubbed my chest, peeking down the front of my scrubs and T-shirt reading "All I care about is my coffee and like 3 people" to confirm that there was bruising. "So if you changed me into a frog, you would be infusing me with frog essence–Oh, come on!" My voice came out in a throaty croak. It went well with my bumpy green skin and the flipper protruding from my left arm pit.

Dr. Gelman laughed. If looking like Kermit was the price of hearing her laugh again, then I'd pay it.

"Infusing you with frog essence makes you a ridiculous looking human," Sienna said, "not a frog."

"Dr. Gelman," I rumbled. Gelman waved a hand and undid the froggy damage. I patted myself down to make sure I was properly restored.

"You witches really did just give us Rasha a fraction of your power," I said.

"Rasha were only given that one sliver of our elimination magic relevant to killing demons." Sienna opened the curtains around the bed once more. "Even that was too much."

"Our magic is pretty cool," I retorted. "Electricity, human blades, super speed, poison skin, shadow manipulation."

"Flashy super powers." Sienna keyed in something on one of the monitors. "Rasha should never have been allowed to exist."

If her attitude was what I could expect from the witches, any hope of co-operation was hooped. "It's not just super powers. We can cast spells."

Sienna and Dr. Gelman laughed. "Spells are the training wheels of magic," Sienna said. "Cast a ward, do a ritual, glamor an object, big deal. Inherent magic is where the real power is and the only inherent magic you Rasha have is that little bit to kill demons."

"Spells are like the channels you get with basic cable," I said. "Got it."

"My analogy was better," Sienna said.

"No, because anyone with a TV can get basic cable. Just as anyone affiliated with the magic world can cast a spell. Rabbis cast spells and they have no inherent magic. Inherent magic are the specialty channels. The good stuff." I appealed to the nice witch in the room. "Can you find out who's behind the binding? Kind of a magic forensic chemist?"

Even Sienna looked to Gelman for her answer.

"No," Dr. Gelman said. "That's not possible. I'll put out feelers about the binding, but it will take time."

"It's a fool's errand." Sienna toyed with the blue bead on the end of one of her short dreadlocks.

"Let's go for a little optimism, shall we?" I squeezed Gelman's hand. "I'll come see you soon."

"Try not to get yourself killed," she said.

"Try not to cough up a lung."

"Insolent child."

I grinned and said she made me seem easygoing by comparison. "Don't disappear on me again, okay?"

"I won't." She gave my hand a final squeeze and I left.

Rohan was going at this from the Brotherhood angle, I'd taken the witches. Neither were delivering any kind of immediate results. That left one other party: the demons. And one demon in particular who was powerful and plugged-in enough to possibly help me get some answers.

Malik.

The only problem with Malik was that the last time I'd seen him, I'd almost killed him. The marid was ancient and probably had perfected the art of holding grudges, so payback was pretty much inevitable. Not looking forward to it. Plus, it would freak Rohan the fuck out.

He wasn't the only one.

The admissions desk had informed me that Naomi had checked out, and after a quick text to Christina to make sure both she and Naomi were doing okay, I headed back to Demon Club to get ready for my birthday dinner.

While I bathed, Ro, shirtless, shaved at my bathroom sink, singing along to the Motown playlist streaming off his phone to my speakers.

I rinsed out the last of my conditioner, a goofy grin on my face at our domestic coziness, and stepped onto the bathmat, drying off.

Ro tilted his chin up for me to inspect. "Did I miss a spot?"

I trailed my fingers over his skin then planted a kiss to his jaw. "Nope."

He rinsed out his razor, washing away all the little hairs in the sink. What a keeper.

Make-up applied, underwear and bra on, and a bright orange towel wrapped around my head, I opened my closet to select my clothes. The jangling first notes of "Ain't No Mountain High Enough" struck up. The Marvin Gaye and Tammi Terrell version, which Ro proclaimed to be the *only* version. I'd been getting quite the musical education dating this boy.

Ro struck a pose for Marvin Gaye's opening line, then the two of us were grooving around, strutting in circles around each other, and striking poses on the bed, all while singing our hearts out in a sassy duet.

I used my fist as a mic and Ro grabbed it, pretending to share with me. We built to the final crescendo, jumping up and down, belting it out.

As the last notes died away, Rohan spun me and dipped me. Silence reigned. My towel fell to the ground, forgotten, our bond, intangible yet absolute, stretching between us to envelop me.

He set me back on my feet. "Get dressed. Don't want the birthday girl to be late for her own party."

Given the choice, I'd have blown it off, stayed here, and wrapped myself in him. Drunk him in like an elixir.

"Can't have that." I shimmied into a short-sleeved blue shirt dress, sweeping my hair up. "Zip me, please?" He zipped up my dress, and I straightened a bend in his stiff collar. "New shirt, just for me?" I teased. "Want me to pick your tie?"

"Tieless today."

"Scaredy cat."

He shrugged into a blazer. "First time seeing your parents as the boyfriend instead of just your co-Rasha. Need to find the balance between 'make a good impression' and 'stop trying so hard.'"

I fiddled with the decorative buttons on my pockets. "You're going to be fine." Or run screaming, but what was a relationship without a few tense family moments here and there?

Rohan's eyes narrowed, but Ari rapped on my door, interrupting further conversation.

"Ready?"

Rohan studied the lightweight pink sweater Ari wore and then my blue dress. "I'm guessing that's not coincidence."

"Nope." Ari smoothed a hand over his V-neck.

"It was our rebellion at age seven at the gendered stereotyping of our clothing." I pulled my damp hair into a high ponytail.

"More like Nava pitched a fit that year that she didn't get to wear this red poufy dress our grandma had given her, because we were always put in blue and pink. Mom insisted we wear what she'd bought us, so Nava gave Mom exactly what she wanted."

I grabbed my purse and led the boys out. "She didn't specify who had to wear what."

"We all know how you love your loopholes," Ari said.

Rohan chuckled. I elbowed him and he caught my hand. "Your brother insults you and *I* get wounded. So unfair."

I interlaced our fingers. "Ari looked adorable in the pink sundress Mom had chosen for me."

My brother nodded. "I really did. Nava just looked like an ugly boy."

"I really did."

We snickered.

"This is going to be some party," Rohan muttered.

He had no idea.

9

Cars clogged the curb in front of my parents' house.

"Two o'clock," Rohan said. "We're being glared at."

Mrs. Jepson's curtains twitched, but not before we caught a glimpse of her trademark floral apron.

I nudged Ace. "Twenty bucks says she finally has an aneurysm about the cars blocking her curb."

Ari snorted. "She's been promising that for years. We're not that lucky."

The cedar and stained glass front door was ajar. We stepped inside, a loud hum of chatter and Céline Dion's "My Heart Will Go On" swamping us, and were immediately approached by a caterer bearing a tray of champagne.

"Why yes, thanks." I helped myself to a flute. Ari, Rohan, and I clinked glasses. "Get Dad off music duty."

Ari grabbed one more champagne flute. "On it."

Two other servers circulated with hors d'oeuvres. I examined their offerings before committing to the order of appetizer consumption.

"Your birthday dinner is catered?" Rohan said.

"But of course." My parents always used the same caterers. Their cheesy zucchini mini quiche were a special treat and I helped myself to two. "I'll make it up to you later."

"For what?"

"So many things." I laughed bitterly. "Just remember that I have no expectations of you playing nice with my family."

"How bad could this be?"

"It's like being disemboweled. You expect it'll be bad, but until you've experienced it you can't actually fathom its awful depths." I ran my hands down his arms. "I appreciate you being here."

"Sparky, be it demons or family members, I've got your back."

I exhaled. "Okay. Game time." I dragged him through the foyer, down the hallway past the grids of framed family photos, and into the living room, opened for this momentous occasion.

The crush of people helped a bit with the room's general soullessness, though most of them wore black, so they kind of blended into the black-and-white brocade wallpaper.

One of the caterers cleared away the drinks and empty small plates strewn over the modular coffee table.

"Whoa." Rohan slowed as the packed room turned and stared at our entrance.

"Wait for it," I muttered. "Blue rinse on your nine."

"Nava!" A tiny freight train of a woman with a blue-tinted perm barreled toward us. She air-kissed my cheek, bestowing birthday greetings, and then turned her gossip-attuned eye on Rohan. "Are you one of the security boys that Nava does secretarial work for?"

I choked on my quiche.

Rohan patted my back with one hand while extending his other to shake. "Rohan. Pleasure to meet you."

"Ellen Tannery. I'm Associate Dean of Dov's Law Department."

I wiped my mouth with the cocktail napkin. "Rohan's my boyfriend."

"Really?" Another women turned with a prim sniff. Awesome, my mom's aunt Alexia had arrived. Ro got full credit for only giving the mildest startled blink at her overly made-up face with her botoxed forehead that wouldn't move with a dynamite blast to the face, and her collagen-injected lips that she swore were merely "good genes."

The Michael Bolton song playing cut out, replaced by Ed Sheeran's "Shape of You." Praise unto Ari.

Alexia waved at Rohan with an asparagus tip. "This handsome young man is really your boyfriend?"

"Will wonders never cease?" I said in a tight voice.

Thus began the Parade of Making Nice, involving Rohan and me circulating from group to group while I smiled through a litany of backhanded insults on my professional status from my parents' faculty friends and blatant disbelief on my love life from my family members. No, that's not fair. There were family members that combined both, like my half-deaf great uncle Moishe, holding court in Dad's recliner, who repeated his slights in a voice only slightly quieter than a stadium announcer's.

Ro was shell-shocked by the time we'd navigated the room once. "These people are horrible."

"Yeah. Come on, Snowflake." I tugged on his hand. "You've done your time. I'm pronouncing you officially freed for good behavior. Leo will have corralled our friends in the TV room. You'll be safe there."

I led Rohan past the charcuterie table first so he could load up on protein because his left eyebrow was twitching, generally a sign he was starving. Though it might also have been PTSD. I shoved a small plate into his hands then waved discreetly at Ari, his elbow caught in a death grip by one of mom's co-workers. He had the same pained expression on his face he always did when she tried to set him up with her douchebag son. I tipped my head to the door to let him know we were making our escape.

Leo, bless her heart, took one look at Ro and stuffed her highball into his hand. "Start now and keep up a steady intake," she said. "It'll make this night go much easier."

He tossed the drink back. "Can't we just go fight demons?"

"What do you think we've been doing for the past hour?" I grabbed another champagne flute from a passing server and chugged it down.

"Going to greet the parents now?" Leo asked.

I shoved the empty glass in her hand. "Wish me luck."

I caught my dad sneaking back into the home office, his phone in his hand. He'd dressed up for the occasion, which meant replacing his sweater vest with a plaid button-down shirt that had been ironed to within an inch of its life. "Freeze."

He stilled mid-reach for the docking system plugged into the house-wide speakers. "You don't even know what I'm going to play."

"Steve Miller's greatest hits."

He blinked owlishly at me. "Are you psychic?"

"I can see your screen."

"They're classics." He huffed. "Besides, you don't have time to worry about music. Go talk more with all your guests."

"Oh, sure." I planted my hands on my hips. "Should I go slip into my *Handmaid's Tale* robe now? Because secretary at a security firm, really, Dad? Uncle Izzy already mansplained how I need to find a nice Jewish boy and get married now that all my dance mishegoss is done with. Haven't heard that one since last Hanukkah, so it was just swell to be told that if I found the right Executive to work for my M.R.S. was assured."

"Sweetheart, no one was going to believe the girl who spent the past year racking up temp jobs was hired for any type of actual security position. Be logical."

I logically wanted to brain him with his phone. I placed my hand on my diaphragm, using a breathing technique from tap to calm the fuck down. "Happy birthday to me."

"Always. What does a clam do on his birthday?"

I exhaled, rolling back my shoulders and visibly bracing myself for the groaner to come. Dad said so many of the wrong things, but he was the first one with a joke to make light of a situation.

I was my father. Kill me now.

"You ready? Can you take it?" Dad asked.

"I've been training. I'm in pretty peak freaking shape. Hit me. What *does* a clam do on his birthday?"

"He shellabrates. Ba-dum. Tshh." He mimed hitting a drum set.

"Wow." I was totally telling that to Ari.

He kissed the side of my head. "Go find your mother. Someone spilled Merlot on her blouse and she's having a clothing crisis about what to change into."

We exchanged wry grins. Mom didn't cope well with on-the-fly decisions.

"Going. Stay away from the music or you'll remember what magic powers I do have."

I knocked on my mother's bedroom door before pushing it open with an "All hail the birthday girl."

Mom stood in a black pencil skirt and black camisole, a variety of tasteful black blouses arrayed on the bed. She frowned at my blue dress, running a hand over her honey-blonde bob. "Really, Nava. Haven't you and Ari outgrown that ridiculous show of petulance?" She dropped her hand. "Dear God. What happened to your chin?"

I blushed, cupping my hand over it. I'd thought the ton of concealer I'd used had done the trick since no one else had commented, but Mom had X-ray vision when it came to finding my flaws. "Demon," I mumbled.

She tsked me. "What's done is done."

I kissed her cheek. "Lovely to see you, too, Mom. What's the problem? Having trouble choosing between black and slightly less black?"

"I had a perfectly good blouse, but your cousin Shauna spilled wine on it." She fiddled with her tasteful gold chain. "I swear that women has nothing better to do than hold a grudge."

I flung her closet door open. "Since it's a party..." *In theory.* "Here." I pulled out the brightest shirt I could find: a jade green number with its tags still on.

"Your father bought me that." She raked a critical eye over it. "I think the color would make me look a bit... desperate."

"You're right. If you put it on, everyone would be like 'cougar it down a notch.'"

She laughed. "You're the payback my mother warned me about. Go enjoy your party. I'll be down momentarily."

Duty done, I fled back to the TV room.

Rohan patted the seat next to him and I gratefully sank into his embrace. "You want another drink?" he said.

"Yes, but no. My mom has enough ammunition for tonight."

Leo sat down on top of me. I sniffed her neck for her Sexy Ruby perfume. "Ooh, smell me, baby." She draped her arms around my neck and smooched my cheek.

Ro put his hand on my knee. "That's mine."

Leo made a raspberry noise. "I pre-date you." She swung her legs onto his lap. "But if you're good, I'll share."

Rohan winked at her. "I'm very good."

Leo leaned back against me. "How good? On a scale of one to ten with one being a pleasant foot massage and ten being Ricky Whittle banging me senseless on the glass elevator going up the outside of the CN Tower?"

Ro cough-laughed.

"What?" she said. "TMI?"

"More oddly specific," he replied.

I tugged on Leo's hair. "Plus, I'm the only one you're supposed to objectify tonight."

"Right." She mouthed "We'll talk later" at Ro.

"Can I get you ladies anything?" he said. Leo requested some more goat cheese-stuffed figs and Ro left.

"You didn't invite Drio?" I asked.

"I did. He said he was too jetlagged."

Or was he still hurt? I didn't say anything to Leo because I didn't want to make her mad and have her drain me dry. I pushed her off me. "Your free trial of my goods has ended. You want me to put out? Sign up. Very attractive lease rates."

"Eh. I'm gonna shop around." She hopped up and straightened her silver velvety sundress, her plethora of silver jewelry tinkling. "Wait here." She skipped off, returning a moment later carrying a large gift.

I ripped open the envelope to find a little kid's card. A "Now you are 2!" button fell out. Leo had added a "one" in red crayon. That explained the button Ari had pinned to his shirt. Inside the card, she'd written "About time you were my friend again, dummy." She'd covered one side of the card in heart stickers.

"I love you, Leo."

She nudged my shoulder. "Love you, too. Open it."

I tore into the gift. "No way. You remembered."

Leo and I used to go see movies all the time, often at this odd little mall downtown that most people only went to for either the theater or the Japanese dollar store. But there was also this art gallery featuring a lot of local artists that we'd hang out in while waiting for our movie to start. The art was weird and wonderful, from pastel portraits of cute monsters to vivid paintings involving fractured fairy tale tableaux. My favorite artist was Camilla D'Errico, who painted these doe-eyed anime girls. One had an octopus hanging off her head, another painting featured a unicorn-horned girl emerging from a Technicolor sea.

Leo had bought me one of D'Errico's framed prints of *Neo New York*, this Blade Runner-type cityscape. A girl with a hot pink umbrella stood downcast in the midst of the hustle and bustle of the city. I'd always said I'd buy it as soon as I had my own place.

I tackled her in a hug until she proclaimed that I was suffocating her, then I slid the painting behind the sofa so no one spilled anything on it. "Hey, can I ask you a work question?"

She pinned my button on me. "I haven't heard anything about Candyman."

"Not that. Ever heard of an oshk?"

Leo laughed. "Where'd you hear that urban legend?"

"Not so legendy. I saw one."

Leo looked skeptical. "Oshk is the bogeyman of demons. It's what mommy and daddy demons tell baby demons when they're bad. Bad in the wrong ways for demons."

"I never thought about demon parenting," I said.

"It leaves a lot to be desired." She scratched her cheek. "Shit. That might explain why some of the demons in town seem to have disappeared."

"I'd noticed. Eaten?"

"Or took off."

"Do oshk hurt people?"

"It's only the one. The oshk is a Unique. But no on the hurting people. Not that I've ever heard."

I hoped this wasn't a first-time-for-everything scenario.

Citrus perfume teased my senses as a woman pressed into my side. My cousin Yael, my favorite family member after Ari. "Who's the hottie?"

I pushed aside her explosive corkscrew curls that I'd envied most of my life to kiss her cheek. "Which one?"

All three of us looked at Ro, Ari, and Kane, chatting in a corner. Rephrase. Ro was chatting with them both. Ari and Kane were standing stiffly in the same general vicinity.

"Start with the one Ari is obviously desperate for."

Leo laughed and stood up. "Good to see you again, Yael."

My cousin beamed up at her. "You too, pipsqueak."

Leo went to join the guys while I examined my cousin. "How do you make middle-age look so hot?"

"I'm thirty-three, asshole." She ran a hand over the gray tank dress she wore. "Also, I have good genes."

I shuddered. "You better hope you didn't inherit those, because you'll be playing tetherball with that rack of yours when you hit fifty. Where's the monster?"

"With the sperm donor." Her expression darkened at the mention of her ex.

"I bet you have photos."

Yael pulled out her phone so fast, she almost brained me with her elbow. She scrolled through each of the hundred photos of her seven-year-old daughter, complete with detailed explanation of what Rachel was doing in each one.

I lasted for about eighteen photos before smothering myself with a pillow.

She pulled the phone away. "You made it through about four photos longer this time. Wow, you're all mature and shit." She elbowed me. "Now spill."

That was all the prompting I needed to give up the gossip between Ari and Kane. Yael knew the truth about what Ari and I did, had known even before he'd hidden out at her place to avoid a repeat of another demon getting to him before his powers had become active.

She rubbed her hands together. "I'm going to make him miserable. But first I plan on interrogating your boyfriend. The one you failed to mention you were dating."

"Ari. That rat."

My brother must have heard us because he smirked and raised his glass in cheers.

Yael stood up, and I scrambled to my feet. "What would it take to keep you away from him?"

She'd terrified Cole with her inquisition. Granted he was young and nowhere near as arrogant as Snowflake, but I didn't want Rohan to freak out.

She stroked her chin. "You really like him, don't you?"

"No shit, considering I'm dating him."

"More than that. Okay. I'll stand down. For now." She broke into an evil cackle.

"You'll also give me my present."

Her cackle got eviler, but she handed me a small gift bag.

I peered inside. "Smutty fridge magnet poetry. How thoughtful."

"Since you'll soon be old enough to have sex for the first time," she said. I snorted. "I'm imparting the sage wisdom of how important communication in the bedroom is."

I flipped the box over to check out the example tiles. "'Body spank want wet.' Yes, I anticipate this facilitating mature and reflective conversations around intimacy."

We cracked up.

My mother entered in one of the black blouses to announce that dinner had been laid out in the dining room. The green one would have really lit her up. Why did I bother? The laughter died on my lips.

Yael nudged me. "Not worth it."

"Damn straight." I pasted a smile on my face.

The meal went by without incident. Since it was a buffet, people were free to eat anywhere, so I loaded up my plate and went back into the TV room.

I'd been stopped by more people wanting to say hello, so I was the last one back. Someone had arranged the seating into a loose circle around the coffee table. I took the last empty chair between Leo and Rohan. Yael sat sandwiched between Kane and Ari on the sofa.

"You know." Kane stabbed at a piece of rotini in pesto-artichoke sauce. "You two being born today makes a lot of sense."

I swallowed my grilled salmon. It was covered in a mustard-maple syrup vinaigrette I was considering getting a dipping bowl full of, next go around. "Why? Because we're Geminis and twins?"

"Laaaame," Leo said.

"No, smarty pants." Kane smirked. "Because every Gemini I've ever known has been stubborn as hell."

"So true! These two especially." Yael scooped up some roasted fingerling potatoes. "The stories I could tell." Which of course she did, though thankfully they were the tame ones.

Ro caught my eye during the tale of me at age six telling my dad that I "rejected his rational opinion in favor of my own." "I find that so hard to believe," he said.

"I know." I pushed the plate away, rubbing my full belly. "I'm so easygoing. You're truly blessed with my low maintenance."

"For which I give daily thanks." Ro helped himself to the remaining rib on my plate.

There was a lot of laughter and silly small talk. It was so different from last year when the only person I'd had here for me had been Ari. I didn't know Rabbi Abrams or any Rasha, not that the hunters had been invited. Even Yael hadn't come, in the midst of her horrible divorce. Leo and I hadn't been speaking and there hadn't been anyone else I was close enough to want to invite.

You couldn't pay me to go back to that existence.

Finally we got to my favorite part: the cakes. Everyone sang "Happy Birthday" as caterers brought in the desserts: a "balls inside" St. Honoré with the cream puffs both inside the sheet cake as well as on top for Ari and a super deluxe chocolate for me. Each had twenty-two candles because there had to be the one for good luck on each.

"Make a wish," Leo called out.

I looked at Rohan, closed my eyes, and blew.

"One boyfriend," Yael said.

I opened my eyes but she wasn't talking about my cake.

Ari muttered for her to shut up and blew his last candle out. Silly boy. Might as well have waved a red flag in front of a bull, because Yael grinned and said, "Let's make a list of candidates!"

Rabbi Abrams had snuck in during the singing, so I brought him a slice of the "balls inside" which Mom always made sure was Kosher.

"Thank you for getting me to Dr. Gelman."

He took a bite with a happy sigh. "You're welcome."

I stood there a moment, fidgeting.

"I'm not mad at you, Navela, but this is a sad situation."

"I know."

"You will keep me in the loop on all of it from now on, yes?"

"Yes."

He nodded. "Happy birthday. You are a good Rasha."

I gave him a watery smile and headed into the powder room down the hall in search of tissue.

"Everything good with Rabbi A?" Rohan held out a piece of chocolate cake to me.

I nodded, throwing my damp tissue in the trash. I hadn't actually cried which was a total win. "I already tried both kinds."

"Yeah, but you want seconds of the chocolate."

I really did. We went and sat on the hallway stairs with our legs nudged together, me occasionally feeding him bites since it was a two-person piece. Fine, it was sharing-sized only because I'd already had two pieces and couldn't plow through this one alone.

I put the empty plate on the stair beside me, braced my elbows on my knees, and dropped my head in my hands.

Rohan rubbed my back. "Talk to me."

"I want a do-over on today." I was rubbed raw. I'd woken up and nearly had a heart attack over Rohan making me think he hadn't given me a gift, I'd seen Dr. Gelman, checked up on Christina and Naomi, and Sienna had told me I was dumb. I'd had more people ask me when I was going to start doing something useful and having kids than I wanted to count. Even the word of the day for today was awful.

Some things were good. Rabbi Abrams believed in me. But my own dad didn't. No one in my family, except for Ari and Yael, thought I had what it took to actually do something cool with my life. My insides were a jagged jumble and any birthday happiness I'd accrued lay broken and battered on their sharp edges.

My mom walked past, her heels clicking on the tiles. "Nava, why aren't you mingling?"

I tensed up.

"She needs a break," Rohan said.

"Your concern is very nice, dear, but Nava can't just selfishly hide away when all these guests have come to celebrate with her."

"Be real," I said. "Four, maybe five of these guests came to celebrate with me, and they'd all understand. The rest came for you and Dad."

"It's not fair to your brother to put this all on him." Her "as usual" was unspoken but very much implied.

"God knows Ari's feelings must always come first."

"There's no dealing with you when you're like this."

I straightened up with a snap. "Like what?"

Rohan stopped rubbing my back. "How about we go outside and get some air?"

"No, Ro. I really want to hear her answer. I've been putting up with insults all night at this sham of a birthday that has nothing to do with me, because in my entire fucking life it's never been about me where she's concerned. So tell me, Mother Dearest, how I should be behaving?"

"I'm not going to make a scene in front of your guests, no matter how much you want me to. I apologzie for my difficult daughter, Rohan, but it was nice to see you again." She turned away. "Now I need to speak with the caterers."

"For fuck's sake, Mom, I'm not being difficult. You're being a bitch."

She flinched like I'd slapped her. "I'm sorry you feel that way." She strode off, holding a hand up to Ari, who'd arrived.

I muttered a curse, curling in on myself.

"You want to go after her?" Rohan said.

"No point right now," Ari said.

I spread my arms wide. "Lay it on me, bro. I'm a horrible daughter."

Ari nudged my foot. "No, you're not. It's been a long time coming. Take her home?" he asked.

Rohan nodded.

"Happy birthday, Nee," Ari said, over his shoulder, already heading back into the fray. "There's no one I'd rather share it with. Even if your sense of timing sucks."

Rohan hung Leo's gift up for me. It looked perfect against the raspberry walls that he'd helped me paint. Now I had the Gregory Hines tap dancing photo on one side of my bed and this print on the other. I'd also tacked up photos of the important people in my life: Leo and me glammed up for a night out, Ari and I at our favorite gelato place, Ms. Clara with a plate of cookies in one hand and her dominatrix whip in the other, Baruch and Rabbi Abrams drinking tea at a café in Jerusalem together, and Kane and Ari mugging with a basketball. Then there were the selfies of Ro and me: us in Prague, here in Vancouver beat up and triumphant throwing devil horns after a nasty demon kill in Stanley Park, and laying on his car at dusk with our best rock star faces on. Ro wore an unbelievably arrogant smirk that made me laugh every time I looked at it, while I'd affected my best sultry pout. I'd get a photo of Drio now that he was back from Rome and stick that up, too.

Rohan tucked me into bed. He wore my "Tap Dancers Need Wood" shirt that was too tight and short on him, fussing over me as he plumped up pillows to go behind my back.

He was amazing.

"I have one more gift for you," he said.

I traced the line of his abs down to his waistband. "Is it R-rated?"

He picked up the acoustic guitar he'd brought in, his hand curved possessively around it, rummaging through the pocket of his shorts for a pick. He had dozens of them scattered about his room, but he pulled out this matte purple one that, according to his fan boards, was his favorite type.

"Did you write a new song?" I'd recently heard the finished version of the theme song for "Hard Knock Strife" and he was writing music again but, even though he was always willing to play for me while I danced, it was either Fugue State Five songs or covers. He hadn't let me hear any other new songs.

Ro put his finger to his lips to shush me and I folded my hands in my lap like a good little listener.

"It's called 'Slay.'" Head bent, a lock of hair falling forward, Rohan's first notes were as rich as aged whiskey. The opening melody wove around me, low and clear.

Sucker-punched by a cherub wrapped tight in barb wire
You skirted the shadows
taught me how to soar higher
It started a game
stand one night on its head
My fallen angel's my home
stack our days end to end

Words poured out of him, his eyes on mine weaving a spell, a story of us, that I wrapped myself in snugger than any blanket. He kept one foot planted on the floor, keeping time, the other bent to support the weight of the guitar.

I listed toward him, drawn in by the warm pull of his smile. My blood heated to a slow drift and my heart kept time with the bass.

His strumming kicked up, his heel driving the rhythm and his voice ringing out for the chorus.

Slay all your demons
I'll slay all of mine
Light up the darkness
you're my bottom line
Let's slay all our demons
I'll lay down my knives
For you, I'll lay down my knives
Why don't you slay?
Come on, just slay,
You know I've been slain.

Rohan danced his pick over his knuckles, swallowed, and pursed his lips. "It's pretty rough. I mean, I haven't been writing for a while and I might need to edit some parts, but that's pretty usual and–what?"

My boyfriend had written a song for me. The best song in the history of all mankind.

Pressing my palms against the mattress, I rose up and kissed him. "I love it."

He set the guitar down. "You needed your own song. For the new album." He tossed the pick on the nightstand. "I wouldn't even be writing again if it wasn't for you."

I kissed him again, more insistent, pouring every feeling I was too overwhelmed to voice into it. He pulled away, breathless and laughing, and from the tender look he shone on me, he'd understood.

"Sing it again?"

His pleased growl shot electric sparks through my blood. But the smile he bestowed on me? It wasn't some sexy wattage or the deadly-deserved arrogance of his hunter smirk that got me hot and wet. No, this one, warm and intimate and a bit shy to fully emerge, swelled me up with light and air and a bittersweet ache like there was this amazing thing if I could only stretch my fingertips one more millimeter to grab it tight.

I couldn't contain it, so I molded it into something I could handle. I got onto my knees, fingering the hem of Ro's T-shirt. "Keep singing." I tugged it over his head, pitching it carelessly at the foot of the bed.

His eyes darkened but he started the song again, a capella.

I snapped the button on his shorts and Ro's voice wavered. I raised an eyebrow and he grinned his apology, singing the chorus in a steadier voice, even as I pulled out his cock, stroking it, luxuriating in the feel of it swelling.

I reached over to the night-table, got the bottle of water-based lube and pressed it into Ro's hands. He was about to stop singing when I shook my head and took out Snake Clitspin, my S-shaped vibe. He smiled and oiled the toy up just at the chorus.

The song ended right as I hit the "on" button and Snake hummed.

Ro reached for me but I wagged a finger at him. "Uh-uh. Keep singing. Mood music. But no touching."

"Come on—"

I sucked his erection into my mouth.

Ro bucked off the bed and burst into song. "Twinkle Twinkle Little Star." Not in my top ten bow-chica-wow-wow songs, but rolling off his tongue, his voice a low growl and the corner of his mouth quirked in a knowing smile, it was positively pornographic.

I squirmed, his answering smirk ruined by the flush on his cheeks and the white-knuckled grip he had on the sheets.

A better musical choice was his rendition of Maroon 5's "Harder to Breathe" accompanied by me on dick and vibe. Ro's breathing was growing harsh, but champ that he was he kept singing, albeit a bit more growly than usual, his eyes darting between his blowjob of the century—I wasn't even using my magic on him, I was just that good—and my writhing, getting myself off on Snake almost as much as on what I was doing to Ro.

By Britney's "Slave to You," he was snapping his hips in time to the music, his erection in my mouth impossibly hard. He strained to stay in control enough to do as I'd asked and keep singing. Keep his hands curled in tight fists so he wouldn't touch me, his voice wavering as he tried to follow my dictate.

With a word I could unleash it all, let the storm of his passions devour me. The knowledge was heady to the point that my wanton moans threatened to drown him out. I rocked Snake inside me in rhythmic pulses; my fingers and toes tingled from the fat coils of pleasure rippling through me. I vibrated, strung taut.

We didn't even make through the first chorus of "Wicked Games" by The Weeknd. Ro sang these filthy lyrics in a ringing voice and I came hard. It sent Ro over the edge, his body bucking, all pretense of singing abandoned.

He mumbled a string of Hindi curses, sprawled against the pillows.

I rode the aftershocks coursing through my body, then mustered up the energy to turn Snake off. The room smelled of sex, drenched in musky good times.

"Your blow jobs are the fucking bomb," he said. I laughed and he nudged my shoulder with his knee. "Happy birthday, Sparky."

I crawled up the length of his body, sliding blankets over us both. The incandescent glow of the firefly lights tapped up around my ceiling made the room softer, warmer. Rohan's chest pressed against my back and my breathing came easier, my heartbeat slowing to match his. "Thanks for making it happy."

He tucked a kiss into the nape of my neck, stretched to switch off the light, and then settled back against me with one arm holding me close. "Always," he said.

And right before I fell asleep, I thought that sounded pretty good.

10

Tuesday morning I ambushed Kane and Ari at the front door, forcing them both to hug me at the same time. "Be careful."

They were headed into the interior of the province which had been affected by extremely bad flooding. Natural disasters: demon's crack.

Twin sets of elbows jabbed me to get free. "We will," they chorused.

"Take care of each other. I refuse to be down a sibling or a friend."

Kane hefted up his duffel bag. "It's always about you." He winked and strode out to his Porsche.

Ari slung his backpack over one shoulder. "Promise you'll talk to Mom. Apologize even."

"I promise that at some point in my life I will once again speak to her."

"Nava."

"Ariiiiii." I squirmed, miserable. "Fine. I promise." I gave him one more hug for the road, waving until he and Kane had driven off.

Drio and Rohan were in the library. Drio, in sweats, was typing on Rohan's laptop, while Ro stood in the corner on the phone in board shorts and another faded T-shirt. He waved hello at me.

I set a foil-wrapped plate down in front of Drio.

He pulled up one edge and peeked in. "This is cake."

"Actually it's cakes plural, but solid attempt on the identification." I tossed a fork at him, hitting him square in the chest. "Next time, come to my damn party."

He glared at me but tore the foil off and dug in, so I figured my point had been ceded.

I sniffed the air. "Wearing Sexy Ruby now, are we?"

He smelled his wrist, his eyes going soft and dreamy for a moment.

I smirked.

"It's on her sheets. Shut up." He dug into the cake with ferocity.

Well, well. I refrained from poking the beast further, especially the beast with a fork and über-speed. I filled him in on what Leo had told me about the oshk's bogeyman status, omitting the part where she'd learned it directly from her goblin father, and letting him think she'd discovered it from the demon clientele she worked with as a part-time Private Investigator. I shuddered to think how the Rasha with the biggest hard-on for killing demons would react when he learned he was sleeping with a half-goblin.

Drio entered the keywords "bogeyman" and "urban legend" into a new search in the Brotherhood's database but it still didn't yield any results for the oshk.

Rohan sat down next to me. "That was Zahir."

"Learn anything useful about Ferdinand?" I said.

"Not exactly. Drio, I need you to go to Palm Springs."

I didn't understand Ro's request, but Drio gave two slow blinks before replying. "You are without scruples."

Rohan wagged a finger at him. "You'll make an old lady very happy."

"Phrasing and huh?" I said.

Drio licked frosting off the fork. "He wants me to visit the widow of the rabbi who ran the Los Angeles chapter."

Rohan spread his hands wide. "Rabbi Soriano has been gone a couple of years and Golda must be lonely. Besides, she loves Drio. It would be such a mitzvah."

Drio kicked his chair. "Golda has early stage dementia and I'm not going to harass her. She can barely remember–" He snapped his mouth shut.

"Aha! I knew you still visited her." He patted Drio's cheek. "Such a mensch."

Drio knocked Ro's hand away, then smacked me with the fork. "Quit gaping. They are pity visits."

I tossed the fork on the table, wetting my finger and rubbing the front of my purple sundress to clean the smudge of frosting. "Sure, softie."

I took his growl for the assent that it was, smothering my fond smile at how much the big meanie was going out of his way to help me. Drio's loyalty to Ro was absolute; having even the tiniest sliver of his support made me more certain that we could pull this off.

"Golda befriended everyone who ever came through the place and Zahir said Ferdinand was based out of there for about a decade, starting in the late 80s," Rohan said. "Not sure why the Brotherhood doctored his record to show Ferdinand was there this past year, but chances are Golda stayed in touch. She might be able to tell us more about his death."

"I understand you don't want to ask the current rabbi in case he's involved, but why don't you visit Golda yourself?" I said. "Los Angeles is your home chapter."

Drio barked his laughter and finished his last bit of cake off with his fingers. "She's never forgiven him for ruining her Passover dinner one year." He nudged Rohan. "Go on. Share."

Rohan stood up abruptly. "Not worth retelling."

"I beg to differ," I said.

"Ro got hold of this–umph!"

Rohan grabbed Drio in a headlock, muffling his mouth. I was totally getting that story out of him one day. Still holding Drio by the head, he dragged his friend out of the room, saying they'd be back in a bit because he was going to buy Drio a cash ticket to Palm Springs.

"Make it one way!" I called out.

Mahmud had texted my burner phone to confirm that other than the possible deaths themselves, there was nothing suspicious about the four Rasha who'd died in Askuchar. Nothing on their records had been redacted and no one was hiding anything about their lives or covering anything up. I thanked him and reminded him to stay in touch on this phone only.

I prepared a few things for the drop later this afternoon. The sooner we nailed Candyman, the better.

My Brotherhood-issued phone beeped madly. I'd never heard that particular sound before and was shocked to see that Orwell had sent me a text with no one else on the chain.

There'd been another Sweet Tooth incident. I called Ro. "We've got a death."

"You want me to meet you? I'm way on the other side of town," Rohan said.

"I'll handle it. Just keeping you in the loop."

"Thanks, Boss."

"Most Superior Goddess works, too."

"Goof," he said, and hung up.

About twenty minutes later, I pulled up to Rocco's Pizzeria, a squat brick storefront off West Tenth Avenue that wasn't too far from our mansion. Close to the University of British Columbia, it was a popular student hangout for its huge portions. I salivated just thinking about their pesto pancetta slices. Yes, pancetta, my not-so-secret love. I was a bad Jew. Jew-ish.

I slung the laminated press pass identifying me as one of the reporters for The Vancouver Sun newspaper over the business casual blouse and linen pants that I'd changed into, and fished a spiral bound notebook and pen from my purse.

Crime scene tape had been strung across the open door, allowing the scent of baking dough and spicy tomato sauce to drift out into the street. Cops milled about.

The first officer I spoke to directed me to another cop who was willing to say that an alleged assault and death had occurred on the premises.

A crying Indo-Canadian woman a few years older than me was inside the restaurant speaking with an officer, but there was no way to get to her. Other than her there were just a lot of gawkers out on the sidewalk speculating on what had happened.

I headed into the alley behind the store. The dumpster hadn't been emptied and the stench of rotting food in this heat made my stomach lurch. Luckily, I didn't have to wait there for very long.

The back door opened and I fished a new pack of cigarettes out of my purse, making a big show of unwrapping it.

"Could I bum one of those?" An unshaven dude in a sauce-stained apron with a dusting of flour along his jaw nodded at the pack.

Thanks to Yael's many stories from her years of working in kitchens, it had been a fair assumption that someone in this place was a smoker.

I held the pack out. "Help yourself."

He jammed a cigarette in the corner of his mouth, flicking open his lighter and lit up. He closed his eyes to better savor that first deep drag. "Need a light?" He sparked the flame for me.

That was the only downside to my plan. Cigarettes were gross. I took the barest drag and then mostly held it.

He gestured at my press pass. "I can't talk about what happened."

"Sweet Tooth is a really shitty drug," I said.

He flicked his tongue over his lips before puffing away some more. "Got that out of the cops?"

I shook my head. "My friend had a bad experience on it a few days ago. Surgery bad. She assaulted someone, too." A long column of ash fell onto my open-toed sandals, startling me out of my daze. I ground the tip into the brick wall.

"Sorry to hear it."

"Everyone affected has friends, family. If you could just tell me—"

He crushed the butt under his shoe. "Sorry."

The door to the pizzeria closed behind him with a reverberating thud.

"Was that just bullshit for the story?" The Indo-Canadian woman watched me from the mouth of the alley with red-rimmed, puffy eyes. "About your friend?"

"No." I walked over to her, glad to get away from the garbage. "One of my friends did Sweet Tooth and was fine. The other one?" I shook my head.

She drew in a shaky breath that racked her slight frame.

I handed her an unopened water bottle. I'd been taught all kinds of tricks for getting victims or their family and friends to open up. This particular purse held all my props. Yeah, it was kind of cold and manipulative, as was exploiting Naomi's tragedy, but if this got me to Candyman and made sure that no one else got hurt, I'd be as manipulative as it took.

"Was it your friend?" I said.

"Cousin. Jake." She twisted the cap off but didn't drink.

"I'm so sorry. What's your name?"

"Harjit."

"I'm Nava. Did you take any?" I checked her pupils but didn't see any dilation.

"No. It wasn't my thing. Caffeine junkie, yeah."

"Can I buy you one? I mean, it is recess time. I generally need a hit about now." She mustered up a weak smile, but I could sense her hesitation, so I bulldozed over it. "There's a café about half a block from here. Blast Brew Bar. You know it?"

"The hipster place?"

"Yeah." I started walking, maintaining eye contact and essentially forcing her to come with me. "They do that handmade, pour-over coffee thing, which yes, is so pretentious, but they're close."

"They're kind of overpriced."

I leaned in conspiratorially. "That's because they factor in the price of the physio from their carpel tunnel. It's my treat. Come on. Let me buy you a hot drink and get some sugar into your system. If you don't want to talk, you don't have to."

Harjit nodded, hesitant, but still agreeing to come. The cops had cut her loose for the moment and she looked adrift. She hadn't immediately gone home so I figured she wanted a chance to steady herself after the loss she'd suffered.

Not letting up my stream of chatter, I led her over to Blast and got us settled in with coffee and biscotti. The Brew Bar was all distressed wood, copper accents, and caffeine condescension with a massive stainless steel espresso maker focal point. The barista rubbed it down like he was jerking it off.

I worried my Starbucks-loving ass might be outed and I'd be run out of the place in a flurry of manbunned indignation, but I managed to place my order with enough ennui to make it seem like I belonged.

True to my word, I powered through my bitter brew, letting Harjit have her space. She broke her biscotti into smaller and smaller pieces until the crumbs mounted on her plate. "I wasn't even supposed to see Jake today. I'd only met up with him to get on his case for ditching his treatment."

"Substance abuse?" I licked my finger and pressed it to the three measly crumbs on my plate. I'd inhaled my biscotti and having gone this far, was committed to leaving no trace.

She pushed her plate away. "No."

"Okay, so you met up and he had already taken the Sweet Tooth?" She nodded. "Was there a sudden shift in his behavior? Like zero to extreme and it was terrifying?"

She glanced up at me, startled.

"It's what happened with my friend," I said gently.

"Jake had ordered his pizza, but he didn't have any cash and I was so mad at him that I didn't want to pay." Her eyes filled with tears. "Rocco? The owner? He's a big guy. He was behind the counter and when he told Jake to come back with money or leave, Jake casually grabbed this decorative vase on the counter and bashed Rocco with it." Harjit lined up the creamer and sugar bowls. "Then Jake jumped the counter and started stuffing pizza slices in his mouth. He wasn't even chewing them, just swallowing them down whole. I was freaking out calling 911."

"Was Rocco okay?"

"Yeah. His head was bleeding, but he was conscious. He and the cook tackled Jake but he didn't seem to care. He fought them for more pizza. He must have eaten two pies." Her voice caught. "He had a heart attack." Grief twisted her features, her eyes bleak as they met mine. "It was over so fast."

"What was he in treatment for?"

She closed her eyes, the answer dragged out of her in a rushed breath. "Food addiction."

I drove Harjit home, making her promise that she would call the number for counseling that the police had given her. I also checked in on Christina, who was doing better because Naomi was doing better. I got it; Naomi was her Leo. Neither of them were up to visitors yet but she did want to see me at some point.

I vowed to make more of an effort with friendships. Or have them at all.

I texted Rohan an address and the words "Meet me?" He texted back his agreement and I gunned my car west.

I parked my car at the lot on top of Queen Elizabeth Park, nicknamed Little Mountain by Vancouverites, and commandeered a wooden bench on the covered boardwalk that curved around the giant fountain. I stretched out my bare legs, letting the sunshine soak away the despondency of this mission.

Kids shrieked with laughter as they dodged and splashed in the dozens of jets spouting water in varying heights.

"Got Drio a ticket for tonight after the drop." Rohan sat down beside me.

I nodded, my attention on a little girl, maybe two or three, naked and dancing like a fiend through the plumes of water.

"Was that you?" he asked.

"I wasn't that young when they redid the park and put this fountain in, so no nudity for me. No, wait, I lie. But that was much later and it was a dare."

"Leo?"

"Good guess." The little girl jumped up and down in the fountain, her laughter shaking her plump belly. I smiled. "Ari and I had many the water fight here." I stood up, my hand extended. "Come on. I need to be in a happy place right now. I'll tell you what I learned there."

The glass and steel dome of the Bloedel Conservatory rose up from behind the fountain like a perky nipple. We jogged down the short flight of stairs by the large Canadian flag waving in the breeze, and around to the front of the building, hit with the warm, moist air piping out of the dome.

"Did you ever have a Snoopy Sno Cone Machine?" I said.

"That thing used to frustrate the fuck out of me. It took half an hour of serious grinding to get a fraction of an inch of ice, but those snow cones looked so cool on TV."

"I know. All that effort for basically nothing and you'd be deaf at the end of it." I nodded at the food truck selling artisan shaved ice parked by the front doors. "They're charging a fortune. We should start a handmade shaved ice truck, but use those things to make them. Tap into the nostalgia factor."

"Sell the interminable wait as half the attraction," Rohan said, holding the door for me.

"World domination through ice. And making people smile on a regular basis. That would be a nice change."

The world transformed from a sunny Canadian day to a tropical bubble, the humid air fragrant with rich earth and tropical flowers.

"Rough time with the incident?"

I nodded and paid our admission and we stepped through the turnstile onto the path marked with one-way directional arrows.

Rohan craned his neck up to the tree canopy brushing the condensation-streaked glass panels. "Whoa."

The flagstone path wove past leafy ferns jutting out of rock beds and Birds of Paradise plants splashing red at our feet, leading us to the small wooden post and rope bridge. Rushing water from a tiny falls splashed into a pool on our right, while on our left was another pond where fat koi swam lazily in ripples of sunlight, framed by spikes of bamboo. Blue and red parrots cuddled on a branch next to giant fronds of plantain banana plants that made me feel like I was in *A Bug's Life*.

"You have a destination?" Rohan said, sidestepping the tourists reading instructional notices about the ecosystem.

"This way."

Tiny white hummingbirds swooped and darted by my head, cawing out to the plump orange fuzzball birds flapping past, cheeping. A brilliant blue and gold parrot carving away at a hunk of wood eyed us suspiciously.

"Did you have a favorite place as a kid?" I asked.

"My mom's studio." Rohan ducked to avoid a blur of brown feathers careening at him. "I fell asleep more times than I could count listening to her and her recording engineer bickering at the soundboard."

I led him to a carved wooden gazebo. We sank onto the bench waiting for a family taking selfies to pass by, soaking in the hum of generators, chatter, and twittering escalating in volume from the doves and finches darting overhead.

Once we had some privacy, I told him about Jake. "The thing that triggers Sweet Tooth? I think it's an addictive personality. Take Naomi, for example. In college she was into extreme sports. Now she's a workaholic. When she had her episode she was acting a lot like she did when she was younger: dangerous stunts, not giving a damn about her own safety, going all full tilt. Jake's compulsive behavior was around food. The drug sparked a serious loss of control in both of them in ways that were fundamental to issues they were already dealing with."

"Christina doesn't have that type of personality?"

"No. We've been lucky that it didn't adversely affect more people." Two tiny yellow birds with orange faces frolicked in a rock pool by our feet. "That looks fun," I said.

"Do you ever wish you were oblivious to all this?" he asked.

"Allowed to frolic my way through life?"

"Something like that."

I pulled him to his feet. "No. I did that, remember? Ultimately, I'd rather be the one slaying monsters than the one not knowing to look under the bed."

He smiled like my answer pleased him.

Passing cacti and some plant dripping with fuzzy pink pods, we stopped at the final wooden perch before the exit. I made him say goodbye to Charlotte, the flame-colored parrot with the electric blue neck plumage, inhaled one last breath of the tropics, and headed outside to the hazy panorama of the city spread out before us, over the pine, fir, and cypress trees stretching out to the edge of the park.

We peeked over the bridge at the top of a tall waterfall, ridged with paths leading down to the manicured gardens below. Neatly landscaped flower beds in a riot of colors were interspersed with a lazy stream and stepping stones. A bevy of brides jostled for the best photo op for their wedding party.

Passing the fountain once more on our way back to our cars, I spread my arms wide, turning my face to the mist. Rohan swung me up in his arms.

"Rohan Liam Mitra, don't you dare." I tightened my hold on him. "If I go down, you're coming with me."

"That's cute." His lips brushed against my ears. "But I know your ticklish spots."

Bastard proved it, too. I shrieked, letting go of him to whack his hands away and stop the torture. He took grievous advantage and tossed me into the water. I landed on a jet that fired up–right up my ass.

Rohan doubled over laughing, half-heartedly fighting me as I dragged him in. Parents smiled indulgently. One cow-licked little guy in a red aqua suit stared at Rohan with wide eyes as my darling boyfriend liberally splashed me with long sweeps of his leg. "Wanna help?" Rohan asked.

The kid hesitated for a second then let me have it, jumping up and down in a frenzy. Water flew up my nose.

"That's it! Water fight!" I corralled a bunch of youngsters onto my team and the war was on. My clothes must have absorbed about seventeen pounds of fountain juice because when I finally sloshed my way out of there, water streamed off me like a river.

I acked on the hair plastered to my mouth and Rohan snickered. "Shut up. You look like a drowned rat, too." I popped my trunk, pulling out the thick beach blanket that Ari and I kept there along with our first aid supplies and an emergency road kit.

Rohan shook himself, more dog than rat. "You got another one of those?"

I closed the trunk and wrapped the blanket around me. "Nope."

He sat on the hood of his car, parked next to my Honda, and wrung out his shirt. "I can't drive back like this. Shelby will get wet."

"Isn't that your dream?" I waggled my eyebrows. "I'm sure you could find somewhere private to service her. Lube her up. Rotate her tires."

"Ha. Ha. Come on. Let me use that."

"No can do. So sorry." I pulled the blanket tight around me. "You're a creative boy. You'll think of something." I finger-waved, got in my car, and with a twist of the ignition, roared off.

11

The drop was scheduled to take place at 6:30PM in Crab Park, a stretch of green on the edge of Gastown. I stared out the window at the crowds milling on the sidewalks in Vancouver's downtown east side. It was home to our most marginalized citizens, many of them homeless, drug addicted, or forced to turn to prostitution to survive. After passing one of the open "markets," with the goods on offer set out on blankets on the grimy sidewalk or stuffed in trash bags and shopping carts, we hit the overpass leading to the waterfront park.

Chinese stone lions carved in intricate detail flanked each side of the road like sentinels. Beyond it, the Burrard Inlet winked blue in the sunlight.

Rohan parked my Honda, the more nondescript of our cars, in a small lot across from the park facing a stand of trees. To our left were the train tracks with an endless stretch of parked railcars, and behind that, gentrified condos in retrofitted brick buildings that still bore traces of their original use. Faded ads painted directly on the bricks proclaimed "janitorial supplies" or "wholesale grocers."

The most mouthwatering smell of BBQ hit us when we exited the car.

We looped around to the water side of the park. Shipping containers in rusts and greens were stacked under the towering cranes at the port terminal directly east. There was the occasional distant siren and scrape of metal wheels and pulleys from the cranes.

Cyclists and joggers used the seawall path, exercising to the cry of seagulls. This stretch of the seawall was practically empty compared to deeper in the downtown core to our west. Even fewer people were in the park itself. It was hard to believe that thousands were close by in densely packed glass office towers, under the towering sails of the Pan Pacific hotel that was designed like a giant ship, or milling around the plaza that was home to the Olympic flame from when we'd hosted the 2010 Games.

Mounds of bright yellow sulfur were stockpiled across the Inlet, with the North Shore mountains looming over it all.

I buttoned up my cardigan against the breeze drifting off the water.

Even though Ro and I had shown up to the drop early, we had no idea if the park was already being watched. Crab Park itself wasn't particularly exciting. Mostly grass, there was that one stand of trees with a scraggly rock garden. Some vagrant with matted hair and dirty clothes slept the snorey sleep of the drunk on one of the scattered wooden benches.

I had to check twice to confirm it was Drio, then I grimaced like a snotty brat. "Do we have to stay here?" I picked up my feet, stepping gingerly like the park could give me cooties. "I want ice cream."

"Anything for my girl."

Gagging loudly at Ro's earnest–and bullshit–tone would have blown the charade so I settled for a soft snort.

We followed the path up to the small stone marker anchoring the rock garden, stopping to guess the language written on its plaque. Really we were checking on the navy backpack full of cash that Drio had tossed into the bushes under a tall pine tree behind the monument. He'd gotten here a while ago with the cash-filled backpack, put it in the drop spot, and then hung around in his guise as a homeless man to keep an eye on it until Candyman showed with the drugs. It was beat up and dirty enough that no one was going to want to abscond with it. To the casual observer, it would look like the backpack had been stolen and dumped here.

Keeping up my whiny persona, I made Rohan go back to the car.

"You sure Drio will spot the guy? His eyes were closed." I wriggled in my seat.

"Are you going to fidget the entire time?"

"It's possible." My stomach growled and Ro shot me an exasperated look. "What? I'm hungry."

"I'll feed you after." He reached across me and rolled up the window. Not that it helped because the car now smelled of grilled meat.

I pulled a granola bar out of my purse. Ro gazed longingly at it, and even though I tsked him, I slapped the extra one I'd started carrying for him into his palm.

He flipped over the package. "This is a real granola bar. Not even dipped in chocolatey coating or with a ton of chemicals and sugar."

"Yeah, you've broken me. Happy?"

"Yup," he said, munching away.

The drop time came and went. At 6:40, a black Trans Am came off the overpass and turned the corner by the trees to the park. It was out of our sight line but three minutes later, Drio texted the word *Go*.

The Trans Am must have pulled a U-turn because it blew by us as we pulled out of the lot. Rohan proved quite adept at blending in traffic farther back, while keeping the car in view.

"Trained, were we?" I said.

"Oh yeah. The driving module rocked."

Hmm. Maybe I could make them teach me all the cool things I'd missed. Not until I'd exposed all the corruption and destroyed Rabbi Mandelbaum obviously, but after that. It was important to make plans for the future.

I fiddled with the radio until I found Beastie Boys' "Sabotage." I relaxed back against my seat, planting my feet on the dashboard. "Appropriate music achieved. Car chase away."

The Trans Am darted down Powell Street. Rohan trailed it, keeping to just above the speed limit with deft surety. Our path took us past one-story businesses painted in colorful murals from the yearly mural festival, Sugar Mountain tent city set up across from the sugar refinery, and a jumble of auto repair shops, light industrial factories, and the microbreweries popping up everywhere in town.

We turned left. Traffic slowed to a crawl, down to a single lane due to construction. I drummed my fingers on the door. "I could run after it faster."

Rohan honked at the bus that cut in front of us, blocking our view of the Trans Am. For several tense blocks we couldn't tell whether or not the car had turned off anywhere, but we caught up with it around the back of Playland.

Right before the Second Narrows Bridge, the driver cut across two lanes of traffic to the off-ramp. Rohan veered sharply and I careened into the door. "We've been made," he said.

The Trans Am blew through a three-way stop, flying under an underpass and whipping down a narrow service road.

I pointed out the window. "À la peanut butter sandwiches." I blew out one of the Trans Am's back tires. The car fishtailed, but the driver regained control.

I fired again and he jumped a curb, drifting sideways into a parking lot and crashing into one of the trees planted in a semi-circle along the fringes. The hood crumpled with a hiss.

Rohan screeched to a stop. "Nice work, Mumford."

"'Amazing Mumford,' thank you very much." I grinned, happy he'd gotten my Sesame Street reference. Flinging my door open, I strolled toward the car and the driver scrambling out, who sported a Metallica T-shirt and a mullet. The haircut was evil, but he didn't sprout horns or shoot fire and pestilence.

"You human?" I said.

"The fuck kind of question is that?" He stomped around his car, running a hand over his busted-up vehicle like he might cry. Rohan's expression was pure sympathy.

Sheesh.

"You trying to get me killed, lady? Throwing nails or whatever is illegal."

"Yeah?" I grabbed the navy backpack off of the passenger seat. "So's couriering for drug dealers."

He frowned. "Huh? I got paid to go to the park and outrun anyone who followed me. Sure as hell not getting my bonus now."

I unzipped the backpack. Rolled up newspapers with the same weight as our stacks of cash spilled out. "Son-of-a-bitch!"

Rohan slammed the guy against the Trans Am's door. "Who paid you?"

"Some dude. Came to the Go-Cart track where I work." The man he described, white, average height, short brown hair, jeans, jean jacket could have been any one of a million people.

Rohan tossed him away. The driver fell on his ass, threatening lawsuits. Ro turned back with a cold smile. "You're going to forget this ever happened or I will find you. Got it?"

The driver threw up his hands. "Yeah, man. No problem."

I took my car keys away from Ro and tossed him my burner phone. "Call Drio."

Soon as we were back in the car, Ro hit the speakerphone button. "What happened?"

"Guy showed up," Drio said. "Walked over to the monument, stared at it a second, and left. Didn't take anything with him, but the backpack was gone."

"Any drugs?" I pulled out of the lot.

"No. Candyman must have found out about the wreta."

"You headed for the airport?" Ro said.

"Yeah, you bastard." Drio hung up.

"Glove compartment," I said.

Rohan opened it and removed a small device. He turned it on. "Hello, Plan B."

We'd gone in to the drop assuming a double-cross, which was why I'd sewn a tracker into the backpack. If Trans Am dude hadn't taken the backpack, then Candyman must have portalled it out of there, confirming him as another demon. The blinking dot on the tracking screen showed an address not far from the wreta house, over by Boundary Road, the street delineating the border between Vancouver and Burnaby.

We hit the address up that night for maximum skulking.

In the daytime, this cozy cul-de-sac would have been filled with kids riding bikes or playing street hockey, overseen by neighborhood watch, but at 2AM, everyone was snug in their beds. We blended into the shadows in our all-black attire and black leather gloves.

The house was a cookie cutter replica of its boxy neighbors. If there was a ward on it, it was nothing we could sense and wasn't designed to keep Rasha out. Rohan made short work of the lock on the back door, and we crept inside, flashlights on. The place was minimally furnished but someone lived here:

there were a few dirty dishes in the sink, some cigarette butts in the ashtray in the living room, and a
rumpled bed.

Glass shattered in the basement. We ran downstairs, flicking on the light, and jumping the stairs
two at a time.

The single unfinished room with its concrete floor
and exposed insulation between the joists was a disaster. Glass was smashed on the floor and boxes of
corn starch were ripped open and strewn over the
walls and floor like a Rorschach test.

The oshk was using its single human arm to rip
apart a moonshine-type still with cattle prods attached to it. Shit, no. I was not being Tased like a
side of beef.

Rohan and I rushed the demon. Ro executed a
roundhouse kick, slicing its arm off, while I trapped
it in a web of current, kicking the cattle prod into the
corner out of its reach.

The oshk's arm slithered back up the demon, re-
attaching itself in place. Where was the Humpty-
Dumpty-couldn't-put-it-back-together-again model
of demon when you needed it?

It flowed its blobby body out of my magic net,
keening in rage. My repeated strikes blew it back,
but for every foot of ground it lost it jumped forward
two more, pushing us back toward the stairs.

I glanced over my shoulder, calculating the distance before it had us trapped in that narrow space.

Rohan upped his assault, a blur of slicing and dicing. The demon slithered its body to surround him.

A glint of a blade, the wet plop of flesh hitting the ground, I couldn't get a clean bead on the demon. Magic danced over my skin as I muttered "Come on," over and over again.

The oshk rippled with a low bassy gurgle and blew Rohan back against the wall.

I heard his back crunch against a fat joist, but my vision was filled with the demon looming over me. I danced back a couple of steps, hit the bottom step, and fell backwards.

The demon bobbed up the staircase without touching me, its features contorted in fury.

"Uh, hello?" I blasted it in the back and it jerked, blowing out a stream of clear liquid that flew over my head to splash the ceiling, mostly absorbed by the exposed insulation.

I lowered the hands I'd flung over my face, and patted myself down, but I hadn't been hit by its secretion. Had I been a couple feet deeper into the room, it would have been a different story. I hopped onto the first stair to follow and was tugged back into Ro's arms. I struggled. "Don't even think I'm staying–"

He nuzzled my neck. "Stop making me chase you."

"What?" I elbowed him, jerking free. "This isn't the time."

"Completely and utterly slain."

I whirled around. Ro gazed at me moonily. "Oh fuck. Rohan."

"Yeah, sweetheart?" He tried to pull me into his arms once more, but I danced out of reach.

His blades, his skin–he'd come into contact with the spawn. The demon had to be the basis of Sweet Tooth and Ro was under its influence. And Rohan had touched me. Was it transferable? I stepped farther away. "The oshk. You touched it."

"Only wanna touch *you*," he said. "Be with you. You're my light."

Something heavy upstairs hit the floor with a reverberating thud.

I cast an anxious glance at the ceiling. Mistake. In the spilt second of taking my eyes off Ro, he'd caught me again.

Sweet Tooth made people go fucking bonkers. I couldn't leave Ro alone if he might hurt himself.

"We need to be together, baby." His hold on me tightened. Ro's eye were tinged with the same mania I'd seen in Naomi's back at the club. I didn't feel any different though, so I didn't think second-hand oshk was a thing.

The demon was tearing upstairs apart and howling. Rohan wasn't fazed by it.

I struggled to free myself without zapping him, but I couldn't. The boyfriend who'd cradled me so tenderly last night was gone.

Glass shattered upstairs.

"Nava?" Rohan's smile was so sweet. I almost fell for it until I saw the off-kilter glint in his eyes.

Oh, Snowflake. I bit my lip. "Sorry, babe. Demon first, creeper stalker boyfriend second." I gave him a vicious electric shock. His face crumpled in bewildered hurt. I tore free and ran up the stairs, bolting the basement door from my side.

Shit. Shit. Shit. Goddamn addictive personalities. Of all the times to be proven right. There were levels of cold hard action I was fine with; disempowering Ro wasn't one of them. I couldn't get his betrayed look out of my head so I drew it in to myself, letting it fuel me.

The oshk waddled into the kitchen, its tiny head bowed in defeat and its body covered in streaks of red rust. The marks corresponded to where Ro had slashed it. Iron poisoning.

The demon jerked at the sight of me and tried to portal out, but it had been injured enough that it couldn't go anywhere. It ballooned up, expanding to take over most of the kitchen real estate, quivering more violently the larger it got.

I dove past it, hitting the living room floor in a sloppy roll, and flattening myself against the wall. Liquid splatted against the walls and floor in the kitchen like a hard rain storm but I was safe in the other room. Gag-inducing cotton candy stank overrode the natural mustiness of the house.

The basement door rattled, Rohan yelling for me.

I unleashed a volley of strikes at the oshk. The demon shrank back to its normal, admittedly still massive size, shooting more trippy liquid. It made a hell of a fire hose.

Bang! Bang! Bang! Rohan threw himself against the door. I prayed it held with Old Faithful geysering in there. If Ro got loose and came after me, I couldn't take both him and the demon on.

Didn't matter how much I peppered the demon with strikes, methodically covering every inch of it, I couldn't find the kill spot. That meant that, as with certain other demons, the kill spot was inside it somewhere. I'd have to open it up.

I regretted not having more weapons training. My magic generally served me well, but right about now, it would have been handy having some expertise with something sharp and iron to cut the fucker up. I'd gotten complacent relying on Ro, never thinking he'd be part of my problem. Though this had been an ambush, so I wouldn't have known to bring a long-range weapon with me.

Rubbing the sweat from my eyes with the inside of an elbow, I raised my arms above my head to dissipate the lactic acid burn in my side, my breaths coming in harsh pants. I was almost tapped out. I tried to shut out Ro's increasingly more furious screams and pounding. Tried to shut out how Jake had literally killed himself at this point of the drug trip attempting to get his object of desire.

Repeating "sorry," I called up all the magic I had left into a tight, hard knot.

It wasn't going to be enough. The basement door splintered. "Nava!" Ro roared. Adrenaline flooded my system. My skin turned blue, lightning bolts sliding over my skin. *This isn't my boyfriend. It's the drug.* "Stay away from her," Ro growled.

My blood ran cold. With Ro lost to this addictive drive to get to me, he was in no headspace to take on the demon. I jumped into the doorway humming and crackling with magic. "Yo!" I yelled, turning the oshk's attention away from Rohan.

I blew the demon to smithereens.

Ever seen those old Bugs Bunny cartoons where the character's eyes bugged out of their head, then snapped back into place? It was like that, but full-body. For one second, the oshk splintered into tiny pieces. It wasn't all nice smooth blob either. There were bits of undigested flesh, bone fragments and one fist-sized piece that was beating–its black lumpy heart. They hung there for one impossible moment, then snapped back together.

I stumbled back. At the same moment that I'd blown it up, Ro had slashed out at the demon to get it out of the way and when the demon reformed, Ro's arm was stuck in the middle of it, buried up to his shoulder, his blade just peeking out.

The oshk and I both froze. Rohan didn't even blink. He jerked his arm upward to free it, slicing through the oshk's heart from the inside.

The demon shriveled in on itself and disappeared, dead.

Ro bestowed this beautiful smile on me like he'd found a treasure. "I saved you."

Say what? "Rohan, listen to me. The oshk produces Sweet Tooth."

"That's nice." He grinned and crooked a finger at me. "Stop being coy and come here."

I tapped my knuckles together anxiously. Could I wait out the effects? He hadn't actually been hit with the secretion, just touched the demon's flesh. Though maybe it was a secretion coating that gave the oshk's skin its oily iridescence?

His expression shot from glorious sun to the most thunderous of storms when I failed to answer. "Nava."

Damn it.

Using a roundhouse punch for more force, I clocked Rohan in the jaw. His head snapped sideways and he went down for the count. I crouched down to check his pulse, then assuring myself he was going to be fine, pressed a kiss to his forehead.

I sat down on the floor next to him and waited it out. The house was silent save for the gurgle of the water intake for the furnace. Yay, I'd killed the oshk and stopped any more Sweet Tooth from hitting the streets. But at what cost? I checked Ro's breathing again, then pulled my knees into my chest, rested my head on top, and kept watch.

The soft dusty rose of dawn tinted the sky.

"Nava?"

I helped my groggy boyfriend sit up. He cracked his back getting up from the linoleum, but he wasn't mauling me so I guess the drug had run its course. That was good. The bruise on his face from my punch, less so.

What was the appropriate greeting in this situation?

He rubbed his jaw. "Your training is working."

"We gonna talk about this?"

"And say what?" His gaze was pure challenge.

That everything I've been scared of is true. That you're rushing us, investing yourself because you need a purpose, and I need us to take things one day at a time because this is all so new and I care about you so much and I don't want us to crash and burn like Cole and I did. That I don't want to end up crying in the middle of the street because you only loved the idea of me. "Are we still good?"

Rohan blinked. "Shouldn't I be asking you that? What I did..." He scrubbed a hand over his face. "I'm sorry. It wasn't me."

Except it kind of was. "I know." My voice was tighter than I'd intended it. I softened my tone as I added, "And I'm sorry for clocking you. I didn't feel like I had any other option."

"I appreciate that, but you sidelined me twice because you decided that the best way to protect me was to keep me out of the fray."

"What would you have had me do?"

"I don't know." His voice was as full of anger and resignation as mine had been. He exhaled, pushing to his feet. "Any useful evidence downstairs?"

Good talk.

"I haven't checked yet. I wanted to keep an eye on you."

"No time like the present." Rohan glanced at the shattered basement door, his expression unreadable, then headed downstairs.

I stepped over some tangled plastic tubing on the basement concrete floor lying next to an overturned chair. Ro pointed to two containers on a metal table. One was a thin, glass vial minus the Sweet Tooth label that held the familiar pink crystals. The other was a plastic container like the sterilized ones they gave you for urine samples. The seal had been broken and it held a clear liquid with pale streaks of blood floating in lazy twists.

Rohan picked it up and walked over near the spot on the ceiling that the oshk's secretion had hit when I'd attacked it. Cotton-candy scented clear liquid had dripped on the floor. "Do you see another sterilized container?"

I sorted through the wreckage until I found one that the oshk hadn't crushed. Rohan collected the liquid and sealed it up.

"Don't get any on you," I said. "With all your issues and the drug in its purest potency?" I mock-shuddered. "I know I'm irresistible, but you were precariously close to *Fatal Attraction* territory there. Boiling bunnies. Yikes."

Rohan raised his eyebrows.

"Too soon?"

That earned me a ghost of a smile. "I'm astounded you held off this long. Besides, my focused, passionate nature–"

"You mean your willingness to obsess?"

"I mean, my absolute commitment and perseverance has served me well. Landed me record contracts, tricky demon kills. You."

I raised my eyebrows.

"Too soon?"

I laughed and swatted him.

We found a trash bag to dump lab wreckage into, taking that and the three containers with us: the vial with the crystals, the blood-streaked liquid already sealed up, and the new clear secretion we'd collected. We dropped the containers off at a twenty-four hour courier service, expedited to a Rasha-owned lab in New York where they could analyze the substances and see if, as suspected, we had a match between the oshk secretion and Sweet Tooth.

My stomach rumbled, so I pulled into a diner that was almost full with a brisk breakfast rush, snagging the last tiny booth in the back. My anger had faded, leaving only hunger and exhaustion. The blueberry pancakes I ordered were light and fluffy with fat fresh strawberries slices on top and a heaping dollop of whipped cream. The bacon was extra crispy.

Rohan's veggie omelet, no cheese, looked very healthy.

"Healthy isn't leprosy. It's actually the opposite," he said.

"Who said a word?" I drizzled melted butter on my pancakes.

"You did." He nudged my leg. His expression of fond exasperation was so familiar and welcome that the vise around my chest loosened.

I held a forkful of strawberry-adorned pancake at him. "Live a little."

He leaned in for the bite, sucking whipped cream off my fingers. "I'm not denying the appetites that matter."

Two could play this game. I slipped off my shoe and snuggled my toes onto his dick. Keeping my eyes on my food, I fought a grin, massaging until he got hard. So, like ten seconds.

Under the table, he grabbed my foot. "Enough," he growled.

I motioned our waiter for more coffee. "Think Candyman screwed the oshk over in some drug partnership? That demon was pissed."

Rohan added some hot sauce to the last third of his omelet. "All I care about is that Leo said the oshk was a Unique and we've eliminated the source of the Sweet Tooth."

The analysis would conclusively confirm it, but the chances were high that the drug was off the street forever. Candyman still needed to be apprehended, but we'd put him out of business. I clinked my mug to Rohan's. "We make a good team."

"The best."

If we both injected a bit too much enthusiasm into our words, maybe that was okay.

With hours until we'd hear back about the Sweet Tooth analysis, we decided to crash so we could hit the ground running finding Candyman. Drio wouldn't be back until tomorrow and depending on what he'd learned from Golda, we'd need a strategy around that as well.

We made one quick pit stop at the cemetery in Vancouver—not the Jewish one, where cremation was forbidden—to meet the Rasha-friendly employee there and burn the trash bag of busted-up lab equipment, and then it was bedward-ho.

I slept okay for a while but a text from Sienna on my burner phone on behalf of Dr. Gelman woke me up.

Esther has a promising lead on the bindings. She'll be out of isolation today if you want to come by. Before I had time to yawn, let alone compose a reply, another message sailed on in: *For whatever unknown reason, your last visit cheered her up.*

I added Sienna to the list of people who were never going to be a fan.

I snuggled back under the covers against my furnace boyfriend, but, hard as I tried, I couldn't fall back asleep again. My promise to Ari to go see my mom weighed on me. I'd let my resentment toward my parents, especially Mom, fester for years and could have easily gone another decade, but I kept seeing Gelman wasted by cancer.

I heaved myself out of bed with a huff and snatched up some clothes.

"Where you going?" Rohan mumbled from under the pillow he'd stuffed on his head when my phone had gone off.

I popped my head out of my sundress. "To see my mom."

He pulled the pillow off and cracked one eye open. "You want me to come with?"

I rumpled his hair. "Best if I don't have witnesses, but thanks."

He flopped over. "When you get back, we can Skype my parents."

I whacked him in the head with his pillow "Not funny."

"You'll have to meet Mom at some point," he called out.

I kept marching down the hallway. "Let's see how things go with the blood-related mother first." I crossed my fingers, not entirely sure which way I wanted things to go, and went to keep my damn promise.

12

Mom was teaching, so I drove over to UBC to catch the end of her class. I slipped into the back of the lecture hall. It was summer semester and this was a third-year history class, so there were few enough students that she noticed my entrance.

She was wearing the green shirt. This weird glowy feeling warmed my chest. Idiot. It was a shirt. It was clean. She didn't know I'd be here today and it had nothing to do with me. Especially since Mom didn't even pause speaking when I came in, her eyes glancing off me from her position at her lectern to the student in the front row who'd raised her hand.

"Can you elaborate on what you meant by 'David was not the underdog of legend?'" the student asked.

"Underdog implies that the odds are stacked against the person because they haven't the skill or experience." Mom had devoted her academic career to becoming the foremost expert on King David. She'd told Ari and me that originally she'd planned to focus on the Roman rule of Judea back in the fifties B.C.E., but after Ari's destiny was revealed, she'd switched her attention to the man who'd founded the Brotherhood.

Even her professional choices were centered around Ari.

I pried my fingers off of my purse and smoothed out my expression. Mom was watching me.

"David was unwilling to follow the rules of honorable conduct that Goliath expected," she said. "He brought a projectile to the fight instead of engaging in hand-to-hand combat. Even King Saul expected the single combat method, as evidenced by him attempting to dress David in his own armor."

"David played dirty," the student said.

"David played to win." Mom adjusted the glasses she wore to clearly see students at the back of the room. I forced myself to remain relaxed. "Hitting Goliath with that slingshot wasn't luck. David was a precise slinger. It was how he'd fought off wild animals as a shepherd. Armor was also heavy, so David kept speed and agility on his side by refusing to wear any. Then there's the fact that Goliath requested that David come to him. Why? Goliath was a seasoned warrior. A giant of a man. He wouldn't have been scared of David. It's now believed that he suffered from acromegaly." She wrote the word on the board behind her.

"Like André the Giant," another student said.

"Yes," Mom said. "Acromegaly causes an overproduction of the growth hormone. That comes with a host of medical problems including vision difficulties." Mom stepped out from behind the lectern. "Why wasn't he an underdog?" She ticked the reason off on her fingers. "David was not lacking experience, nor did he only have a slim chance. Instead, he assessed the facts in a way that no one else had. Everyone else had read the situation differently, dependent on their understanding of how things had always been resolved. David had his own unique lens on events. He did what had to be done to win. It's to be admired, not sold short as merely luck."

Once more her eyes met mine. I didn't understand the takeaway. Mom didn't know what I was up to with the Brotherhood. It's not something Ari would have shared and I certainly didn't tell her.

The bell rang and students gathered up their books. Mom reminded them about their papers due next class.

I made my way down the stairs to her, wondering what I was missing. "Mom."

She stilled, a folder of lecture notes and a couple of fat hardcover books pressed to her chest. "Yes?"

"I'm sorry."

"It's fine."

"No, it's–"

"I said it was fine." She brushed past me.

I stood there, warring with myself. New students filed in and the professor gave me an odd look, so

I took my indecision out into the hallway, standing next to the vending machine.

Mom's departure was my cue to get back in my car. To quote the immortal Snagglepuss, "Exit, stage left ev-en." It's not like we had to interact all that much since I'd moved out, and when we did, we'd both be civil. We'd perfected that.

I stormed her office before I could second guess myself. She sat at her desk, staring out the window. She'd added a red and blue throw rug since the last time I'd been here and the small sofa in the corner was a bit shabbier, but otherwise it was as I remembered it. It still smelled of sun-warmed books and her Chanel perfume. Framed photos of Ari and myself at different ages, always grinning at the camera with our arms draped over each other, lined the window sill. They were even stacked in front of history books, along with photos of her and Dad on various trips.

"I meant it, okay? I was tired and sad and just done with that party and I know that's not a good excuse, but please understand that I mean this." I closed her office door. "I shouldn't have called you a bitch."

Mom swiveled in the chair to face me, cleaning her glasses with more vigor than required. "No. You shouldn't have." She didn't offer anything in return.

Students' conversation out in the hall about their tuition payments drifted in through the closed door. Since I'd rather have a kappa demon suck my guts out through my ass than have Mom start in about my UBC status again, I gestured at the door. "I'll leave you to it."

One of the photos on the bookshelf caught my eye. I picked it up. The camera had caught me pulling an over-the-top, my head tilted and lips curled in a sassy smirk, wearing a tux costume.

"Your last competition," Mom said. My Achilles had snapped soon after and it was off the stage and into the emergency room and physical therapy.

I rubbed the back of my neck. "Another life."

"You blew everyone else out of the water." She didn't sound proud, exactly, but she didn't sound indifferent either.

I replaced the photo on the shelf with a dull thud. "Why did you tell that story about David not being an underdog?"

She leaned over her desk to close her blinds on the afternoon sun slanting into the room. Out in the hall, the classroom door shut, leaving the two of us in the hush of this darkened office. "Why do you think?"

I hated it when she answered my question with a question. I hated it even more that I wished I had the answer, especially since there was an expectation in her measured stare. A stare that was going to flash with disappointment in a moment, the way it always did.

I flicked on the overhead lights, making her blink. "No clue. Why did you?"

"Mallory asked."

"Right." I didn't have the guts to ask why she'd worn that shirt, but there was a question I could throw her way and actually get a useful answer on. "Did you ever hear anything about King David and witches?"

Mom raised her eyebrows, an intrigued glint in her eyes. "There are witches?"

"Big time."

Mom was already opening her laptop. "Is that how David originally got the magic for the Rasha?"

"Yup." She didn't respond, her gaze vacant and her attention to me lost. I bid her a soft "bye" and left.

I got back to Demon Club in time to hear the results of the analysis of the Sweet Tooth that Rohan and I had sent to the lab. It was such a beautiful day, we took the call out back by the pool. The albezia tree's leafy fronds cast dappled shadows around the edges of the flagstone deck, though its Dr. Seuss-like purple puffy flowers wouldn't bloom for another couple of months.

Rabbi Abrams had joined us, pulling up a teak chair next to the water. His eyes were closed and his face was tilted up to the sun and I wasn't positive he was awake.

I'd kicked my sandals off and was dangling my legs in the cool water, watching the refracted sunlight dance along the concrete at the bottom. Ro dipped a foot in, then joined me, the cell on the warm ground between us.

The Rasha on the other end of the speaker phone confirmed that Sweet Tooth and the two other substances were the same. I high-fived Rohan, and the Rasha told us to hang on, he was transferring our call to HQ.

"You think Ms. Clara or Baruch want to talk to us from Jerusalem?" I scooped up some water, drizzling it down the back of my neck.

"How would the New York tech guy know?" Rohan wet his hands, flinging drops onto my chest. "Cooling you off."

"What a mensch," I said.

He nodded and leaned in. "That plus your dress is really thin."

I glanced down at my nipples now showing through the wet spots, made sure my back was to Rabbi Abrams, and splashed my boyfriend.

"You got the source of the drug?" Rabbi Mandelbaum barked at us over the line in his Russian accent.

"You mean did we kill the demon responsible for producing it?" I said. "Why yes, we did. And thank you, Nava and Rohan, for valuable insights when our database had such meager intel on it."

"If it was a Unique as you claim and it's dead, then the information is perhaps not so valuable anymore." If he sneered any harder, he'd strain something. "When will you apprehend the other demon involved. This Candyman?"

"We're working on it." Rohan poked the corner of my frown and I bit his finger. But I stopped scowling at the phone.

"Not you, Rohan," Mandelbutt said. "I want you back in Los Angeles. I have another mission for you."

"The investigation isn't finished yet," Ro said.

"Nava is the only Rasha listed on the assignment," Mandelbaum said.

Ice filled my veins. The bastard couldn't take Ro away from me. "We're working together on this."

The rabbi spat something in Hebrew.

Rabbi Abrams opened his eyes, sighing. "Boris."

I snorted. "Must catch Moose and Squirrel," I said in a Russian accent.

All the men went silent. Rohan pressed his lips together, his shoulders shaking.

"What?" Mandelbaum said.

"Nothing." I smiled sweetly, even though he couldn't see it.

Rabbi Mandelbaum jabbered on in angry Hebrew.

"Maspik!" I'd never heard Rabbi Abrams snap.

Mandelbaum sputtered to a stop.

"With Kane and Ari away, we can use Rohan. You have enough Rasha in Los Angeles." Abrams patted my shoulder.

"Grown fond of her, have you, Isaac?"

"I thought we were speaking of Rohan. I've grown fond of him, too." His voice was placid, but his smile chilled me.

"It's settled then," Rohan said. "I'm staying."

"You mean you won't leave your girlfriend." Mandelbaum made a smug noise at our collective silence. "It's understandable. She's Rasha. She's there. Fighting together forges a bond."

I couldn't look at Rohan as Mandelbaum so eloquently voiced every single fear I fought to keep at bay.

"Don't. Push. Me." Rohan snarled. "And stay the hell out of my personal life." His voice turned to silk. Silk hiding an iron bar. "You know better."

Was he thinking of Asha? I curled into his side, rubbing his back. He was rigid, but slowly relaxed under my touch. He caught my hand and laced our fingers together.

"This investigation continues," I said. "You can list both of us on it, but I'm still lead."

Ro laughed and Mandelbaum hung up.

"Douchebags gonna douche." My hand flew up to cover my mouth. "I'm so sorry, Rabbi Abrams."

"I think you said it perfectly." He rose from the bench, slowly, but every inch a fighter. "Keep on

Candyman, and step up your activity on everything else."

Rohan waited for Rabbi Abrams to leave, then he kissed me. "We're in this together. Nothing can change that."

So why did it feel like I was waiting for the other shoe to drop? Fucking Mandelbaum and his insinuations. I wanted to nail his hide to the proverbial door. I hopped out of the pool and grabbed the basketball sitting on the edge of the court. "Did you Skype your parents?"

I fired off a quick lay-up. The ball hit the backboard and bounced off. Rohan stole it. "Yeah. Mom was running out to a session so it was a quick chat, but Dad gave me a detailed run-down of the golf tournament details." He shot, but didn't fare any better.

We both ran for the ball, leaving a trail of wet footprints on the court.

"I like your dad," I said. Rohan collided into me and I rubbed my hip. "You, not so much, pushy."

Ro tossed me the ball. "I like my dad, too. I think he's been travelling too much for work, though." He bounced on his bare toes, arms out, blocking me from getting near the basket. "How'd it go with your mom?"

I bounced the ball, looking for my opening. "I want to run an idea past you, but you have to keep an open mind."

"Score and you got it."

There was some universe in which I feinted right and put Ro in the dust, shooting a perfect basket from center court, but in this one, I pivoted and ran to the other basket that we weren't using and flung the ball.

It teetered for a precarious second on the rim then dropped through the basket, bouncing along the court until I scooped it up.

I fist pumped. "Nailed it."

"Cheated it."

Something flashed through my head. I sauntered back to Ro. "Won on my terms."

I thunked the ball into his chest.

He patted his pecs. "Strong like bull," he said in a Russian accent. "You realize that Mandelbaum will now forever be Boris Badenov for me."

"You're welcome. Will you listen to my idea?"

"For the record?" He bounced the ball, dodging my every block. "I hate it already, but go ahead."

"In terms of everything we've been investigating about who is binding demons and the connection to Askuchar, we've been going about it in expected ways. You're investigating the Brotherhood and I've roped Gelman into helping with the witches."

"How else do you want to do it?"

"Demons."

"You tried the zizu. They didn't know either."

I steeled myself and went for it. "Malik might."

Rohan fumbled his bounce, dropping the ball which rolled away. "You can't be serious."

"Gelman's promising leads could take weeks to pan out. If ever. We don't have that kind of time. If there's a demon who's capable of narrowing down our search? It's worth pursuing."

"No." Rohan cleared the court in fast, angry strides.

I jogged after him. "Why not? Like you said, I already dealt with the zizu."

"No past history there. You're not going to see the marid demon who's thousands of years old, who you almost killed, who almost certainly wants to kill you back. Who probably will."

"I learned a new word today. Autocratic. Look it up."

He stopped at the bottom of the back stairs, his expression grim. "I lost Asha because I was an asshole. But if I have to be an asshole to save you, I'll do it."

"Then you'll lose me anyway."

Rohan raked a hand through his hair. "'He wants me dead.' That's a direct quote from your debrief."

"I remember. But Malik is also very interested in his own self-preservation and the goings-on in his world. He'll have a vested interest in finding out who's behind this."

"It's a suicide mission."

"Every time we step out the door as Rasha, it's a suicide mission. Take emotion out of this."

Don't make me your new cause. It would be an easy mantle to assume for a man with an overdeveloped sense of responsibility towards those he wanted to protect, but our relationship had to stand apart from all that.

"Fuck." He shook his head, the fight draining out of him. "You're a glutton for punishment."

"Not really. I like being alive." I shrugged. "I do seem to see things differently from the other Rasha."

"Do we get to be in this together?"

"I think that between what I have to tell him and his fascination with Ari, I'll be safe. I can't say the same for you and I won't risk having you there."

"New word for you. Hypocrite."

"I can live with that." I slid my arms around his waist. "Can you?"

His lips flattened into a stern line before he shook his head with a weary sigh. "Promise me you'll be careful." His hold on me tightened. "People who keep their promises get very good rewards."

"Cuntessa is very happy to hear that."

"Cuntessa?"

I screwed my expression into adorable confusion and pulled away. "What?"

"Cuntessa? Nava," he purred. "Spill."

"Tell me the Passover story."

His counteroffer was to tickle my hips.

"It's my clit," I gasped, batting his hands away. "Cuntessa de Spluge."

"You named your clit Cuntessa?"

"Like you're one to talk, dude who is cheating on me with his car."

"Aw, Sparky, you're a close second in my affections."

I shoved him away. "I'm leaving and you suck."

He snickered, then swung me in to his chest. "Promise me."

I kissed him. "I promise."

Man, was it gonna bite if he was right and I ended up dead.

13

"I love home delivery." Malik lounged in his doorway, eyeing me the way the wolf must have with the three little pigs. His British accent was pure sin.

"I love your arrogance that you didn't bother moving after I almost killed you."

He laughed, flashing straight white teeth against his bronze skin. He was still the only being I'd ever met who could pull off a Caesar cut, and was still the stuff of billionaire romance cover fantasies in his soft gray trousers that were artfully tailored to the hard lines of his body and navy shirt, carelessly folded back at the cuffs. "Oh, petal. I'd say I missed you, but I didn't. Now, unless you brought the more interesting twin?" He peered into the hallway. "No?"

He shut the door, but I stuffed my foot in to block it. Not like he politely stopped trying to close it. "Ow." I pushed my shoulder into the door to keep my poor bones from breaking. "If you weren't wondering why I was here, you wouldn't have let security buzz me up or let my toes cross the wards I'm sure you've got strung across this door."

"Ten seconds."

"That's not—"

"Five, four..."

"Demons are being bound." I rushed my words as he made a buzzing noise.

Malik yanked me inside by my collar and slammed the door.

I wrenched free.

His penthouse apartment hadn't changed. Still to-die-for sweeping views of the city, a massive glass wine storage unit in the open concept space, and a loft bedroom. He pointed at one of the leather sofas, custom made to hug the curved walls. "Sit and talk."

I told him about the gogota and the purple magic. I left out the spine modification, the yak-sas, and Askuchar. I'd meant what I told Ro about enjoying my continued existence, and bringing up any Brotherhood involvement severely reduced my chances of walking out of here.

Malik listened in silence. A look of crystalized rage flashed over his face, but he sounded positively insolent when he said, "Why ever would you care about all this?"

It was a good question, but I had a good answer. "Leonie."

Malik knew my bestie was half-goblin and I hoped that fact would make him amenable to helping me, because saying that I wanted to make sure humanity was safe from people binding demons and using their magic to further nefarious human agendas would just get me tossed out.

He weighed my answer, rubbing a finger over his chin. "What do you want from me?"

"A name." I followed him to the kitchen.

He removed two stemless wineglasses from a glass-fronted cupboard, yanked the cork out of the half-drunk bottle of red on his counter, and poured us both a liberal dose. He shoved the drink at me. "I have no love for my fellow demons. If they're stupid enough to get caught, they deserve what's coming to them."

"I got the better of you once and I'm not as powerful as a witch." I took a sip of the wine and yes, it was as smooth and expensive as the fancy cream label promised.

"Your concern is touching. Misplaced, but touching."

I savored one last sip. "Don't say I didn't warn you. Thanks for the wine. Have a nice life."

I crossed the room. Every hair on the back of my neck stood up, and my shoulder blades prickled, tensing for an attack.

"Halt."

Malik prowled toward me, circling me. He had that gleam in his eyes, the one that spoke of an ancient intelligence, an inhumanity barely buffered by a thin veneer of civility, and a power too complex for me to comprehend.

I forced myself to affect a semblance of nonchalance and a tight control of my bladder.

"How did you do it?" he said.

I flinched away from the whisper of his breath over my skin, even though he smelled yummy, like zingy citrus and spearmint. "Do what? Snuff you out like a candle? That's for me to know and you to find out."

He stepped away from me. "But that's my price, petal. That and a small job."

"What's the job?"

Malik studied me a moment longer, then laughed, returning to his wine. "You have no idea, do you? Could you hurt me a second time?"

My heart hammered in my ears. My skin turned blue, electricity pouring off me. "Test me and let's find out."

"As you wish."

I gasped, all the air forced from my lungs. My limbs twitched, muscles seizing as my magic slammed back inside me. I jerked up off the ground, my head snapping back, and my mouth howling a silent scream while my lungs burned and black spots danced at the end of my vision.

"I'd say the answer is 'no.'" He let me flail a bit more before flicking his fingers sending me crumpled to the ground. "An answer and a job and I let you live."

I had to get my lungs working and my heart beating again before I could form words. Meantime, I remained sprawled facedown, the floor muffling my words. "I don't know how I did it."

"We'll work on it." Malik hooked a hand under my elbow and yanked me to my feet. He had to physically escort me to his couch, because when he let go of me, my legs trembled and gave way.

"Then you'll know my secret and I won't know any of yours." I twitched with the aftershocks of his assault.

"I doubt you only have the one." He went into the kitchen, returning a moment later with a glass of water. "Salt. You need your electrolytes."

His knowledge about Rasha never failed to impress and horrify me.

By holding the glass in both hands, I managed to keep my tremors at bay and drink most of the liquid without sloshing it on myself. I tried not to taste it as I knocked it back because salt water was the worst. "The job?"

"There's a painting of mine. It was lost to me centuries ago and I want it back." Weirdly, Malik was actually a talented artist, beloved by all in the artists' collective that he painted out of. I'd seen a few of his works. One of them, an abstract of a woman called "Lila: on waking" had stuck with me for the vibrancy, life, and passion captured in the half-suggested lines.

"What's its evil purpose?" I said. "Suck people's life force? Turn the viewer to stone?"

Malik crossed his arms. "It's a very fine painting and I think it would go perfectly on that wall."

"Why can't you port in and get it?"

"Think about it for a moment and get back to me."

I almost laughed because that sounded like something I'd say, but I didn't want to set off the psychopath who was barely tolerating me. "It's behind a Rasha ward."

He slow-clapped me.

"Whatever. Give me the address."

He scribbled it down, plus a few other things, but didn't give me the list right away. "The canvas is stretched over a frame. Do not touch that one. Simply remove it from whatever other larger frame it was placed in. Bring pliers and a screwdriver to remove the canvas from the new frame. Wrap it in buffered, acid-free glassine paper, wrap it a second time with bubble wrap and put it into a cardboard box that's at least three inches larger on all sides than the wrapped canvas. I've noted the dimensions down for you."

"Why can't I just transport it as is?"

"Because I said so. I don't want it damaged."

He handed the paper over and I leveled him with an unimpressed look. "This is in Orlando."

"Very good. You're functionally literate. That bodes well for a bright future."

"How am I supposed to get there?"

"Ask your boyfriend. He's got cash."

"Get a hobby that isn't me, you stalker."

He picked up his wine again, running a finger around the rim. "Oh, petal. You flatter yourself if you think you're the twin I'm most interested in."

I bared my teeth at him, stomped to the door, and wrenched it open.

"Tick tock, Nava." That reminded me about the prophecy, but I wasn't about to share that tidbit with him. "You have forty-eight hours."

"I can't pull this off in that time frame. I need a week."

"Seventy-two hours." He shooed me toward the door.

"Get stuffed." We both knew I'd do it.

I laced up my new beautiful tap shoes. "Why aren't you predictably furious?"

Rohan, once more in my "Tap Dancers Need Wood" shirt, plucked a string on his guitar, plucked it again, then tightened it. "I live to fuck with you."

"No, you live to fuck me." I crossed into the center of the floor, my taps ringing out.

"Don't pigeonhole me." He strummed a few chords.

"Okay, but seriously. What gives?"

"I looked up autocratic and was shamed into humble submission?"

"Next."

He scooted forward on the sofa, the guitar in his lap. "You were right. It was worth pursuing and there was nothing you could have done differently. You're alive and we'll go get the painting together."

"Next time can we skip all the blustering and jump right to this part?"

"How about next time we both agree to try and do better? Together."

I nodded. "I'd like that." Fighting demons as we did, we'd find ourselves in critical situations where talking things out wasn't going to be an option, but when it wasn't life-or-death, then yeah, we had to face it as equals.

"Good," he said. "Now, you dictating the playlist or can I surprise you?"

I batted my eyelashes at him. "You're full of surprises tonight, baby. No reason to stop now."

We made it through "Bohemian Rhapsody," and most of "Blank Space" when Drio showed up. He took in Ro's shirt and his gleeful rendition of Taylor Swift and glared at me. "You've wrecked him."

I ended the song on a heel scuff. "Or I've thirty-seven percent improved him."

Ro ran a hand down his body. "You can't improve perfection. Got the goods on Ferdinand?"

Drio had learned Ferdinand was killed outside Palm Springs. According to Golda, that's where he'd been living. "Hell of a commute into L.A. every day."

"The L.A. affiliation is bullshit." Rohan stuffed Ferdinand's address that Drio had gotten in his pocket. "How's Golda?"

Drio brightened. "Still hasn't forgiven you."

"She will."

"You'd have to face her first, chickenshit." He knocked the wall twice. "I'm going off-duty. Don't call. Don't text."

I made a "squee" face and ran into the hallway after him. "Are you going to see Leo?"

"No."

"Total lie. You're all prettied up and you put on cologne. You like her. Do you like her?"

"She's great."

I jumped into the stairwell, blocking him. "I know she's great, but that wasn't my question."

Pain flashed across his face so fast, I wasn't sure I'd seen it. "Leave it, Nava."

I blinked because he so rarely used my name. "Leaving it."

"I'm glad you and Ro are happy." He rubbed his hand briskly over his hair. "Don't fuck it up."

"Why do you assume I'd be the one?" That earned me a level stare. "Forget it. Thank you for going to Palm Springs. We're going to get these assholes."

"Do you remember what I told you about the thrill of the fight? How we could get hooked and nothing else compared to this big noble cause?" He rolled onto the outside edge of one foot, his eyes growing distant. "Other shit matters. Don't forget that."

I opened my mouth to press him further because you didn't just drop something that heavy without context, when he caught me in a stare so ferocious, I took a step back, my hands up. "I'm not asking."

He stalked off.

I fired Leo a quick text of apology for possibly making her booty call ragey and quickly turned off my phone.

It took us another day to make a plan and arrange everything. Rohan and I headed to the airport on Thursday morning to fly to Orlando and retrieve the painting. The Shelby roared along Southwest Marine Drive, the windows down, and the wind streaming in our hair. Despite being blackmailed into working for Malik, I was in an irrepressibly good mood, singing along with "Can't Stop The Feeling." Rohan joined in for all the falsetto parts.

My Brotherhood phone rang with the "Imperial Death March" theme, assigned to all secret society numbers.

"Hello?"

"Ms. Katz."

I slapped the stereo button off. "Hello, Rabbi Mandelbaum."

Rohan cut me a wary look and I shrugged.

"What have you done since our last conversation in regards to stopping Candyman?" the rabbi asked.

"Our last conversation that was only two days ago?"

"Yes. I assume you are investigating right now and that you aren't merely going out for brunch with your boyfriend?"

I frantically motioned for Rohan to veer past the Arthur Lang Bridge leading to the airport because Mandelbaum was tracking us. This was a bullshit phone call designed to let me know he could get to me. "We're following up on some of the lab equipment we found at the house. Whether it was purchased or stolen. There might be something that leads us back to the demon."

There was nothing. We'd sent Drio down this road yesterday while we planned our Orlando mission. All the pieces were too widely available; even cattle prods could be purchased on Amazon.

"Don't waste Rohan's time. He's too valuable a Rasha." Mandelbaum hung up.

I shoved my Brotherhood phone in the glove compartment.

Rohan found a security-patrolled lot and paid for parking, while I called for a taxi on my burner to take us to the airport. Ro borrowed the phone to call Drio to let him know where both the car and the spare key were, so he could drive the Shelby around and it didn't sit in one place for hours. Brotherhood-issued phones automatically sent out locations after twenty-four hours of inactivity, in case a Rasha needed to be rescued.

Rohan would rather get a root canal than let anyone drive his car, so whatever had bonded these two had bonded them but good.

The cabbie had turned off the main road to one of the hangers near the south terminal before I spoke. "I hate Boris Badenov."

"I know, sweetheart," Ro said. "But you have to let him keep underestimating you."

I pulled my seatbelt away from my chest like I needed room to breathe. "It's not a matter of 'let.' There's nothing I can do that would make him see my worth."

Except taking him down. He'd see it then.

The cabbie pulled up to a private terminal not far from the Flying Beaver, which was this cool pub on the water with views of the floatplanes. We grabbed our one small carry-on and the cardboard box with the packing supplies.

Rohan paid him and we walked directly on to the ramp where the private jet Ro had chartered awaited us.

"I am so turned on right now," I said.

Carlos, our steward for the journey, greeted us. He checked the tickets on Ro's phone, ensured we had our passports for customs when we landed in the U.S. and gave us the tour of the jet. There was a lounge with a large screen TV and DVD system and a telecommunications center. He got us settled in, saying that drinks and a choice of hot meals would be available after take-off.

Ro made himself comfortable on the couch while I paced the plane. "Did you find Mandelbaum's timing suspicious?" I said. "Why would he phone when we were headed for the airport?"

"He couldn't know. Only the three of us did."

"Yeah." I did another lap.

"Nava. Drio didn't tell him."

I stopped. "I honestly don't think he did, but we had our phones. Could they be listening in to our conversations even if we're not on the phone?" I wasn't worried about that on this flight since we'd left them in Ro's car which Drio was going to take back to the house.

I was however, extremely worried about what Orwell might have overheard up to this point.

"You're being paranoid," he said.

"Justifiably paranoid."

Carlos entered the cabin to tell us to get ready for take-off and we strapped in.

Keyed up though I was, when the engines rumbled to life and the jet sped down the run-away, my stomach still flipped in exhilaration. It was a fairly smooth ascent and soon we were cruising comfortably at altitude and able to move around.

I signed on to the secret email that Kane had set up for me, swearing it was safe from prying eyes, and called Rohan over to review the blueprints and dossier we'd compiled on the owner of the painting.

Rabbi Paskow had served the New York chapter for forty years before retiring to the sunny climes of Orlando, where he lived with his wife in a gated community on a golf course. His son and three grandchildren still lived in Queens, and the rabbi and his wife were currently on their yearly visit up north.

We wouldn't encounter them, but we still had to get into the alarmed and monitored house in full view of all neighbors and community security. The easiest solution would have been for Kane to stage an alarm issue that we could have responded to, but he was busy with his mission, so no hacking job for us.

We didn't have time to match the uniforms of the groundskeepers but we did have two things: Ms. Clara, who had access to the rabbi's cell number, and a Florida-based minion who owed Malik a favor. Neither Rohan nor I were happy about the latter part of the plan, but desperate times.

Before we'd even landed in Houston for the first leg of our flight, Lackey Demon had burst a pipe feeding into the rabbi's home. The water line fed in to the laundry room so hopefully the damage would be minimal. Drio had called it in at an appointed time, then after the agreed-upon waiting period I'd phoned Rabbi Paskow, who'd already been notified by the community's management company. I said I was from the restoration company and I needed authorization to enter his premises to assess the damage.

He'd promised to call the clubhouse immediately to let main gate security know to expect us. Our entire plan was dependent upon the snail's pace of all bureaucracy. When my family had had a flood, the restoration company hadn't been called until the next day. I was counting on a similar procedure here—that they'd be so focused on containing the leak and fixing the pipe that they wouldn't have called the restoration company themselves.

The plan was held together with metaphoric Scotch Tape and a prayer, and there were more places it could derail than not, but Malik had given me an impossible timeframe and I needed to find whoever was behind the purple magic.

The walk to the rental car from the airport terminal in Orlando was short but with the humidity here, it was like walking through a swamp in scuba gear. I was sticky by the time we reached the Corolla. Once we cleared the rental lot, we pried off the stickers on the rearview mirror and windows that the company used to track the cars in and out of the lot. Driving up in an obvious rental would have given us away.

We didn't see much from the highway beyond some strip malls, lots of entrances to gated communities, and even more palm trees, though it was a lot greener than I'd expected.

When the security guard at the gate took the identification into the booth, I tensed. We'd doctored them up yesterday with Photoshop and a laminate machine. All she did was check it against something on her computer, hand them back, and give us directions to the rabbi's house before lifting the gate.

Billboards on an undeveloped area of the grounds advertised homes starting at $300,000, which wouldn't buy you a shoebox condo in Vancouver proper, but got you a pretty swank place here. Like Rabbi Paskow's: a yellow villa-style home set back a couple of blocks from the golf course that was a decent size for two people but not enormous. A spectacular pink bougainvillea dominated the front yard.

Workers milled about outside. Rohan and I approached the one woman in business casual who was supervising, correctly guessing she was from the management company. We introduced ourselves, presenting business cards with fake names from the area's largest restoration company. She was a bit flustered that the rabbi had called someone in before she'd had a chance, but we brazened it out and someone else soon claimed her attention.

Other than the fact that she could later describe a brown-skinned man and white-skinned woman, any other details would be wrong. Rohan and I had both put in brown contacts after we'd disembarked. He'd styled his hair into the most boring cubicle drone look to go with his khakis and plaid shirt and I wore a wig of short, straight, light brown hair.

We didn't bother taking down the Rasha ward around the house. Theft and tampering was bad enough, we didn't want the rabbi left open to an actual demon attack.

My blouse was sticking to me by the time we snapped on latex gloves, grabbed all necessary supplies and got inside into the air conditioning. Framed prints of grapes and Province pastoral scenes hung on pale yellow walls, with sandstone tile and floral print-furniture rounding out the decor. Fresh flowers sat in brightly colored hand-blown glass vases on fussy side tables, making the place smell like a hothouse.

The damage in the laundry room was minimal. One small corner had flooded, so we cleaned it up and lugged the industrial fan we'd rented inside to dry it out. The sanitation engineers hadn't had to open the concrete floor inside, which was good because we were alone in the house.

We didn't have to snoop for long. There was only one original painting in the place, which hung in the rabbi's cluttered study on a shadowed wall away from any damaging sunlight. I turned on the small spotlight to see it better. A small plaque mounted next to the painting read "The Birth of Our Prince."

Upon first glance, it was the unlikely subject matter of the birth of Jesus. A raven-haired woman, her coarse features twisted, gave birth in a manger, the night sky twinkling with stars beyond the open manger door. Except she had black wings with edges like razors, so unless Mary had had a few additions that no one else had seen fit to document, this wasn't her.

A man wearing a crown kneeled beside her, his face etched with grief. The baby he held in his blood-soaked hands, still connected to the woman by a thick, purple umbilical cord glistening with fluid, was a monstrosity. It had three heads: an ogre, a ram, and a bull.

"Rohan!"

He came running at my screech, bringing the cardboard box and a small pouch with the pliers and screwdriver. "What?" All I could do was point at the painting. "Asmodeus?" Rohan dropped the stuff onto the rabbi's desk, but didn't tear his eyes off the artwork. "Does Malik know you killed Asmodeus? Is this some kind of message?"

"It didn't come up in conversation but Malik makes it his business to know things and Ari is a topic near and dear to him these days. It's possible he knows what happened."

Malik hadn't lied about painting this because his signature was legible in the corner. But of all the paintings in all the world, why have me get this one?

"Who are Asmodeus' parents?" I said. "Who would come after me for killing their son?"

Rohan didn't know either, but there was someone who might. It was worth the long distance charges on my burner. "Rabbi Abrams?" he said. "Nava and I need your help." He described the painting to the rabbi, providing specific details at the rabbi's prompting. Rohan's expression grew grimmer and grimmer. "Yes, Rabbi. Thank you."

"Holy Hell." He rubbed his fist against his temple and I tugged on his sleeve. "Malik intended for us to know this. It's going to open a Pandora's box."

"Why?" I was vibrating.

"The raven-haired woman is the demon Mahlat. See this?" He pointed to a genie's lamp tossed on a bale of hay to one side. "According to certain Kabbalistic legends, Mahlat was put into a vessel like this and locked in these cliffs on the Dead Sea by King Solomon."

"So that's Solomon?"

Rohan shook his head and touched what looked like a tiny baby's hat with very long strings, woven from rope.

"I don't understand."

Rohan traced his finger along the protective glass to point out a rock that had rolled slightly away from a larger pile. "It's a slingshot."

"*That's King David*?!" I twisted my gold ring, with its engraved hamsa that marked me as Rasha, as if it could ward off this information. "No. He can't be Asmodeus' father. He formed the Brotherhood to stop demons, not birth them."

Rohan pried the painting off the wall, and flipped it over, removing the glass. He held out his hand, and like an operating room nurse, I placed the screw-driver in it. He made short work of the staples then carefully pried the canvas away from the large out-side frame.

As it slid free, an orange flame-shape slithered from between the frame and the canvas. No heat emanated from it and no sparks cracked as it wound itself around Rohan's chest. He slashed at it with his finger blades, but as I'd learned from Ari's shadow magic, that wasn't a thing.

The painting thudded to the thick area rug at my feet.

Part of the flame creature reared up like the head of a cobra at me, so I bombarded it with magic. The crackling voltage passed through it harmlessly, but my presumption in attacking pissed the thing right off. It settled on Rohan like an anaconda, squeezing hard enough to bug his eyes out. The flaminess of it was similar to one of the magic types that marids possessed but this wasn't a demon. More like... a trap.

I couldn't fire because the only thing my magic would hurt was my boyfriend and I wasn't done with him yet. I scrabbled for a hold on it, fear making my fingers clunky.

Grabbing at flames: also not a thing.

I ended up grabbing Ro's shoulders, elbow deep in this entity that seeped into my skin like a toxic spill. My flesh split and reddened with burn lesions bulging with pus.

Rohan was turning blue, his thrashing growing weaker.

There was no way to fight and my flight instincts were screaming at me, so I grabbed the painting in one hand and yanked on Rohan. Magic bloomed inside me, not the white hot crackle of electricity, but a slow sensual unfurling of something more primordial.

The world shifted. The library disappeared, replaced by the shadow of the palm tree in the rabbi's backyard that we now stood under.

Rohan gulped air down. His shirt was torn, his torso and arms a mass of bluish-purple bruises overlaid on blistered, burned skin.

I dropped to his side, ignoring the searing burn from the blistering mess running from my elbows to my fingertips and the melted latex on my hands. I patted him down, checking for injuries, but before I could ask him if he was okay, he jerked away and in a voice laced with dread asked, "What are you?"

14

What are you? Rohan's question rang 'round and 'round in my head. Why hadn't his first reaction been to have my back? Or a simple "Thanks, Nava. So glad I'm not dead." Was he scared of me now?

I stared out the plane's window, flexing my gauze-encased fingers, the skin pulling tight over my knuckles. I can't imagine what Carlos thought when we returned all beaten up, but he'd provided a first aid kit and dressed our burns. I'm sure charter jet employees were paid for their discretion.

I'd always been different from the other Rasha, just by the fact of being female. If I had magic abilities that they didn't, why did that matter? Was Rohan viewing me differently now?

The leather couch squeaked as Rohan sat down beside me. "Are we going to talk about this?" He was still hoarse from the attack.

I shrugged, keeping my focus on the clouds.

"Will you please look at me?"

I stared at him, impassive.

He pressed an ice pack to his ribs, his shirtless torso a mass of pulpy bruises. Luckily, the burns were healing quickly. "What I said. I didn't mean–it came out wrong."

"Ah. So you don't think I'm a freak among freaks?"

"No. But you aren't like the rest of us, either." He shifted stiffly and winced. "Our powers don't grow stronger over time, but you keep getting layers."

"That's on my trainers for their failure to know the full spectrum of my electric magic."

"Maybe. But you portalled us. That's not connected to your magic."

Like I hadn't been circling back to that for the past six hours.

I headed to the telecommunications center at the far end of the jet. Every step sent fresh hell blazing down my injured arms. I traced my finger over the canvas, but the delicate brush strokes had no further secrets to yield. "Ari portals."

"Ari shadow transports. It's at least connected to his magic. Though, after this afternoon, I can't help wonder if that ability is a result of your twin thing and you not being tested in the first place. That he can do it because you can."

He wasn't the only one wondering that.

"Did you know?" Rohan stood directly behind me.

The painting was rich with shadow, but Malik had captured pools of light, a certain radiance affiliated with holy births and moments of awe that was both chilling and captivating in this context. But then, that was that marid for you. "Know what?"

"That you could portal."

I spun around, fists clenched. "Hell, yeah. I'm also waiting for the right moment to spring my invisibility and flight on you." I shoved past him but he caught me by the waist in a gentle hold.

He tossed the ice pack onto the table. "I'm sorry. Please talk to me. This is upsetting you way more than it should."

I didn't want to talk to him. His words after I'd rescued us still stung. I could pull away, slam my walls up, and let him stew. Hello, comfort zone.

It was so tempting, but scary as it was to break that pattern, I didn't want to be that person anymore. I couldn't be, not in this relationship. I bowed my head, silently repeating the words until I had the courage to say them aloud.

"What if I'm a witch?" I helped myself to a Coke from the small tray of drinks that Carlos had left out for us so I didn't have to face him as I spoke. "Because if I am a witch, I'm not Rasha."

"Technically, Rasha are kind of mini-witches. Witches lite." Rohan planted himself in front of me, tipping my chin up to meet his gaze. "You'd be better than Rasha."

I doubted that. The snag in my hypothesis was that my magic signature wasn't red and neither Dr. Gelman nor Sienna had pegged me as a witch, so if I was one, I was a pretty pathetic shadow of one. No longer unique, merely one of a multitude–and a half-assed one at that. I ran my unburned thumb along the edge of the tab. "Right. The Brotherhood would totally see me as better."

"Like you care what they think."

I popped the tab on the Coke hard enough to send up a fine mist of soda. "I care what some of them think."

"Some of us would think it's pretty fucking cool." My mouth fell open and Rohan grinned at me. "What? It'd be like dating–"

"Wonder Woman?"

"Not even remotely." He looked like he was about to elaborate so I clapped my hand over his mouth. He nipped me and I dropped my hand. "Sabrina," he proclaimed.

I pulled my punch to his shoulder at the last second out of respect for his injury. "The *teenaged* witch? Rethink that, you perv." I snapped my fingers, which was a terrible idea because a) they made no noise with my bandages on and b) snapping fucking hurt when burned. "Doctor Strange."

Rohan grabbed a water bottle and twisted the cap off. "Quit it."

"Quit what?"

He took a sip and wiped his mouth off. "Whatever weird shit you're imagining with me and Benedict Cumberbatch."

"You should be so lucky. For an old guy, he's pretty hot." I chugged back the pop. It was warmer than I liked, but I appreciated the sugar rush tingling my teeth and burning my throat. "I like being the only girl Rasha."

"You like shit disturbing. If this is true and we've got a witch in our ranks?" He whistled and made a bomb exploding noise. "We're in this together. Along with Ari, and Kane, and Drio, and Rabbi Abrams, and Baruch and Ms. Clara if you'll let me tell them. Not to mention Mahmud, and at least a half dozen other guys that will have our back."

"Against all the other Rasha and the Executive."

"No. Against a few corrupt assholes. I'm willing to bet that most of the Rasha have no clue this is going on and if they did, they'd be as mad as we are. They'll be on your side."

"Even if I'm not Rasha?"

"You're making this either or." He tugged on my hamsa ring. "We were always told that this ring was a covenant with the Brotherhood, but maybe the fact you could be a witch and it still doesn't come off means that it's a covenant with the greater fight against evil. Wherever evil is to be found. And you, Nava Katz, seem to be leading the charge."

I scowled at him. "How am I supposed to stay mad at you when you say things like that?"

He pulled his shirt back on with a wince. "You can't. I'm perfect."

True. Even with all his issues, Rohan was pretty damn great and thoroughly comfortable in his own skin. Me, on the other hand? Growing up, I'd had such a clear sense of myself. There were the jocks, the bunheads, the drama kids, and me, the tapper and Ari's twin. Eventually, my identity had expanded to include being Cole's girlfriend since we were joined at the hip.

When I'd lost two of those three, I'd floundered. Neither had been my choice to walk away from like Rohan leaving the band. I'd crafted the only identity I could to keep the hurt and loss at bay. The one way to feel like I had any say in my own existence. Then once again, I didn't. I was told I was Rasha and that was that. Even worse, no one, from my parents through to Rabbi Abrams and the other Rasha were happy about it. I was some freak they'd all gotten stuck with.

That's why I'd been so determined to get Ari by my side. Not just because this was his destiny, but because if I'd lost him, lost that one final essential link to myself... I exhaled and tipped back the rest of my drink.

I'd been fighting for so long and I'd just gotten to the point where I could breathe. I had allies and I'd adjusted to my new life as a hunter. Now it seemed I wasn't the only girl at the party: I was some second-rate witch at best and some weird mutant at worst.

Outside the window, all was gray. There was no horizon to orient myself. I shivered, telling myself that I'd be on terra firma again soon.

"Do you think David was covering up his fuck-up?" Rohan was examining Malik's painting.

I got him a fresh ice pack, cracking it to activate it, and pressed it against his ribs over the gauze taped there, the edges shiny with ointment. "How so?"

"This painting basically states that he fathered Asmodeus." Rohan took over ice pack duty. "That he slept with this demon Mahlat. What if the reason he struck the deal with witches to create Rasha wasn't out of some noble desire to kill all demons, but to have a handpicked team to clean up his mess?"

"Yikes. It's entirely possible. Oh! The lovers." I raced for the carry-on and pulled out our laptop. "The second part of that prophecy. 'Tick tock goes the clock, the lovers reunite.'" I jotted down my thoughts as fast as I could type, which wasn't all that fast with my bandaged hands

"David and Mahlat are the original lovers. Rasha and demon." I tapped a finger against my lip. "That pairing doesn't work if 'the lovers reunite' in the prophecy refers to Mandelbaum and whoever is doing the binding. Like symbolic lovers slash partners kind of thing. It would need to be rabbi and witch and David wasn't a rabbi."

Next to me, Ro went still. "Rasha and witch, Sparky." He gestured between us.

"First off, we don't even know I'm a witch. Second, wrong combo. We haven't 're' anything. We're united. Full stop."

"It's a prophecy. Things yet to come. We haven't broken up yet, but–"

"Ro." I slammed the laptop shut. "I didn't go through all sorts of hell to lose you so easily, okay? Don't even think that bullshit."

He nodded, but for the rest of the flight home his words hung heavy between us.

"You put my painting in a garbage bag?"

Malik was practically hyperventilating as he drew it out, muttering what sounded like endearments to the canvas. Some lively symphony played from inset speakers and his place smelled like tomato sauce.

I crossed my arms. "Nice job trying to get me killed, asshole."

"Cardboard box," he said, still running a hand over the canvas, checking for wounds. "Layers of packaging. Was I or was I not exceedingly clear in my instructions?"

"Boo hoo. I wasn't going back in the house after that thing attacked us."

"If I have to pay a restorer, you're footing the bill." He carried the painting down the hallway leading off the open concept living room and kitchen.

I followed him, chewing him out and being totally ignored.

Malik opened a closet door. Inside was a glass door with a keypad. He typed in a code. There was the hiss of a decompressing seal as he opened it, and cool air flowed out. Inside were several other paintings. Malik stowed this one carefully on a rack a few inches off the ground and sealed the unit up again. All that trouble and the jerk wasn't even hanging the damn thing up. "You better hope it's not damaged," he said.

"*I'm* damaged, you dick."

"You're alive." Malik raked a slow, thorough gaze over me. "Interesting." He returned to his kitchen, picked up a wooden spoon and lifted a lid on the stainless steel pot burbling on the stove. Steam curled out. "Your boyfriend's knives couldn't have sliced my trap and your magic couldn't have destroyed it. That means you escaped it."

"How'd you get past the ward to set the trap for me?"

"Don't flatter yourself. I set it years ago. It just happened to be a handy way to get my answer of what you are. So answer." He swiped some tomato sauce off the end of his spoon and tried it before adding a dash of salt. "Did you use some magic not in your Rasha starter kit? How did you escape?"

"A bad attitude and a fast car."

"If you're going to waste my time, leave."

I didn't even get a flick of his fingers in warning. I flew out of the kitchen, slamming into the wall in the hallway and cracking my skull before sliding to the ground.

The world swung sideways. I sat there, breathing through the vertigo. When I could open my eyes and the room held steady, I pushed to my feet, touching a finger to the back of my head. Blood.

The smart thing to do would have been to walk away. Keep my suspicions about what I was to myself and wait for Gelman to track down the witch. Except the marid had set me up with a very specific test. There had only been one of two ways I was getting out of there and if I was alive, he already knew.

He'd done his stupid test, now it was my turn. Still, it took me a moment to move in his direction. I kept the counter between us, standing stiffly on high alert. "I portalled. Disappointed I'm not dead?"

He filled a second pot with water and set it to boil on the stove. "Not yet."

"Rohan and I could have been killed if your hunch was wrong."

He shrugged like that was acceptable collateral damage. "The level of magic ability you accessed when you attacked me occurred when you'd been in an extreme state of distress. I needed to recreate those same conditions and see if I was right about you."

"You know what I am, yet you just stand here making dinner."

He reached up to a high cupboard to remove a bright blue box of rotini. I was so angry with him, I almost couldn't appreciate his tight ass and the way his back muscles rippled when he stretched out his arm. "I'll worry when you actually know what you're capable of."

"You got your answer and your painting. Give me my name. Who's binding demons?"

His doorbell sounded. I planted myself in his way, but he lifted me up and set me aside so he could pass.

I stomped into his living room while Malik greeted someone in Arabic. I sat down on the sofa, intending to crash his dinner party.

He led a gorgeous woman with lustrous black hair and lush curves who was maybe a few years older than me into the room. Malik was thousands of years old so talk about cradle robber. "Lila, Nava. Nava, Lila."

She approached me, hand outstretched, more for me to kiss than shake, her eyes aglow. "You are not what I imagined." Her lilting voice with its trace of a

Middle Eastern accent made my nipples harden and a low lick of heat unfurl inside me.

"I never am. You're the Lila that Malik painted." I stood up, pressing her hand between mine. Everything about Lila was flawless, from her dusky skin to the gentle curve of her smile.

"Yes." Lila regarded Malik fondly. "I see my reputation precedes me."

No reason why I should be the only one.

Malik chuckled. "Always playing coy, Lilith. You put a lot of work into your reputation."

I crashed back onto my ass. "Lilith? Like Lilith Lilith?"

She settled into the chair beside me. "Guilty as charged. I prefer Lila these days."

I sputtered for a few minutes while Malik got a platter of olives and assorted cheeses from the fridge and Lila watched me like I was amusing but not too bright.

In the Garden of Eden story, Lilith was human, not a demon. She was supposed to be Adam's first wife. Gelman had said she was a witch. It was only later mythologies that referred to her as a demon. Granted, those were written by men and being both a witch and a woman with a strong sexuality would have been enough to earn her the demon label, but at some point, had she truly become something other than human?

"How the hell are you still alive?" I said. "What are you?" Heat slashed across my mouth, searing my lips together. Panicked, I thrashed in my seat, struggling futilely to open my mouth.

"Lila," Malik chastised.

Lila reached for an olive, taking three dainty bites to finish it. "I don't like her tone."

I clawed at my face with icy fingers, making pleading noises. I no longer had lips, just a smooth expanse of skin. Bitch had eliminated my mouth. I hadn't even liked that scene in *The Matrix*. Living it now was terrifying.

The lid rattled on the pot of boiling water. Malik ripped open the box of pasta and dumped some in the water. "She'll make that infernal racket all through dinner and ruin my excellent sauce."

"That's on you for letting her stay." Lila glared at me. "Stop whining."

My jaw fell open. I gulped down air, running fingers over my lips. "Now would be a good time for that wine you're so fond of."

Malik set the timer on the stove with a beep, plucked the bottle off the counter and procured some glasses.

"Can I safely ask some questions?" I took the glass Malik gave me with shaking hands. At least they were no longer burned.

"You may ask, but it will cost you." She accepted the glass Malik held out to her.

My heart was hammering in my throat, my magic slippery and uncontrollable. Sparks jumped off my skin.

"Watch the furniture." Malik sighed. "Every time you people come over I have to call in my decorators to fix it."

Lila chuckled. "Not like that. I want to experience a passionate memory of yours."

Cautiously, I powered down. "Steal it?"

"No. Simply experience it. Relive it through you. It won't hurt you in any way."

"It won't," Malik said. Was I really going to trust the word of one psycho that the other one wouldn't hurt me?

I examined the proposal for all the ways it could go wrong versus this opportunity to get answers, but no matter how I turned it over the request seemed fairly benign. "Deal."

Lila placed her hand on my shoulder. "Think of a pleasurable sexual memory."

My body went hot and tight, assaulted with images of Rohan's hands on me, his lips, his cock.

Lila inhaled with a husky gasp and a shiver.

"What did you do?" I whispered, wrapping my arms around myself. My skin was prickly and ill-fitting, my core cold and queasy.

"I told you. I lived your memory. The rush off that one small hit... You are a very lucky girl."

She glowed with satiated vitality, but I ached with a deep sorrow. She was right that it hadn't hurt–physically. It was one thing to enjoy public sex, even get off on someone watching Rohan and me. That was from the outside. Lila had come into my memory and experienced it as I had, and in doing so diminished and tarnished it. I felt violated.

I wanted a shower. And to curl up at Rohan's side and let being with him make everything better. I wished he was here now. I'd gotten used to us working as a team. "My questions?"

Lila waved a hand at me. "Ask away."

I visualized Snowflake sitting behind me, lending me the strength to get through this shit show. "Do the witches know you're still kicking?"

"I don't know and don't care. I don't concern myself with witches, but I'm willing to make an exception about this binding business since Malik asked so nicely."

More sputtering from me, this time narrowly avoiding splashing my clothes with the wine. "You're the one who can figure out the purple magic?"

"Did you not tell her anything?" she chided Malik.

"It's more fun not to." He dropped into his chair, legs crossed. Lila tsked him.

My incredulity morphed into excitement. "Were you the witch that David made the deal with? To create Rasha?"

"The betrayer? Much to my everlasting regret." Lila had only presented a beautiful human face up until now, but with that question, her eyes glittered with malice.

I hugged one of the sofa cushions to my chest, like that could protect me, seriously considering jumping out Malik's thirty-story window.

Again.

"I told you she was entertaining." Malik helped himself to some goat cheese and a cracker.

Lila hissed at him.

I sat very still, not stupid enough to access my magic in her presence. "Was it because he'd fathered a demon?" Apparently, I *was* stupid enough to ask her another question.

Sprawled in his chair, one foot propped on the coffee table, Malik raised his hand. "Can I take this one?"

Lila reached for another olive. "You're annoying and you never have anything sweet on hand."

He quirked an eyebrow. "Asmodeus wasn't a mistake, petal. David wanted demon pets. He thought that fathering one would give him an unexpected weapon in the fight against us. He always did think out of the box."

"He was a hypocrite." Lila's lip curled in a sneer. "A man with big appetites and aspirations trying to justify them in a moral righteousness."

Reeling, I slugged back the rest of my wine. Was this why Mandelbaum was teaming up with the witches? To fulfill David's crazy idea? Why didn't anyone else in the Brotherhood know about all this? I had to talk to Rabbi Abrams. "But–"

"One more question." Lila stared at her hands, her shoulders drooping like my continued harping on the subject had sucked the fight out of her.

"Are you all right?" I said.

Lila's turn toward me was slow and measured. "You would waste your last question on that?"

When she put it that way, no, but I'd already gotten invaluable information and taking back my concern was too rude, even for me. "Yes."

"I don't like reminders of that man. Mahlat was my favorite daughter."

Whoa. My brain was one more revelation away from imploding. "If you did become a demon, when?" I said this more to myself. "It had to be before David because by the time he came around you'd be..." I counted off years on my fingers.

Lila smacked my hand down. "I have lived for so long that labels are irrelevant."

The timer went off and Malik walked toward the kitchen. "As you can see, it's a touchy sub–" He gasped, clawing at his throat.

I winced in sympathy. But better him than me.

"You may have a proper final question," Lila said.

Malik jerking around, attempting to breathe was distracting. In a funny way, like a cat chasing after a laser pointer. Fireballs spurted off him, his limbs sporadically blurring into flame, but he couldn't get past the hold that Lila had on him to lock into his protective fire form.

The timer continued to sound, a shrill beep.

Lila was more concerned with spreading the goat cheese onto her cracker than Malik, which was a pretty brutal way to treat a friend, or lover, or whatever he was to her.

I shook my head. "If you were so mad at David, why make the deal at all? Why hand over any magic to those men?"

"Demons still needed killing." She shot a wry glance at Malik, releasing her hold.

He slumped over, hands braced on the counter, his chest heaving, and swore in Arabic.

I blinked. "But–"

"You had your questions." Her tone brooked no further argument.

Malik silenced the timer and shut the stove off with a snap of the dial, sliding the pot off the burner. "Tell her, Lila, or I will."

"I don't want to talk about him." The temperature dropped several degrees. Lila half-turned toward Malik.

Malik dissolved into flame. That familiar dancing blaze of gold and orange contained within a human outline with the merest suggestion of a face.

"If the Brotherhood is trying to repeat history?" he said. "Your peaceful isolationism is over."

"I have survived much. These games mean nothing to me."

"No? Not even if they carry out David's plans? If your ex-lover wins even while in the grave?"

Eww. David had slept with both mother and daughter? Tacky.

The floor-to-ceiling window spiderwebbed with cracks. My wine was crystalizing. Shivering, I put the glass down in case it shattered.

It was an unholy showdown. Malik was pure flame. Hot. Bright. Awesome.

Lilith was a deep freeze. Winning in the scary-as-fuck department. She relaxed by degrees: the lowering of her shoulders, the looser clasp of her wine glass. "Like I said. These games mean nothing to me."

"What games?" I had to say it twice because my vocal chords didn't want to cooperate.

Malik became flesh again with nary a soot mark on his person or the furniture. Running the water in his sink, he dumped the pasta into a colander. "The deal with David was supposed to be a one-time thing. Get some more warm bodies to help fight us." He snorted.

I inspected my glass and finding it unbroken after the mini ice storm, finished up my wine. "There's a ritual to test babies. Initiate the next generation. That doesn't imply single-use."

"The ritual was to test David's *adult* potentials. To see if they could handle the magic." Malik took the water out of the colander. "David was a slick talker. He convinced another witch to create the initiation and induction rituals in order to keep the world safe for future generations. Witches are big on that." He didn't sound impressed.

"Why are you telling me all this?"

"I like this world. I like my toys and my playmates. Make sure that's not disturbed."

"Make sure yourself. Help me." I looked to Lila to include her in that, but she was gazing out the window, giving no indication she was listening.

Malik laughed and laughed, putting final touches on his sauce while I scowled at him, arms crossed. "Oh. You were serious."

"Lila." When she turned, I handed her the gogota finger still purple from the magic signature spell we'd cast. I'd retrieved it from Rabbi Abrams before going off for the painting. "What's it going to cost me to find out who did this?"

"One night with your lover."

"You're not his type," I said lightly, tamping down a hot flare of "over my dead body." Who was I kidding? She was everyone's type.

"You are though. I want to possess your body for one night, habibty."

"No."

"Why not? You're the host. I'm just a passenger allowed to experience your passion."

That cold calculating part of my brain said to pay her price if it meant answers. The rest of me recoiled.

Lila sipped at her wine, her eyes intent on mine.

"Even if I was willing, which I'm not," I said, going with my heart and my gut, "he'd never agree." I didn't want her knowing me that intimately. Didn't want her perverting a precious experience.

She stroked a hand over my hair. "He doesn't get to know."

"No way. That's wrong." I ducked out from her creepy touch and grabbed the gogota finger. It may have been my body, but I wouldn't be alone and I'd never do that to Ro. I wouldn't take his choice away.

Malik blocked my route to the door. "Don't be ridiculous. This is nothing."

The marid may have appeared as an attractive, civilized man but in the end, he was still a demon and he was old. To him, time and life were an impressionist painting where any of the individual dots failed to matter.

"It's everything." Magic erupted out of me. "Now get out of my way or so help me we'll both find out exactly what I'm capable of."

Hands up, he let me pass.

15

I sped through the city, hell-bent for the chapter club, white-knuckling the steering wheel. Barely holding myself together from the adrenaline and yeah, fear, still pumping through my system. I'd texted Ro that I was coming back but hadn't answered his questions on how the delivery had gone.

I curved onto my dead-end street, the car fishtailing. The trees on each side that afforded us privacy from our neighbors pressed in on me. I floored the gas pedal that final millimeter, my body straining forward in my desire to get home.

The gate was open, Ro waiting for me to slow to a stop. The stiffness in his pose wasn't all from his injuries. He strode past the wards out to the curb, stuck his head into my rolled-down driver's side window, clasped my face in his hands, and kissed me. Leaning further into the window, he pressed me back against the seat, his hum of relief vibrating down to my toes.

I gripped his wrists, refusing to be let go of.

"You're giving me gray hairs, Sparky," he murmured with a shaky laugh, before kissing me again.

I rested my forehead to his.

"Are you okay?" he said.

"Better now that I'm back." I leaned across the car and opened the passenger door. "Get in. I'll drive us up."

An oshk materialized out of nowhere, denting the hood right as Ro walked past it.

I jumped out of the car and blew the demon back against the stone fence. While this oshk had the same blobby body as the one at the wreta house, instead of a single human arm, she had a fully defined female face with short blood-colored hair.

Her amorphous body expanded to deflect the impact. The oil slick pattern on her skin momentarily sucked all the light into it, creating the illusion of a massive void that was oddly hypnotic. I tore my eyes away, checking Ro for possible contact and repeat symptoms.

The glint in his eyes and hard set of his jaw was directed at the oshk, not me. He snicked out his blades as the oshk peeled herself off the fence.

I shoved him out of the way and blew a steady stream of electricity at the demon. "Are you kidding me?" I made a mental note to get some kind of long folding switchblade.

"I can't just stand here." A muscle ticked in his jaw.

I respected him enough that this had to be his choice, even if getting another hit of secretion wasn't worth him lending his magic to this battle. "Your choice," I said.

"Stop being reasonable," he snapped. But his knives went away.

The oshk curled in on herself, her flesh rising up over the gash I'd caused and sealing it. "Where is he?" Her screech was a broken rasp. "Where is Candyman?"

"We don't know," Rohan said.

"You killed Five." Was that a name and were there four more like her? Her eyes flashed red.

I launched a new offensive, but she ignored my magic like the deadly voltage was a gentle mist, and flew at us.

Rohan pulled me behind the open car door, swinging it outward to collide with the demon. The oshk slammed into the metal hard enough to rattle the hinges and disappeared.

"Bhenchod!" Rohan stormed up the driveway.

I got back in my car, driving past Ro and giving him space.

Drio was home so I dragged him into the library, filling him in on what had just happened.

The front door slammed. Rohan marched in wearing a deadly smile. "Leo needs better intel. Oshks aren't Unique. Time to have a little chat with her."

Ro had covered for Leo at every turn since I'd known him. Was the oshk in front of the chapter house really the final straw? Was he just frustrated or was he done keeping her secret? I stepped forward, but Drio gripped my arm, expression bland.

"That's not Leo's job." He waved a hand around the library, deceptively mild, but leaving no doubt whose job it really was. "An urban legend's got to have documentation somewhere."

Rohan returned Drio's impassive smile. "It better."

The first time I'd met Drio, there'd been a moment when I thought Ro was going to kill him. I'd never seen that again from him and I wasn't freaked out because I was seeing it again now. What had my palms clammy and my heart galloping was that Drio looked a blink away from methodically dismantling my boyfriend over my best friend.

Drio pulled the laptop close and ran a new search for the female face in the database.

I gripped the top of a chair watching the anger rolling off Rohan meet the implacable front that was Drio. It scraped my already raw nerves to fine wire. I opened a window but the fresh sunny breeze failed to ease the powder keg vibe.

Screw it. I jogged downstairs and rapped on Rabbi Abrams' door.

"Come in." His voice was a bit muffled.

I threw open the door. "What's wrong?"

He crumpled up a Kit Kat wrapper. "Found them."

I placed a hand over my heart. "Stop at one, please, and no more honey in your tea today."

"Agreed. Do you have an update?" He waved me at a chair.

"Yeah."

Give the man his due, he stayed pretty calm while I told him about his illustrious founder. I left out the deal Lilith had proposed because there wasn't enough money in the world to make me talk sex with the guy. "You think Rabbi Mandelbaum knows this? Or that he's up to the same thing? Making demon pets to help fight this war?"

"I've never heard any of this, and I've been around this Brotherhood much longer than he has." He stroked his white beard. "It is, however, possible. Does Esther have anything to add?"

"She doesn't know yet. I'll go see her soon, but first I need your help with something else. Ever heard of an oshk?"

He sat forward with an interested gleam. "No. A demon?"

I gave him a brief run-down, asking if he could think of the best place to search for it since it wasn't in the database or any of the texts we'd tried. He reached for another Kit Kat from the stash on his desk, leaning back with a grumble when I shook my head at him.

Denied his treats, Rabbi Abrams heaved himself out of his chair and pulled a thin book off his shelf.

I took it from his gnarled hands. "It's a journal."

The leather binding was brittle to the touch, the ink on the parchment was faded with time, and many of the pages had come loose. Entries were written in a spidery handwriting in a combination of English, Hebrew, and Russian while the pages were filled with illustrations of demons I'd never heard of, not that that meant anything. I didn't have as complete an education in demonology as the other Rasha. "Are these Uniques?"

"The Brotherhood doesn't believe them to exist. According to them, Rabbi Shokovsky made it his life's work to record the whisperings of madwomen."

"Witches?" I said.

"The Brotherhood wanted facts, demons that were confirmed in different cultures, not crazed rumors and fanciful tales. He died alone and reviled." He ran a wrinkled finger along the edge of the page. "You said the oshk was an urban legend told by other demons. Perhaps Shokovsky heard the story."

I stopped flipping pages at one covered in rough scribbles, all the sketches a variety of the oshk I'd met. "I'd say he did. How'd you get this contraband, Rabbi?"

"He was my great-great-great-grandfather." Rabbi Abrams winked and tossed me a Kit Kat. "My family doesn't precisely toe the party line either."

I skipped into the library, clinging to this small victory like a lifeline. "I have returned triumphant."

The mood had thawed between Rohan and Drio, but both the men seethed with frustration, open half-drunk beer bottles on the table in front of them.

"Did you bring us chocolate, too?" Drio asked.

"No. Rabbi Abrams gave this to me because I'm his favorite. He also gave me this." I lay the open book down on the table, tapping the demon's name that Shokovsky had written at the top.

"A matryoshka," Rohan read.

"Like the Russian dolls?" Drio humphed, studying the drawings. "We're dealing with eight of them?"

"Seven," Rohan corrected. "We killed one of the versions with an arm."

"Seven out there for Candyman to make more Sweet Tooth with? That's plenty," Drio said.

"The matryoshka is a Unique. She just comes in parts. Leo wasn't wrong," I said pointedly, dropping into a chair.

"No, she wasn't." Rohan hooked an ankle around my chair and tugged me close. It was all the apology that I was going to get.

The journal entry confirmed that the matryoshka ate other demons with no apparent interest in humans. Its secretion worked as a paralytic on demons.

"We're lucky it doesn't work as a paralytic on us," Drio said.

"It's bad enough," Ro replied.

"Speaking from experience." Drio smirked.

"Don't start," Ro said. It was unclear whether he meant me or Drio. Drio's smirk grew wider and I pressed my lips together, pointedly looking away.

We poured over the drawings, learning everything we could about the rest of the forms. A head, an arm, a leg–put the eight parts of the oshk together and she made a complete human figure.

The guys discussed how best to track it, as well as what protective gear we'd need to keep from getting splashed with its secretion. Ro agreed not to tempt fate by using his blades so he and Drio made a list of weapons we had on hand that would get the job done.

I told them that the heart was the sweet spot then tuned them out, needing to properly regroup after the shit show at Malik's. Needing to release the breath that had been stuck in the base of my throat these past couple hours. I pressed up against Rohan. With every inhale, I filled up a little more with him. My skin heated, my tension eased, and my muscles became pliant. I shifted closer as if the hard warmth of his side could keep me upright when my spine so clearly couldn't.

He didn't look at me, didn't speak to me, listening to Drio expand on an idea. His only movement was the idle play of his fingers on the neck of his beer bottle but his utter awareness of me emanated outward. So when the table got jostled and he reached past me for the box of tissue to blot the pooling liquid with a murmured "kitchen," I had to shut my eyes to steel myself because the unease humming in my system had become low grade arousal and that one word skyrocketed me.

Rohan left the room carrying his beer and the soggy tissue.

Drio kept reading the journal. "Go after him."

I didn't need to be told twice. I scampered into the kitchen.

Rohan caught me, pushing me up against the cabinets. "I hated letting you go to Malik's by yourself."

"But you did." I slid my arms around his neck. I didn't want to think beyond this moment, so I kissed him deeply, and whatever else he might have said died as his lips met mine. The kiss danced on the edge of violence, grinding against each other, working through all the anger, fear, and frustration we both had penned up.

Our darkness banished, our lips became a sweet tease. Rohan wrapped his arms around me and we held each other, our heartbeats slowing in tandem.

"Want to tell me what happened?"

I pulled away with a shaky sigh. "Yeah. But let's get Drio. And food. Lots of food." I hadn't eaten since breakfast on the red eye flight home, and using my magic had long ago metabolized it.

Excellent boyfriend that he was, Rohan made sure I was stuffed with my favorite Szechuan food, even ordering the ginger beef extra crispy for me. He stayed at my side, a steady presence, while I caught Drio up on Orlando, and told them both about meeting Lilith.

Ro took the bit about Lila making my mouth vanish better than I expected. His vibrated fury only lasted a few seconds. He stuffed it down to focus on me, pulling me into his arms and rubbing my back in slow, steady strokes, as I recounted everything else that had transpired.

Almost everything. I couldn't tell them about Lila reliving my memory or her offer. I tried three times, and on each occasion broke into a coughing fit. The third time my coughing was so violent that Drio actually got me some water instead of his expected response of letting my brains leak out of my ears. When I was able to speak again, I ended up saying I'd pissed her off with my questions and it was a no-go.

I yawned, my lids half-closed.

Ro tugged me up. "Let's get you to bed."

As soon as he climbed under the sheet with me, I gripped his hand, wrapped my leg over his, and stuffed my cheek against his chest. He was something real and solid to rest against; someone caring and fierce and mine. I finally felt secure enough to let sleep claim me.

I woke up in the middle of the night because I'd kicked the sheet off and I was cold. I reached for

Rohan, but he wasn't there. My hand hit something crinkly. I switched on the light to find a note Ro had left me on his pillow.

Gone to Palm Springs. Back in the morning. Don't worry.

He'd snuck out in the middle of the night to fly to California. Why would I possibly worry? I tried to go back to sleep, but his absence left me raw and empty, like a demon had sliced me open, casually thrust in a claw, and yanked out my insides.

Dawn was a long time coming. Rohan's reappearance even longer.

I'd been sitting on the front stairs for two hours, consumed six cups of coffee and two bagels, and worked myself into one righteous fury by the time Rohan rolled up.

A smoke-infused haze covered the sky, the sun a bright orange ball from forest fires burning hundreds of kilometers away. The air was heavy and stagnant with no hint of a breeze coming off the water through the trees.

He got out of the car, saw me, and flashed me his rock fuck grin. "You won't believe what I found. Women's clothing and a fairly recent photo of Ferdinand with some lady. I don't know who she was to him but I'll find out. It's a great lead."

"Don't patronize me." I spoke in a low voice, my eyes locked on his. "And don't lie to me. Ever."

"How did I lie?" He sat down next to me. "I checked out Ferdinand's place."

"Red-eye flights aren't that red-eye. You didn't charter a jet in the middle of the night. You kept it, didn't you?" My hands tightened on my coffee mug, now cold and empty.

"I called them to arrange it when you went to deliver the painting."

"Why didn't you tell me?"

He twisted his Rasha ring around. "I was going to, but I was waiting for you to come home, and then the oshk happened and..." He leaned back on his elbows against the stairs. "I didn't want to worry you."

"I wouldn't have stopped you."

"No? You were locked onto me last night so tight that I couldn't even turn over. You'd have asked me to wait and I would have." He looked away. "I didn't want to."

"Better to ask for forgiveness than permission, huh?" I'd lived that way, but I'd never figured Ro would pull that on me. Never figured he'd strip the connective threads that bound us with his manipulations. Funny how fast "doing better and doing this together" flew out the window when it didn't fit with Ro's wants. I crushed the remnants of my bagel into a pulpy mess and tossed it onto the grass. "If I ask you to wait, then convince me otherwise. Don't sneak around." I jabbed a finger into his chest. "You know who sneaks around, Ro? Addicts."

And addictions never ended well.

"Here comes the melodrama." He stomped up the stairs.

"Better than the death wish."

"Oh, okay. You fight the oshk and you take down the Brotherhood. I'll just sit here enveloped in bubble wrap and you tell me when it's safe to move."

I jumped to my feet. "I have a better idea. How about you pull your head out of your ass and examine your behavior? You're spiraling. Acting on emotion, not logic. Great way to get yourself killed."

"Spare me the bullshit. You want this blown open more than I do."

"I thought I did." I clenched the coffee cup, stifling the urge to check it at him "But you're getting obsessed. Running full tilt on everything. You need to slow down. You were the one who said we were in this together."

"We are," he growled.

"Then keep your promise. And don't break us."

16

Naomi and Christina's dingy lobby had been renovated since the last time I'd been here, the new flashy disco tiles in varying shades of sea green a dazzling pop upon entry. The faded red carpet in the hallways had been ripped out and replaced with hardwood which brightened things up, but the plaster was still cracked in the far corner and the ill-fitting stairwell door still stuck.

Amazing how easy it was to make something look surface shiny. Kind of like the smile I'd perfected on the drive over.

I knocked on their door, balancing a cardboard tray with coffee cups and a large brown paper bag. Christina opened the apartment door and I held up the bag. "I brought bagels with lox and cream cheese."

"From Siegel's?"

"Where else."

She grinned, taking the bag from me and calling out for Naomi to join us. I braced myself but other than the turtleneck sweater Naomi wore that was out of place on this beautiful June day, there was no sign of what she'd suffered. Externally, at least.

"I got you chicken noodle soup because I wasn't sure you were eating solids after the surgery." I handed Naomi the take-out container and plastic spoon, half-expecting her to throw it back at me. Definitely expecting her to say something cutting.

"Thank you," she said, in a raspy voice, her throat still healing. She took it and curled up on the corner of the sofa.

I grabbed my own sandwich and sat down, making bright chatter with Christina about all the beach traffic on my drive over. The conversation progressed to a restaurant we'd both heard good things about and on to the mind-numbing topic of our recent weather. If we discussed house prices, we'd have run through the greatest hits of Vancouverite small talk.

Even though Christina was keeping up her end of the conversation, she kept shooting glances at Naomi like she was waiting for her to tell me something.

I pushed my mostly uneaten sandwich away, wondering if I should make my excuses and leave.

"I'm quitting the firm." Naomi put the soup on the table, pulled a worn fleece blanket off the back of the sofa, and laid it across her legs.

I did a double take a Naomi's words. "Why? You sounded so glad about making associate soon."

"She was happy about what her parents would think," Christina said. "She's going to put herself first for a change and go traveling. Rock climb in Copper Canyon and slackline in the Moab Desert."

"I'll go back to law eventually, but not in the corporate world. The attack..." Naomi fiddled with her turtleneck. "It put a lot of things into perspective. Made me realize it was time to go for things I didn't think I deserved."

Christina smiled at Naomi and took her hand.

"Oh. *Oh*." I said. "Good for you two. I'm sorry for being kind of a bitch to you all those years, Naomi, and I can't really discuss it but I wasn't lying when I said I was in the security business. I promise you that we're going to get those responsible for the Sweet Tooth."

"I'm sorry, too," she said.

"Now that we're all friends," Christina said.

"Weellll," Naomi and I said in unison and laughed.

Christina glared at us. "Shut up or I'll hurt you both."

"Vicious. Good luck with that," I said to Naomi.

She shot Christina a heated look. "I like her feisty."

I covered my ears. "Nope."

Christina kicked her foot out at me. "I think we should all go out sometime soon. You can bring hot stuff that you're dating."

"I'd like that." Something good was coming out of the Sweet Tooth tragedy after all. I needed, no, I *wanted* more friends in my life. It was an unexpected victory. Our lunch relaxed into a much more upbeat affair after that, though I couldn't stay long. With firm promises to get together soon, we said our good-byes and I headed for the hospital.

Along with visiting Naomi and Christina, seeing Dr. Gelman out of isolation and surrounded by flowers and get well cards went a long way to brightening my shitty morning.

"You can't portal." Dr. Gelman took a bite of the fruit compote on her tray and made a face.

"Out of everything I've told you, that's the part you're most interested in?"

"One thing at a time. Portalling is elimination magic."

"Which Rasha have."

"Not that type of elimination magic. You eliminate demon life, not the spaces between two points." She pointed her knife at me. "Don't be obstreperous."

"I'm not difficult."

She hid a smile like she hadn't expected me to understand. That Word of the Day app was brilliant.

"Ari shadow transports," I said.

She poked through the rest of her food. "That definitely shouldn't be possible."

"It is if I'm a witch and Ari got some kind of echo of some of my ability."

"Figured that out all by yourself, did you?" She pursed her lips. "It's our fault, really, for not seeing the obvious. There wouldn't be a female Rasha. That's redundant."

"You agree?"

"Yes. I pronounce you witch." She tapped my shoulder with an imaginary wand. "Welcome to the club."

I still wasn't convinced I wanted to be a member. "No badge? No cake?"

"Here. Mazel tov." Gelman pushed the corner of her tray with the bland white cake square close to me.

"Pass, thanks. The sticking point in all this is that my magic is pink, not red."

"That's because you're a mess." She wiped her mouth and threw her napkin on the tray, covering the food.

"No. I used to be a mess. A hot one even, but I'm only lukewarm now."

"That too, but I was referring to this twin business. Seems it affected you as much as it did Ari." She picked at her fruit salad, eating around the maraschino cherries. "In some ways it would have been better if he hadn't had magic at all."

"Why?"

"As the two of you developed, gestated, Ari's magic must have inhibited yours. His lay dormant, waiting for the induction ritual, and that leeched onto your magic."

"But when the ritual happened, it was my magic that burst free."

"Because your magic is innately stronger. It overpowered his."

I rubbed my temples. "Even so, why didn't I get all my magic at once?"

"The induction ritual freed it, but that ritual is designed to only call out the magic bestowed upon Rasha." She shrugged. "That's what you got."

"The elimination magic pertaining to killing demons. Right."

"Give your magic time to fully manifest and stabilize."

Sienna pushed the door open, letting in the hum from the floor polishers outside. Her scrubs were printed with teddy bears and she'd changed the beads on the ends of her dreadlocks from blue to glittery green. She saw me and groaned. "My day is complete."

"Happy to brighten your world. Anyhow, Rabbi Abrams is totally a candy sneak which can't be good for his diabetes." I babbled on, while Sienna placed her hands on Dr. Gelman's chest and closed her eyes.

"I have a nurse on this ward, you know," Gelman said. "She's lovely and takes very good care of me."

Sienna finished her magic treatment before responding. She opened her eyes, shaking out her hands. "She doesn't have my vested interest. I lose you, I lose the best rugelach around."

I clasped my hands under my chin. "You make rugelach?"

"She does." Sienna headed for the door. "If you want any, next time spring for something better than crappy hospital store flowers."

Dr. Gelman frowned. "Why didn't you want her to know?"

I made sure Sienna had disappeared down the corridor before answering. "I get the impression she hates the Brotherhood."

Gelman snorted. "To put it mildly."

"For all intents and purposes, I'm still Brotherhood." My Rasha ring glinted under the lights. Was there a way to get this stupid ring off me if I wasn't Rasha?

"You'll need to be trained in the full extent of your infusion and elimination magic."

"Are you offering?" Having Dr. Gelman as my mentor was my dream.

"Depends. There's a test to verify you are a witch and not a mutant Rasha." Gelman nudged me with her blanket-covered foot. "This is where you come in."

"Shouldn't this have happened before you welcomed me to the club?"

"I was trying to make you happy. You so desperately looked like you wanted to belong."

I rolled my eyes. "What kind of a test?"

"Enough questions. There is a test. You will take it." Gelman plucked a flower out of the vase beside her bed. Not from the bouquet I'd brought. Mine were at least all alive. "Restore the azalea to its natural beauty."

"Is most infusion magic healing?" How boring. I exhaled in a hard "oomph" like I'd been punched in the gut. My lungs started bubbling, going at it like a pot of water on full boil, getting larger and larger, pushing everything else inside me aside. I was going to pop.

"I'm infusing your lungs with air. Blowing them up like a balloon. Does that feel very healing?"

I flailed around until she released me, then rubbed my chest. "Can I learn that?"

"We'll see." She squeezed my hand and warmth unfurled inside me, taking the pain away.

The azalea sprig had only a single white-tipped pink bloom, brown curling one shriveled edge. I carefully took the wilted piece of compost...

...and two of its three remaining petals fluttered to the ground.

"Brilliant start."

Everyone was a critic. I wasn't warm and fuzzy at the best of times so pulling some latent Mother Nature instinct out of my ass didn't exactly come naturally. I waved my finger over the flower like a wand.

"Say 'abracadabra' and I'll stab you,'" Dr. Gelman said.

"Like that plastic cutlery's gonna inflict hella damage." I scrambled for a different plan. "You're not such a bad little flower. You just need a little love." The words had worked for Linus and the Christmas tree. Thinking good vibes, I sent the tiniest spark of magic into the sprig, hoping that might jump start it back to life.

Its last petal fell off.

"Let's table this for now." Figuring that electricity was at the heart of all things and perhaps the flower simply needed a good long soak, I infused the sprig with a constant low-grade stream of magic. "Did you know about Lilith or what the painting implied? Any of it?"

"No."

I peekd in at the petal. Nada. "Could Lila be the one binding demons? Even if she's part demon or whatever now, she was a human witch at some point so she could have both red and blue magic giving us the purple. She's got to be massively powerful."

"She's not a demon."

"She has to be. Mahlat was her daughter and Asmodeus her grandson. Weird though. That would have made him only a quarter demon, but his power was immense. He was like demon royalty, not some wannabe. And he didn't dissolve into gold dust when I killed him like other halflings do. Like his own two spawn did."

"Lilith isn't an ordinary human." Gelman adjusted her blankets. "By the time she'd birthed Mahlat, she was already suffused with dark magic. If Mahlat and her sisters presented as full demons in every way that counted, then I imagine the demon and dark magic formed a genetic mutation resulting in this superbreed of creature. And remember, David already had Rasha magic when he slept with Mahlat and had Asmodeus. The mother of Asmodeus' offspring must have been a regular human."

"Insanely powerful mutant demons. That's terrifying. But what about Lila feeding off my sexual memory like a succubus?"

"No, Nava." She cut off all further protest. "Lilith is not a demon. It doesn't work that way. There is no spell to make a person part demon. You can't be turned or bitten. The only way she could still be alive is through magic so dark I don't know how it hasn't killed her." Her brows drew together. "No one else has ever survived its practice for very long."

I opened my fist again but there was only the same flowerless stem. "Everyone is so certain they know how this all works. Except when they don't."

"I do. Lilith offered to find you the witch. She never would have done so had she been the one binding those demons, and you can be sure Malik would have known if it was her."

"But she isn't helping me." I glared at the azalea, frustrated with my lack of a name, a lack of answers, a giant fucking lack.

Gelman poured herself some water. "She isn't helping you because you refused whatever price she put on the job. Yes?"

I raised startled eyes to hers and she nodded. "Your Rasha may not have understood your coughing fit, but I did. Lilith is not the one you seek."

"Then who is? Your leads aren't panning out but someone has to know something about the bindings. I'm a witch. Introduce me. Get me into the community so I can actively investigate."

"Give me a week to get through this final round of chemo. If I haven't found anything then I'll bring you in."

"Like a witch debutante. I'll start shopping for my gown."

"You're impossible."

Sweet Tooth 911. Orwell had texted me.

I tossed the azalea sprig onto her bed. "I have to go."

"Nava."

I waved at Gelman over my shoulder.

"Nava." More insistently.

I turned and she held up the sprig. A single green bud had formed. She tossed it to me. "You're a witch. And probably a damn good one with enough training. But more importantly, you really are part of our group, and we're going to find whoever is betraying us."

Us. I tucked the precious bud behind my ear. "Yeah. We are."

"Are we sure this was Sweet Tooth?" I said to Rohan and Drio. I'd texted them the second I'd left Gelman's room and they'd gotten there first.

"They fucked themselves to death." Drio moved away from the rooftop ledge so I could take his place. He handed me the camera. I knelt down to get the best angle, loose rocks digging into my bare knees, and peered through the telephoto lens. "Holy hell. They look like they were torn apart by wild animals."

The crime scene bedroom on the sixth floor of the building across from the roof I stood on was destroyed. This wasn't an overturned lamp or shit knocked off shelves during a bout of crazed sex with red scratch marks and a couple of hickeys. This was every photo and stick of furniture smashed, holes in the plaster with blood smeared at the edges, and–

"Fuck me!" I shoved the camera at Drio. "She's got a chair leg stuffed up her vagina. She's impaled on it."

"To be fair, his dick broke off, so..." Rohan said.

I grabbed the camera back.

"It's in the far corner," Ro said.

I swung the lens over. "That's not a lumpy sock?"

The cops and the coroner left the room, missing the appearance of the oshk. The one with the female face. She flowed over to stand directly over the victims for a moment, her expression downcast, and blinked out.

"Visitor." I told them about the oshk.

Drio packed up the camera case. "That thing needs a tracking chip."

"Oh. What about a location spell?" I tossed him the lens cap that had fallen on the ground.

"Rasha can't do those," Rohan said.

Drio snickered. "You'd know. The Passover dinner," he told me. "But he's right. It's not something you cast. It's something witches do and I'm not bringing any witches into this."

"Too late," I said. "Ta da!" I threw jazz hands, giving him my brightest smile.

Drio gave me his Torture Time smile in response and blurred out. Ro jumped in front of me with a winded omph as he collided with Drio, who flickered into place.

Ro grabbed Drio's arm, wrenching it up behind his back. "Not happening."

Double checking that Rohan had Drio secured and was calming him down from the bombshell I'd dropped, I moved to the far end of the rooftop and phoned Dr. Gelman to ask what I needed to do.

Gelman explained that location spells were misnamed because there wasn't a spell, it was elimination magic. Removing the distance between a single item and its source, like a hair and a person's head or a prized possession and the owner. It didn't work on compounds, so I couldn't use the Sweet Tooth. However, if the oshk had left any secretion behind in the crime scene room, that would work.

"What do I do with it?" I said.

"You ask Sienna really nicely. I'm going in to chemo and you can't pull this off without training."

"I portalled. Isn't this the same idea?"

"You portalled under extreme stress. Try it now and get back to me. Besides, this may be the same idea, but it's far more complicated to execute. Sienna's still on duty. Bribes work. She likes sambuca." Gelman hung up.

"Ack!"

Drio had flash stepped to stand directly in front of me.

I fumbled my phone.

"You're more powerful than me?" he said.

I bounced on the balls of my feet. "You gonna try and take me, suckah?"

He chucked me under the chin again. This was starting to be our thing. "Training is going to be fun."

"You're a weird puppy. You know that, right? Can you zip on over to the crime scene and check for oshk goo? You got gloves? Something to collect it in?"

Drio rummaged in the camera bag, snapped on a pair of latex gloves and dumped a thin filter out of its case. He flashed out.

And then there were two.

I fiddled with the flower behind my ear. "Sorry I didn't get a chance to tell you first about Gelman confirming me as witch."

Rohan jammed his hands in pockets and shrugged. "That's the least of the shit between us."

My lack of a protest lasted a second too long. He gave a bitter laugh and turned away. Only a few feet separated us physically. Emotionally, we were across a chasm I didn't know how to breach.

My phone rang. It was my mom and I debated ignoring the call but it couldn't be worse than this pained silence. "Hi, Mom."

"Can you come over?"

I gripped the phone. "Did something happen?"

"No. Why would you ask that?"

It's not like you call me for social visits. "No reason."

Drio returned and shook his head. Damn. No secretion and no bribing Sienna necessary.

"I can come now." I stuffed my phone into my pink capris. "Gotta go."

Drio ignored me and Rohan nodded. There was no goodbye kiss.

I stewed on that fact for the entire drive over to my parents.

A charred, slightly sour smell hit me when I unlocked the front door. My knotted-up stomach lurched because the one time Ari had let the coffee burn off, Mom had torn a strip off him. My ass nothing was wrong.

I turned off the coffee maker and put the carafe in the sink to cool. "Mom?"

No answer. I ran through the house, searching, my panic escalating, and images of her dead on the floor whipping through my thoughts.

She was sitting at her desk in her study, her back to me.

"Mom? Mom. Shana!" I shook her shoulder.

She blinked at me. "You got here quickly."

"You could have burned the house down. The coffee maker." I clarified at her blank stare.

"Oh." She stood up, but I pushed her back down.

"It's handled. Thanks for giving me a heart attack." I peered at her screen to see what had had her so engrossed. It was open to a search on witchcraft in Judea. "You know you can't publish anything on that, right?

"What? Oh. Yes." She closed the laptop. "Have you considered the possibility that you're a witch and not Rasha?"

I pressed a hand to my heart, my relief that nothing bad had happened supplanted by a rushing in my ears as she regarded me with professional curiosity and not an ounce of maternal concern. "Uh, yeah.

Turns out I am. Ari doesn't know yet, though. This other witch I know confirmed it." Mom didn't say anything and I kept babbling. "I think you'd hit it off with her. She's in the hospital now, but I'll introduce you when she gets out. She's a physicist."

"Maybe she'll influence your academic choices," Mom said dryly. Goody, there was the mother I knew, and well, knew. She opened her desk drawer and handed me a letter. "If you don't confirm your registration by the end of the month, UBC will force you to withdraw. I've pulled all the favors I can."

I took the letter, not bothering to complain that she'd opened my mail. "No one asked you for any favors."

"From what I understand, most of the Rasha have degrees. You won't get anywhere within the Brotherhood with your high school diploma."

I stuffed the letter in the back pocket of my capris. "I won't get anywhere because I don't fit the definition of 'brother.' Aside from that, I think the only real criteria is staying alive and I'm not dead yet."

"Don't be so morbid."

"You're right. It's all sunshine and rainbows fighting demons."

Mom slammed the drawer shut so hard that I flinched. "You think I don't worry every single day about my kids dying?" I shrugged. Mom muttered something under her breath about me.

"I'm not going back to school. Not now. You can bask in your golden boy's achievements." A tight smile on my face, I spun around. I couldn't get out of there fast enough.

"What 'golden boy?' Nava, stop."

I froze, conditioned to obey that sharp tone. I forced out a breath to the count of three. "Ari. It's what you always called him, right?" I didn't mean to sound so bitter. I mean, I was, I just hadn't intended for her to hear it.

A fleeting sadness crossed my mother's face. "Nava," she said. "He wasn't my golden boy. He was my golden-haired boy. The same way you were my raven-haired girl. You and Ari shortened it to Golden Boy and Raven, when you were about three. You told me they were your superhero names."

I wrapped my arms around my chest. "Nope. No memory of that." Mom pushed me out of the room. "What are you doing?"

"Disabusing you of this ridiculous notion of yours that Ari is more important to me."

Mom forced me down the stairs and into the TV room. She pulled an album off the bookcase, quickly flipping through the pages. "Here."

The photo showed me as a preschooler, sitting in our kitchen on top of a pile of candy. "Yeah, the year I went as a crow." Good haul.

"The year you went as a raven."

I took the album from her. "Are you sure?"

She glared at me. "Yes."

"Why did you stop calling me that then?"

"Because you're the most stubborn child imaginable. I don't know what your brother had done to set you off, but you stomped in one day when you were about seven and announced that name was done."

I sat down hard on the sofa. Those were pretty much the exact words I'd said to Ro when I'd told him to stop calling me Lolita. That part was plausible but... I bit my bottom lip. "You treated Ari like your golden boy. My entire life."

Mom sat down next to me, fiddling with her wedding ring. "When Rabbi Abrams told me about your brother, I cried for three days."

"Because you were proud of his big destiny."

She tucked a curl behind my ear. "Because I was terrified. How could this tiny baby fight demons? Would I," her voice cracked, "outlive him? I swore to enjoy every second I had with him."

I ripped a tissue out of the box on the coffee table and blew my nose. "Never mind that you had twins."

"You had Ari and you had dance and you seemed so together, I didn't need to worry about you." She reached past me for her own tissue and her Chanel perfume teased a memory from when I was little of falling asleep in her lap all the times she and Dad had stayed up late playing cards. How she'd held her cards with one hand so she could keep me snuggled against her chest with the other.

I blew my nose again.

"Sweetheart. You suffered the fallout of my fears and I'm so, so sorry." She gripped my hands. "The day you realized you couldn't keep tapping and accepted your place at UBC? My heart broke for you."

I'd lost the battle not to cry. "Why push so hard for me to go to school then? Even now?"

"I was scared of how empty you were without dance. But I was always proud of you."

"Really?" My skin was tingling, a warmth radiating through my body.

"Well, except maybe the past couple years. You've been a disaster, my girl."

I choked out a laugh through my tears.

There wasn't much talking after that, just the clock ticking and Mom's arm around me as we looked at the photo of the girl I used to be.

17

Any lingering anger at Rohan evaporated after my visit with my mom. She and I had wasted too much time on misplaced emotion and misunderstanding and I wasn't about to do the same with him.

Ro waited for me on the front stairs at Demon Club, but he jumped to his feet when he saw my red-rimmed eyes. "What happened?"

"A good thing." Things weren't fixed between Mom and me, but they weren't broken either and that was better than they'd been in a long time. I kissed him. "I don't want to fight and I don't care about anything except us being okay."

"I don't either. I love that we get to share everything about our lives, but it's hard." He gave me a wry grin. "I'm used to my autocratic ways."

"I may be somewhat intractable myself. Not confirming or denying."

"Best not to. We deal with danger all the time and I don't want to add to yours. I never want to be the reason you get hurt. Physically or emotionally."

Rohan stroked my cheek. "Being thrown into all this? The way you've held your own and proven time and time again you can hunt with the best of us? You're amazing."

I blushed and mumbled my thanks.

"This is touching. Now we will all go into the bathroom and discuss douching together, sì?" Drio lounged in the front door.

I batted my eyelashes. "You're the douche expert."

His lips quirked.

"I had an idea about Candyman." I led them back into the library, scooping up water bottles from the fridge on the way, and tossing them to the guys. "What if his name applies to a physical attribute, not a dealer handle?"

We entered all kinds of keywords into the database, scoring a match with "sugar."

"Hoc demon. Rings a bell." Drio spun his bottle on the table.

"Hoc is an acronym," Rohan read. "Hydrogen, oxygen, carbon. They survive off this compound."

"They eat sugar?" Drio said.

I picked at the label that was damp with condensation, a thought niggling at the corner of my brain.

Rohan dug deeper into the database. "They absorb it through their skin like plants with photosynthesis. Their intake cycle is twenty-four hours. Dusk to dusk. They need to be in their natural form to absorb the sugar."

Drio snapped his fingers. "They're related to fix demons." The demons who fed off addictions.

I studied the drawing. The hoc looked like a hairless cat, but with a tiger head. "How big is it? Kitten or giant feral predator?"

"Cougar-sized," Rohan said.

Drio tipped back in his chair. "How do we find a demon giving himself a sugar scrub before his night out?"

"Buying all that sugar, rubbing itself down, it's a lot of hassle." I drummed my fingers on the table. "Candyman used the wretas to distribute Sweet Tooth. Their home was in East Vancouver along the water. The drop was in Crab Park, also along the water on the Downtown East Side, and the first address we had for him?"

"East Van. Along the water?" Drio said.

"The most east, and not that far away from the water," I said.

"What's your point?"

"Guess what else is in that general area?" I took a sip of water. "The sugar refinery." I pushed Ro's bottle at him so he'd hydrate.

He nodded his thanks and drank some. "We may not be able to question the hoc while it's in its natural form."

"I could flash in, slap it with a tracking device, and get out," Drio said. "We follow it, question it wherever we want. No problem."

"Slight problem," Rohan said. "Hocs have strong pair bondings and don't tend to go anywhere alone. We'll all go in case one of them needs distracting. Better to have us and not need us."

"Slight other problem," I said. "The refinery is at the port and we need clearance. Everything down there is fenced off with manned booths at every entrance."

Drio fired off a text. "Sending in an ID request. The Brotherhood won't be able to pull anything together for tonight, though."

"Even better," Rohan said. "Gives us time to match employee uniforms, get a layout, and figure out the most likely place to find the hoc."

"We'll do that tomorrow. Tonight we're going out. Double date. I'll tell Leo." I cut off the men's protests. "No. People need balance in their lives. There is always going to be another demon, something else we need to deal with. We can't go to the sugar refinery until tomorrow and I don't have it in me to deal with the purple magic tonight. I need fun downtime to regroup. *We* need this. Shit like this matters."

I didn't understand why Drio looked so uncomfortable with the idea. "Didn't you tell me we needed balance? Come on. I will brook no dissent. We're going to have fun and then we'll save the world tomorrow."

I gave them the details. I'd been waiting for a chance to put my plans for Rohan into motion, but including a double date made the night even better.

A couple hours later, I wheeled a small suitcase into the foyer and whistled. Rohan stood there in a skinny black suit with white piping along the edges of the lapels, worn over a crisp white shirt, with his sockless feet stuffed into a pair of shiny black shoes. He sported a silver thumb ring and a leather cuff, his hair gelled spiky, and his eyeliner making his gold eyes pop.

He took in the scarlet fall of my silk dress, held up by a thin ribbon around my neck, and motioned for me to turn around.

I closed my eyes, the warmth of his body behind me palpable.

He ran his hand up the inside of my thigh under the fabric, his calloused fingers reverent, but with a bite of sandpaper. The fabric rustled, slipping against my bare ass.

Rohan bit the hollow between my collarbone and neck. "You expect me to sit through dinner knowing you're naked under this?" His finger dipped inside me, his lips ghosting my skin. "Knowing how wet you are?"

I dragged in a ragged breath.

The shrill beep of his phone receiving a text was the spell breaker I needed to step away from him. I had plans for a long night but I'd been about ten seconds away from taking what I wanted here and now and fast.

Really needed to practice the virtues of delayed gratification.

"Drio's leaving Leo's place now." His gaze licked over me and he took a step back, noticing the suitcase for the first time. "Going somewhere?"

"We're staying at a hotel tonight."

The smile he turned on me was pure wolf. "You're right. A night off is exactly what we need."

He insisted on driving, and though I'd never admit it, riding in the Shelby was a rush. The leather seats molded to my ass like they were custom made, the sound system was top-notch, and the car didn't so much drive as prowl. I rolled down the window, letting the sweet summer breeze tamp down my fevered need to a manageable simmer.

First stop was dinner at a downtown fancy steakhouse. Suited men drank tinkling highballs in a dozen shades of amber and women in cocktail dresses enjoyed good wines in a room lined with wood paneling and dangling chandeliers. The muted hum of conversation filled the restaurant over the live pianist playing jazz standards and the smell of grilled meat had me salivating in seconds flat.

We joined our friends at a private booth with leather upholstery and a high curved wooden back. Leo was beautiful in a floral vintage dress with a poufy skirt, her red hair pulled back in a bun and secured with a large flower barrette. A stunning shawl in fiery reds and purples was draped over the back of the booth. This must have been the gift that Drio had brought for her from Italy. I couldn't fault his taste.

Drio's slim black suit was only a couple of shades lighter than the scowl on his face. He sat stiffly in his seat across from Leo, greeting us only with nods.

"Girls' side of the table? Yay!" I slid in beside my bestie, giving her a hug. "What's his deal?" I whispered.

"No clue. If he wasn't so pretty, I'd never take him home again."

I opened my menu. "Good to know you're a sure thing."

"Says the chick not wearing underwear."

Drio may have been having some kind of hissy fit not wanting to sit beside Leo, but I'd seen women on the Atkins diet gaze at chocolate cake with less hunger than him drinking her in. I caught my reflection in the mirror behind the bar. Oh. Shut up, Katz.

Leo was my best friend; Rohan was Drio's. The talk should have flowed fast and furious.

Dead. Silence.

We all studied our menus way too carefully. It wasn't until I'd surreptitiously checked Ro out for the fifth time, Drio had wrenched his eyes from his date yet again, and Leo had given her third quiet sigh, nibbling her bottom lip, that I clued in to how our collective sexual tension could power the next Mars mission but was doing sweet fuck-all for scintillating conversation.

"Would you care for something to drink?" our waiter asked.

"Wine," we all chorused.

The waiter smiled. "That type of day?" He recommended a Malbec. "I'll bring it for you right away."

"That was pathetic." I wiped away tears of laughter and rubbed my finger. "My mascara is smudging."

"Waterproof. I keep telling you. It's an amazing cosmetic technology." Leo stood up and smoothed her skirt down. "Come on, we'll go fix it."

Drio shot her a wry look. "That's code for they want to talk about us in private."

Leo planted her hands on her hips and arched an eyebrow saucily. "Anything we could possibly say about you, Ricci, could be said before we left this table. There's just not that much there," she said.

Drio put his hand to his heart and fell back, mock wounded, a smile so sweet on his face, that I checked for cameras to see if I was being pranked.

Rohan wore the same gobsmacked expression that my face had frozen in. Drio shot me the finger, but when he turned to Ro, he shifted in his seat, his eyes dropping to his lap.

"Oh. No, man." Ro clapped him on the shoulder, without a word. Some unspoken message passed between them, some permission granted, then Drio nodded and relaxed, smiling at Leo again.

Leo looked as lost in this little exchange as I was, though she also preened under his attention.

"Snap out of it," I hissed as we scootched sideways through the tightly packed tables.

Smirking, Leo skipped her way into the restroom.

"How serious is this?" I said.

Leo wagged a finger at me. "Uh-uh. I can see the hearts and flowers dancing around your head. Not all of us are you and Le Mitra. Or want to be. Boy toy. That's it."

"That's fine." Better than fine, because Leo had a small chance in hell of keeping her demon secret if the two of them stayed casual.

She uncapped her lipstick. "I don't think I'll sleep with him tonight."

I blotted my smudged mascara with a paper towel. "I can see that. Those piercing green eyes, that olive skin against his blond hair, that hard body. Meh."

Leo paused to glare at me in the mirror. I grinned. "I didn't say I didn't like him or want him," she said. "I'm not dead. I said I wasn't going to sleep with him tonight. You made Rohan work for it." She gasped theatrically, covering her mouth with her hand, her eyes wide. "Oops. Sorry. Wrong friend." She smirked. "You rolled over like a cat in heat."

I threatened her with my mascara wand. "Piss me off and your friend base goes into negative numbers."

"I have plenty of friends. Drio is my friend."

"Drio may be many things, kitten, but friend?" I screwed up my face.

"Harry."

"Harry is your boss and mentor. Different dynamic. I'm it." I puckered up. "Give me some sugar."

She twisted her lipstick into the tube, popped the cap on, and dropped it into her small clutch. "Drio has a masochistic streak. I make him work for it, things go very nicely for me."

"Gross."

She snapped her fingers. "Kane is my friend. Kane who tells me all sorts of TMI things."

"You're a pervy voyeur and you're not allowed to gossip about me."

"*Pfft.* Whatever. You're a raging exhibitionist."

"True." I dropped my mascara back in my clutch, then checked the stalls to make sure we were alone. "Get this. I'm a witch, not Rasha."

"Reaaaaallly? That ought to liven things up. Can you give me bigger boobs?"

I grimaced, remembering the frog fiasco. "No. There's more. I met Lilith."

"You met Sarah McLachlan?"

"Why would I have met Sarah McLachlan?" I scrunched up my hair, plumping my curls.

"You met Lilith. Lilith Fair? Sarah founded it and she lives here in Vancouver."

"Garden of Eden Lilith."

Leo tugged up her sweetheart neckline. "Oh."

"Meeting the person out of the Old Testament is less exciting?"

"Those SPCA videos Sarah does?" She sighed and patted her heart.

I shook my head and headed for the door. "Why do I bother?"

"You gonna give me more details later?"

"D'uh." And with a wink, I left the bathroom.

Ro and Drio were almost finished their first glasses of wine. Drio had switched seats to be across the table from Rohan.

"What'd we miss?" asked Leo brightly.

"Me." Drio stretched his arm out along the top of the booth.

Leo dropped into Rohan's lap, curling a finger into his hair. "Not so much."

Rohan wrapped his arms around her, mugging at me.

"Bella." Drio's purr rumbled through *me*, so Leo, as its intended target, was probably creaming herself.

On my boyfriend. Ew.

I jerked a thumb at her. "Off."

Then I sort of got distracted by Drio shrugging out of his jacket, revealing a tight black shirt that was kind of shiny and somewhat see-through, but not in a cheesy way. I swallowed, mesmerized by his intensity as he tipped his head to watch Leo from under his fringe of lashes, before flicking his hair out of his eyes with strong fingers.

"Ahem." Rohan tugged me down beside him.

I hadn't even noticed Leo vacate his lap and plant herself at Drio's side. He tilted his head down to murmur something to her. Leo blushed, caught herself, and said something back to make him laugh.

"You really want to remind me he's your type?" Ro said.

"You're my only type." I patted Ro's abs absently, my eyes locked on Drio's physique.

"At least look at me when you're being patronizing, Sparky. Put some effort into selling the lie."

"His shirt is just so shiny." I tilted my head, all the better to see the light catch the translucent fabric, and the teasing glimpse of olive skin stretched taut over sculpted abs.

Ro clapped a hand over my eyes.

"Looking is allowed," I said.

"Is it? I'll remember that." He removed his hand.

A flare of jealousy for this wholly fictitious girl spiked through me. I tore my eyes from Drio and hooked my fingers in Ro's belt loops. "Try it and I'll gut you like a fish."

His answering smile was a tad smug.

The waiter carried over a tray laden with plates.

"You ordered for us?" Leo said.

"Appetizers." Drio rearranged the wine glasses to make room for the crab cakes, beef carpaccio, seared scallops, and oysters.

"Is there anything you guys didn't order?" I said.

"We figured we needed energy." Rohan threw me an exaggerated wink.

"Less so with every passing second," Leo chirped, but she speared a scallop and held it out for Drio to eat off her fork.

I kicked her under the table because the expression on her face was pure infatuation.

"Ma che cazzo!" Drio kicked me back. "Did you just kick me?"

Leo, who'd just eaten her own scallop, began choking with laughter, then actually choking. Hurriedly she downed a glass of water.

"Don't think so," I said.

Rohan held a paper-thin piece of carpaccio out for me, his eyes twinkling. "Oh, how she lies."

I ate the beef, pleasantly surprised by the tangy, citrus reduction drizzled on it, then held up my glass of Malbec. "Eat, drink, and be merry for tomorrow we die."

Drio dropped his napkin and swore. Leo's fork clanged against the china plate. I could swear that even the restaurant dimmed, conversations petering out around us as the candles fluttered nervously.

"Lovely, Nee." Leo topped me up. "Only happy drunk girl allowed tonight."

"Sorry. The saying just popped into my head. And well, let's face it, we don't know what's going to happen tomorrow. We never know." I raised my glass in cheers. "I know it's sappy, but there's no one else I'd rather be with."

Drio was the first to clink his glass to mine.

Rohan took my hand. "We're gonna make it." I didn't know if he meant us personally or the general us versus them, but either way, I agreed.

Drio slurped an oyster. "Let me tell you about the time I had to track a lunatic troll from Oslo to Rome." Soon he'd swept the somber mood away with his witty tale. I never thought I'd hear about Drio in a fur coat disrupting a Vatican tour by climbing out of a sewer, but here we were.

"He's being charming," I whispered to Rohan. "Should I be scared?"

Ro looked relieved. "No. This is what he's really like."

Well, damn.

18

The rest of the night panned out according to expectation, with a lot of banter and laughter. Time flew by after that until it was 10PM and the real games were about to begin.

Shocker, Leonie totally took Drio home. It was a good thing she could use the excuse of wanting privacy to never come back to Demon Club, because as a half-goblin she couldn't cross the wards without help from one of us. One bounce off those invisible shields and Drio would know the truth and kill her. I didn't think that his feelings for her outweighed his intense hatred of all things demons.

Rohan dropped me off in front of the Robson Plaza Hotel, a snazzy boutique accommodation at the bottom of Robson Street, our main shopping district downtown. It was within walking distance of Stanley Park and my favorite beach, English Bay.

I retrieved the suitcase from the trunk and handed him a gift bag. "Come back in one hour."

The suite I'd reserved was perfect for my needs. I hurried to set everything up and get myself ready.

Rohan knocked on the door sixty-one minutes later.

I smoothed down my clothes about four times more than I needed to, resisting the urge to run for the bathroom and change. This was our chance to step out of being us for a night. To connect without all the other bullshit and reset things, get back to what was great about our relationship without the stress.

I opened the door, only sticking my pigtailed head out.

He held up the mask I'd gifted him with. The rest of the costume was nowhere in sight. "Whatever are you up to, Sparky?"

My heart sank at the sight of his regular clothes, but I mustered up a smile and stepped aside to let him into the short entrance hallway of our suite. "Call me Harley."

Rohan gaped at my red and blue satin short shorts with the black hip belt and T-shirt reading "Daddy's Lil' Monster." Blessings for online cosplay stores. "Harley Quinn hates Batman," he finally said.

My cheeks flamed. I toed at the ground but it didn't conveniently open to swallow me whole. "Plenty of fans ship them." I'd checked.

My boyfriend stepped back like I might infect him. "We're roleplaying fanfic? It's not canon. It's wrong. I mean really wrong. Weirder than that alternate universe with the zombie Alfred."

Save me from fanboys and screw you, buddy. I'd subsisted on Chickeny Delight to save up the cost of hotel rooms and cosplay outfits, not to mention stepped way outside my comfort zone in dressing up in the sexual foreplay miscalculation of the century. We needed this night.

I needed this night.

Except Rohan was still frowning at me. I wasn't getting this night.

"My bad." I gestured for him to head into the main part of the suite, ripping out one of my pigtails. Would it be too much to skip the glass and just stick a straw directly into the champagne bottle chilling in the stainless steel bucket over in the corner on a stand?

He did a double take at the bed's spiffy little addition of an under-the-mattress restraint system. Four nylon and Velcro cuffs, one for each arm and leg, were connected with cords under the mattress. No headboard or footboard needed. "You were going to let me tie you up?"

"Yup." I slingshot a blindfold onto the bed.

"Fuck canon." He turned the Batman mask over in his hand, then stuffed it in his pocket, and poured us each a splash of champagne. "Breaking into my home? You can't get to Wayne Enterprises that easily, Dr. Quinn."

Bruce Wayne, the guy who didn't want to reveal himself.

I accepted the glass. "I never thought anything about you was easy, Bruce." I swallowed my champagne, savoring the fizziness dissolving on my tongue, and ran a finger down his chest. While he was distracted, I whipped out the miniature wooden toy bat I'd had tucked against my back.

Rohan disarmed me in a second. He spun me, pulling me tight against him, the bat to my throat. "Nice try."

His voice vibrated up along the base of my neck, into my skull.

My nostrils flared, my empty glass bouncing onto the plush carpet. I rubbed my ass back against him. He was half-hard, his biceps tense as he kept himself in check.

"Safe word," he whispered.

Ms. Clara had discussed this with me, had patiently answered my many, many questions about what I could expect, but happily imprisoned against him like this, damned if I could remember the word I'd come up with. "Chair?"

He chuckled, then his grip on me tightened, back in character once more. "Didn't think I could get to you that quickly?"

"No," I said hoarsely. "I thought I had more of a chance against you."

"This game was decided the moment you invaded my space." He forced me to the bed, cuffing my wrists above my head. "Too tight?"

I tugged on them. "No."

I swung my legs in a scissor kick, catching him around the waist and locking him tight. "I'm not that easy."

"I never thought you were." Rohan pulled the metal, bat-shaped throwing star that had come with his costume out of his pocket and sliced my shorts off me. I was so surprised I dropped my legs, allowing him to catch my feet and cuff me, spread-eagle.

My heart pounded.

Rohan stood at the foot of the bed, his hooded gaze on me.

The straps were pretty comfortable. And strong. No matter how much I jerked and strained against them, I couldn't get free. Believe me, I tried. Laying here, naked from the waist down was a vulnerability I hadn't counted on.

"Any time you need to, say it." That was my boyfriend, not Bruce.

"Got me where you want me?" I asked in a throaty murmur.

"Not even close." Ro wielded that throwing star like a pro. Okay, more professional chef than ninja, but he got the job done. The rest of my clothing fell off me in tattered shreds, leaving me in only the hip belt. Remarkably, there wasn't a mark on me. He picked up the blindfold that had fallen off the bed, twirling it around his finger.

I jerked my chin up. "You can strip me but I won't break, Wayne."

He slid the blindfold over my head. "I don't want you broken, Harley. I want you desperate."

I took a deep breath, my ribcage tight.

My lack of vision made everything more intense: Rohan's cologne, the air conditioning humming over my skin, the scrape of the belt along the base of my spine.

Rohan ran a finger down the side of my neck and along my collarbone. I suppressed a gasp at the contact. He whipped the belt off me, using it to stroke me everywhere: toes, hands, stomach, legs, breasts, mapping my body.

Goosebumps trailed in its wake.

The leather creaked and then the buckle clattered against something. "Next time, Harley, bring leather, not this cheap shit that falls apart."

"You seem pretty sure there's gonna be a next time."

He gave a dark laugh that shivered through me. "I'm fairly confident."

My nipples hardened.

I canted my hips. His hand splayed over my stomach, pinning me in place. A bite where his hand had been, then nothing. The sting of his teeth faded quickly. I strained to hear a footfall, to pinpoint his location, but the carpet was too thick and Rohan too practiced at moving silently.

The minutes ticked by. I rubbed my ass against the mattress, seeking relief and finding none.

My stupid boyfriend crunched ice instead of getting me off.

"Desperate yet?" His cold tongue swiped a line from between my breasts to my pubic bone.

Ooh. I arched off the bed. "You'll have to work harder than that."

"Can't ever be easy with you, can it?"

"Wouldn't want you losing inter-eeest." My voice jumped two octaves because he'd rubbed an ice cube against my clit.

"Not a problem." The ice against my clit disappeared. "More? Use your words."

"I'm not begging for anything." Didn't need to. My writhing worked just fine as consent.

"Your first strategy doesn't have to be war." He ran the cube over Cuntessa in slow, even strokes. "Haven't you heard you can catch more flies with honey?"

Cuntessa pulsed with a vengeance. The ice was rapidly melting, running down and out along the crack of my ass. "But you don't want honey. Maybe you did at one time, but now? It's too sweet for your tastes."

My thighs were soaking and I had no idea how much of that was the ice. I dug my heels into the pillowy mattress top, muscles clenching.

The ice melted and his strokes stopped, leaving me on the brink. I arched my back, clamping my mouth shut so I wouldn't whimper for more. My pulse thudded in my ears.

He drizzled sticky grape-juice-smelling liquid over my tits. The champagne. "You think you know what I want?"

I barely had time to register the fizzy booze sticking to my skin before the cool liquid was replaced by the heat of his mouth, licking and suckling in exquisite torture. He squeezed and pinched my breast, thrusting the fingers of his other hand between my lips.

Like he didn't want me to answer.

I sucked on them greedily until he withdrew them, lavishing hot, messy kisses along my body.

The sting of his teeth nipping my skin, his rock-hard cock pressed against me through his pants, his lips worshipping me, Rohan was branding me and it still wasn't enough.

My fingers flexed, wanting Ro but closing on thin air.

The warmth of his body disappeared. A thud and rummaging. "Trying to discover my secrets by going through my purse?" I said.

"No. Looking for… ah." The squirting sound of lube and skin moving on skin.

"Are you jerking off?" I bucked against the cuffs. "Without me?"

"Definitely not without you. I'm staring at every inch of you spread open for me."

I rocked my hips and moaned.

"Are you picturing me?" he growled. "Shirt open, one hand running over my abs." His slaps grew louder, faster, his breath quickening, his harsh exhales matched by my own. "I'm so hard for you. I can see how wet you are and all I can think about is plunging into you."

"Scared you won't measure up if you actually try it?" My voice wasn't so much sultry as frantic with sexual anguish, but he sounded too far gone himself too notice.

He laughed. "I'm not scared of anything you can dish out, Harley."

I tugged the restraints. I didn't want to be anybody else. Not with Rohan. Not now. "Chair." I was practically thrashing against the bonds, my heart trying to punch its way out of my ribcage. "*Chair*."

"Hey." He tore the blindfold off.

I blinked, my eyes adjusting expecting a harsh brightness, but he'd turned the lamps off in the room. Any light spilling in from outside was dim enough not to hurt, but having my sight again, being rooted in a physical space instead of the sensual one I'd floated in was disorienting.

He stroked my hair back from my face. "Sweetheart, it's okay."

"Is it?" I arched toward him. "I don't want to be Harley. I want to be me."

His face was inches from mine, his gold eyes wild and fiery. "And who am I in this?" His hands curled around my biceps.

A wild laugh tore out of me. "You think I don't know it's you? Always you? Rohan. Liam. Mitra. My Ro. My Snowflake."

He ripped my cuffs off me, plundering my mouth. Under the coolness from the ice, was the taste of licorice thanks to the candy-coated fennel seeds he always popped.

Rohan plunged his cock into me in a single ferocious stroke. "My beautiful girl."

He pulled out an inch, pushing forward again slow and filthy until the exquisite fullness of him so deep inside me made me tremble. "Fuck. Being inside you like this?" His expression was full of dizzy wonder. He cupped the back of my head, nipping my bottom lip.

"Oh God, Ro. Please." I wrapped my legs around his waist, scrabbling at his shoulders. I sounded unhinged and didn't care so long as he kept going. I pled incoherently for more, sweat trickling between my breasts and down the backs of my knees.

He fucked me into the mattress, riding me in short, hard pounds, my shredded costume floating through the air with each bounce, like streamers at some kind of sex parade. With each thrust, he danced in and out of the slanted shadows: his muscles contracting, his eyes slits of gold, and his hands a dark caress of my slick, hot skin from my shoulders to my waist and back again.

I raked my nails down his back, thrilling at his hiss. Blood roared in my veins and static buzzed my brain. We were tangled up, taking up residence under each other's skin.

His hands fisted in my curls, and growling low, he bit the hollow of my neck. "You taste like music, you know that?"

I whimpered, my body caving into his touch.

He grazed his teeth along my neck. "This tastes slow and dreamy like one of Chopin's piano concertos. But here?" He palmed my breasts, sucking my nipples into his mouth. "Mmm. A fat R&B groove."

My breath came in greedy gulps. "Yeah?" I ran a hand down my side. "What about here?"

Ro held my hands over my head, and ran his lips along my skin, his thrusts slow rolls. "Bouncy Top 40. The infectious kind that you find yourself humming all day."

I wrapped my legs around him, drawing him in even tighter. I'd spent so long convincing myself I didn't want this connection, this attachment, and I'd been right. Wanting meant craving something that could be taken away without catastrophe, like candy or alcohol, something you liked, something that maybe even had its hooks in you, but that ultimately, you could survive without.

I could not survive without this.

"I think we're both music," I said. "We're like two different parts of the same piece: separately we're cool and interesting, but together we're transformative."

"God, Nava." His eyes blazed molten gold. "I meant it. You've slain me. I–" Rohan shuddered and came, his face twisting in ecstasy and his fingers clutching mine.

My orgasm slammed me sharp and hard and bright, sparks erupting off my skin to singe the blanket.

Rohan watched me with those expressive fucking eyes of his and chasing hard on the heels of my dreamy flying state, came the sensation that I was unbound. Unmoored. My entire being undone for him.

I buried my face in his neck, light-headed and shaking, like a butterfly had been trapped in my chest, its wings madly fluttering, except it had just revealed that it was really a pterodactyl, its teeth bared.

Rohan gathered me into his arms, wrapping himself around me, and pulling the blankets half over us while he stroked my hair, whispering how incredible I was. My breathing slowed. Every heartbeat drove me closer to him.

Rohan kissed my eyelids. "How are you?"

Threadbare, I could only nod, unable to speak in the wake of these emotions breaking wide-open inside me.

He didn't let go of me and I was grateful, letting myself succumb to his embrace. "It's intense," he said.

Understatement. My eyes hadn't fully slid back into focus yet and my soul ached. Role-playing was supposed to be an escape from all these feelings, not something that made me feel them even more. Not something that forced me to tell the truth to myself when I wanted to pretend.

I tried to get up, but my arms wouldn't support me.

Rohan kissed me, slow and sweet. "Stay there. Let me take care of you." He wiped me down with a warm washcloth. "Are you dehydrated? Do you want water?"

"Juice box. In my purse." I motioned with a shaky hand.

"Someone came prepared." He pulled the straw free with a crinkle of plastic and punctured the top.

"Ms. Clara was very thorough about what I could expect." I sucked about half the juice back in one go.

Rohan winced, blushing. He sat naked and cross-legged on the bed and massaged my leg. "You told Ms. Clara?"

"Are you embarrassed? That's adorable. Of course I told Ms. Clara. I needed to talk to someone about this."

"It was good? For your first time?"

"It was perfect." I smiled. "If I'd known I was going to get a spa treatment after, I might have signed on for this faster."

"Think we can do that again sometime?" He said it with a studied casualness, pressing his thumb into the arch of my foot.

I flexed my toes against his hand. "Next time you're paying for the outfit."

Ro grinned down at me. "Do I get to pick the toys, too?"

"We'll see. I'll have to run your suggestions past my sex mentor. See if she thinks it's a good fit."

The full-body massage he gave me left me boneless. When he finished, he kissed the precise spot at the corner of my mouth to send shivers through my body. "Do you want a shower?" he said.

"If you'll help me. Buddy system and conserving water and all."

"We gotta do our part for the environment."

"That we do." And we did, though there was no more sexytimes. Both of us were too exhausted and shower sex sucked. Rohan lathered me up, letting me close my eyes as he massaged my scalp. Kissing me pressed against the tiles, his fingers laced with mine until the hot spray finished, and believe me, it took a long time in a hotel to make the water turn cold. The walls ran with rivulets of water, the bathroom now a steam room, but all that, including my pruney fingers, was worth it.

I dried off, wrapping a towel around my head and slipping into underwear and one of Ro's T-shirts. I felt light as air and so very, very happy. Giddy even. I bounced on the bed. "Can I have room service?"

Rohan towel dried his hair. "Baby, you can have whatever you want."

I kept bouncing. This mattress was pretty great. "Oh yeah? Will you get me a pony?"

"And rent a stable to keep it in. You gotta be practical when it comes to equine care, Sparky."

I laughed. I didn't care about Ro's money, but after the past few days, silly teasing was a welcome relief. "Will you get me gadozens of fancy purses?"

"Gadozens?"

"A gazillion dozens." *Bounce. Bounce.*

"A gadozen gadozens." He pitched the damp towel into the bathroom and grabbed the boxers I'd brought for him.

"Will you take me to Paris for dessert?" Rohan stilled. I hadn't meant to say that, especially since I only knew about this part of his romantic history because I'd been eavesdropping. Except, I guess I had meant to say it, to let Rohan know that I knew about the lengths he went to for Lily. I didn't like that about myself. I didn't want to be the girlfriend threatened by his past.

"Cheeseburgers," I said gaily, to cover the impending awkward silence. I hopped off the bed, picked up the receiver, and hit the room service button. I ordered for both of us, then stared at the phone, wondering who else I could call so I wouldn't have to deal with the loaded tension.

He wrapped his arms around me. "Do you want dessert in Paris, Sparky? You can have it."

"I don't. Not really." I turned in his embrace and raked his damp strands of hair out of his eyes.

"I gave Lily that, but I never fully gave her myself. Not like I do with you."

"It's fine, honestly. I mean, Cole never had me like this, either." I snapped my lips together against that final truth that had just slipped out.

"Phrasing," Ro snickered.

I rolled my eyes, but I was secretly thankful to put things on a more lighthearted track.

Half an hour later, we were eating cheeseburgers in our underwear and T-shirts, watching an old Fugue State Five documentary that Ro had bitched about putting on. The mattress dipped under his weight as he returned to the bed and tossed me one of the two tiny bottles of Scotch he'd liberated from the mini bar.

"You're one classy motherfucker, Mitra."

"Right? L'chaim."

We lifted our bottles in unison and clinked them. I shot back a hefty swallow, clenching my jaw against the burn.

"Cheeseburgers after bondage are the best." I couldn't shovel the food in fast enough.

He licked ketchup off the corner of my lip. "Agreed." He grimaced, watching his younger self talk at length about the poetry of his lyrics. "Please shut this off. It's painful."

"Your lyrics are beautiful."

"My lyrics are fine, but I was hardly Leonard Cohen. Fuck, I was pretentious." He polished off his cheeseburger and lay on his side, propped on his elbow, inching his hand up my thigh.

I snorted my laughter, pointing at the screen. "Oh my God! They did make you guys take dance lessons!"

He sighed and flopped back against the bed in resignation, pulling a pillow over his face to hide his embarrassment and deter further questions until the interview finished or I changed the channel. And it would have been the perfect night, cheeseburgers, and lyrics, and Rohan and I wrapped up in a warm bed with good jokes and music, except that's when the Man in Black broke in.

19

A balaclava obscured his features and black leather gloves covered his hands, but this guy had to be Rasha. He had the build and that familiar coiled tension. His presence wasn't random either, because he went straight for Rohan as the greater threat. Ro held his own, the two of them grappling for a hold on the other with a flurry of punches and kicks.

Magic would only escalate the situation and I wasn't about to have him unleash some unknown power. I grabbed the wooden toy bat.

Rohan slammed a fist into the attacker's body. He grunted, his entire frame curling around Ro's punch but recovered pretty damn quickly, slamming both hands to either side of Ro's head. Rohan's blades flickered out for a second, snapping back inside him under the thin coat of ice that formed over his skin.

I swung the bat at the back of the attacker's head but the weapon froze and splintered before contact. The Man in Black turned on me with a menacing smile. Still deep-freezing a struggling Rohan, he grabbed my arm, wrenching it up my back.

Ice filled my veins. Literally. My heart stopped and my blood crystalized into miniscule sharp-edged snowflakes. The world crackled black.

He dropped me on the floor and cracked Rohan's skull into the wall. Once. Twice. Frost slithered down the wall. "One warning. Back. Off."

He stepped over me and left.

I curled in a ball, dragging in a deep breath. Big mistake. I shook with a wracking cough, air hitting my half-frozen, tortured lungs.

Blood dripped out of Rohan's ears as he knelt over me to scoop me into his arms, the drops falling in slow motion. Each plump droplet hit the carpet with a rumbled thud before fracturing, staining the fibers.

He ran the water in the jacuzzi in the bathroom, only letting go of me long enough to strip us of our clothes, before lowering me into the tub braced against his back.

"Cold." My words came out a garbled mumble. My teeth wouldn't stop chattering.

"Here." He shifted for maximum skin contact, wrapping his legs around me.

There was enough hot water in the tub that feeling seeped back into my toes. I cried out, breathing through the blazing agony of having what amounted to my entire body coming off the world's worst brain freeze.

Ro's tears hit the water in pretty pink streaks. "Don't cry," I said, my chest tightening at how upset he was over my injuries. No, he wasn't crying. It was blood. His hair was matted with it. My too-tight ribcage convulsed with fear. The water was only a few degrees below boiling and if he was concussed, hot water was a bad idea.

I peeled myself off him. "Out."

"Yeah." He climbed out of the tub and collapsed on the floor.

"Ro? You okay?" Still trembling and seeking heat, I slid further into the tub until only my mouth and nose peeked out above the water. I didn't have the energy to move. Defrosting took a lot out of a girl. Now I finally understood why my Chickeny Delight always tasted so exhausted.

"Dizzy. Need a sec."

Eventually we recovered enough to throw on our evening clothes, grab our stuff, and get the hell out. Rohan had cleaned up any traces of his blood and had reached the end of his patience with me checking his pupils for a concussion.

"Hey." Ro took my purse from me. "You're shaking." He pressed a hand to my skin. "Are you still cold?"

"No." My reflection in the burnished gold elevator doors showed a rosy cheeked Nava. I stabbed the elevator button, storming inside the empty car when it opened with a ding. I curled my hands around the metal railing, trying and failing to get my fury under control. "They tracked us here tonight. Came after us, trying to scare us."

"The further we go down this road, the more the Brotherhood will be gunning for us. We won't even be able to properly watch our backs, because it might be a friend who sticks the knife in." Rohan tilted my chin up to face him. "You heard the guy. One warning. Do you want to stop? Walk away?"

"We can't. And I wouldn't. Would you?"

He shook his head.

I slid my hand in his. "Thank you."

"For what?"

"You were fighting the guy but it wasn't because you were trying to protect me."

The elevator opened into the parking garage, revealing the Shelby. Ro had snagged a spot right by the elevators.

"Slugger, you didn't need protecting." He unlocked my door and placed my bag on the floor mat.

"Still," I said. "Thank you. We need to be smart and way more stealthier from this point on."

"Plans C through Z. Be more careful. Told you." Rohan blocked me from getting into the car. He brushed my damp hair out of my eyes. "You're hooking into me, Sparky and I want to be caught for a long, long time."

The words didn't scare me this time. He wasn't saying them because he was under the influence of a demon drug or even because of the Man in Black. Our night together had shifted something between us—stripped us down and gently deposited us here—a place of cautious optimism.

I curled my toes, rolling onto the sides of my feet. "You're hooking into me, too."

Rohan glanced down at the ground, a pleased smile tugging at his lips. "Well, all right, then."

The first person we called back at the chapter house was Kane. Rohan and I had holed up in my room, leaving our Brotherhood phones downstairs. We used my burner phone and called the landline in Kane's hotel room in Osoyoos, a small town in British Columbia's interior.

"Sorry to disturb you." I put the call on speaker, the cell sitting on the mattress between Rohan and me. "But we've got a situation."

Kane yawned. "This better be an emergency. We've got a gong show on our hands between the demons and this flooding."

"Put your cell in the bathroom and turn on the shower," Rohan said.

Kane muttered about paranoia but did as he was told. "Speak freely."

I told him what had happened.

"What do you need?" He sounded wide-awake.

"What Rasha has ice magic?" Rohan said.

"Hang on. Gotta get my laptop." We heard Kane moving around and keys clacking.

"Is it secure from Brotherhood prying?" I asked.

"Don't insult me." More typing. "Hold off on telling your brother about this, babyslay."

"Why?"

"Because I'm more than mildly annoyed hearing what went down, which means Ari will go ballistic and I need his head in the game right now."

"Got it."

"Let's see what we've got." Kane hummed under his breath. "Fuck."

I leaned forward. "What?"

Kane didn't answer me.

"Kane," Rohan snapped.

"Wait," Kane snapped back. "Fuuuuck!"

I gripped Ro's hand. "Kane?"

"There's only one Rasha in the past fifty years with ice magic. Ferdinand Alves."

I needed a moment to absorb the fact that a supposedly dead man had attacked us.

Ro paced in a tight circle. "Search for all Rasha killed in the past, say, six months."

Kane came up with a list of twelve. Four of the men were the hunters that had been killed in Askuchar.

"You sure those Rasha are dead?" Kane asked.

"Yeah. Mahmud saw their bodies and I trust Mahmud." Ro pinched his nose. "Any correlation between missions? Chapter houses?"

"No and no," Kane said. "Other than the fact that they all supposedly died, there's nothing connecting them."

"Thanks, Kane," Ro said. "Be careful, man. We don't know what the Brotherhood has managed to piece together about who's working with us, but just being our friend is enough to throw you in the danger zone."

"I'm hard to kill. And no one else is getting hurt on my watch."

As soon as Kane had hung up, Rohan grabbed the burner phone. "I'm gonna call Drio. He needs to be warned."

I flopped back against my mattress, rubbing my eyes. "He'll want to come back here because it's safer for us to be together."

"It is safer."

"And if he decides to bring Leonie with him?" I stared at the print Leo had given me, wishing I could grab her and disappear into that neon cityscape.

"I'll convince him there's no point coming back here tonight. But she has to tell him."

No, that was the one thing she could never do.

Ro's conversation with Drio was short and to the point. True to his word, he assured Drio there was no reason to come back tonight. Ro didn't expect any more visits and the attacker had done what he came for. At least until we made our next move.

We had one final call to make and I insisted on making it.

Rabbi Abrams took the development in stride, even the news about my witch status.

"I always knew you were an interesting girl," he said.

I switched the phone to my other ear. "Does this change anything?"

"Should it?"

"Well, no?"

He chuckled. "Beseder. Then get some sleep." He said he'd arrange privately to beef up the security at the chapter house. A ward could be set to keep all Rasha out, but that would include us, so Muggle security solutions it was.

I chucked the phone onto my rug and rolled myself up in my blanket like a burrito. If Rohan was able to confirm that those eight hunters left on Kane's list weren't actually dead, then they had to be the ones working with Mandelbaum on whatever was going on. I edged my head out of my cocoon. "Can I see the photo you got at Ferdinand's house?"

"Sure thing." Rohan jogged downstairs, returning with the snapshot.

In his forties, Ferdinand was ruggedly good-looking, with a crew cut and the deep tan of someone who spent a lot of time outdoors. His clothes were neatly ironed. He had his arm around a woman with long blonde hair with gray streaks, wearing a tie-dyed dress in brilliant swirls of color.

"One of these things is not like the other," I said.

"Huh?"

I tapped the photo. "He looks like he's in the military and she's a Woodstock refugee."

"Love is blind."

"Is it? Really? Check out her pendant."

"A crescent moon. Witch?"

"I'd say love knew exactly who it was tapping." I yawned. "I'll see if Gelman can identify her."

"First, sleep. We need to hit up the sugar refinery in a few hours."

"The excitement never stops around here." I didn't bother leaving my blanket roll.

Rohan crashed out on my bare mattress.

I was woken up by someone shaking my shoulder. "Five more minutes, Mom," I mumbled.

"Sparky, wake up. Sarah needs to install the safety bars on your window."

I flung a pillow at Ro's head.

"Sorry." A dimpled woman who had to be close to retirement poked her head in to my room. She had a large red tool box in one hand. "I'd have let you sleep, but Uncle Isaac told me this was urgent."

I blinked through my grogginess, squinting at my clock. I couldn't see it from this angle, but my room was flooded with bright sunlight. "Yeah. Of course."

I had never been so happy to be wearing sweats and not my dress from last night.

Last night!

I stumbled out of bed, scanning every available surface for the purse I'd so cavalierly tossed somewhere and any bondage systems that may have tumbled free.

"Smooth," Ro murmured, brushing my hip. "I put it in my room."

"But it's mine."

He grinned, booped me on the nose, and left.

Sarah tested her cordless drill. "You two are adorable. New relationship?"

"Yeah." I shrugged on Ro's hoodie that was draped on my chair. "I'll get out of your way."

I followed the rumble of the coffee maker down the curved staircase, my hands jammed in the pockets of his hoodie. I rubbed my cheek on the shoulder because the fabric smelled like him.

"Navela." Rabbi Abrams beckoned at me from the front porch. I almost tripped off the last stair. The man wasn't in a suit. Just dress pants and a long-sleeved shirt. "Come see what we've done."

I threw a longing glance back down the hallway toward the kitchen and found Rohan behind me holding out my already doctored coffee. "Remind me to thank you in sexual favors," I whispered.

Rabbi Abrams showed off the new front door. He hadn't changed the hand scanners because he didn't want to alert anyone, but this door was some heavy duty shit. It had rebar running in a "T" pattern. When the door was locked, the rebar sunk deep into the frame of the house. No one was breaking in through this puppy. The back door was now the same model.

My burner phone trilled. I glanced at the text as I finished off my coffee.

Thank me in sexual favors.

I snorted my drink out, coughing. Ro patted me on the back, a pious expression on his face as he asked the rabbi questions about how the new security bars on all the windows opened from the inside.

Rabbi Abrams walked us around the house, pointing out all the hidden camera that would be recording twenty-four seven with the data on a server in-house for our eyes only.

"Does your niece own the security company?" I said.

"She's not really my niece. Daughter of my wife's best friend. But yes. She's discreet, trustworthy, and very good at her job." Rabbi Abrams lowered himself into a chair on the back deck, rubbing his knee. "Do you have your phones on you?"

We shook our heads, having left the Brotherhood-issued phones in Ro's room, and got comfortable on the wicker sofa. I leaned against my boyfriend, my legs curled into my chest.

"Update me," Rabbi Abrams said.

Rohan told him about the list. Rabbi Abrams asked for each individual name, closing his eyes. Once again, I'd have sworn he was asleep if he hadn't been fidgeting with his kippah. "Stop," he said at the seventh name. "Ilya. He trained here as an initiate many many years ago. His brother still lives here. Mischa didn't carry the Rasha gene, but they were inseparable. I can put you in touch."

"Wouldn't his brother have been told he was dead?" I asked.

The rabbi opened his eyes. "Most definitely, but Mischa was his twin. How well did you believe being told Ari was no longer Rasha?"

I pulled Ro to his feet. "We're in business. But first I have to see a witch about some demons."

Gelman was in-between chemo treatments and looking a lot better today. In fact, she was dressed and waiting around for her green light to return to her sister's house. That was the good news. The bad news was that when she glowered at me, holding the photo of Ferdinand and the woman tight enough to turn her fingers white, she was healthy enough that if she decided to blame the messenger, I was toast.

Fuck it. What was one more target on my back? "Do you know her or not?"

"This photo is a fake." She flung it back at me.

I picked it up off the ground and brushed it off. "Based on your savvy Photoshop skills?"

"Based on the fact that Tessa would never have anything to do with a Rasha. She isn't working with one and she certainly wasn't involved with one."

I picked up the photo and shrugged. "Looks pretty chummy to me."

"Then she's being coerced."

"Yeah, at a patio restaurant with a good view and a fancy-ass bottle of wine. Scary."

Gelman slammed her hand on the arm of the chair. "She hates the Brotherhood."

"You sure? Love makes people do stupid things."

"Yes, I'm sure, you insolent girl. Who do you think I got the Vashar from?"

"Whoa. Hang on," I said. "She made the Vashar? Is that not a case for her being involved in black magic?"

"That magic was gray at best."

"Tomato, tohmahto. How can you defend her when she sicced the gogota on you? Those demons may have been modified by the Brotherhood, but Tessa was the only one who could have forced them to attack us. Bad enough the demon came after me for the Vashar, it came after you, period."

Gelman crossed her arms, jutted her chin out, and looked pointedly away.

"This is your last warning. Quit upsetting her," Sienna said, entering the room.

I glared at her. She had bags under her eyes and her cartoony penguin scrubs were a glaring contrast to her listless shuffle. Even her dreads hung limply.

"Do you have an APB out for my visits?" I said.

"Yes. The nurses on this ward call me when you show up. Did you pack your toiletries?" Sienna went into the bathroom.

"I already checked," Gelman said.

"Uh-huh." Sienna returned, holding up a tooth-brush. She hipchecked me off the hospital bed to toss the toothbrush into Gelman's open suitcase.

"You're a total witch," I said.

Sienna raised her eyebrows. "And?"

Grr. I pulled up a chair. "Lure kids to your gin-gerbread house, much?"

"Nah. I have celiac. It's straight up puppies and candy out the back of vans."

"Your patients must love you."

"They do." She rubbed her temples.

"Pulling overtime again?" Dr. Gelman said.

Sienna blinked at her confused for a second, be-fore nodding. "Yeah. Rough night." She pointed at me. "I don't like you and I certainly don't trust you."

"Sienna, enough. Nava is annoying, but her inten-tions are good."

I pressed my hand to my heart and fell back in the chair. "Such praise. I'm verklempt."

Sienna picked up the photo. "Since when is that Tessa's type?"

"It's not," Gelman said. "He's Rasha."

The room went absolutely, eerily still. Sienna's lip curled and any trace of tiredness vanished. "Who is he?" she growled.

"Since you both seem to be so chummy with her, how about one of you call her and find out what the deal with this guy is?" Suddenly, I was levitated horizontally, then crashed onto the ground. Hard. On my tailbone. Bypassing the nice chair I'd been sitting in altogether.

I rubbed my butt, letting Sienna see the magic crackling over my hands. "Are you fucking kidding me?"

"You want to earn a drop of trust with any witch who isn't Esther? Give me his name."

If Sienna went after Ferdinand, I suspected it wouldn't go well for him. I shut down my magic and hauled myself back into the chair. "Ferdinand Alves. I don't know where he is but he attacked me and he has ice magic, so if you want to rip his balls off for taking advantage of your friend or whatever? Go nuts."

Sienna dropped the photo in my lap. "Bloodthirsty. There may be hope for you yet." She scanned the empty closet and closed up Gelman's suitcase. "Call me if you aren't feeling well tonight."

I didn't rate a goodbye.

"Will I be able to levitate someone like Sienna did? Or wait." I slid the photo into my pocket. "Fly?"

"Levitating, even a split-second elimination of gravity, takes years to master. So I'm going to go with no. You want to fly? Book a plane ticket." Gelman rummaged through her purse for her phone, scrolled through her contacts, and called Tessa. She left a message saying it was urgent. "We'll be lucky if she gets this any time soon. This week was solstice. She's probably at the Santa Barbara celebration."

"There are witchy vacation destinations?"

"There are places of interest for our community, but Tessa lives in Los Angeles. It's not far."

"Is Tessa powerful enough to wield black magic?" I said.

"Possibly, but she wouldn't do it for the Brotherhood. Tessa's a very talented witch who fervently believes that organization is to blame for our community losing strength."

"How so?"

"What do you know of the Laws of Thermodynamics?" she asked.

"Nothing."

She muttered a few choice words about the dumbing down of humanity. "First Law. Energy can't be created or destroyed. Same with magic. Think of all magic as a cup of rice. The number of grains are finite. They can be divided into piles but to do so you must take from one pile and give to another. No adding in new grains."

My stomach growled. "Hold that thought. I'm just gonna run to the vending machine." I'd forgotten to restock my purse stash of snacks in all the excitement of the past couple days.

Gelman rolled her eyes, reached into her bag and tossed me a granola bar.

"Aw, thanks, Mom." It even had chunks of dark chocolate in it. Sweet!

"Feel free to chew before swallowing."

"I'm channeling my inner anaconda. So what you're saying is the more Rasha, the smaller the witches' pile?"

"Yes." She unwrapped her own granola bar, eating it with pointed slowness. "Tessa figured she could reverse the problem. Magically castrate the Brotherhood and all would be replenished."

"Hence the Vashar."

Gelman smiled.

I gasped. "You cold-hearted snake." I tipped my head in acknowledgement. "You stole the amulet from her so she couldn't use it and then handed it over to the Brotherhood. Why would you do that? If not having Rasha means witches get stronger, don't you want the same end goal?"

"Take away the hunters, do you take away the demons?"

"No."

"Precisely. So we stop future Rasha from being made and in, what, thirty years? Fifty? Demons run wild over the earth. We witches are not trained to handle it anymore, and most in my community have other concerns. We need hunters. Also." She waved a hand dismissively. "The amulet was a crude solution. Stopping Rasha one at a time would be futile."

I made puppy dog eyes at her purse but no more treats were forthcoming. "Is it less magic or weaker magic as well?"

"I suspect both. Historical records report witches' magic had once been strong, come easily, and incurred less of a personal cost. That's changed." She cleared her throat. "We seem to succumb to disease faster these days."

I closed my eyes briefly. Was it her magic, not her smoking that had caused the cancer? On the surface, magic seemed so cool. It was necessary; I just wasn't sure it was worth it. And from the wistful expression on Gelman's face, I couldn't tell if she did either.

20

Armed with Tessa's full name and place of residence, I went to an internet café and Googled
the shit out of her. What I found floored me.

I leadfooted it back to Demon Club, parking the
car practically sideways in my haste to get inside.

Rohan and Drio were clipping their Brotherhood-
crafted employee passes on beige overalls. A set of
work boots and a hard hat sat on the table for each
of us.

I waved the record I'd found and printed at the
café, mouthing the word "Phones?"

"All clear." Ro tossed me my overalls.

"They're married. Ferdinand and Tessa. I don't
think her friends knew about this." I stripped off my
sweats to step into my uniform. Changing backstage
or in coed dressing rooms all those years for dance
meant I didn't give a crap about stripping down to
my underwear in front of people.

Rohan smacked Drio across the top of his head
when he stared at my boobs more than listening to
me.

Drio shrugged. "Leo's are better."

I plumped up my girls. "You wish. Pay attention. Even if Ferdinand charmed Tessa into marriage, convincing her to use her talents to bind demons, why would she go along with it if she hates the Brotherhood?"

"Table it." Ro zipped up my overalls and I smirked at him. "We gotta get to the docks." Ro left the room but before I could stop him, Drio stepped in front of me.

"Wanting a peek for the road?" I said. "Smart to wait for Ro to leave, but still not happening."

He scowled at me, rubbed his neck, and then scowled again. "I want to do something nice for Leo. Take her out. The two of us." He jabbed my shoulder. "Why aren't you making one of those little comments you think are so funny? You don't think I'm good enough for her?"

"This isn't just hooking up. You want a serious relationship with her?"

"Forget it."

"No." I grabbed his arm. "You just caught me off-guard." To say the least. I wasn't going to out Leo and I wasn't going to cast aspersions on their relationship, but I was going to have a very serious talk with my bestie very, very soon. "Take her to a Whitecaps game. Our soccer team," I clarified.

His face lit up. "She likes football?"

"European football, she's nuts about. North American football, not so much."

"Who would be?" he said.

"That's cute. Your confusion does double duty as Italian condescension."

Rohan popped his head back in. "You two planning on coming?"

"Grazie." Drio gave me another chin chuck and bounded out of the room.

From the road, the sugar refinery was confined to a series of connected, six-story brick warehouses with arched windows that were over a hundred years old, but once we got through port security with our passes and identification very thoroughly checked and onto the site itself, we saw how large the property actually was.

Fellow workers in white or beige overalls, all with hard hats and work boots milled about, going between the different buildings that facilitated the various aspects of the sugar refining process.

After careful study of the map, we'd pinpointed the most probable area for Candyman to show himself. He wouldn't be in any of the packaging centers, nor did the buildings for storing or melting sugar seem likely.

"This way." Drio led us to our destination along the waterfront like he'd been here a million times before. There were so many employees that no one glanced twice at us, plus if we'd cleared port security, we'd obviously been vetted. We kept our stride purposeful and not hurried, despite the fact the brilliant gleam of pink and gold sky was already shot through with inky purple, the sun starting its descent, and Candyman needing to feed for his next twenty-four hour cycle.

The shed where they stored the raw sugar looked like it had been built for a giant. The huge bay doors were open, revealing massive piles of sugar the color of wet sand. I could easily picture some baby cyclops sitting in here building sandcastles, spinning turrets stretching up to the slanted ceiling.

A group of workers were busy using the crane to transport the raw grains. We bypassed them and stepped inside the shed, only to be immediately hit with the smell of molasses that was so pungent, I tasted it at the back of my throat. The air was so thick with sugar that even this short exposure left my skin skim-coated in it.

Steel beams ran the length of the ceiling, illuminated in pools of light. There were plenty of shadows for the hoc demon to portal in up there and never be seen.

First rule of monster hunting? Always look up.

We climbed the metal staircase to the catwalk, talking quietly, occasionally pointing at the sugar like we had some logistical problem to solve, scanning for any hint of movement.

"There." Rohan tilted his chin the tiniest bit to indicate the shadowy creature sitting at the juncture of two beams overhead.

The hoc scrubbed at its mottled gray skin with its front paws, a long pink tongue lolling out between two very sharp fangs. Hairless cats were fugly. Demon hairless cats that were the size of a cougar with gremlin ears and wrinkles I could count like tree rings were profoundly disturbing.

"Where's the mate?" I asked. "Is this Candyman or the other one?"

"Doesn't matter," Drio said. "We tag this one, we follow it back to the other one. Va bene."

I leaned over the catwalk. "Clear."

Drio flash stepped the length of the catwalk. Our only sign that he'd jumped onto the railing and pulled himself up onto the beam with the hoc was when the demon swatted his ear with a heavy paw. Drio had tagged the hoc with a subdermal tracker.

A sharp whistle sounded from down below. Drio stood at the bottom of the stairs, throwing a thumbs up.

Ro and I kept our attention on the sugar, bodies relaxed as we clomped down the stairs, pretending we couldn't feel the weight of the demon's tawny-eyed stare on our backs.

As soon as we hit the street, I pulled off my hard hat, scratching the top of my head in relief. According to the tracker, the hoc was still in the sugar shack, completing its sugar synthesis process, so we waited in my car.

Drio sprawled in the back seat, fidgeting and tapping his feet. Every few seconds he let out an annoyed huff.

"Quit it before I fry you," I said.

Another huff. "Your witch friend going to train you to fully use your magic?" he said.

"I hope so, but I'm not sure when that's going to happen." I twisted around and ruffled his hair. "Worried about me?"

He pushed my hand off his head and sank back against the seat. "Leonie is worried. Call her."

I hid my smile because that wasn't actually a denial on his part.

"You're growing on him," Ro said, his eyes trained on the tracking screen in his hand.

Drio kicked the back of his seat.

Ro shot him the finger, then held up the tracker. "Brace yourself, kids. It's recalibrating."

The screen buffered for a second and redrew the map. We hightailed it to the next location. The hoc had set up shop in an empty storefront a few blocks away, its windows papered over, and a faded To Let sign on the outside wall.

We parked in the alley around back, next to a stack of pallets, and exchanged our cloth employee overalls for brand new chemical protective suits and facemasks in case the oshk showed up, wriggling into them as best we could in the car.

Ro picked the lock on the back door and I stepped through, magic on, ready to short-circuit any alarm panel. Good thing there wasn't one, because in light of what I found in this back room, disarming any system went clear out of my head.

One of the matryoshka, this one with a blood-encrusted female human torso, was bound to a metal folding chair with thick iron chains. The fat iron vise gripping her chest was overkill.

Oozing sores dotted the raw red skin along the top of the chains and her tiny head was missing a chunk, like it had been bitten off. The demon had lost all blobbiness, her body more a teardrop than a water balloon. Ribs protruded from her human torso and she'd shrunk to about a third of her size, though slumped over unconscious as she was, her exact height was hard to determine.

Clear plastic tubing was attached to her nipples with metal clamps. The other ends of the tube fastened on to a still, like the one we'd found at Candyman's previous residence. That still was some kind of fucked-up mad science, with a humming box dispensing corn starch into the glass beaker collecting the oshk's dripped secretions.

The person-sized cartoon cake doughnut painted on the wall from the previous tenant, smiling merrily at us with the words "Add some YUM to your day!" floating in the clouds around it, really added that je ne sais quoi to the tableau.

With a mechanical rumble, the vise clamped down, squeezing the oshk. Bloody liquid glugged out of her nipples and into the plastic tubing. The oshk was being milked, emitting a hot gush of cotton candy-scented stank with each spasm.

I gagged, covering my own boobs in sympathy. Rohan put his hand on my shoulder to steady me.

Wind whispered against my face. Drio was gone.

Whistling in the front of the store cut off with a strangled shriek. Drio dragged Candyman through the doorway, into the back room. The hoc flickered between his human glamor of unremarkable brown-haired, white guy and his wrinkly hairless cat form. He fought hard, but Drio had skewered him through the shoulder on the end of a short iron spear. With the iron coursing through his system, the hoc was unable to portal.

The hoc finally managed to lock into his demon form, sinking his fangs into Drio's arm. Trying, anyway. His teeth snapped together with a sharp click, closing on thin air.

I backed up against the wall, one eye on the back door and one on the exit to the front office. Chances were if the mate showed up, she'd portal in, but I didn't want to be taken off guard because she used a door.

"Here kitty, kitty." Drio crooked a finger at him.

The hoc leaped for Drio. Another miss. He bellowed a roar and pounced on me, knocking me to the ground with all four paws, but immediately bounced off with a yelp when he got the electric shock of his life.

Snarling, the cat swung his head at Snowflake.

"Where's your mate?" Rohan casually flicked out all his blades.

The hoc growled and charged him, knocking Ro off his feet. My idiot boyfriend was grinning as he wrestled with the demon cat. The hoc snapped his fangs at him, barely missing Ro's nose.

Ro sliced the demon's belly open. Liquid gooshed over his gloved hand and when Ro jerked away, it glistened, stretching like taffy.

Candyman was coated in a fine sheen of sweat, his skin streaked with black from the iron now poisoning his system thanks to both Ro's blades and the spear. Leaping away from Rohan, the demon changed back to his human form and tore the spear out with a wet plop. The iron tip splintered, leaving part of it embedded in him. It was designed to do that, but the demon didn't know it.

The sugar syrup that made up his blood streamed from both his shoulder and his gut. He was grayer as a human than his natural demon skin color.

I grabbed the broken spear. One good tight grip and a little magic elbow grease and my current heated the broken tip until it glowed white hot. "Hold him, boys."

They pinned the hoc to the floor and I jammed the tip in a fraction of an inch away from the kill spot in his stomach. His flesh seared like a good steak, though the smell was more fetid flesh than delicious BBQ. I kept up the heat and soon he was bubbling, charred human hair falling to the ground.

The demon mewled.

I crouched down so I was eye level with him. "This is a new trick for me, and I'm happy to spend the next three hours practicing increasing the heat on all the parts of your body. Or you can answer our questions and I'll put you out of your misery. Where's your mate and how did you capture the oshk?"

The demon lasted another fifteen minutes before he cracked and admitted that he'd trapped this oshk after it had eaten his mate. There were no other Sweet Tooth production centers. It was kind of hard to understand him because half of his head was a ruined, blackened mess, but we got the gist.

I drove my fist into his gut, firing my magic through my gloves into his kill spot. There may have been justice for Naomi and Jake and that poor couple, but there was no satisfaction. Soon as he'd disappeared, dead, I tore off my protective head gear and fired it at the wall, snarling at the single whisker left of the demon, beyond done with this entire mission.

"You brutalized him." Drio nodded approvingly, pouring the beaker of oshk secretions into a patch of weeds just outside the back door. He and Sienna would get along beautifully.

Rohan unplugged the still and the humming quieted. He found a dented cardboard box and packed the still and tubing into it.

I stood up and unscrewed the vise. The oshk flopped over in her chains, her smaller head blob jiggling. Her flesh overhung the side of the chair like a slime toy. "What do we do with her? The matryoshka doesn't hurt humans. She eats other demons. Isn't that something we want to leave alive?"

Drio flicked something squishy off his suit and pushed up his face mask, cheeks ruddy. Being in these suits was like being roasted alive. "Kill her."

"She suffered."

"Demons are never victims." Drio looked around the room for anything we'd missed. "We kill them. It's what we stand for."

"The only good demon is a dead demon, I know." But there were exceptions to every rule and he was currently sleeping with one of them.

"Drio's right." Ro remained fully outfitted from head-to-toe.

Drio shook his head, as if that was obvious, picked up the box of drug-making paraphernalia, dumped his helmet on top, and carried it all out to my car.

"How can you say that?" I demanded. "What about Leo?"

Ro squatted down, working on the locks imprisoning the oshk. "I make an exception for her."

"How magnanimous."

"Yeah, it is." The chains binding the oshk to the chair fell to the floor with a clang. "If I had my way, Malik wouldn't be around anymore either. I appreciate he has his uses, for now. You've taught me the value of squeezing every drop of assistance out of demons I can before killing them."

"That's not at all—Argh." I threw up my hands.

"Nava, things may not be black and white, but there's still right and wrong." Rohan kicked the chains aside, catching the oshk before she fell over.

"Why is it still alive?" Drio was back.

"We're discussing what to do with her." I picked up the chains.

"What's to discuss? It doesn't matter if she doesn't gun for humans, her secretions can harm us, and she has to die," Drio said. "It's not open to debate."

"The basic element of right?" Ro said. "Don't fuck people over."

"This isn't about the Brotherhood," I said.

"Demons, Brotherhood, it doesn't matter," Drio said. "Listen to your boyfriend."

"Bite me."

"It turns out we do have one more use for this one." Ro threw the oshk over his shoulder in a fireman's carry. He was fully protected by the chemical suit so I wasn't worried about another episode. "She's going to help us kill the rest of the matryoshka."

Drio nodded. "That works."

The oshk had some use as a demon-eater, but ultimately, it didn't matter if she had to die. One day I'd kill Malik, too. No, I was incensed over Ro's high-handed attitude about Leo. She wasn't an exception. They'd become friends. Could he really flip on her that easily if push came to shove? Drio's reaction didn't surprise me, but I'd been counting on having Ro's help in protecting Leo if things went sideways and Drio's feelings got hurt. Now? Would Drio's rights as a full human automatically trump hers as a half-demon? Would her human half even matter?

Driving home, ignoring the guys chatting about some Rasha that Drio had run into on his jaunt to Palm Springs, I got my anger under control. I'd promised to have Leo's back. I glanced at my two passengers and their combined deadly force and my heart sunk. In another world where Drio didn't hate demons and Leo didn't have that unfortunate parentage, they would have been great together. With all that baggage? There was only one way to keep her safe: convince Leo to stop seeing Drio before she went from an exception to a statistic.

Ro and I carried the oshk from the car to the iron chair in the torture room. She remained limp and unconscious, as far as we could tell without her having eyes. I leaned into the oshk with the side of my body, keeping her upright so Ro could tape her in place with the special duct tape threaded through with iron and salt. Under my gloved hands, the demon had the blubbery consistency of Silly Putty.

Ro ran the duct tape over her raw sores to pin her torso to the chair and the oshk jerked violently against me.

Startled, magic snapped out of me like a whip. "Jeez!" I laughed, placing my hand to my chest. It had only been a spasm. The oshk was still limp, out cold.

Ro tore off his glove, reached for my ribcage, and abruptly dropped his hand before he touched me. "Does your skin feel wet?"

"Shit." I flung off my gloves, grabbed the chemical suit and twisted the material to examine it. My magic, born of surprise and therefore, uncontrolled, had torn a hole in the suit.

There was a single glistening drop on my skin that I wiped away with the fabric.

I bit my lip. "One tiny drop. It didn't even sink in. How much damage could it do?"

"Right." He slung an arm over me. "Besides, I'm here to keep an eye on you. Go all crazypants and I'll take you out."

I bumped his hip with mine. "And to think some women only get jewelry. I get my own personal assassin."

"Anyone can buy jewelry." Rohan slapped his hand against the scanner to open the door and let us out into the Vault. "I'm full-service."

"Oh yeah?" I ghosted my lips over his. "Prove it."

He did. Three times.

It was yet another night of very little sleep, but I wasn't complaining. In fact, when Ro woke me the next day, I bounded out of bed. Meaning, I opened my eyes on the first try and didn't brain my boy-friend with sleeping implements.

"How you feeling this morning?" he asked.

I stretched. "Sore, but good."

Ro crossed his arms, wearing another pair of board shorts–these a dark plaid–that rode low on his hips. "Demon-wise, Sparky. I figured when you woke me up that last time begging for it, that you were probably good."

I was momentarily struck dumb by the dip be-tween his hips and his abs in the strip of skin visible between his shirt and waistband. One bite of that beautiful brown skin, please and thank you. Maybe a couple of licks.

He snapped his fingers. "My eyes are up here."

"Yeah. Not really interested in that feature right now."

Rohan tackled me and I squealed. "Just because I'm the hottest lay you've ever had," he said, "doesn't mean you can objectify me."

I beat him with the pillow until he rolled off me. "One of these days," I said, "your arrogance will outweigh your use in providing orgasms."

"With you? Not if you had three lifetimes."

I reached for him, fisting my hands in his shirt. Pulling him close, I kissed him. "Let's test that theory."

He groaned. "Drio's waiting for me. Rabbi Abrams got us a meeting with Mischa."

Sighing, I let him go, smoothing out the wrinkles I'd put in his shirt. "All right. Go confirm his twin is still alive."

"What are your plans?"

"I gotta talk to Leo. Then I'll check in with Gelman, see if she got hold of Tessa."

I lay in bed a bit longer after hearing the front door close and the Shelby drive off. I texted Leo asking if I could come over and got a thumbs up emoji. Got my word of the day as well: *indomitable*. Why yes, I was, thanks.

As I hopped out of bed and grabbed my headboard, the room swung sideways, my vision blurring at the edges. I'd stood up too fast. Coffee would fix that. Hmm. Since I was going downtown to Leo's anyways... I sent her another text and grabbed a clean towel for the shower.

If I was going to convince my bestie to dump the best sex of her life, a Belgian waffle bribe was in order.

21

Leo stabbed her Liege-style waffle in the pool of syrup on her plate. "Was this supposed to be a bribe?"

"Think of it as an offering. Well? Ready to cut loose from the Italian Stallion?"

"For the last time, and I do mean last, I'll take my chances." She chowed down, oblivious to how much danger she was in.

I gripped her hand. "I don't think you understand. He'll find out at some point and then he'll kill you. Very slowly and painfully, because he hates people who betray him only slightly less than he hates demons and you're both."

Leo tried to pry herself loose but I had to impress on her how serious this was. I tightened my hold.

"Are you insane?" she hissed. "Let go of me." She picked up a fork, raising it over my forearm.

"Stab me. I'm not walking away until I get your promise."

"Then you'll shrivel and grow old here. I'm not ending things with him." She pressed the fork into me until I released her. "The sex is phenomenal."

"He wants to date you. This is getting serious."

A small smile tugged at her lips. "I'm worth being serious about."

"No shit, but that isn't the issue. I'm sorry, Leo, and I wish I was wrong, but there is no happily-ever-after for you two. For whatever reason, he won't be able to get past this. Please, please break up with him. It might hurt, but at least you won't be dead."

Leo flung her fork down. "Back. Off." She pushed her plate away and marched out of the restaurant without a look back.

I called after her, but she ignored me. This was a disaster of epic proportions. Leo had fallen for him. Fuck.

I called for the bill. My Eggs Benny quivered un-eaten on the English muffin, all of it drowned in Hollandaise sauce. Poached yellow vomit. My stomach twisted and sweat beaded my neck. I dragged myself to my car, fanning myself with the front of my shirt, wobbled into the driver's seat, and lay my head on the steering wheel, ignoring the honks of the car wanting my parking spot.

Driving home was a bitch. I swear my brain was stuffed with cotton. I pretended I was in a video game and had to exactly follow the car in front of me, because I kept veering sideways.

What a time to get sick. How long would it take my healing to knock this flu out of my system? My entire body ached, my skin hot and itchy. I'd have taken an oshk drug freak-out over this, but the flop sweats that punctuated my drive home, while extreme, hadn't ever been a side effect of Sweet Tooth. Plus, my generous tip back at the restaurant had been the opposite of punching the waitress and wrestling her for the maple syrup jug to drink from until I fell into a sugar coma, so this wasn't caused by the drop of oshk secretion I'd gotten on my skin.

I blacked out briefly waiting for the scanner at the chapter house gate to identify my car and let me onto the grounds, barely managing to throw the car in park, and stagger up the front stairs into Ro's bed, where I passed out into a restless sleep.

"Nava." Drio shook me. "Wake up!"

Wincing, I sat up. My stomach muscles screamed in protest. "Was I doing ab curls?" Why was Ro asleep next to me? "Is it night?"

"Are you drunk? Look at him."

Ro's face, the one part of him not wrapped in blankets, was blue. His eyelids were closed, fluttering madly, his jaw was badly bruised, and he had an angry red scrape across his forehead. Ice crystals dotted his hair, melting and running in tiny pearl droplets down the side of his head.

My heart slammed into my throat. I burrowed my hands under his covers, frantically searching for a pulse.

Drio pulled me off. "He's breathing." He lay his hand on Ro's head. "He's breathing," he said, quieter.

I beat on Drio's chest, lost to the wild fury whipping through my blood. "Why didn't you have his back?"

"Cosa?"

"That's it, isn't it?" I snarled. "You and him. You screwed up with him before and he got hurt."

Drio grabbed my wrists and pushed me away. "You–" He dropped his head, almost deflating, then shook himself off and picked up one of the hand warmers that he'd thrown on the bed, kneading and cracking it to activate it. He tucked the warmer inside Ro's blanket.

Magic flared off my skin, flinging Drio sideways. "Don't. Touch. Him."

I didn't hear him leave, busy inserting the rest of the warmers in key points between Rohan's skin and his blankets and checking every few seconds that he was still breathing. When that was done, I reswaddled him, needing something to keep busy with, to keep my choking panic at bay.

I couldn't tell. Oh, God. I couldn't tell if he was getting better.

I rubbed my hands together to warm them, then placed them on either side of his head. I'd made the azalea sprig bud; I could heal Ro. I visualized a bright white light emanating from my palms, burning away all other magic in his system.

My hands tingled and even though I kept it up until I shook with the strain and my vision fogged, I didn't feel any magic pouring out of me. I grabbed the lamp on his bedside table, thrusting it close to his face to check. He was so cold. So still.

Time blurred. I changed the IV that Dr. Sousa had set up, sleeping in fits and starts between my repeated attempts to heal him, terrified I'd miss him waking up, or worse, him taking a turn for the worse.

Rabbi Abrams brought me food and water. I think I drank a bit. Food held no appeal.

Drio darkened Ro's doorway. He was shirtless, gauze taped over some white ointment smeared on his side. "How is he?"

I gave up trying to wrestle Ro out of his shirt myself to sponge him down. "Make yourself useful and then get out."

We stripped him. I fished in the bowl of warm water for the sponge, gently wiping away the sweat glistening on Ro's forehead.

"You need to hear me out," Drio said. "Ilya's alive. Ferdinand ambushed us when we left Mischa's."

"Yet here you stand unscathed."

Drio flashed up, grabbing my throat. The sponge hit the floor with a splat.

I jutted my chin up, meeting his eyes. "Try it."

"Rohan is the last person I'd ever hurt," he said, his expression pleading. He stepped back, raking a hand through his hair. "The fight was nothing. Barely started. Ferdinand hadn't used his magic on us yet, but we were swarmed by shedim."

If Gollum had gotten drunk and fucked the monster in the original *Alien* movie, their spawn would be the prettier version of these demons.

I wrung out the sponge, cleaning under Ro's chin and along each arm, my fingertips lingering over his palpitating pulse.

"Ferdinand was their main target, but we were caught in the crossfire." Drio's hands balled into fists. "That betraying Rasha fuck caught Ro right as one of the shedim pinned Ferdinand down. The demon sent his magic into Ferdinand, Ferdinand's ice flowed into Ro and..." Drio glanced at the bed, then cleared his throat. "Ferdinand is dead, but that attack wasn't random."

He tossed a pointed leathery ear onto the bed. A *purple* pointed leathery ear. Shedim were burnt-orange.

I dropped the sponge in the water, wiped off my hands and reached for the ear. It had been cleanly severed. "You did the signature spell?"

"Being attacked right after learning what we had about Ilya? Ro didn't think it was a coincidence. He'd sliced the ear off for us to test so I tested it. I want the witch behind this."

"What will you do to her?"

"If he doesn't pull through? It's going to be war." He glanced at Ro one last time and left.

Rohan was going to pull through, but Tessa had to pay for what she'd done.

I whipped out my phone. "Where is she?"

My eyes were glued to every twitch of Ro's, constantly checking him for fever, for an improvement in color, for his continued breathing.

"Who?" Gelman said.

"Tessa. Don't give me any bullshit about her being in Santa Barbara. She's here. She attacked Rohan." My voice cracked.

Gelman dragged in a breath. "Tessa's dead."

"Impossible."

"Her burned body was found."

My hand tightened on my phone. "Murdered?"

"Burned from the inside. Black magic. The Los Angeles coven was trying to keep it a secret."

"When?"

"Nava." Gelman sounded wrung out.

"*When*?" I growled.

"Last week."

If that was true, then Tessa wouldn't have been able to bind the shedim. But if it wasn't Tessa, then every lead we had just came to jack shit. I hurled my burner phone at the wall with a screamed curse.

My attempts to wake Ro up yielded nothing and more nothing. I kept at it until I was lightheaded and my whole body ached. Every breath was energy I resented expending on myself.

Finally, deep inside me, a faint bloom of magic unfurled. That same primal silkiness as when I'd portalled. I caught my breath, barely daring to hope. Eyes screwed tight, I visualized stoking that bloom from a pale pink nub to a deep red bloom, the flower growing and stretching, pushing into every inch of me and flowing out into Rohan.

"Nava." It was a whisper and his eyes only fluttered open for the briefest millisecond, but my heart soared.

"I'm here."

It was like a fever breaking. He didn't wake up, but he became warm to the touch, his color turned normal, and his breathing evened out, deep and steady.

Exhausted, I crawled onto the bed beside him and let myself sleep.

"Nee?"

I rubbed my eyes, but Leo wasn't a hallucination. "You shouldn't be here. You'll get sick."

"I'll be okay for a short period." She already sounded strained from being on this side of the wards. "Rabbi Abrams helped me across."

"You told him?"

"Old news." She stood at the edge of the bed. "Ro's okay?"

Rohan stirred and rolled over, the first movement he'd made.

Tension ebbed out of my body. I motioned for her to follow me out of his room so we didn't wake him.

"He will be."

"And you?" she said.

"What about me?"

Leo grabbed my hand and pulled me up the stairs into my room. She planted me in front of my mirror.

Daylight highlighted my every flaw better than HD. My hair was a snarled mess and my eyes were bloodshot with dark circles under them.

"Have you showered?" she said.

"I was busy."

"You didn't eat or leave his side for two days. You gave Drio third degree burns. Not to mention how weird you were at breakfast with me. Something's wrong with you." Leo shoved me onto the bed, snagging my arm in a death grip.

"Ow!"

"Hold still," she snapped. She screwed her eyes shut, face scrunched in concentration. "You've been poisoned."

"I had the flu."

"It's poison and it's making you crazy worrying about the people you love. Was it the oshk?"

"Impossible. It was only a drop and it didn't behave like Sweet Tooth." I tugged but was held fast. "Naomi and Jake with the drug, Ro touching the oshk, the effects hit them immediately. They got a happy high followed by this intense darker moment when they were denied the object of their desire, and then, well, they either died or came out of it. Mine was more groggy, sleep for a week sickness. It wasn't the secretion."

"It most definitely was. You absorbed a drop in its pure form," Leo said. "You can't use humans *or* Rasha as a template for the secretion's behavior when affecting someone with witch magic. Come to mama, you little bastard," she muttered, twisting my arm like she was wringing out the poison.

I curled double, panting. Her touch had woken the venomous snakes in my veins, hissing and snapping and not wanting to be pulled out from my skin into the light of day. I let out a low moan.

"The poison is in deep." Leo's voice was reedy, sweat dripping off her brows.

"Leonie?" Drio stepped into the room. "What are you doing here?"

My head snapped up and I prayed he wouldn't understand what he saw. I tried to jerk free but Leo hissed for me to stay still, that she wasn't done.

"What's going on?" he said.

"I'm just… I'll come find you later," she told him.

He didn't budge, brows furrowed, his gaze locked on her hands doing their poison-removal.

"She has her industrial first aid," I said through gritted teeth, racked with tremors from the de-poisoning process.

Leo gave a pained laugh. My forearms, Leonie's hands, all were slick with black goo.

Drio grabbed one of her hands, forcing it against my iron bedpost.

"Sorry to disappoint you," she said, returning her hand to my arm. That little amount of iron wouldn't hurt. She ate salt, too. No, the only thing hunching her head deeper and deeper into her neck and bowing her spine were the wards.

Drio recognized the effects on her. "But you crossed the ward line."

"I'm a riddle."

"I'm good now," I said brightly. "That first aid certification really came in handy."

"Nava." Leo sighed. She pulled the poison away from me, stretching it like taffy before condensing it into a small, hard ball and crushing it to dust between her hands.

"No. *No.*" Drio was a blur, flash stepping up to Leo and away again. He came into focus, ramming his fist into the doorframe on the other side of the room hard enough to splinter the wood.

I flinched.

Leo got to her feet, pale, her still-coated hands planted on her hips. She sneered at him. "You're a smart man, Drio. Did you really not put it all together before now? Or did you know deep down and not want to admit it?"

"You're a PD."

"Yeah. I'm also the woman you've been sleeping with and the person who just healed her best friend. If you can't reconcile all those parts of me, then fuck you."

Drio scrubbed a hand over his face, half-curled over like he'd been punched.

I crossed my fingers that I was wrong about him. That when faced with the truth, he'd choose the reality of Leo over his prejudices.

He snapped straight up and jerked a finger at her. "You have two minutes to get out of my sight. After that, I see you? I'll kill you. Clear?" he snarled.

Leo didn't back down from the menace rolling off him. In fact, she looked a breath away from taking out her silver eyebrow ring and stabbing him with it. "Crystal."

He flashed out.

She dragged in a breath, her hands trembling. "Guess you were right about him. I thought…" She shrugged. "Doesn't matter now."

I pulled her into a fierce hug. "I didn't want to be right. Do you have somewhere to go?"

"Yeah. You good?"

"Only because of you. It's out." I stepped back, searching her face. Clear-headed once more, I didn't regret my efforts to heal Ro, but my behavior over the past couple of days had been crazy messed up.

I practically strong-armed her out to her car. "Go. I almost lost Ro. I can't lose you, too. Get out of here and go away for a few days. Hide."

One more hug and a promise from her to call me if she needed me. I jogged down the drive, following her car, standing guard until she'd turned the corner at the end of the block. Leo had been forced into hiding and I couldn't be there for her lest I risk the Brotherhood finding out about her.

I locked down any telltale emotion and went in search of the massive loose end.

Drio, still in his street clothes, was in the Vault laying into the bag with murder in his eyes. He pounded on it bare-fisted, his knuckles split and bleeding. "You let me be with that—"

The hits intensified.

"Not a 'that.' Leonie. Beautiful, wonderful Leo."

"She's a demon."

I swallowed, inching closer, my hands up. "She can't help who the sperm donor was. And you know how amazing she is. Why does it change things? Why are you acting like it's personal?"

"Because it is!" he roared.

I tensed but he just stood there, head bowed, one hand pressed over his eyes. He slid down the wall onto the padded flooring.

I'd given up on this conversation continuing when he spoke.

"You know how I met Ro?" he said.

"You were paired up for a mission?"

"I was fifteen." To Rohan's thirteen. I blinked. He'd known him ten years? "My father is a civil engineer, specializing in water conservation. He was transferred to L.A. for a year, so I had to train at that chapter house." Drio gave a faint smile. "I took one look at Rohan's emo bullshit and thought 'fuck, no' but the only other initiate was this eight-year-old brat called," his voice went flat and unimpressed, "River."

"Like you'd hang out with some hippy kid." I folded myself onto the floor.

"I picked Rohan as the lesser of two evils. Not that I was always sure I'd made the right choice, but there was one good thing about him."

"What?" The faster I humored him, the faster I got an answer about what really mattered here.

Drio was silent a long time before he fished his phone out of his pocket with a shaking hand. He opened his photos, flicking through them, then slowly handed the cell to me, like he was parting with some great treasure.

I sat down beside him.

The photo in question depicted a girl of East Indian heritage with a pixie cut and nose ring. Her knowing grin was coupled with gold eyes that were startlingly familiar. "Is this Asha?"

Rohan's beloved cousin.

Drio swallowed and nodded, taking the phone away from me and pressing it close to his chest.

"Were you? Did you…"

"It took me two years to convince her to be my girlfriend." His smile was filled with such pain and love that it hurt to look at it.

It was my turn to drop my head in my hands, my heart breaking for him. "How long were you together?"

"Five years."

From the moment I'd met Drio and Rohan, I'd been obsessed with knowing their history. Their big bomb of a secret. Now, I'd do anything *not* to know because I knew how this ended.

"I killed her."

I flinched at the words fired like gunshots. "No. Demons killed her because Ro was too fucked up from fame and he wasn't there for her."

Drio laughed harshly. "Asha announced she was coming to live with me in Rome. I had other ideas. For me, the thrill of the hunt was the greatest rush in the world. After two years, I'd become one of the best hunters. One of the most addicted. It was a high that being tied in one place to a long-term girlfriend couldn't compare to." He rested his head against the concrete wall, turning the phone over and over in his hands. "I'd given her some bullshit excuse about the importance of the mission to keep her away." Drio didn't look at me as he spoke, each new detail striking a blow into my heart at what they'd all suffered. "Ro found out and we had a huge fight. He said if I wasn't going to treat his cousin properly I didn't get to have her, and he told her the truth."

"He had no right." Rohan had said he'd gotten cruel. That his opinion of himself had been arrogantly off-the-charts. Fame might have been the cause, but Asha was the tragic consequence. That didn't mean it was anyone's fault other than the demon's.

I curled my fingers into my palms so I didn't reach out for him. Drio wouldn't want my sympathy. "Your flash stepping," I said. "It's because you run into danger."

"It's because the moment I became Rasha, I was running away from her." His voice was thick with self-loathing.

"Did you still love her?" He glared at me for even having dared asked that. "Exactly. And you'd stayed with her those first two years of hunting. That's not running, Drio. Trust me, I know what is."

Hope flashed across his face, but he shook it off. "Asha flew to Rome to confront me but Mandelbaum said all the right things to keep me hopped up, fighting the good fight, and I told her to go home. I'd make time for her later." His voice cracked in pain. He exhaled. "I guess the demon I was hunting spied us together. She got to Asha, then disappeared. Asha…" He pressed his lips together. "Asha is dead."

Was this the first time he'd said that out loud? My heart cracked a hundred times more. I reached for his hand, but he jerked it out of reach.

"The one bright part of my life was gone, and it was my fault because I stupidly believed that something else mattered more. Because I betrayed her."

"Stop," I pleaded.

Drio flexed his fingers, wincing. "Leo betrayed me and you betrayed me."

It hadn't occurred to me that he'd lump me in on the blame, but yeah. "I didn't mean to."

"I don't care."

I listened to his fading footsteps. All the trust and goodwill and friendship that I'd built with him was gone. He wouldn't rat me out to the Brotherhood because that would mean ratting Ro out but the man that had walked out of this room was no longer on my team. I'd lost Drio and my world was bleaker for it. I already missed the stupid psycho with his fierce devotion and wry take on the world.

No one would ever be Asha for him, but him and Leo could have been something new together, calming each other's rough edges and brightening the dark parts. But if they each spiraled fully and completely into that darkness? I pressed the heel of my hand into my breastbone, rubbing at the sting, but it didn't ease the hollow worry.

22

Ro was awake when I checked on him. "My magic," he whispered, white-knuckling the sheets. "I can't get it to work."

Adrenaline spiked through me. I reached out for him, then froze. "At all?"

He rubbed his hands briskly over his arms. "When I reach for it, I hit a dead zone. I can't..."

The anguish in his voice lashed me.

"It's still there." It had to still be there. "I'll be back."

I ran out of the room, sprinting into my bedroom to call Dr. Gelman. The screen on my burner phone had cracked in my outburst earlier, but it worked. I counted the rings, willing her to answer.

"Nava, now's not a good time."

"Please. I tried to heal Rohan and now his magic doesn't work." I slid down the wall, my hand pressed to my mouth, swallowing the metallic bile in the back of my throat.

"Coming," she said and hung up.

I stood at the gate, gripping the iron bars, waiting for her to arrive. I hit the scanner the second I saw the car. Dr. Gelman's sister, Rivka, was in the driver's seat. She popped the locks on the door and I scrambled in the backseat. "Thank you."

"No more breaking into my house." The resemblance between her and Dr. Gelman, her younger sister, was strengthened by the aging that Gelman's cancer had added to her features.

"Never again, I swear. I'm sorry."

Rivka nodded and sped through the grounds.

I helped Dr. Gelman out of the car and up the front stairs, forcing myself to accommodate her slow pace.

"Isaac." Rivka stopped inside the foyer.

My eyes darted between them. They'd dated years ago and he'd broken her heart. Should I have cleared this visit with him?

"Rivka. Esther." He gave a half-bow, clearly puzzled.

"They need to help Ro," I pleaded.

He patted my shoulder. "It's all right, Navela. Take them to him."

Ro was sitting in bed, his eyes closed. He kept tensing his muscles. No blades popped out.

"Ro?" I said.

"Not now."

"Ah. The illustrious Rohan. We didn't get a chance to meet in Prague."

Rohan opened his eyes at the sound of Dr. Gelman's voice. "Sorry?" He was giving me a what-the-fuck look.

I helped Dr. Gelman into a chair. "This is Dr. Gelman and her sister, Rivka."

"Also Dr. Gelman," Rivka said, moving to the side of Ro's bed. "A real doctor, unlike this one."

My Gelman snorted.

"I understand you're having some trouble with your magic?" Rivka reached for his hand. "May I?" He placed his hand in hers. She clasped it, asking him what had happened. After he'd finished up, she nodded and placed his hand on the blanket. "Your magic is still there."

"What's the bad news?" he asked.

"It's tangled up with the magic of the shedim and the other Rasha to such an extent that I can't unravel it."

"Is that all it is?" I backpedalled, seeing the flash of hurt on Ro's face like somehow that wasn't bad enough. "I mean, who can? Unravel it?"

"The demon and the Rasha are the sole causes," Rivka assured me. Her sympathetic smile faded. "But I don't know of any witch who has the power to break this. I'm sorry."

Rohan swung his feet out of bed. "Forget it. Thanks for trying." He strode to the door.

"Ro."

He didn't glance back.

The two women murmured platitudes about giving him time before they left. Their concern was wasted on me. I thanked them and walked them to their car, but I couldn't get rid of them fast enough.

I'd scoured every inch of the house and most of the grounds before I found him.

Rohan had hidden away in a secluded back corner of the garden, sitting on the ground, his back against a tree. His knees were drawn up to his chest, his arms covering his head, the only sound his harsh, broken exhales.

Giving up his music had cost him, but he'd been able to get back to it. Losing his magic? It would destroy him. He had to have his powers. That's all there was.

And I could get it back for him even if it was the worst thing I ever did.

"Who says the offer is still on the table?" Lilith had accepted my container of red velvet cupcakes from the finest cupcake store in town as her due. She licked the last of the frosting off her fingers. "Especially with your new condition on the agreement."

A light breeze provided relief to the evening heat, teasing the strands of her hair and the hem of her coral sundress. White-capped waves danced under a brilliant blue sky, and the beach-goers here at English Bay were in a festive mood.

Where was the rain and gloom when you needed it? If I was going to step into the role of cold-hearted betrayer, I didn't need the fucking sun mocking me. I wanted my treachery on an appropriate stage, my villainy for all to see, because the thought that I could do this and get away with it, even coming out like some kind of hero, was killing me.

I am David, thinking outside-the-box. Fighting on my own turf and playing to win.

I sipped my iced latte, shifting to take up more room on the bench so the couple who approached us would find somewhere else to sit. "The memory you experienced before was nothing compared to the passion between Rohan and me now."

"I'll be the judge of that." Lilith took my hand and I focused on the night in the hotel. When her hold slackened, her eyes were half-glazed with lust. Her skin was luminous, her breasts higher and tighter. She'd fed off the memory.

"Told you." Taking this precious memory and offering it up like so much smut when what had mattered was the trust and the tenderness and the raw intimacy made me wish I could scrub my skin bloody. I dug my nails into my palms, riding the pain. She couldn't know how every second propelling me forward into this deal was flaying my soul.

"What about your pesky morals?" she said.

"They don't matter in the scheme of things. You were right."

She nodded. "I know better than anyone what it takes for a powerful woman to blaze her own path. Decide what's important; let the rest go. Once you understand that, you can take anything you want if you want it badly enough. You will have near infinite power."

I didn't want power over Rohan, I just wanted to save him. "What Ro doesn't know won't hurt him. He won't know, correct?"

"Neither of you will be aware of me. To be clear, you're offering one night with Rohan in exchange for the name of whoever is behind the purple magic and the return of his Rasha magic. That's the agreement."

"The purple magic on all three items and no using black magic to fix him. The deal is off then." I pulled the gogota finger, the yaksas horn, and the shedim's ear out of my purse, arranging them on the wooden bench between us.

Lilith picked up the items, curling her fingers lightly over them, staring out at the freighters far out on the water. She handed me back the gogota finger and horn. "The witch who did this is dead. She is of no importance."

Tessa. This was the definitive connection between Prague and Askuchar, between the Brotherhood and a witch able to bind demons to do her bidding, but there was no surge of sweet triumph. "How about the ear?"

She turned it over and over in her hand, caressing its ridges. Super creepy. "I know this magic. No, something close." She sniffed the leathery ear. "Millicent," she sighed.

Millicent? It took me a moment to remember where I'd heard that name. "The witch who practiced black magic? She's dead." I looked at my companion. "Isn't she?"

"She is," she said sorrowfully. "This isn't her magic. But similar."

"Sister? Daughter?" I held out my hand for the ear, dropping it in my purse with the other items.

"Daughter. Yes. The one she gave up."

Leo might be able to help me search adoption records, except she was hiding. I hoped. "Got a last name for Millicent? Her daughter's name? Anything useful?"

She shrugged, like she'd lost interest. "She was white; the father was black. Her family didn't allow her to keep the child."

My latte hit the ground. "How old would this kid be now?"

"Thirties?"

Sienna was in her thirties. Brotherhood-hating Sienna who had been furious to learn about Ferdinand and was very upset the last time I'd seen her. Around the time of Tessa's death. It had to be.

"We need to formalize our deal." Lilith took my hand, scoring her thumb across it. My palm split, drops of blood welling up.

"Wait." *You're doing this for his magic. He'll never know and it's still me that he'll be with. It'll merely be like someone watching us.* "You swear it's only one time."

"Yes. Tonight."

"He'll just have gotten his magic back. He may not be in the mood."

"Then convince him." She cut her own hand open and pressed our skin together. I repeated the words of my vow to uphold the oath. Our gashes sizzled, scabbing over like a pink, twisted burn. "It'll fade once the deal is completed."

There'd be no mark save for the blemish on my psyche. "Can you get through the wards?" I said.

"I don't need to. I'll be in you, and you can cross them no problem."

No problem. What a joke. Ro lived by the code that you didn't betray your team, and in making the deal with Lilith I'd done just that. It didn't matter that the ends justified the means, because if I didn't save him this way, I'd lose him. It didn't matter that he'd never know what I'd done.

I'd know, and I hated myself already.

Lilith sashayed to my car, throwing coy smiles at all the turned heads.

I clutched my purse strap so I wouldn't clock her.

She slid into the front seat and, pulling down my visor, applied some lipstick she had stashed in her bra.

"You said he wasn't going to see you." I wrenched the engine on, grinding it. It went well with the still-dented hood.

"I want to look my best for me. Now, let's see what we're working with." She pumped my arm up and down.

"What the hell are you doing?"

"Do you have to know every little detail?"

"Uh, yeah." I tried to swat her hand away but she swatted me right back.

"You have a bit of healing magic, but it's weak. No one trained you?"

"No one knew I was a witch. How did you?"

"Who'd ever heard of a female Rasha?" She kept pumping my arm.

I squirmed, checking that no one was staring in through the windows at us. "This is ridiculous."

"I'm priming the magic up for one good shot. You want your boyfriend fixed, don't you?"

"Yes, but there's no way you're really doing anything."

"Ye of little faith." She pumped my arm one last time.

"Ye of big bullshit. This doesn't work, our deal is off."

"Be careful when you release it. There's a bit of a kicker on this."

"Fucking hell." What a joke.

She brushed off her hands. "Don't say I didn't warn you. Ready?"

I snapped my seatbelt in. "As I'll ever be."

One second she was there, the next she wasn't. A feather-light touch skimmed my shoulder blades, my skin stretching like the not-unpleasant sensation of flexing my fingers with tight, dry skin and that, apparently, was that.

I searched my eyes in the rearview mirror but there was no sign of her. Nothing about me looked different, nothing felt different, yet driving home, my fingers twitched, itching to claw off my own skin, find her, and rip her out.

I called Dr. Gelman over Bluetooth. "Sienna's taken over from Tessa."

"You're doing wonders for my recovery. Would you like to come over and throw some nuclear waste on me?"

"Sienna is *your* friend. Did you know she was Millicent's daughter?"

"Bat zona!" A long drawn out pause, followed by a flick, and a deep inhale.

"Are you smoking?! Put that out!"

"One drag. Rivka," she called. There followed a fast and furious conversation in Hebrew and I was put on hold.

I scrolled through the dial: Paula Abdul's "Cold-Hearted Snake," Bon Jovi's "You Give Love A Bad Name," and "Burn" from Hamilton. I punched off the radio.

"Sienna's cell is out of service," Gelman said. "My ward nurse said that she up and quit suddenly after seven years on the job."

"Could Sienna take over from Tessa? Binding demons?"

"She would have had to be training in secret for years, but that's how it works, isn't it?" Her lighter clicked on and off. "Working for the Brotherhood, however? Tessa may have been charmed into it by Ferdinand, but Sienna? No. Whatever she's up to, she's not helping them."

"Did she kill Tessa for it?"

"No. That was the magic." She said it with absolute certainty.

I pulled up the chapter house gate, expecting alarms to blare, and my flesh to boil when I passed the ward line onto the property. I crossed my fingers, hoping for the out, and gunned forward. There was no bouncing off the invisible shields, just a smooth slide onto the grounds.

"How's Rohan?" Dr. Gelman asked.

"He'll be fine." *Help me.* I coughed.

"Are you all right?"

"Fabulous. Gotta go." There'd be no help for what I'd done, but I could fix what was broken.

Unless Ro and Drio, sparring in the Vault, killed each other first.

They'd left the door open. We had an air conditioning system that did a pretty good job keeping the sweat stink at bay, but they'd propped open the door because it was steamy in there. I stayed in the shadows of the hallway.

Ro, wearing gi bottoms and a T-shirt, swung a thin curved blade mounted at the end of a long iron pole at Drio's head. His pecs tensed and flexed with the movement.

The pole whistled over Drio, who'd flattened himself backward before springing back to his feet, a similar weapon at the ready. Drio's gi bottoms encased his rock-hard thighs and his bare chest gleamed with sweat. Dude was so ripped, his six-pack had a six-pack. In a flash, he was behind Ro, his blade arcing toward Rohan with a hard whoosh.

I eeped at the ensuing decapitation, but Rohan had it under control. He sidestepped the weapon, not even flinching as it brushed by the end of his nose. He swept his pole under Drio's and would have torn a chunk out of Drio's side had Drio not blocked it with a ringing clang.

Both men strained, their weapons locked. Tendons popped on their arms, their teeth grinding, keeping each other at bay. Rohan stepped back, knocking Drio slightly off-center. Taking split-second advantage, he delivered a roundhouse kick to Drio's thigh, hefted the pole high, and swung the blade down.

Drio blurred out, reappearing on the other side of the room.

The two circled each other. Rohan lunged suddenly, flipping the stick to knock Drio under the chin with the handle. Drio parried with his own weapon, sending Ro's arm out of whack, but it wasn't enough to block the hit entirely. Drio may have saved himself a pole through the underside of his jaw, but the blow still landed on the side of the head.

He staggered back, blood flowing from his ear.

Rohan went in for the kill. Even without his magic, he drove Drio to his knees.

"Basta," Drio said. He pushed up off his knees, wrestling Ro's staff to take it away from him. "Enough, Rohan."

Ro's hair was plastered to his forehead, his T-shirt soaked through. He grabbed the cloth wraps laying in a pile beside some discarded boxing gloves and began wrapping his knuckles. "What happened with the oshk?"

Drio grabbed his T-shirt off the floor and used it to staunch the bleeding. "Took her outside the wards again today, but if she's calling the others, they're not coming for her. I'll try again tomorrow. Come upstairs. You've done enough training for today." Drio spied me at the door and his jaw hardened, but his concern for his friend overrode his animosity towards me. "Talk some sense into him."

"I'll do better than that. Ro, come here."

"Kinda busy." Wraps on, he tkihrew a couple of shadow punches.

"This is important." I hugged him tight, laying my head against his chest.

He tensed, but his arms finally came around me. "What am I going to do?" he whispered.

"Not a damn thing." I smiled up at him, reaching deep inside me for that magic Lilith had given me. This was no small sprig, but a massive rich bloom. I unfurled its petals, magic like dust motes flitting through me to fill my every inch.

Red magic shot out of me into Rohan, snapping my head back. Each dancing particle was visible; the world cranked to eleven. The floor wasn't blue, it was infinite depths of the ocean. Rohan's heart glowed pink through his brown skin, Drio's hair shone like spun gold. Could have done without seeing the individual drops of sweat flying off the men, but the rainbow prisms refracted in them were pretty.

My amped-up power was a waterfall, a deafening roar lifting me off the ground, cool and pure and majestic. It lasted a single heartbeat and then turned off like a tap. I crumpled to the floor, mourning its loss. In that moment, I'd have agreed to anything to feel that way again.

"O cazzo!" Drio held the poles like a cross.

Rohan's laugh bounced off the walls. Every single blade on his body was extended, his face lit up. I let his joy satisfy my craving for more of that magic. It was a salve, but it worked well enough.

I collapsed back against the padding and feebly fist-pumped. "Healing, bitches."

He dropped to his knees beside me. "They said it couldn't be unraveled."

"Scientist witches. They had to find a solution." Lilith allowed the lie.

"And you're just that good." Was it my imagination or did his eyes meet mine a little too pointedly? Was his smile a bit too wide?

I held out my hand and he pulled me up. "You better believe it. With a little help from my friends." I coughed. "I'm going to take a shower." I trailed a finger down his chest. "You could make me dinner in thanks."

My stomach was knotted up and my mouth tasted like ash.

Drio still watched me with hostile suspicion, but he lowered the poles, disappearing into the weapons room.

My beautiful boy kissed my forehead. "You got it."

As kisses went, it was a passing sweetness. I'd like to say that I'd have cherished it for the rest of my life, but the memory had already faded by the time I joined Ro in the kitchen forty-five minutes later, my hair loose and damp.

He'd laid out a candlelit table, which would have been romantic were the candles not pumping out a constant stream of smudgy smoke. Rohan presented me with crusty bread with olive oil and balsamic to dip it in, wine, salad, and fish.

It looked delicious. The taste, on the other hand? I poked at the halibut. "This salt-crust is really… salty."

"Good, right?" Rohan ate with gusto. "It's this Spanish recipe I've been wanting to try."

I muscled another bite past my gag-reflex. Figured the last meal he'd ever want to cook for me was this disgusting disaster. "Yum." I knocked back my wine, pouring more into my glass. Nerves steady, I pulled the fridge magnets that Yael had given me out of my terry cloth bathrobe. "You game?"

He laughed. "Smutty poetry magnets. Why not?"

I dumped the tiles out. Have. Give. Slow. Explore.

"Did you get burned when you healed me?" Rohan picked through the tiles for his selection.

I stopped rubbing the scar Lilith had given me to seal the deal. "I guess."

Ro countered with: suck, stroke, quiver, throb.

"Jumping a few levels there, Snowflake." Naked. Make. Me. Moan.

"I like this game." We. Caress. Rub. Quiver.

"My turn." Girl. In. My. Body. The tiles jerked sideways before he could read them, slipping to the floor. I doubled over in a hacking coughing fit, tears leaking out my eyes, my esophagus trying to escape out my mouth. All the words I wanted to say and couldn't were a tight pinch, choking me.

It had been worth a try.

Rohan got me some water, patting my back until I waved him off. I dropped my head in my hands.

"Clusterfuck of a day, baby," he said. "Come on. Let me take away all your tensions."

I could close the fraction of an inch between us, let him lead me to the bedroom, rock his world, and wake up treasured in his arms the next morning.

I lay my hand on his cheek, not trusting my voice yet. Wishing there was any way other than this way outside-the-box plan. "I tried, but I can't do this. I don't want to be with you anymore. We're done."

Rohan jerked away. "That's not funny."

"I'm not kidding." A maelstrom of jagged edges and burning gusts swirled inside me. Lilith voicing her displeasure. My lawyer father would have hung his head in shame that I'd negotiated without reading the fine print about the consequences of breaking this deal. The section pertaining to my death. I grit my teeth. "There's no separation in our lives and it's too much. I can't breathe." For someone without blade magic, I fired those metaphoric knives like a pro. "We can't be together."

I stood up, crashing into the table, bent over double, feeling for my way out, wondering if I'd even make it to the door before the searing pain ripping me apart, consumed me. My vision tunneled down into a single dot.

"Nava! Come back here. Please."

His pleading was wrecking me. One touch and I'd take it all back. I sped up so that couldn't happen. "I'm sorry. This is how it has to be."

"*You can't.*" That hadn't been Rohan. That was Lilith, roaring up inside me. "*Nice try. But you can't get out of our deal that easy. I'll take it from here.*"

My consciousness was shoved to one side, manhandled into a tiny ball, and stuffed into a black box. I fought her with everything I had, but my efforts were laughable. *You said I wouldn't even know you were here.*

"*You won't,*" she purred and slammed the black box shut.

I woke up the next morning naked in my bed. The scar was gone.

I turned over to find Ro watching me. I cast about for the appropriate salutation after one had dumped one's boyfriend and then been unconscious through body-possessed sex. "Have fun last night?"

"You tell me," he replied in a bland tone that clarified exactly nothing.

Oh, how I wished I could. I stretched out my limbs, checked in with Cuntessa, tested for unfamiliar soreness. Nothing. Whatever had gone down last night, Lilith hadn't been freaky. "About what I said last night?"

"Forget it." He got out of bed and pulled on his pants. "We're going to try contacting the other oshk again. Meet us out back."

There was no good morning kiss before he left.

I pressed my fists into my eyes until I saw stars.

Rohan knew. I don't know how, but he did. I'd broken up with him thinking it was my one way to save him, and instead Lilith had tricked me and fucked him and I'd lost him anyway. There was no point being mad at the duplicitous witch. My self-loathing, on the other hand, was endless.

My phone trilled merrily with my Word of the Day notification. *Specious*: adjective. Having deceptive attraction or allure; having a false look of truth or genuineness.

I deleted the app.

23

Drio deposited our oshk bait on a stump in the woods behind our back fence–outside the wards. Her body was wrapped in iron chains, not that she was in any condition to portal or fight back. Her sores hadn't healed on her human torso, and her oshk skin had turned the color of rust. She was vibrating, emitting a sound like sizzling butter, and she smelled like mold.

The three of us were back in full protective gear from head-to-toe. Drio gripped one of the iron poles with the curved blade that he and Ro had been fighting with in the Vault, while Rohan had three canisters of liquid nitrogen, modified with spray nozzles. He'd volunteered for the position, saying that with Drio's flash stepping and my magic wielding from a distance, we were better equipped to deal with the direct attack. For Ro to take this support position was huge. He'd always been ready to sacrifice himself for the people he cared about–like me on more than one occasion–which wasn't healthy.

I was proud of him recognizing that fact and desperate to know if him not wanting to throw his life away in a fight he didn't need to have was tied into our future at all, but he was sticking close to Drio. I could have pushed the point but things were so strained between us that any conversation was likely to explode into ugly truths and put the mission at risk.

I kept telling myself that was the reason, anyway.

Drio kicked the oshk. "Call the rest of your spawn squad."

A laugh burst out of me, dying at the look of malevolence he fired my way. Situation normal all fucked up. I wouldn't forget again.

I squatted down on the ground, scratching at a gnarled tree root through my gloves, not bothering to check for any support from Ro. Other than a quick glance when I'd first arrived, after which he'd pulled his mask down, my boyfriend hadn't bothered with me. Though he might not be that anymore so... I snapped the root in half and kicked it aside.

A faraway truck backed up, its beeping drifting in on the breeze and a neighbor had left their dog outside barking, but no matryoshka.

The sun rose high in the sky. We'd pulled off our head gear and unzipped our suits, moving from shadow to shadow to stay cool. Waiting for the rest of the matryoshka to show was tense enough, couple it with the fact that the men barely acknowledged my existence the entire time, and I was ready to snap harder than that tree root.

The oshk's torso became brutally sunburned, and still the other matryoshka didn't show.

"This is bullshit." Rohan drove the curved blade that Drio had tossed on the ground through the oshk's heart. The demon disappeared, her chains slithering off the stump into the dirt with a rattle.

"Way to make a unilateral decision there, Ro." Drio scuffed one foot back and forth in the dirt.

The forest stilled like a sound-dampening blanket had been tossed over it. The air shimmered and the remaining six oshk appeared.

We scrambled to suit up.

Drio grabbed the weapon and fist-bumped Rohan.

"Go forth and fucking conquer," Ro said.

I wasn't included in the rallying cheer.

With my own war cry, I bombed the shit out of the matryoshka, keeping them disoriented enough for Drio to slice and dice them open for one of us to reach their heart kill spot.

The ground became littered with oshk parts. Ro doused each one with liquid nitrogen, stomping it to dust beneath his feet so that it couldn't reattach to the demons. The liquid nitrogen swirled around him like an eerie cloak.

Drio and I had whittled a couple of the oshk down enough that one more well-placed strike would open them up, but the two melded with each other, resulting in instant regeneration, before separating once more hale and hearty.

"You've got to be kidding!" I snarled.

The battle raged on, trampling saplings, overturning mounds of dirt, exposing startled spiders that skittered away, and decimating one long ant formation. Not only were we starting from scratch with the two regenerated demons, but we had to keep them all away from each other so that regeneration couldn't happen again.

The outsides of our suits dripped from their secretions, eating away at the protective material. By the time we killed two more of them, I was slick with sweat, my limbs jerky from the magic I was expending.

That left four against three and we were tiring. The oshk weren't.

The left-legged oshk drove me backward. For every hit of my magic on her skin, my suit took an equal blast of her secretion. Cool air blew across my thigh. I glanced down to see the tear in my suit, missed my footing and tripped over a fat fallen tree branch, falling on my ass.

The oshk glided toward me, wound some blobbiness around my leg like an evil Barbapapa and pulled me toward her now-grotesquely distorted mouth. I dragged my gloves along the ground, scrabbling for a hold on anything, magic flying off my body.

The oshk ducked and wove, avoiding my strikes. I went slack, letting her lift me up and position me over her fetid pie-hole, willing myself to remain still, remain calm even as the black hole of her mouth filled more and more of my vision. The demon lowered me, my toes brushing her lips. I held on another second until my foot was now inside her mouth, the hole closing around my ankle, and blasted my current out through my shoe, down her esophagus and into her body. It bounced around inside, lighting her up like a pinball machine before dinging her heart.

She disappeared, dead. I fractured my ankle with the ensuing fall. Better that than my nose.

Rohan and Drio weren't faring much better. The last three oshks had forced them back-to-back and were taking their time circling in for the kill.

The demons flowed together to form a huge misshapen woman with a human head, a right leg, a left arm, and a whole lotta blob.

Drio fired his pole, impaling her in the heart but the iron weapon didn't even stop her. She shook herself and expelled the pole without breaking her stride.

Drio grabbed Ro and flashed out.

Finding them gone, the huge oshk turned her gaze on me.

I scrambled back in the dirt using my one good foot, my magic tapped out. I let her come for me, trusting that while the guys were mad at me, and my relationship had been ground into dust, that at least for this mission, they had my back.

The oshk loomed over me, blotting out the sun.

Drio and Rohan appeared behind her. Drio swung, decapitating her human head with a meaty thwack.

The oshk fell apart into three separate entities and in the split second before they could regroup, Ro firehosed them with an entire canister, freezing them on the spot. I blew them up, demon blobs hitting the ground around us like hail.

Drio located each of the larger blobs that was their hearts and drove the iron blade into them. The pieces disappeared, the forest once more tranquil.

I tore off my face mask, unzipped my suit and rolled it down to my waist, exposing my sports bra and letting the breeze cool my fevered skin. My hair clung to my face in dank strands. The men had done the same as me, both equally sweaty and red-faced.

Rohan gave me an inscrutable look before he and Drio left, canisters and the bladed pole tucked under their arms. I sat down on a log, my injured leg stretched out and the fingers of my left hand digging into the rough bark, breathing in the rich dirt, cedar, and pine.

The mission was over for Ro and I, but the question remained: were we?

A hand tangled into my hair, yanking me up off the ground. Malik's face edged in close to mine. "Where's Lila?"

I stretched as far as I could for my tiptoes to remain on the ground, scrabbling at his fingers. "I don't know."

Malik's hold tightened. His hair was unkempt like he'd been running his fingers through it, his shirt buttoned incorrectly.

Blood rushed in my ears and my heart threatened to break free of my rib cage. I stared into his glittering eyes and saw death. So I did the only thing I could do: I kneed him in the balls as hard as I could.

Malik gasped a wheeze and dropped me.

Ignoring the red-hot agony blazing up from my injured ankle, I scramble-hopped back inside the door to our warded backyard, tripping safely behind it as Malik lunged.

He bounced off the invisible shield of the ward with a snarl. "Did you kill her?"

"I voided our deal." Or I carried it out in grand style. I had no idea.

"Things not go as planned? Poor petal."

My foot throbbed, I was exhausted, and yet, the waves of deadly hostility rolling off him only amped up my own fury. It didn't matter that I'd gone to Malik to begin with: I wanted to savage him for putting me in Lilith's path. For facilitating whatever the hell state my relationship was now in. "Get lost, demon."

The marid nosed right up to the ward line. Only inches separated us. "You've got everyone poised to attack each other: your friends, the Brotherhood, witches, demons. There's a war coming and you better be ready, petal, because I intend to survive it. And when I do?" He raked his fingers through his hair, smoothing it down, and smiled a polished smile. The one the wolf wore for the Three Little Pigs. "I'll expand your lexicon with the true meaning of the word hurt."

He portalled out.

I had no doubt that my day of reckoning was coming with him–with all of them–but right now there was only one person whose words meant anything.

I hopped my way into the kitchen and cornered Rohan. "Can we talk?"

He grabbed a bottle of water from the fridge and jumped up on the counter. "Go nuts."

I tried, but dissolved into a coughing fit, still not at liberty to voice our deal. I swiped his water bottle, chugging it back, and wiped my mouth. "You go first. Last night."

I toyed with the cap, a hollow pit opening in my stomach. I didn't want to hear the details, since she'd probably rocked his world, but I couldn't not know, either.

He studied me. "You really can't say anything? Dr. Gelman wasn't kidding."

My head jerked up. "Dr. Gelman?"

"Nava, I figured there was something going on the second you restored my magic."

"Oh." I grabbed an industrial bottle of extra-strength ibuprophen and dry swallowed two before swiping a pack of frozen peas from the freezer. I sank into a chair, slipped off my shoes, and slapped the bag against my ankle. "I guess you wouldn't have believed I could heal you."

"I know you healed me once. I felt it when I was unconscious. It was the same honeyed warmth as when Rivka tried. But the second time? It was a sharp snap, more like an electric shock from all your magic at once. It was too much to believe you suddenly had the power to unravel the magic knot when Rivka didn't know any witch strong enough."

"So you called Gelman?"

"I did. She figured out what must have happened. Drio zipped over and picked up what I needed while you were in the shower."

"Those smudgy candles and the world's saltiest fish." Now it made sense.

"We tried to pull Lilith out of you." He rubbed his neck.

I may not have had the Word of the Day app anymore, but I was pretty solid on my grammar. Tried implied that an attempt had been made. The silence that followed implied it hadn't gone well. "And?"

"She was too strong. Her hold on you was too deep. The best we could do was trap her unconscious inside you."

I probed deep inside but I could feel no trace of her. That wasn't a win. I'd rather have had a handle on her. Nothing. I had a ticking time bomb living in me with no idea what might trigger its explosion. It was terrifying, but it wasn't the reason for my icy fingers and stuttery breath.

"When?" I mumbled, staring at my feet.

"What?"

I cleared my throat and met his gaze. "When did you knock her out?"

He crossed his arms, his eyes blazing, and his body rigid. "You want to know if I'd already fucked her? If last night I believed I was making love to my girlfriend and it had been like nothing I'd ever experienced? Will it ease your conscience if I enjoyed it?" He leered at me, lowering his face close to mine. "You were the best, baby."

I slapped him.

The sound lingered over the gurgle of the dishwasher kicking in. Neither of us spoke, the air charged like the seconds before the eruption of a thunderstorm.

He rubbed his cheek. "How could you make that deal?"

Would the frozen peas work on my heart? "How could I not? You'd lost your magic."

A muscle jumped in his jaw. "I told you before that I didn't need saving."

"Really?" I adjusted the bag on my swollen ankle. "I saw you outside after you'd learned the bad news. You were devastated."

"I'd have dealt."

"Like you did with Asha?"

"You have no idea—"

"Drio told me."

"Then how the hell could you betray me?" he said. "Basic concept, right from wrong. Even you understand that."

Even me. I dug my nails into my palms. "I tried to keep things from playing out. I tried to spell it out with the fridge magnets and break up with you and—"

"And at the end of the day, you made that deal with whatever the fuck Lilith is, involving me, without my consent." A literal brick wall springing up between us would have been easier to breech than his unyielding stance.

I reached for him, desperate for him to understand, but he stepped back.

Was it me or this thing inside me? I was too scared of his answer to ask.

"After Drio told me about Asha, and you were out there broken," I said, "I understood wanting to do whatever it took to protect someone I cared about. I'd have done anything to help you. 'If I have to be an asshole to save you, I'll do it.' Your words."

"'Then you'll lose me.'" He jabbed a finger at me. "*Your* words."

"Have I lost you?" I could barely croak out the words through the thickness in my throat.

At least with his anger, he'd still felt something toward me. Rohan standing here, hands hanging limply at his sides, his eyes closed, not answering? That was him giving up.

My skin tingled from the strain of holding in my sharp sorrow. It weighed me down in pieces: knotted behind my breastbone, pulsing in my temples, and pooling in my feet. Lilith didn't rouse to gloat, though.

I pressed my fists to the side of my head. "Where do we go from here?"

"On which part?" He slumped over the counter, his back to me, his head braced in his hands.

"All of it. Is it…" I took a deep breath. "Are we over?"

His phone rang. Rohan glanced at the screen and answered it. "Hey Mom, this isn't a good–" He straightened up. "What? When? Is he–?"

Concerned, I stood up, hissing when I put my weight on my foot. Ro's expression softened in sympathy for a second before hardening once more. His gaze flicked away.

"Yeah," he said on the phone, "I'll get a flight today. Okay. Bye."

I placed my hand on his arm and he flinched. My eyes watered. "What happened?"

"Dad had a heart attack."

I opened my arms without thinking, immediately correcting to wrap them around my chest. If he'd flinched at my touch, I couldn't take seeing what he'd do at the full body contact of a hug. I dug my fingers deeper into my ribcage, moving to the opposite side of the island to give him space, but no matter how hard I tried to keep myself upright and dignified, my body leaned toward his. "Is he all right?"

"He's alive, but he's in the hospital." He clutched his phone, staring blankly at it. Then he shook himself off and headed for the door. "I need to go home."

When Rohan had sung me "Slay" he'd proclaimed that I was his home. The loss of status was numbing.

But I had my answer about us.

I pressed my hand against my mouth, but there was nothing I could do about the tears streaming down my cheeks.

He stopped in the doorway, his back still to me. "Nothing happened. With Lilith. I would never…"

"Okay." I dragged in a shaky breath.

In three strides he was back at my side, kissing my wet lashes. With my eyes closed, I could pretend that his lips on my tears were in comfort, and that the nausea swirling in my stomach was giddy anticipation.

But I couldn't keep my eyes shut forever, and when I opened them, I was hit full force with the cold vertigo of my splintered heart, his touch and warmth lost to me and the broken look on his face more devastating than all our words.

"This isn't the end of us," he said. "Just..."

I sniffled. "A break?"

A coffee break? A bone break? A heartbreak?

He rested his forehead on mine. "A slowing down. We kept saying we wanted each other desperate," he said. "And as much as it had been a joke, it wasn't. We can't do that anymore. Can't crave each other so much that it's this all-consuming mess of fucked-up power dynamics and who gets to keep who safe and happy."

"I know. And the harder we tried, the harder we trampled each other." The problem hadn't been making *ourselves* vulnerable, it had been accepting the times when the other person's vulnerability was on the line.

I lay my hand on his cheek, wondering when he turned into it, his stubble scratching my palm and his eyes damp, if this would be my last memory of him.

Of us.

Rohan was right. We needed to slow down. I understood that intellectually. Emotionally, I was howling, laying bleeding and gutted on the floor, the ruins of what we'd had strewn around me in shattered disarray.

He stepped back and I mourned the loss of contact. "I'll call you when I get there."

I struggled for breath to form the correct, careful platitudes, gripping the counter behind my back to keep myself from going with him. No longer having any right to be his source of comfort. "I hope your dad gets better quickly."

"Me too." We held a look that wasn't so much mutual recrimination as tragic acknowledgment.

Ro half-raised his hand in a wave and I nodded. All this time, I'd been so worried about Rohan and his bad behaviors, but it turned out that the real danger to our relationship had been me all along.

I didn't watch him walk out the door.

END OF BOOK FOUR

Thank you for reading!

Dear fabulous reader,

Things are getting intense, aren't they? *grin* There's more to come in Nava's journey with a lot of twists and turns along the way.

Thank you so much for all your emails and Facebook comments. I'm loving getting to know you and hearing your thoughts on these characters who are near and dear to my heart.

Now, I have a favor to ask. It's your reviews that help other readers to find my books. You, the reader, help make or break a book. So please, especially if you want more Nava and Rohan, spread the word. Leave an honest review of *The Unlikeable Demon Hunter: Crave* on Amazon, Goodreads, your blog, etc.

xo
Deborah

Get a free download!

If you enjoyed this book, then how about a couple of free short stories set in this world from the guys' POVs? Demons and sexytimes, galore! There are mild spoilers in each one, so it's best to enjoy them in the proper reading order.

Go to: http://www.deborahwilde.com/subscribe

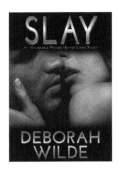

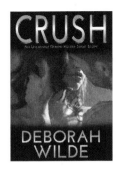

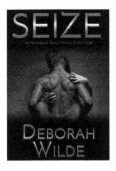

Nava explains awesome Yiddish and Hebrew words used in this series.

- Bat zona (Hebrew) - Daughter of a whore! (Enlightening you on swears from around the world.)
- Beseder (Hebrew) – Okay.
- Maspik (Hebrew) – Enough. Sounds way better growled at someone than the English equivalent.
- Mazel tov (Hebrew) – Congratulations. Can be shortened to "mazel mazel" which sounds super snarky and may leave the recipient in doubt as to how to take it.
- Mensch (Yiddish) – a person of integrity and honor. Technically it's gender neutral, though I see it applied way more often to men. Go figure.
- Mishegoss (Yiddish) - Craziness. Senseless behavior or activity. I thought this was my grandmother's nickname for me when I was little.
- Mitzvah (Hebrew) – A good deed. As in "Not punching Drio in the head was my mitzvah for the day."
- Oy vey (Yiddish) – A very handy exclamation of dismay and grief conveying everything from "aw, man" to "kill me now."
- Verklempt (Yiddish) – Choked/overcome with emotion. "I was so verklempt after disrupting Ari's induction ceremony that I had to eat my body weight in chips to calm down."

Acknowledgments

Big thanks to Jessica Massey Golson for the "Karma" T-shirt gag. You nailed Nava on that one! I just have to say that my Wilde Ones Facebook group is the absolute best and I love (virtually) hanging out with you all.

To my daughter, Kiki, I owe you, kid, for always being willing to talk story with me, and for the smutty fridge magnet idea. You are my joy and my delight and I'm so proud to be your mom.

Alex Yuschik, are you getting tired of me raving about your editorial brilliance, yet? Because I'm not going to stop anytime soon. I owe you so much and I love working with you.

Much gratitude to my family, for supporting me in this crazy endeavor 150%.

To my readers, I have no words. (Okay, I lie. Here I go. Words.) You people are incredible and I am so glad that you love reading these books as much as I love writing them! Thank you from the bottom of my heart for choosing Team Nava.

About The Author

I'm Deborah (pronounced deb-O-rah) and I write sexy, funny, urban fantasy.

I decided at an early age to live life like it was a movie, as befitted a three-syllable girl. Mine features exotic locales, an eclectic soundtrack, and a glittering cast—except for those two guys left on the cutting room floor. Secret supernatural societies may be involved.

They say you should write what you know, which is why I shamelessly plagiarize my life to write about witty, smart women who kick-ass, stand toe-to-toe against infuriating alphas, and execute any bad decisions in indomitable style.

Catch me at:
www.deborahwilde.com
Twitter: @wildeauthor
FB: www.facebook.com/DeborahWildeAuthor

"It takes a bad girl to fight evil. Go Wilde."

Printed by Amazon Italia Logistica S.r.l.
Torrazza Piemonte (TO), Italy